"One of the most i

"*Deadtown* was good, but *He*
writing is airtight; her charact
There is comedy, drama, romance, and a whole lot of ass kicking. *Hellforged* is the total package." —*Fantasy Literature*

"The thrills are nonstop in Holzner's latest Deadtown novel as the action races from continent to continent and into the reaches of Hell itself. Even better than the first book; this series is becoming highly addictive!" —*Romantic Times*

"Gripping the reader from its highly entertaining opening scene, the terrific *Hellforged*, the second installment in the Deadtown series, maintains that hold until the very end . . . Holzner's expertise as a mystery author shines brightly throughout the narrative as she flawlessly connects threads of both the tale told in *Hellforged* and the overall story arc of the Deadtown series. This fabulous novel skillfully combines several distinct elements into a highly satisfying whole: action, adventure, suspense, Welsh mythology, humor, and pitch-perfect characters that live and breathe on the page . . . This excellent series belongs in the collections of all urban fantasy fans." —*Bitten by Books*

"The demons Vicky chases in *Hellforged* are bigger, badder, and so much more fun. I love the unexpected twists and turns . . . I cannot wait to see what is in store for my new favorite demon hunter!" —*Intense Whisper . . .*

"The second Deadtown novel is jam-packed with action. A quick and satisfying read, *Hellforged* will have readers on the edge of their seats for more. Vicky is a very likable and headstrong lead . . . a fun yet serious novel; fans of Laurell K. Hamilton, Rachel Caine, Kim Harrison, and Karen Chance are likely to enjoy this series." —*Night Owl Reviews*

continued . . .

"Vicky is the kind of kick-butt heroine fantasy lovers can get behind—rough and tough, afraid to jump into the fight but too stubborn to stay out of it . . . Aided by a whole cast of interesting characters, including her aunt Mab, who is a perfect mix of hard taskmaster and sweet and comforting aunt, Vicky and crew are ones you can't help but root for in the battle of good versus evil . . . *Hellforged* is a novel lovers of fantasy, urban fantasy, and paranormal fiction in general won't want to miss." —*Romance Reviews Today*

DEADTOWN

"Fresh and funny, with a great new take on zombies."
—Karen Chance, *New York Times* bestselling author of *Hunt the Moon*

"Holzner's prose combined with a spunky protagonist with a dark side, woven together with fast-paced action, emotional reveals, and engaging plot twists, makes *Deadtown* a must-read. I'm looking forward to more adventures in Deadtown with Vicky Vaughn—this heroine totally kicks butt!"
—Phaedra Weldon, author of *Revenant*

"Fast, fun, and feisty, Holzner's *Deadtown* is chock-full of supernatural action, danger, and creatures who do more than go bump in the night." —Devon Monk, author of *Dead Iron*

"Zombies, demons, and a sassy slayer. *Deadtown* sparks with an incredibly realized world and a cast of vivid characters. I can't wait for the next book!"
—Chris Marie Green, author of *Deep in the Woods*

"Full of dangerous magic and populated with characters so realistic they almost jump off the page. I loved this book. Nancy Holzner is a master of characterization, and I'll be buying her next book the moment it hits the shelf."
—Ilona Andrews, *New York Times* bestselling author of *Magic Slays*

“A perfect blend of mystery, fantasy, humor, and even modern-day social issues. It’s Boston as you’ve never seen it . . . where the shapes shift, the zombies gnaw, and the blood flows warm through the oh-so-delicious veins of the area known as Deadtown. Victory Vaughn gives evil a run for its money.”

—Anton Strout, author of *Dead Waters*

“Welcome to Holzner’s fascinating world, where a plague has turned much of the Boston population into zombies. Part demon-busting tale, part political thriller, Holzner’s take on urban fantasy is exciting and fresh. Here’s to the future adventures of Vicky Vaughn.” —*Romantic Times*

“Holzner applies humor with a deft hand, enhancing the reading experience of this superb addition to the urban fantasy genre. This reviewer will be first in line for *Deadtown*’s sequel.”

—*Bitten by Books*

Ace Books by Nancy Holzner

DEADTOWN
HELLFORGED
BLOODSTONE

BLOODSTONE

NANCY HOLZNER

THE BERKLEY PUBLISHING GROUP
Published by the Penguin Group
Penguin Group (USA) Inc.
375 Hudson Street, New York, New York 10014, USA
Penguin Group (Canada), 90 Eglinton Avenue East, Suite 700, Toronto, Ontario M4P 2Y3, Canada
(a division of Pearson Penguin Canada Inc.)
Penguin Books Ltd., 80 Strand, London WC2R 0RL, England
Penguin Group Ireland, 25 St. Stephen's Green, Dublin 2, Ireland (a division of Penguin Books Ltd.)
Penguin Group (Australia), 250 Camberwell Road, Camberwell, Victoria 3124, Australia
(a division of Pearson Australia Group Pty. Ltd.)
Penguin Books India Pvt. Ltd., 11 Community Centre, Panchsheel Park, New Delhi—110 017, India
Penguin Group (NZ), 67 Apollo Drive, Rosedale, Auckland 0632, New Zealand
(a division of Pearson New Zealand Ltd.)
Penguin Books (South Africa) (Pty.) Ltd., 24 Sturdee Avenue, Rosebank, Johannesburg 2196,
South Africa

Penguin Books Ltd., Registered Offices: 80 Strand, London WC2R 0RL, England

BLOODSTONE

An Ace Book / published by arrangement with the author

PRINTING HISTORY
Ace mass-market edition / October 2011

For information, address: The Berkley Publishing Group,
a division of Penguin Group (USA) Inc.,
375 Hudson Street, New York, New York 10014.

ISBN: 978-0-441-02100-0

ACE
Ace Books are published by The Berkley Publishing Group,
a division of Penguin Group (USA) Inc.,
375 Hudson Street, New York, New York 10014.
ACE and the "A" design are trademarks of Penguin Group (USA) Inc.

PRINTED IN THE UNITED STATES OF AMERICA

10 9 8 7 6 5 4 3 2 1

To my parents, Harold and Lois Brown,
with love and appreciation.
Thanks for reading my books even though
they're not always your cup of tea.
I could not have chosen better people
to love and guide me throughout my life.

ACKNOWLEDGMENTS

It was a great pleasure to work with Kat Sherbo, who took this manuscript through several drafts, editing them all with great care and attention. Kat's questions weren't always easy to answer, but they were always perceptive, intelligent, and aimed at making *Bloodstone* a better story. Thanks, Kat, for all your hard work. You're awesome!

The kick-ass cover art comes from Don Sipley, who does an amazing job of bringing Vicky to life. Thanks also to Edwin Tse.

I'm also grateful to the other professionals who worked on this book: text designer Tiffany Estreicher, production editor Michelle Kasper, assistant production editor Andromeda Macri, copy editor Jessica McDonnell, and proofreader Pam Barricklow.

My agent, Gina Panettieri, works hard on my behalf so I can focus on writing. She even sent me chocolate!

My friends and fellow writers Emily Johnson, Pat Carlson, Jeanne Mackin, Nicola Morris, and Janis Kelly offered helpful feedback on parts of the first draft—not to mention fun conversation and good company. Thanks, all!

My daughter, Tamsen Conner, thinks it's cool that her mom writes this stuff, and listens patiently when I moan about the writing process. She's the best.

Many friends just made life more fun while I was writing, including Kathy Giacoletto, Maria Giacoletto (you're still an inspiration!), Michelle Brandwein, Deborah Blake, Kate Laity, Margaret Strother, Sydney Chase, Chris Schjoth, Carlos Thomas (who appears here in a cameo and who created a video game avatar based on Vicky), Keith Pyeatt, Christina Henry, and my fellow bloggers at *Dark Central Station*: Sean Cummings, Wayne Simmons, Erin Kellison, Gary McMahon, Thomas Emson, and Darren J. Guest.

Thanks to Cam Dufty for making my Deadtown series possible in the first place. And thanks to everyone who reads my books—it's such a thrill to know that people are following Vicky's adventures.

Most of all, thanks to my husband, Steven Holzner, who may well be the most patient man on the planet. I know for sure he's the most loving.

1

BAYSIDE HEALTH CLUB, A FORMER GYM ANGLING TO GO upscale, is where Bostonians go to pump some iron, get sculpted, and trade in their beer bellies for the sexier kind of six-pack. I'd read the brochure. It has a weight room, state-of-the-art exercise equipment, a lap pool, and full-time personal trainers and nutritionists on staff. Everything you need to get motivated and get buff.

But I wasn't here for a workout. The duffel bag I carried didn't hold gym clothes. It was loaded up with bronze-bladed daggers and two bottles of holy water. This afternoon, I was here to kill a demon.

As Boston's only professional demon exterminator, I kill other people's personal demons for a living. Often, that means I get rid of the demons that give you nightmares or gnaw at your guts with guilt or worry. Harpies—revenge demons sent by a sorcerer—are also big business.

Today, though, I was after a different kind of demon. Bayside Health Club had an out-of-control Peccatum infestation.

Peccatum, Latin for *sin*, describes a type of demon that contaminates people's personal behavior. A Peccatum looks kind of like a giant octopus, but with seven tentacles instead of eight. Each tentacle represents one of the seven deadly sins—Anger, Greed, Pride, Lust, Envy, Gluttony, and Sloth—and can branch into an infinite number of tendrils. The tendrils snake out and wrap themselves around their victims, ensnaring them in whichever sin the Peccatum has sent forth. When a victim indulges in that sin, the demon feeds.

Bayside, like a lot of businesses, had paid for this Peccatum, buying it on the black market. A whiff of sin in the air can make a place feel edgy, a little dangerous, and a whole lot of fun. Bayside's owner had told the sorcerer who conjured the demon to keep it small and to stunt all the tentacles except for Envy, Pride, and a thin strand of Lust. Those sins were good for business. But the Peccatum had gotten out of control, and now Gluttony and Sloth had taken over. How—who knew? Maybe someone showed up for their workout feeling lazy, calling Sloth forth from the demon. Maybe a nutritionist appointment made a client fixate on forbidden foods, stirring thoughts of Gluttony. Or maybe the sorcerer did a sloppy job of binding the demon. Since conjuring demons is illegal, anyone who buys demons on the black market takes that risk. No money-back guarantees from a sorcerer. If you complain, you might find a Harpy handling customer service.

As I pulled open the door and walked inside, the receptionist barely glanced at me. She leaned back in her chair, feet up on the desk, eating a cupcake. Frosting dotted the tip of her nose, and the number of empty wrappers that littered the floor around her would do any zombie proud. (Zombies are world-class eaters. They don't go after brains so much, but they adore junk food.)

"I'm Victory Vaughn," I said. "I'm here to . . ." I glanced around. Business owners don't like to advertise that their business is infested by demons, but there was no one else in the lobby. "I'm here to fix your Peccatum problem."

"Yeah, whatever." She waved a hand vaguely toward the club's interior and let the empty cupcake wrapper fall to the floor. Then she sat forward and put her head down on the desk. Her snores riffled Post-it notes like a gentle breeze.

Great. Sleeping Beauty would be no help at all. I checked my watch. This was supposed to be a quick-in, quick-out job. Tonight my werewolf boyfriend, Kane, would be meeting my sister for the first time. In a few hours we were due at her home in Needham for dinner. For all kinds of reasons, being late would spell disaster.

I'd have to track down this Peccatum myself. I opened my senses to the demon plane. The room dimmed, and the stink of sins filled the air, making me cover my nose against the stench. Gluttony smells like flatulence and belches, Sloth like long-unwashed bodies caked in shit. The sounds of a Peccatum at work filled my ears: burps, openmouthed chewing, farts, sighs, snores—a symphony of gross bodily functions. The receptionist let loose a gentle burp in her sleep. Peccatum tendrils coiled around her, wrapping her tightly in their embrace. Gluttony and Sloth both gripped her. Gluttony is sickly yellow and sharp-edged, like a serrated knife to saw at the guts with hunger. Sloth is gray and more diffuse. It enfolded her like a warm, fuzzy blanket.

I let her sleep. Cutting off the tendrils would do nothing more than alert the Peccatum I was here. To kill the demon, I had to get its head.

Of course, "head" might not be the best term for the blobby main part of a Peccatum. It had no eyes, no ears, and no mouth, although it could sense people around it, mostly through their weaknesses. The demon's main body was a roiling mass of oily mist, globbed up into a big ball of ugly.

I opened my duffel bag and removed a belt that looked like something a Wild West gunslinger would wear. But instead of guns, the holsters held water bottles. I hadn't brought a pistol for this job; shooting the demon wouldn't work. Although bronze is lethal to a Peccatum, as it is to any demon, the bullet passes through the thing's misty head too quickly to do any lasting damage. The mist merely fills in the hole. It takes a thorough dousing with holy water or prolonged contact with a bronze blade to kill a Peccatum.

I put on the belt and fitted my liter bottles of holy water into the holsters. Then I strapped on two thigh sheaths, each loaded with a bronze dagger. I checked that everything was snug, the caps on the bottles tight. I was ready to track down the demon.

Unlike other demons, which manifest only after the sun goes down, Peccata are active around the clock. After all, sin is a 24/7 affair. But Peccata don't like sunlight, so the sorcerer would have conjured it in a dark place, a closet or a windowless room. I set off to explore.

The first room off the hallway was the weight room. Inside, bodybuilders lay on benches, sleeping or staring into space. Some sat on the floor, slumped against the wall, heads nodding forward. The whole room was filled with a thick, stinky fog of Sloth.

That was the trouble with Sloth. It's so lazy and diffuse it has a hard time holding its own shape, so it's difficult to follow Sloth tendrils back to their source. I needed to find some gluttons. The tendrils that enwrapped them would lead me to the demon.

But, really, what was the hurry? I yawned. It was only late afternoon, but already I'd had a long day. I deserved a break. My eyelids drooped. My body felt too heavy for my legs to hold up. I could just lie down right here and . . .

No. I *was* in a hurry. I shook off the sleepy feeling and stepped back into the hallway. Fluffy gray tendrils puffed toward me, following. Bits of gray fluff clung to my legs.

There are two ways to avoid a Peccatum's tendrils. One is through virtuous living and iron-clad willpower, and I'm sure that works great for some demon-killer, somewhere. But I'd come prepared with option number two.

From my pocket, I pulled out a crystal atomizer and misted myself with its contents. Not perfume; holy water. It makes the wearer temporarily invisible to the Peccatum. I'd misted myself before I entered the health club, but the effect wore off as soon as the holy water evaporated.

The fresh misting of holy water did its thing, and the

reaching Sloth tendrils drifted toward the floor. They lay there like dust bunnies.

I went back to the receptionist and picked up the trail of Gluttony. The jagged yellow tentacle snaked down the hall, branching off into several rooms. I ignored the branches and followed the main tentacle, which grew thicker and sharper as it went deeper into the club.

The tendril led to a door marked CONFERENCE ROOM. Next to the door was a placard: WINNING LOSERS SUPPORT GROUP. Gluttony—in a dieting club? Uh-oh. I spritzed myself with holy water and opened the door.

Half a dozen people sat around a conference table stacked high with extra-large pizza boxes. With my senses open to the demon plane, I couldn't see their faces. Gluttony tendrils covered them like kudzu in a Georgia forest. All I could see was slice after slice of pizza disappearing into Gluttony-possessed lumps.

"Did you bring food?" a lump demanded.

The holy water made me invisible to the Peccatum, but not to the humans it possessed. I reeled my senses back from the demon plane, making the tendrils disappear, to see who was speaking. A plump woman of about thirty had paused mid bite to address me. Pizza sauce was smeared on her face, and a string of mozzarella dangled from the corner of her mouth.

"No, I—"

"Then get out!" she shrieked. "There's not enough for you!"

Five other angry faces glared at me. "Yeah!" a man yelled. "We're starving here." He turned to a college kid who wore a baseball cap adorned with a slice-of-pizza logo. "Call your boss and order a dozen more. Extra large with everything."

"Double everything!" someone added.

"And garlic bread!"

"I want a calzone!"

"A meatball sub!"

As the dieters clamored for more food, the kid pulled a cell phone from his pocket. Between bites of pizza, he placed the order. Or tried to. It was impossible to keep up with all the shouted demands.

Looking at all the empty pizza boxes, I was glad Tina had quit being my apprentice several weeks ago. Tina's a teenager and a zombie, and that combination makes her a nonstop eating machine. Plus, like all zombies, she's super strong. Holy water or not, if Tina had walked in on this pizza fest, she'd have taught everybody here a lesson in Gluttony. And it's a little distracting when your apprentice gets possessed by the demon you're trying to kill.

"Didn't I tell you to leave?" the plump woman snarled. "There's not enough to go around."

"Don't worry about me," I said. "I'm not hungry. I'm here to do some maintenance." I didn't have time to waste with the Winning Losers, anyway. I had to find the Peccatum. Another spritz of holy water, and I stepped inside. I opened to the demon plane a little, enough so I could make out both the faces of the support group members and the tendrils that gripped them. They regarded me suspiciously, ready to fight to defend their pizza. I stayed near the wall, studying the floor, trying to see where the main tentacle left the mass of tendrils. Soon they forgot about me and started arguing over the few slices that remained.

The conference room had a folding wall, the kind that could be pulled back to accommodate a larger meeting. The tentacle, much thicker than it had been in the hallway, passed through it. I skirted two support group members who were playing tug-of-war over a pizza crust, and left the room. The door to the next room, the one on the other side of the retractable wall, looked ordinary. No tendrils passed underneath it. In fact, it was the only door in the hallway clear of tendrils—kind of like a big, flashing neon sign proclaiming, "Nothing to see here. No demon behind this door. Move along." I'd bet my fee the Peccatum was inside.

I misted myself with holy water and tried the knob. It turned. I cracked open the door and slipped inside.

The room was dark, but that made no difference in the demon plane. A dim gray twilight, the constant half-light of the demon plane, permeated the place, along with a stronger stench. A huge blob, bulging and distended from gorging on sins, was sprawled on the conference table. The head, which looked like a muddy garbage bag filled with sludge, sat on top of two huge tentacles—Gluttony and Sloth, each as fat as a fire hose—and five shriveled ones: one for each of the other deadly sins. The head pulsed and shivered as the demon fed on the sins of those it trapped. Finally. Now to kill this demon, go home, and dress for dinner.

I could douse the Peccatum with holy water or gut it with a bronze dagger. Either way, I'd have to get in close.

I stood with my back against the wall and inched the door closed. There was a soft click as the latch caught. Immediately, exploratory gray tendrils—Sloth—sprang from the Peccatum and wafted toward me. The holy water kept me hidden. The tendrils felt their way around the door for a minute, then receded.

Another self-misting with holy water—I'd used up most of the atomizer already—and I stepped forward. I loosened the caps of the bottles of holy water in my holster and took another step. A few tendrils snaked from the gray tentacle and swept back and forth across the floor, as though the demon suspected that there was someone in the room but didn't know where to look. I advanced cautiously, watching the searching tendrils, moving toward the demon then pausing. The holy water's protection held. Whenever a tendril got near me, it changed direction, as though glancing off an invisible barrier.

Halfway across the room, I removed the caps from both bottles. When I got close enough, I'd dump their contents on the demon. A half gallon of holy water should be enough to dissolve the Peccatum into a puddle of goo.

I eased the left bottle from its holster and held it ready. Another step. I tugged on the right bottle, but it was tight in the holster. I pulled harder. The bottle came out, but some water sloshed from its neck. I looked down in time to see a drop splash onto a tendril near my foot.

Yellow steam, stinking of sulfur, hissed and shot upward like a geyser.

Immediately a mass of tendrils sprang from the gray tentacle. I ran toward the Peccatum, but I'd barely gone two steps before a fuzzy gray net wrapped around me and yanked me to the ground. A bottle of holy water flew from my hand, hitting the floor and rolling to a far corner of the room, spilling its contents as it went. Tendrils wrapped around my other arm, holding it immobile, as more tendrils plucked the second bottle from my grip and flung it away. It rolled under the conference table.

Peccatum tendrils are usually wispy and insubstantial, a creeping suggestion, but these were like bands of steel. I struggled, but the Sloth-woven net weighed me down. The more I tried to move, the tighter it got. As it tightened, Sloth claimed me.

Sleep. More than anything, I wanted to sleep. I was so tired. I knew there was something I was supposed to be doing, but remembering what, exactly, took too much effort. Better to rest now, just for a little while, and worry about it later. Whatever "it" was. My eyelids drifted shut.

The tendrils loosened slightly, letting me curl up on my side. They didn't feel like a net anymore; they felt like a soft, warm sleeping bag, enveloping me in coziness. Nice. The floor, covered with thin, cheap commercial carpeting, was surprisingly comfy—except something dug into my thigh. I reached down to see what it was. Oh, right. My dagger in its sheath. How odd that I'd strap on a dagger before taking a nap. I adjusted the sheath so it wasn't directly under my leg. There, that felt better.

I let my consciousness sink toward oblivion. It felt good, so good, to rest.

I wanted to sleep, but I couldn't. A strong, unpleasant smell, like dirty diapers mixed with month-old body odor, wrinkled my nose. I forced my eyes open, but I could barely see through the warm, gray mist that clung to my face. Tendrils slithered into my nose and down my throat. They squeezed my body. *This is bad,* I thought, strangely calm. The Peccatum was cocooning me in Sloth—and that was where Sloth became a truly deadly sin. If I didn't do something, the demon would smother me. Sloth would seep into my body until my lungs couldn't be bothered to draw in air, until my own heart grew too lethargic to beat. Yet the realization felt far away and unimportant. Sleep was so much more appealing.

Stinking gray tendrils clogged my nose. I couldn't breathe. My mouth opened in a gasp; invading Sloth filled it like dirty cotton. I gagged. A spark of self-preservation flared in me, and I snorted, trying to clear the tendrils from my nose. My hand lay near the hilt of my dagger. In the tight cocoon, I couldn't move enough to get my hand around it, but my fingers walked the dagger, inch by inch, from its sheath. Each inch felt like a mile; all I wanted was to stop and rest. But I kept going. When the blade was clear, I angled it upward and poked at the Sloth that smothered me. It gave a little, and I forced the dagger upward. Sloth dissolved around the blade, adding the stench of sulfur and brimstone to the stink in the air.

I pressed my advantage, cutting a bigger hole in the cocoon. When I managed to grip the dagger's hilt, I swept the blade back and forth. In a moment, my arm was free, and I sliced away the Sloth that was wrapped around my head. Sloth recoiled, the cocoon loosened, and I pushed myself into a sitting position. I drew my second dagger and sliced with both hands, cutting the tightly woven cocoon to shreds.

More tendrils reached for me, but I severed them as they approached. Stinking yellow smoke filled the room. I crawled toward the conference table, where a bottle of holy water rested against one of the legs. I got under the table and grabbed the bottle. About a quarter of its contents remained. I splashed holy water over myself and stayed where I was, directly beneath the Peccatum. Tendrils of Sloth slithered on the floor around me, searching, but the holy water kept me hidden, even as I coughed Sloth out of my lungs. Gray clouds puffed from my mouth as I hawked up the last of it.

Bam! An explosion shuddered the room. Fire blasted out, rife with the smell of smoke and charred meat. I ducked and covered my head, then peered out from between my arms. A massive new tentacle, red and fiery, streamed from the demon and through the wall. Anger.

The door burst open. One of the dieters—the woman who'd

told me to get out—stormed into the room like an avenging Fury. She was no longer a yellow lump of Gluttony; now she was burning with Anger. Her face was scarlet, and she was wrapped in flames. Behind her loomed two bodybuilders, both of them also in the fiery clutches of Anger.

The woman scanned the room until her eyes locked onto me. "What the hell do you think you're doing?" she screamed. In the human plane, she couldn't see the demon that wrapped her in flames. Only me. And I was the target of a massive Anger overdose.

She rushed into the room, fingers curled into claws, and swiped at me under the table. When I drew back, she kicked. I tossed some holy water on her leg, extinguishing the flaming tendrils that clutched her. She staggered back, confused.

Her bodybuilding friends charged me. I threw holy water at one. The other made it to the far side of the table and grabbed my ankle. I shook the bottle over his hand, but the few remaining drops of holy water barely dimmed the flames. He dragged me from under the table.

I slashed his forearm with one of my daggers—barely a scratch, but he let go. I scrambled to my feet. He bellowed and charged at me, arms swinging. I ducked and ran around behind him. When he turned, his arm drawn back for another punch, I sliced through the tendril of Anger that held him. He staggered as it let him go, and gazed at his own fist as if wondering where it had come from.

With a screech, the woman launched herself at me, her fingernails aimed at my eyes. I sidestepped her and stuck out my foot, tripping her and sending her sprawling. As she fell, I slashed through the Anger tendril that clutched her. But then one of the bodybuilders charged again.

I could take him. I could take all three of them. As a shapeshifter, I'm stronger than any human, even one who spent most of his time pumping iron when he wasn't in the grip of Sloth. Fighting off these norms wasn't what worried me. The Peccatum could keep this up forever. As soon as I severed a tendril, it sent out a new one, possessing the human with Anger again. Shouts and footsteps came from the hallway, as more Anger-possessed norms stormed the conference room. And the holy water I'd doused myself with was wearing off—I didn't have any more.

Tendrils of Sloth snaked toward me. I could sever them with bronze, but they'd keep coming. Eventually they'd get me. And I'd stand still, indifferent, while a throng of enraged dieters and bodybuilders beat me to bloody mush.

I had to get close enough to drive my blade into the demon's head.

Again, all three norms in the room flamed with Anger. They spread out, trying to encircle me. The woman snarled.

Her fury gave me an idea. The thing about sins—they're equal opportunity. They don't care what their object is.

"Hey," I said to her, "did you hear what that guy said about you?" I pointed at the closest bodybuilder. "He called you a fat cow!"

The dieter stopped in her tracks. Her head whipped toward the bodybuilder, her eyes narrowed with rage.

"And you know what she called you?" I asked the bodybuilder. "A stupid slab of meat!"

The two of them bellowed and charged each other. They went down, wrestling on the floor. As soon as they hit, the other bodybuilder ran at me. When he got close, I pointed at the wrestlers and said, "That guy said you're a wimp and his grandma can bench-press twice as much as you." He ran right past me and jumped into the fray.

I didn't waste any time. I ran to the Peccatum and plunged both my daggers into its head. I moved the blades around, making as much contact with the oily mist as possible. Tentacles thrashed. More norms, possessed by Anger, barged into the room. Barely glancing at me, they were drawn to where the Anger was strongest, the three people pummeling each other on the floor. The newcomers leapt into the brawl.

Anger lashed at me, too, cutting into me with fiery whips. I gritted my teeth. Let it. I channeled the fury into my attack on the demon, stabbing and slicing and slashing the disgusting blob. I hacked through the Anger tentacle at its root. My rage diminished, but that didn't slow down my attack on the head.

The Peccatum began to deflate. It tried to regenerate its Anger tentacle, but the result was thin and pale, barely flickering. One by one, tentacles dropped from the body and withered, curling like dried-up slugs. Across the room, the grunts and smacks of fighting ceased. I moved the bronze blades through the demon's body like I was stirring a big vat of sludge. The vat got smaller and smaller, until the Peccatum collapsed on itself. A puddle of grayish glop spread across the table. Thick, viscous strings oozed over the edge.

I wiped my blades, resheathed the daggers, and turned around. People stood in the room, looking dazed. The Anger had worn off, and they weren't quite sure what had hit them. The bodybuilders were helping the dieter to her feet. Her dress was torn and she had a black eye, but she'd held her own. She clutched a big clump of hair (once she noticed it in her hand she flung it away with a gasp), and the faces of both bodybuilders bore long, bloody scratch marks. All three apologized profusely to each other. Those who'd joined the fight late slunk quietly out the door.

As I left the conference room, one of the bodybuilders was making a date with the dieter. "Dinner?" he asked. The idea made her turn green—not surprising after all that pizza. They agreed on a movie instead.

Back in the lobby, the receptionist looked bewildered and a little green herself. She dialed the gym owner to come and fill out the final paperwork and cut me a check. He'd been smart enough to stay far away from the club once the Peccatum got out of control. Now, I assured him over the phone that it was safe to come back, and he said he was on his way.

I hoped he'd hurry. This job had taken way longer than planned, and I still had to get ready for dinner at my sister's house. *Mmm, dinner.* I wondered what we'd have. For some reason, I was feeling kind of hungry.

2

IN MY APARTMENT IN DEADTOWN, THE PARANORMAL-ONLY section of Boston, I checked myself in the mirror, wondering if pearls were too formal for a family dinner. Probably not for *this* family dinner. To my boyfriend, Kane, a high-profile lawyer as well as a werewolf, "casual" meant loosening his tie. And my sister, Gwen, was all about appearances. Ten to one there'd be a silver candelabra on the table tonight. Now that I thought of it, pearls might not be enough. Oh, well—they'd have to do. Too late now to rent the crown jewels.

The phone rang. It was Kane, letting me know he was waiting in the no-parking zone in front of my building. I threw on my jacket—the mid-March evening was chilly—and headed for the elevator, before some zombie meter maid threatened him with a ticket.

Downstairs, though, I paused at the mailboxes. Mine held an electric bill and a couple of junk-mail flyers. I shoved them back into the box to deal with later, disappointed that the one piece of mail I was hoping for hadn't arrived: a postcard from my vampire roommate, Juliet.

Six weeks ago, Juliet had gotten mixed up with the Old Ones, shadowy super-vampires so reclusive most vampires thought they were a legend. Then she'd disappeared. Since her disappearance, she'd sent me a series of postcards with cryptic messages, suggesting she was on the run from the Old Ones but letting me know she was okay. I'd received five postcards so far, mailed from locations all over the world, but the last one had arrived nearly a week ago. I was worried. The Old Ones prey on vampires the way vampires prey on humans—and they have no scruples about killing their victims. If they'd caught up with Juliet, she could be in serious trouble.

There was nothing I could do to help her now. I didn't even know where she was.

I went outside. Kane's BMW purred at the curb. My Jag was in the shop again—one of the hazards of owning a vintage car—so he was driving us out to Needham.

I opened the door and slid into the passenger seat, tugging the skirt of my dress to a reasonable level of decency.

"Wow." Kane gave a low whistle—I'd call it a wolf whistle if I were into puns—and leaned over to kiss my cheek. "You look great."

"Thanks," I said, putting my hand on his face. I turned his head until our lips touched. He smelled like summer forest at midnight. His lips, slightly rough, pressed against mine.

With a sigh, I sat back in my seat. "We'd better get going." It took about half an hour to drive out to Needham. Traffic should be light on a Saturday night at seven thirty, but I didn't want to keep Gwen waiting.

"Damn," Kane said, but he pulled the BMW away from the curb. He shifted gears, then put his hand on my thigh. "I was kind of hoping you'd brought a little Lust home from work."

I let his hand linger for a moment, feeling its warmth through the thin fabric of my skirt. His fingers curled around the hem, inching it upward, and I shivered. Then I picked up his hand and placed it back on the gearshift. "No, you weren't. If that Peccatum had nailed me with Lust, I would've already scratched that itch. You forget I was at a gym full of prime, grade-A beefcake." Most of them had been firmly held in the clutches of Sloth, Gluttony, or both, so they weren't exactly in peak form. But I didn't have to paint that picture in Kane's imagination.

He growled deep in his throat and jabbed the accelerator. Almost immediately, we were at the checkpoint out of Deadtown. He hit the brake, and we jerked to a stop.

As the checkpoint guard reached to open his window, I leaned over and whispered in Kane's ear, "Besides, I'm saving the Lust for dessert."

Kane grinned and gave my thigh another squeeze. Then he pulled out his wallet and removed his ID. I handed mine over, too. The guard, who had the gray-green skin and red eyes of a zombie and the bored expression of a public employee in a routine job, checked our cards. He looked at each of us, comparing pictures to faces. Then he swiped the cards through his machine and handed them back to Kane. The gate raised. The guard nodded as we drove through.

"Lust for dessert?" Kane did that thing with his voice that made my insides go all fluttery. "Too long to wait. Let's make it an appetizer. We could turn around right now and spend the whole night feasting on it."

His look smoldered, but tension—not lust—strained his voice.

"You're nervous!" I exclaimed. The attorney who regularly argued high-profile paranormal rights cases, who spoke on national television more often than some people brushed their teeth, was afraid to meet my suburban housewife sister and her family.

"Can you blame me?"

Well, no. In the couple of years that Kane and I had been dating—off and on until recently—Gwen had basically pretended Kane didn't exist. Like me, Gwen was one of the Cerddorion, a race of Welsh shapeshifters whose origins reach back to the goddess Ceridwen. Unlike me, Gwen had chosen home and family over shapeshifting. Cerddorion females gain the ability to shift at puberty, and lose it if they give birth. When Gwen decided to go norm, she went all the way, aspiring to be even more human than her middle-class, white-bread human neighbors. Although she said she accepted my decision to retain my shapeshifting powers and carry on the Cerddorion tradition of fighting demons, my sister sometimes acted like she was uncomfortable having a monster in the family. She'd never accepted my paranormal friends, and she'd tried to fix me up with a never-ending norm parade of potential boyfriend material, mostly her human husband's coworkers and acquaintances.

So when she'd asked me to come out for dinner and casually added, "Oh, and bring Kane if you like," the invitation seemed nothing short of miraculous.

"You'll do fine," I said. "Gwen is the world's most gracious hostess."

And Kane was the world's most charming werewolf. It wasn't just his good looks—silver hair, gray eyes, and a be-still-my-heart smile. It wasn't just the coiled strength that radiated from his muscular body and gave grace to his movements. It was who he was, the way he combined the best of everything human—a passionate belief in justice, true concern for his fellow beings, an appreciation of the finer things—with the power and sensuality of his beast.

Hmm. An extended lust feast did sound tempting right now.

At the far end of the block, we reached the second checkpoint, the one into human-controlled Boston. Here, the guard was human, but his scowl made him look scarier than the zombie we'd just encountered. Again, we presented our IDs. I also passed over a sheaf of papers for the guard to inspect. Lately, restrictions had been tight on Deadtown residents who wanted to venture out of Boston's paranormal-only section into the wider world. I'd spent half the morning filling out forms so we'd have the required permits to drive out to Needham for dinner.

The guard shuffled our papers, taking way longer than seemed necessary to rubber-stamp our permits. Everything was in order; I'd double-checked to make sure. But sometimes you got a jerk at the checkpoint. A lot of the norm border guards were card-carrying members of Humans First, a political action committee whose goal was to expel all paranormals from Massachusetts. If this bozo was one of that crowd, I'd bet he recognized Kane and was slowing us down on purpose. Kane's white knuckles on the steering wheel showed that was his opinion, too.

I wanted to tell the jerk to hurry up, that we had places to go. But this guy could refuse to let us pass, for any reason or for no reason at all. So I waited and didn't say anything.

Finally the guard returned our documents and raised the gate. Once we'd gone through, Kane blew out a long breath.

"Asshole," he muttered.

I knew what he was thinking. Kane was trying to get a paranormal-rights case in front of the Supreme Court, to establish federal-level rights for PAs (short for "Paranormal Americans," Kane's preferred term for what everyone else called "monsters"). His case had been postponed when the court's chief justice, Carol Frederickson, was murdered. But if the case went forward and Kane won—a big *if*, in my opinion—PAs could live anywhere. We could vote, travel, do anything the norms could do. Checkpoints like the ones in and out of Deadtown would be a thing of the past. And so would asshole border guards.

"It's worse at night," I said. "That's when they put all the Humans First hardliners on duty." I'd had no trouble crossing the border on my way to and from today's job.

"It's more than that," Kane said. "Haven't you listened to the news today?" He clicked on the radio.

A man's voice was in the middle of relating the gory details of Boston's latest murder. Of course I'd heard about that—everybody had. In the past three days, two bodies had been discovered in the South End. The first, sprawled in a park near Rutland Square among the just-blooming crocuses, had been bad—sliced up beyond recognition, with strange symbols carved into the victim's flesh—but nobody freaked out too much. Boston's a big city; murders happen. Then, less than forty-eight hours later, in the wee hours between last night and this morning, another victim was found a few blocks away. The second victim had been dumped in the middle of Harrison Avenue, not far from Boston Medical Center. The cops refused to say whether the killings were related, but no one had any doubts. A serial killer stalked Boston. Some reporter for the *Herald* had even come up with a nickname, based on leaked information that the killer used a curved blade, like a sickle: the South End Reaper.

The newscaster continued: "Boston Police commissioner Fred Hampson has put code-red restrictions in place on Designated Area 1, popularly called Deadtown." Code red—no wonder that guard had taken so long with our papers. Code red meant zombies couldn't leave Deadtown at all; no permits would be issued for them under any circumstances. And it tightened restrictions on the movements of other paranormals between dusk and dawn. I'd thought I was going for overkill on the forms I'd filled out this morning. Apparently, I'd done just the right amount.

The possibility of a serial killer worried me. Not because I expected the South End Reaper to jump out of the shadows, slashing at me with a curved blade. I could take care of myself in a knife fight. I patted the dagger sheathed inside my knee-high boot, thought of the other two tucked in my purse. In my world, "be prepared" was more than just the Boy Scout motto. No, I was worried there might be a supernatural force driving this killer, a force darker and more deadly than anything the norms could imagine.

A month ago, a really nasty demi-demon named Pryce Maddox had attempted to lead demons out of their own plane to overrun the human world. Pryce called himself my cousin—a far-fetched claim—but even if we were related, he was a thoroughly rotten branch of the family tree. Believing that an ancient prophecy pointed to his own ascendancy over both the demon and the human realms, Pryce had busied himself freeing the Morfran, a spirit of insatiable, destructive hunger that's the essence of all demons. My Cerddorion ancestors had imprisoned much of the Morfran deep underground in an old slate mine, binding it inside the stone. Pryce had discovered the spell to release it, and he believed various signs indicated the time was right for him to set the Morfran free. As the Morfran fed, demons would grow stronger—and the demon plane would no longer contain them.

Free-floating Morfran takes the form of monstrous crows that rip and tear at their victims with cruel beaks. Crows are carrion eaters, and Boston's two thousand zombies looked like an all-you-can eat buffet to the ravenous Morfran. Pryce sent the spirit there to feed. At an open-air concert, to celebrate Paranormal Appreciation Day, the Morfran had attacked, killing nearly a dozen zombies before I managed to trap it again. Or most of it; some of the Morfran got away. And when the Morfran possesses a human, the spirit drives that person to kill—over and over and over.

If the South End Reaper was Morfran-possessed, could Pryce be behind it? The last time I'd seen my demi-demon "cousin," he'd been lying on the ground, alive but little more than an empty shell. During our fight, I'd killed Pryce's demon half, leaving his human form comatose. And then Pryce's body had disappeared. The two human cops who'd been guarding him were dead, every drop of blood sucked from their bodies. It was how the Old Ones, those über-vampires my roommate Juliet feared, killed their prey.

It seemed clear the Old Ones had taken Pryce—but why? Demons and vampires didn't get along. Even if the Old Ones could revive Pryce, what would they want with him? Pryce was thoroughly evil and cared for no one but himself. Besides his ambitions to subject the human world to demons, he'd tried three times to kill me—and that was to test whether I was "worthy" to be raped and forced to bear his child. Personally, I hoped the Old Ones had drained Pryce dry, as they'd done to those cops. I hoped I'd never see or hear of

Pryce again. And I hoped the South End Reaper was just some run-of-the-mill psychopathic killer, with no ties to demi-demons, the Morfran, or the Old Ones.

But as we drove through the night, the voices on the radio edging toward hysteria, a quieter voice inside me whispered that any such hopes were utterly foolish.

3

GWEN GREETED ME AT HER FRONT DOOR WITH A WARM hug. Hints of Italian herbs underlay her expensive perfume. My throat got a lump as it hit me how much I'd missed her. It had been too long. The strength of her hug showed she thought so, too.

She stepped back and offered a hand to Kane, welcoming him. Nick, Gwen's husband, repeated the routine—a hug for me, a handshake for Kane—and took our coats.

"Where are the kids?" I asked, stepping into the living room. As soon as I cleared the doorway Maria, my eleven-year-old niece, rocketed over and threw her arms around me. I stroked her fine blonde hair and kissed the top of her head. She was getting so tall.

"I see you found Maria," Gwen said. "The boys are already in bed." *The boys* meant Zack, six, and Justin, who was two. "That's why I invited you for a late dinner, so I could wrestle the little hooligans into bed and have a grown-up evening for a change." She put a hand on Maria's shoulder and drew her back a step. "And that's why Maria is on her way to bed, too."

"But Mom, I want to talk to Aunt Vicky."

"We agreed you could say hello, and then you'd go to bed. No arguments. Remember?"

"Yeah." Maria looked at the floor.

Kane came forward, holding out his hand. "Hi, Maria," he said. "I'm Kane. Vicky's told me lots about you." He smiled. "All of it good."

Maria squinted at him, giving him the once-over, as she shook his hand solemnly. "Are you Vicky's boyfriend?"

He and I exchanged a glance, and his eyes were so full of warmth and light I melted a little inside.

"Yes," we said together.

Maria nodded, and her serious expression morphed into a grin. "Okay."

A timer dinged. Gwen looked toward the kitchen door. "That's the lasagna," she said. "Upstairs now, Maria. I'll come up in a minute to say good night. Then you can read for a bit, but lights out by nine, all right?"

"Okay, Mom."

Gwen squeezed the girl's shoulder and went into the kitchen.

Maria stood on tiptoe to plant a kiss on my cheek. "Come back soon, okay? When it's not just for grown-ups."

"I will. But you listen to your mom now."

She nodded, said good night to Kane and her dad, and climbed the stairs.

"Who wants a drink?" Nick asked.

Nick poured me my usual club soda. Kane had a Scotch. (His werewolf metabolism would burn off that, plus any wine served with dinner, long before it was time to drive home.) Gwen returned and announced that dinner would be on the table in fifteen minutes.

Conversation flowed easily. Kane asked Nick about his work in a downtown Boston investment firm and talked knowledgeably with Gwen about the novel her book club was reading. Once we moved into the dining room, he admired the table and complimented the food. She caught my eye and touched her chin as she tucked her hair behind her right ear, a signal we'd developed in high school. It meant, "This guy's a good one."

Halfway through dinner, the conversation slowed down for a minute. During the pause, Kane turned to Gwen.

"I enjoyed meeting your aunt last month," he said.

Gwen stiffened, but Kane didn't notice.

Oh, no. Don't bring up Mab. Not when everything was going so well. I tried to kick him under the table and missed.

"I don't think—" I began, but he talked over me.

"Wales is such a beautiful country, and her home is magnificent. I know Vicky used to visit Mab every summer. Did you also spend a lot of time with your aunt when you were growing up?"

Gwen's face was ghost white. She bit her lip, and I could almost hear her mentally count to ten. Very precisely, she laid her fork on the edge of her plate. "We do not mention that woman's name in this house."

Kane froze. Then he glanced at me, perplexed.

Damn it, I should've warned him. I'd been so caught up in thoughts of Pryce and the Morfran and the South End Reaper that it hadn't occurred to me to tell Kane to leave Mab out of the conversation. My aunt had trained me as a demon fighter; I'd been her apprentice for seven years. She was tough and strict and rarely showed her emotions, but I loved her like a second mother. Kane had liked Mab, too, during his brief visit to Wales. He'd never have suspected how much my sister hated her.

There was no way I could explain it now.

Kane's eyes darted back and forth between me and Gwen. Nick reached over and put his hand on Gwen's, but my sister stared at her plate like she was trying to set it on fire with her eyes. The silence extended, then graduated to a whole new level of awkward. I flailed around for a safe topic.

"Gwen," I said, reaching for the bread basket, "this bread is delicious. Did you get it from that new Italian bakery near the train station?"

She looked at the basket in my hand as if she'd never seen such a thing before, then blinked and nodded. "Yes, I did. And the tiramisu we're having for dessert, too."

"Ooh, yum. I *love* tiramisu," I said, so heartily I almost peeked into the demon plane to see if any stray wisps of Gluttony clung to me. But of course Gluttony wasn't the problem.

Nick came to the rescue—or tried to. "So," he asked Kane, "do you think the Celtics are going to make it to the playoffs this year?"

Kane is a workaholic who doesn't know the meaning of the phrase "spare time"—he's too busy crusading for paranormal rights. It would never occur to him to go to a basketball game or other sporting event for fun. But sports sometimes tied in to his work, and he kept up enough to discuss whatever sport was in season when he was schmoozing with influential people. Just last week he'd taken a couple of congressmen to a Celtics game, courtside seats and everything.

Kane and Nick talked about basketball for several minutes. Nick was enthusiastic, certain the Celts would go all the way this year. Kane made some informed comments, but mostly he listened to Nick, who glowed with pleasure as he reeled off statistics.

Gwen, on the other hand, seemed to have lost her appetite, pushing food around her plate. Kane kept glancing her way. He wrapped up the conversation with Nick by inviting him to a game—courtside seats again—in a couple of weeks.

Whoa. Courtside seats. My brother-in-law rated as highly as a senator. That must mean Kane . . . My commitment-shy brain dug in its heels and refused to go down that path.

Kane turned to Gwen. "Do your kids like sports? Any budding basketball stars in the family?" Smart move, bringing Gwen back into the conversation by asking about her kids. It was a topic my sister and her husband could discuss for hours.

"Not basketball." Gwen looked up slowly. "Not yet, anyway. Nick promised Zachary he'd teach him to shoot baskets when he gets a little taller. But Zack is only six, so he's got quite a bit of growing to do."

"He's a pretty good shot with that kid-sized basketball hoop we got him," Nick pointed out.

"Oh, and you should see him when Nick lifts him up and lets him shoot at the hoop over the garage." The image made Gwen smile. "He's so cute when you do that." She turned back to Kane, her face softened with pride in her kids. "Zack and Maria both play soccer, although I think Maria is going to give up soccer for ballet. She's crazy about dance. She says she still wants to play softball this spring, though. She's a good shortstop."

"She's a *terrific* shortstop," Nick corrected. "You would not believe this one play she made last season . . ." He launched into a description, Gwen jumping in here and there with more details.

Kane listened, asking the right questions in the right places. Soon, the stiffness had melted from Gwen's shoulders and she was laughing and enjoying the conversation again. Crisis averted. No wonder Kane was so good at his job. He was a master at getting people to relax and open up.

In my peripheral vision, the kitchen door cracked open and Maria peered through. I pointed at Gwen to ask whether she wanted me to get her mom's attention, but Maria's eyes widened and she shook her head vigorously. She pointed at me, and then crooked her finger.

I stood and picked up my plate. Gwen pushed back her chair, but I put a hand on her shoulder. "You sit and talk," I said. "I'll clear the table. Everyone want coffee? I'll get that started, too."

"The tiramisu—"

"I'll take care of it. You worked hard putting together a great dinner. I can handle dessert."

Balancing the stack of dirty dishes, I shouldered open the swinging door into the kitchen. Maria sat at the table in her PJs. She slumped in her chair, one bare foot swinging back and forth.

"Hi," I said.

"Hi." She glanced at me, then examined her hands.

"So what did you want to talk about?"

She shrugged and chewed at a thumbnail.

Okay. Maybe she didn't know how to broach the topic, whatever it was. I'd let her get to it in her own time. I slid the plates onto Gwen's spotless counter. "Aren't you supposed to be in bed?"

"Yeah."

"I think I hear a 'but' coming."

"But . . ." A faint smile curled her lips, then faded away. "I couldn't sleep." She murmured her next words so softly I almost missed them. "I'm scared to."

I turned on the water at the sink. "How about you rinse, and I'll load the dishwasher?"

"Okay." She got up and padded over to where I stood. Her small feet looked cold on the tile floor, so I moved over to make room on the rug in front of the sink. We worked for a minute or two in silence, Maria squinting at each plate with concentration.

"Bad dreams, huh?" I asked.

She gave half a nod, then shook her head. "Not bad. Some of them are good. But they're weird."

Now we were getting to it. "Weird how?"

"It's like I'm not *me* anymore." Worry clouded her face as she handed me a plate. "Mom said I should tell her if I have dreams like that."

"Have you? Told her, I mean."

Her wet hand gripped my wrist. "What will she do if she finds out?"

I curled my fingers around hers and gave a little squeeze. "It'll be okay, sweetie. I promise." I picked up a dish towel and dried both our hands. She nodded, but doubt furrowed her forehead.

"Dishwasher loaded," I announced. "How about some hot chocolate? That helps me sleep sometimes."

"Okay." Maria sat down again at the table.

I put two mugs of milk into the microwave. As they heated, I got the coffeemaker started.

"You look weird in a dress," Maria observed.

Yeah, I could agree with that. Felt weird, too, not to be in my usual jeans. "That's because I don't have cool pajamas like yours."

Maria looked down at her pajamas, blue flannel covered with yellow peace signs, and grinned. "Mom would freak if you wore pajamas to a dinner party."

"You're right, she would. But at least I'd be comfortable."

Maria laughed. I stirred in the cocoa and carried the two mugs to the table. She took hers in both hands and sipped, then sipped again. She put down the mug and wiped off a cocoa mustache with the back of her hand.

"So tell me about these dreams of yours," I said.

Maria drank more cocoa. "They start off normal—you know, just dreams. But then they change." She wriggled in her chair, sitting up straighter. "Like, I had this one where I was walking down the hall at school, except all of a sudden I realized I was underwater, swimming. It scared me because I thought I'd drown. I kept thinking, 'I need air. I need to breathe.' But then I realized I *was* breathing. I could breathe the water." Her eyes went wide with amazement as she remembered how that felt. "After that, it got fun. Except I was worried I couldn't open my locker because I didn't have any hands. Just fins. And then I laughed at myself because I thought, 'Silly. Why would a fish need a locker?' The laughing made lots of bubbles." Amusement lit her eyes but dimmed at once to worry. "Do you have dreams like that?"

"Sure. When I was your age, I had them all the time. Swimming, running—but on four legs, right?—burrowing, flying . . ."

Maria leaned toward me. "Flying dreams are the *best*. It's like, suddenly I'm up the air and I'm *flying*. And then somehow I realize I always could; I just didn't know it before. It's great. I can go anywhere I want. And part of me thinks, 'Why do I even bother to walk?' "

"Yeah, I know what you mean. It's like—"

The kitchen door swung open. "How's that coffee coming?" Gwen stopped and stared at the two of us. From the heat that rose in my cheeks—and from the way Gwen watched us through narrowed eyes like we were conspirators plotting an assassination—I knew we looked way guiltier than a girl and her aunt sharing some cocoa.

"What are you doing up, young lady?" Gwen asked Maria.

"Um, I . . ." Maria's round eyes implored me for help.

"She came downstairs for hot chocolate," I said. "It sounded like a good idea, so I made us each a mug. She helped me load the dishwasher, too."

"Well, you get back to bed now, Maria. I'll be up in a few minutes to tuck you in. Again."

"Okay. Night, Mom. Night, Aunt Vicky." Maria gave Gwen and then me a peck on the cheek. She fled up the back stairs.

I put the empty mugs in the dishwasher and got a carton of half-and-half from the fridge.

"So, what were you two talking about?" Gwen took the half-and-half and poured it into a cream pitcher, which she set on a tray. The tension was back in her shoulders, and her hand shook. That was Gwen. When upset, make things even more perfect.

"Oh, you know . . ." I *so* didn't want to get between my sister and her daughter on this issue. Maria should confide in Gwen about the dreams, yes. But not until she felt ready.

"She's having dreams, isn't she? Preshifting dreams."

"They're just dreams, Gwen. She said she had a couple of odd dreams lately—flying, swimming, stuff like that. Norms get those, too. It doesn't necessarily mean anything."

"But it might." Gwen's biggest fear was that her daughter would become a shapeshifter. That was a big part of why she'd married a norm; she'd hoped human DNA would make her children something other than Cerddorion, something closer to "normal." But as Maria grew, so did Gwen's fears. It didn't help matters that a crazy scientist with an ambition to map the shapeshifter genome had tried last fall to kidnap Maria and use her as a lab animal. I'd brought Maria home, but Gwen's protective instincts had kicked into overdrive. Yet she couldn't protect Maria from herself. She couldn't shield the girl from her own nature—whatever that turned out to be.

"We'll have to wait and see," I said. "There's no point in worrying yourself sick about it now."

"We'll talk about this later." Gwen's tone made the words sound like a threat.

I held open the door as she carried the coffee tray into the dining room. She'd forgotten the tiramisu. But it didn't matter. The evening was over. Not even Kane could pull Gwen back from whatever dark place she'd gone in her worries about Maria, in her anger and hurt that Maria had chosen to talk to me—not Gwen—about what she was going through. Within fifteen minutes, we were saying good night.

4

"THAT WENT PRETTY WELL," I SAID AS WE PULLED OUT OF Gwen's driveway and headed back to Boston.

"Are you kidding? If that had been a trial, and the jury was starting its deliberations—like your sister and her husband are doing in their living room right now—do you know what I'd be doing? I'd be pacing the hallways, chewing my nails until they bled and trying to figure out how to tell my client we were going to lose."

"Oh, come on. It wasn't that bad. Okay, there were a couple of tense moments. But Gwen likes you. She gave me the secret signal."

He scowled like he thought I was teasing him. "I wish you'd told me not to mention your aunt."

"I should have. I'm sorry about that."

But even if I hadn't been distracted on the drive out here, I might have neglected to bring up the issue. In my mind, Mab's household and Gwen's family existed in such completely separate spheres that I probably wouldn't have thought to warn

Kane. Of course, without that warning from me, he'd think bringing up family would be a natural icebreaker. He'd probably expected that saying he liked Mab would win him points with my sister, not send him three giant steps back.

"What happened between them?" he asked.

"I don't know, exactly." The animosity had started nearly twenty years ago. "When Gwen was thirteen, she went to Wales for her first summer of demon-fighter training. Or that's what was supposed to happen—she was home within a month. When I asked her why she came back, she burst into tears and told me to leave her alone. She never said what went wrong. But whenever anyone mentioned Mab's name, Gwen would shout, 'I hate her,' and run out of the room."

Gwen's rejection of Mab had changed our family. No more Christmas visits to Maenllyd, Mab's manor house in north Wales. Gwen flat-out refused to go. And all those summers I spent in Wales, Gwen never once asked about Mab or acknowledged that I'd been away. She hadn't invited Mab to her wedding; she hadn't sent announcements when her children were born. Because of Gwen, Mab hadn't attended my father's funeral.

"Do you think the training was too tough for Gwen? Your aunt isn't exactly a softie."

I shook my head. "It was more than that. Mab wouldn't speak of the incident, either." I'd asked her about it when I began my apprenticeship. "She told me it was none of my business. That I was there to focus on my own training. She said so in a way that made me think it would be a bad idea to ask a second time." Mab never said she hated Gwen; she never talked about her at all. Whatever had happened, it erased each of them from the other's world.

"Families can get so complicated," Kane said. "It's easier being a lone wolf."

"Oh, yes? Should I stay at my place tonight, then, and let you do your lone-wolf thing at yours?"

He gave me a sidelong look, and then made a sharp right into the empty parking lot of a closed mini-mall. He stopped, turned to me, put his hands behind my head, and pulled me to him for a kiss. All the tension, all the pent-up frustration of the evening, was transformed into the urgent pressure of his lips against mine. A thrill went through me. The kiss deepened, making my heart pound. Then Kane sighed and rested his forehead against mine, his hand stroking the back of my neck.

"I said easier, not better."

Whichever. Right now it all felt pretty damn good. I tilted up my face to kiss him again when his cell phone rang.

He groaned. He pulled out his phone and checked the number. "Damn. I'm sorry, Vicky. I should take this call." He ran a finger along my lips as he pressed a button and put the phone to his ear. "Alexander Kane." He listened for a couple of seconds. His finger stopped moving on my mouth. "Hold on." He muted the phone and turned to me.

"It's about Juliet. She's in Goon Squad custody."

My heart lurched. The Goons had Juliet? At least she was safe from the Old Ones. But she was being held by the cops who police Deadtown—and that wasn't good news.

The Old Ones weren't the only ones looking for Juliet. She was also wanted for questioning in connection with that Supreme Court justice's murder, the one that had derailed Kane's paranormal rights case. Witnesses had seen Juliet in Washington on the night Justice Frederickson was killed. But what the cops didn't know—or wouldn't believe—was that the Old Ones had been there, too. Kane had seen them. Three Old Ones had tried to prevent him from reaching his werewolf retreat that night, the first night of a full moon, and force him to change in the middle of the city. They'd almost succeeded, too.

When Justice Frederickson's body was found, her throat ripped out, Kane was initially the prime suspect. But the D.C. cops hadn't been able to charge him because of his airtight alibi: Just before moonrise, he'd made it to a werewolf safe room at the National Zoo, where he remained locked in until dawn. Kane was convinced the Old Ones had murdered Frederickson and tried to frame him for it—and that Juliet was somehow involved.

Had Juliet admitted her involvement? Was that the reason for this phone call? I couldn't believe it.

I listened, but I couldn't make much sense of Kane's one-sided conversation. When he ended the call, I asked what was going on. "When did the Goons pick up Juliet? Where?"

"They didn't. She turned herself in three days ago. Said she needed protective custody."

The Old Ones. They must have been closing in on her.

"But why did the Goons call you?" Unlike humans, paranormals had no right to legal counsel. We weren't guaranteed a phone call, either. The cops could legally hold Juliet indefinitely, without ever telling anyone she was in custody. There had to be a reason they were calling now.

"Juliet says she'll cooperate fully if she can talk to a lawyer first. She asked for me." He turned in his seat and put a hand on my arm. I didn't like the look in his eyes. "You realize it's impossible for me to represent her."

"What do you mean? Of course you have to."

"Vicky, somebody murdered a Supreme Court justice and tried to pin it on me. Juliet was involved. I can't imagine a bigger conflict of interest."

"She didn't frame you. I know she didn't."

"You can't say that. I know she's your friend, but you haven't even heard from her in, what, six weeks or longer."

I hadn't told anyone about Juliet's postcards, not even Kane. It was like she was confiding in me, and they were too secret and too urgent to share.

"So you're just abandoning her to the mercy of the norms? That doesn't sound like you."

"That's *not* like me." His glance reproved me for thinking otherwise. "Did you hear me mention Betsy Blythe? That was a referral. Betsy is a terrific defense lawyer. She's a human who has a decent track record in paranormal cases. In fact, let me give her a call now."

He placed the call, waited several seconds, and glanced at me. "Voice mail," he said. At the beep, he said, "Hi, Betsy. It's Kane. I gave your name to the JHP"—JHP was short for Joint Human-Paranormal Task Force, the Goon Squad's official designation—"as a referral for a vampire they're holding. Her name is Juliet Capulet, and she's wanted for questioning in connection with the murder of Justice Frederickson down in D.C. She says she'll cooperate after she's spoken to a lawyer, so they're allowing her access. She asked for me, but for obvious reasons I can't take her on as a client. Of course, I immediately thought of you. If you could meet with her, I'd really appreciate it. I'll touch base with you in the morning, but call any time if you have questions. Thanks, Betsy."

He put his phone away and took my hand. "All right? Betsy's top-notch, Vicky. Juliet will have competent counsel. I promise."

"She asked for you."

"It's the best I can do."

I pulled my hand away. It sat in my lap, clenched into a fist. When I spoke, my voice sounded tight. "You won't help her, even for my sake?"

"It's not a matter of 'won't.' It's 'can't.' I cannot represent Juliet when there's a cloud over our relationship." He put a finger under my chin and turned my face toward him. His gray eyes were sincere. "If I did, it wouldn't be fair to her."

He was right, damn it. But that didn't mean I had to like it. I jerked my head away and stared out the side window.

Kane laid a hand on my shoulder. He pressed my arm. I didn't turn. After a moment, he sighed and started the car. We pulled out of the parking lot and back onto Route 9.

My chest felt tight as I watched the wood-framed houses of Newton go by. Most of them were dark, their norm inhabitants asleep. Maybe they were having flying dreams. Maybe they dreamed they were being chased by monsters like the two who drove silently past in a late-model BMW. Whatever. They were lucky. They weren't sitting alone in some Goon Squad cell waiting for a lawyer who wasn't coming. I turned in my seat. "I want to see her, Kane."

"All right." He nodded. "I'll tell Betsy to try to get you on the list of approved visitors."

"No, I want to see her now. Tonight. I want you to drop me off at the Goon Squad's holding facility."

We stopped at a red light. He looked at me as though I'd just told him I wanted to run the Boston Marathon route in my dress and high-heeled boots. "I don't think that's a good idea."

"I'm not asking your permission."

A muscle twitched in his jaw. "Okay, you're not asking my permission. And you won't let me talk you out of it, either."

"Just drop me off."

"They won't let you in." The light turned green, and we crossed the intersection.

"I've got to try. You say you can't represent Juliet because she's mixed up with the Old Ones. That's exactly why I need to talk to her. She might know where Pryce is."

It was my best argument. Kane knew what Pryce had tried to do to me, and it bothered him that my demi-demon "cousin" was still out there. No one knew where Pryce was or why the Old Ones had taken him—except maybe Juliet.

"All right." The words were more growl than agreement. And I didn't really care whether or not he dropped me off—we both knew I'd try to see Juliet tonight, wherever I got out of the car. Yet his willingness meant something, an acknowledgment of my friend's importance to me. Perhaps even an acknowledgment that I could be right about her.

I needed to make sure Juliet was okay. I needed to find out what she knew about Pryce and the Old Ones. I needed to find out what had happened that night in Washington. There were lots of reasons I needed to talk to Juliet. And they couldn't wait until my name showed up on some officially approved list.

5

KANE PULLED THE BMW OVER JUST BEFORE THE CHECK-point out of human-controlled Boston. "Mind if I let you off here? I want to stop by the office and pick up some papers, and I don't think they'd let me back through." He nodded toward the checkpoint, where a bored guard paged through a comic book. Spider-Man. I could see the cover from here. With the code-red restrictions in place, there wasn't much traffic between Deadtown and the rest of the city. Kane's office was on the norms' side of the barrier, near Government Center. But since it was past eleven, well outside norm business hours, the guard might insist he stay put.

"Sure. I'll go through the walk-up booth." There was only one open tonight. "We're practically on the Goon Squad's doorstep, anyway." The first building in the New Combat Zone, the block between the checkpoints into Deadtown and the rest of the city, was my goal: a nondescript concrete structure that served as the Goon Squad's headquarters and detention center.

"Thanks for dropping me off here," I said.

Kane put a hand on my leg. His fingers toyed with the hem of my dress. "This isn't how I'd imagined tonight ending."

"The night's not over yet." I leaned over and kissed him. "I'll see you back at your place."

He put an arm around me and pulled me to him. As we kissed again, longer, his fingers caressed my neck, bringing up shivers.

"I'll be waiting," he whispered.

It was my damn high-heeled boots that made me stagger a little on my way to the walk-up booth.

The guard barely glanced at my ID before he swiped it. The norms don't care who's leaving their part of town half as much as they care who's entering it.

I went into the Goon Squad building. The main activity—headquarters and offices—was upstairs. The holding facility was deep in the soundproofed basement. I clacked down the stairs in my boots and pulled open the glass door at the bottom.

A human woman looked up from the reception desk. She was about forty, had on no makeup, and wore her hair slicked back in a ponytail. "Yeah?"

"I'm here to see Juliet Capulet."

Her eyes narrowed. "You're her attorney? I thought you said you couldn't come in until morning."

Betsy Blythe had already called back. That was a good sign. Maybe Kane's faith in her was justified.

I decided to ignore the receptionist's question—no point in lying to the police unless absolutely necessary—and responded to her statement instead. "If I waited until morning, there'd be no point, would there? Vampires sleep during the day." Juliet was old for a vampire, with all of the powers age conferred. She could stay up half the day if she wanted, but most vampires conked out as soon as the sun cleared the horizon.

The receptionist considered, then shrugged. "Sign in here," she said, turning an open book toward me. "I'll need to search your bag."

As she opened my purse, I scrawled a signature that could be anything from *Betsy Blythe* to *John Hancock.*

"No weapons allowed in the cells. I'll give you a receipt for this knife." She removed a bronze dagger and set it on her desk. "And this one."

The second dagger made her raise an eyebrow. But both eyebrows went up when the third dagger, the one in my boot, set off the metal detector. I handed it over. "Jesus, how many blades do you carry?" She crossed out the number she'd been writing on my receipt.

"I'm, um, taking a self-defense class."

Uh-huh, said her look. *In a cocktail dress and pearls.*

"Can't be too careful in the Zone, right?" I added.

"Well, that's true. I never go to any of the monster bars. I walk straight between work and the checkpoint. And the place still creeps me out." She handed me a ticket. "I'll get a guard to escort you to the prisoner. Use this to reclaim your weapons on the way out." She handed me a slip of paper, which I stuffed into my purse.

The uniformed guard was also human—six two, buzz cut, with shoulders that might even give him an edge in a wrestling match with a zombie. He jerked his head to indicate I should follow. We went down a hallway and turned a corner. I waited while he removed a ring of keys from his belt and sorted through them to open a metal door. Near the end of another long hallway he stopped and again went through his keys. He opened a door and gestured me inside.

"Fifteen minutes," he said.

I went in. The door shut and locked behind me.

Juliet sat on a narrow cot, on top of a scratchy-looking beige blanket. She was thin. Not concentration-camp-victim thin, but she'd lost her voluptuousness. Her elbows looked knobby in the short-sleeved orange prison shirt. Her long black hair was stringy and lusterless.

This was not the Juliet I knew. My Juliet had made Romeo fall in love with her at first sight more than six centuries ago. Since then, countless others had fallen for her sultry gaze, the curve of her mouth, her effortless allure. This Juliet looked frail, like the years (if not yet the centuries) were catching up with her.

If she was surprised to see me, she didn't show it. I wanted to hug her, but she made no move toward me. Just a steady stare.

There was a chair against the wall by the door. I sat in it.

"Hi," I said. "Orange is so not your color."

She pressed her lips into a tight, tiny smile—a vampire's smile. "They told me this style doesn't come in black."

We stared at each other. Juliet's face was as still and unblinking, as if carved from marble.

My questions tumbled out all at once. "So what's going on?" I asked. "Where have you been? Who are the Old Ones? What the hell happened in Washington?"

She said nothing but shifted on her cot, crossing her legs. A chain rattled. A silver shackle was locked around her right ankle, connected to thick links of silver chain that coiled on the floor and disappeared under the bed. Around the shackle, her skin was mottled purple and black, covered with large blisters. That had to hurt.

Juliet flicked a glance toward a corner of the room, behind me. I turned in my chair to see a mounted video camera winking at us rhythmically with its red eye. The room was probably bugged, too. So much for lawyer-client privilege. Not that any such thing existed for us monsters.

"Are they treating you okay?" I asked.

Juliet sniffed. "I turned myself in to get protective custody. That means they're supposed to keep moving me to different facilities, not leave me here chained to the wall like some pathetic Andromeda waiting for the sea monster." She rattled the chain. It looked long enough to let her move around the cell. Not that there was anywhere to go in the eight-by-ten room. "If they don't torture me to death with silver, they'll drive me insane with that camera. The way it's always blinking, blinking, blinking. I can't ignore it." As a predator, Juliet's vampire senses were hyperalert to any movement. She could probably see the pulse of the recording light even through closed eyelids. "Or else they'll starve me with diluted blood." She wrinkled her nose. "They serve it cold. In a bottle."

Blood loses vitality when it leaves the body, and vampires need living blood to thrive. The Goon Squad should know that. But obviously they didn't care. They were giving Juliet enough nourishment to keep her alive, but weak. She'd be easier to handle that way. "I'll see if there's anything Kane can do."

"Why didn't he come? I asked for him specifically."

"He said . . ." I looked around, wondering where they'd hidden the microphone, and didn't finish.

How the hell were we supposed to have any kind of meaningful conversation? There was so much to talk about, but nothing we could say, given the circumstances. We went back to staring at each other.

Coming here to talk with Juliet had been a bad idea. In the morning, her real lawyer would show up. There might be trouble for Juliet because I'd dropped by tonight. And I hadn't gotten an answer to even one of my million-and-two questions.

So much for helping my roommate.

At least I could try to play lawyer, then get advice from Kane. What would he be asking if he were here?

"Have any specific charges been brought against you?" I asked, trying to sound like I knew what I was doing.

Instead of answering, Juliet gasped. "What on earth?" She was looking over my shoulder, toward the camera.

I twisted around. It took me a moment to realize what she'd seen. There was no blinking from the video camera. Its light had gone dark.

Out in the hallway, something crashed, making the cell's cement floor shudder. The crash was followed by a protracted scream, a sound twisted with unfathomable fear and pain.

I jumped up and went to the door. There was no knob on the inside. We were trapped. More crashes, more bangs shook the cell. Maybe whatever stalked the hallway wasn't looking for us. Maybe it would pass us by.

I held my breath and waited.

A blow from outside jarred the door. So much for passing us by.

Behind me, Juliet made a strangled sound. "It's them," she whispered. "They've found me." She looked wildly around the cell. Her gaze landed on me, darkened with something like sorrow. "I'm sorry, Vicky," she whispered.

Her words chilled me more than the scream had. Vampires never apologize—ever. Not even as a figure of speech.

Another blow bulged the door inward.

I reached into my purse for a knife—and pulled out my weapons-check receipt. Stupid visitors' policy. I picked up the chair I'd been sitting in and lifted it over my head, pressing myself as flat as I could against the cinder-block wall beside the door. When whatever was on the other side rushed into the room, I'd knock the crap out of it.

With a screech of tearing metal, the door was ripped from its hinges. A robed figure sped through the doorway. I slammed the chair down on him, and he collapsed in a heap of black cloth.

Right behind him came a second one, this one in a brown robe. He flew—literally flew—over the first, straight at Juliet.

Juliet sat perfectly still, her hands folded in her lap, her face expressionless except for the terror that screamed silently from her eyes.

What the hell was wrong with her? Why wasn't she fighting?

She didn't move, didn't even flinch, as the brown-robed creature lifted her from the bed.

I picked up the chair and rushed him from behind. As I brought the chair down, the creature flung his arm backward, knocking me sideways. There was ice and power in the blow, and more-than-ordinary strength. I flew across the room and hit the wall headfirst. Stars exploded through my vision. Pain and the warm, metallic taste of blood filled my mouth. I'd bitten my tongue when I hit the wall. I wiped my mouth, smearing blood across my cheek.

The room felt twenty degrees colder than it had before the Old Ones entered.

I shook the stars away. Brown Robe held Juliet like an undead groom about to whisk his bride over the threshold. But her shackle held her back, the silver chain stretched taut. The creature grabbed the chain and pulled, trying to yank it from the wall. He shrieked as a cloud of black-and-yellow smoke billowed from his hand. The creature dropped both Juliet and the chain. He spun around, clutching his hand to his chest, his bulging eyes searching the room.

His face. I'd forgotten how hideous the Old Ones were. Yellow skin stretched taut across the skull. His eyes protruded from their sockets, the whites tea colored. A hole gaped where his nose should be. But it was the fangs that made the Old Ones redefine ugly. They stretched from this Old One's lipless mouth past his chin, ending in razor-sharp points. Saber-toothed vampires. Just what I wanted to fight without my weapons.

Brown Robe didn't share my dilemma. Smoke still streaming from his right hand, he drew a short sword with his left. I tensed, preparing. But the Old One didn't attack. Instead, he picked up Juliet, threw her onto the cot, and began hacking at her leg with the sword, just above the shackle.

Juliet screamed.

Oh, no, you don't.

I rushed the Old One from the right. He tried to swat me away again, but I dodged the blow. I grabbed his sword, and we grappled for it.

The Old One's grip was strong. His icy fingers made my joints ache. Gritting my teeth, I stuck a finger in his eye socket. Brown Robe recoiled, and I twisted my body. I got the sword away.

Immediately I thrust, but Brown Robe jumped impossibly high. Something grabbed my ankle and yanked backward. I fell, cracking my head again on the side of the cot. More stars. They filled the room, swirling over my head like the goddamn Milky Way.

When my vision cleared, I lay on my back, a weight pinning my limbs to the floor. Inches above me, the faces of two Old Ones hovered like a nightmare. The cold, stale smell of ancient death—of mold and rot and grave dust—flowed from them like an arctic wind blowing through a tomb. I struggled, but I couldn't move. The Old Ones looked at each other. The black-robed one nodded. Brown Robe yanked his sword from my hand and rose. Immediately, Juliet's screams began again, louder and more frantic than before.

Black Robe lowered his face to mine. A tip of black tongue poked out from between his fangs. Slowly, carefully, he licked the corner of my mouth, tasting the blood smeared there. It felt like an ice-coated slug slithering along my skin. Revulsion clenched my stomach, and I turned my head away. Mistake. Pain stabbed my neck and shoulder as the Old One sank his fangs into me. These creatures could drain a person dry in a couple of minutes. I'd seen the empty husks they left behind.

My neck ached and burned, and I could feel myself weaken as the creature sucked the life from my body. My toes and fingers were cold, going numb. I wiggled them, and my left hand brushed something. I heard a faint *clink*. The silver chain. It had burned Brown Robe's hand to a cinder. I had a feeling that Black Robe wouldn't like it much, either.

Black Robe had my hand pinned to the floor, but I got my fingers around the chain. One flick, and the silver made contact with the decrepit yellow flesh. Smoke billowed. Black Robe reared back, batting at his burned hand.

The moment his weight left my arms I was up on my knees. I wrapped the chain around his neck and yanked hard. Black Robe snarled and bucked and clawed at me with both hands. I looped the chain around my own hands so I wouldn't lose my grip on it. The silver links grew hot in my fists as smoke billowed, spewing the smell of charred, rotten meat throughout the room. The links of chain seared my palms, the backs of my hands. I clenched my teeth against the pain and kept the chain taut.

A blade sliced toward me. I dropped sideways, dragging Black Robe with me, rolling as we hit the floor. With the second strike, Brown Robe drove his blade deep into his buddy's gut. I kicked Brown Robe's wrist, and he dropped his sword. In my hands, the burning chain went slack as Black Robe's head toppled from his body and rolled under the cot.

I held two lengths of chain, one in each hand. Contact with the Old One's flesh had melted the links, breaking the chain. The Old One's headless corpse lay at my feet. The contact hadn't done the creature's neck any good, either.

The length of chain attached to Juliet's shackle was the longer of the two pieces. I lashed it like a whip at Brown Robe. The Old One jumped back, but not far enough. The chain hit his face, burning through his cheek. He shrieked and flew up to the ceiling. I whipped the chain at his legs, his feet, whatever I could reach. The smoke that choked the room showed I'd hit him more than once.

Brown Robe swooped toward me. I ducked, spinning the chain over my head like a helicopter rotor. But Brown Robe wasn't attacking; he was running away. The Old One rocketed through the door. I let go of the silver chain, snatched up the dropped sword, and ran after him.

The hallway was empty. Cell doors hung crookedly, any inhabitants long gone. I ran toward the entrance. The metal door that sealed off the cell block had been torn from its hinges. Beside it, the guard who'd walked me down the hallway lay crumpled on the floor. I passed him, then stopped where the hallway turned right. Keeping my back against the wall, I peered around the corner.

No sign of Brown Robe—except for more bodies left behind. Two here. The receptionist who'd signed me in lay sprawled across her desk. Another guard, one I hadn't seen before, had been tossed aside like an empty candy wrapper. All three of the dead norms had been drained of blood.

Through a half-open door, I could see the building's surveillance center. It looked like a tornado had blown through, and then someone had taken an ax to what was left.

What a disaster. After this, Juliet wouldn't be safe from the Goon Squad or the Old Ones. I had to get her out of here. I gathered up the knives I'd left with the receptionist and returned to the cell block.

The ruined door to Juliet's cell lay against the far wall, where the Old Ones had hurled it. A quiet moaning issued from the open doorway.

Juliet sat on the cot, her injured leg pulled up and resting on her other thigh. The silver chain trailed from her ankle. She rocked back and forth, back and forth, cradling her leg.

I went over to her. "Let me see—"

She snarled, baring her fangs, and shoved me away. Nail marks scored my arm.

"Juliet, we have to go."

She snarled again, her eyes flaring with rage and pain but not a spark of recognition.

"Hey, it's me. Vicky. Come on, you know me." I stayed out of scratching range, trying to make my voice both gentle and urgent. "We need to get out of here. Those Old Ones killed the guards. The one that got away might come back with reinforcements."

"The Old Ones," she whispered, and I saw a flicker of the Juliet I knew. Her forehead wrinkled, like she was considering a difficult problem. "You *killed* one of them."

I nudged the headless body with my toe. Yup. Killed it dead. Juliet stared at the corpse as if she couldn't fathom what it was.

I tried again. "How badly are you hurt? Can you walk?"

She extended her leg toward me. The bloody wound where Brown Robe had tried to saw through her leg gaped. The bone, absurdly white, showed in the ragged cut. That wasn't good. Juliet should have started to heal already.

"It's the silver," she said. "It slows healing. As long as that's in contact with my skin . . ." She hugged herself. "And I'm so famished."

She looked terrible. Purple crescents, so dark they were almost black, ringed her eyes. Her skin, always pale, looked dead white, like those guards who'd been drained of blood.

The guards. The one who'd let me into Juliet's cell carried that huge ring of keys. One of them had to open Juliet's shackle. Once the silver was off her, she'd gain strength and start to heal.

I hoped.

I hurried to the guard who'd fallen in the hallway. His key ring jutted out from his hip. I removed the keys and started back to Juliet's cell. Along the way, I noticed that one of the gray metal doors was stenciled with the word *Kitchen*. I tried the knob; it opened.

The Goon Squad's kitchen looked more like a break room. In its center stood a table, magazines and newspaper sections strewn across its top. There was a microwave and a coffeemaker on a counter to my right. Beyond the counter was a refrigerator.

I opened the fridge and surveyed its contents. On the top shelf sat a carton of milk, a couple of brown bags, and a Tupperware container of some kind of pasta. The next shelf down held what I was looking for: bottles of blood. Juliet had complained it was cold and watered-down, but it would give her some nourishment.

With four bottles clenched in my arms, I left the kitchen and returned to Juliet's cell. She was still on the cot, rhythmically kicking the dead Old One with her good foot. As soon as she saw what I carried, she reached for the bottles. She downed the first two without taking a breath. I started to uncap the third, but she shook her head.

"Can you get this silver off me?"

I sorted through the keys until I found a few that looked like they might fit the shackle. On the third try, the lock clicked open. Juliet sighed with relief as the silver fell away from her skin. I dropped the shackle on the floor, away from her. A puff of smoke went up where some silver links touched the Old One's body. I picked up the chain again, considering—it made a pretty good weapon against the Old Ones.

I wrapped the length of chain around my waist, like a belt, the perfect accessory for my ruined dress. My kind of fashion statement: Mess with me and you're dead.

Juliet scooted forward to the edge of the cot. "I'm a bit better now," she said. "Let's go."

I checked her leg. It didn't look better. If anything, it looked worse: foul-smelling, greenish pus mixed with the blood that ran toward her ankle. I cut a strip of cloth from the fallen Old One's robe and used it to bind up the wound.

I looked at Juliet's bright orange prison outfit, PRISONER stenciled in bold letters across the back. Not exactly subtle. "Would you wear that thing's robe?" I asked. "We could pull the hood forward to hide your face."

She wrinkled her nose with distaste, but she nodded. I stripped the robe off the Old One, revealing an emaciated body. Yellow, leathery skin clung to elongated bones.

Juliet shuddered. "And to think I once wanted to join them."

It was the first piece of information she'd given me about the Old Ones. But we didn't have time for more questions now. Black Robe had been about a foot taller than Juliet, so I had to cut more fabric from the bottom of the robe. But once the garment was on her and the hood pulled up, she was impossible to recognize. You almost couldn't tell there was anyone inside the robe at all.

Juliet stood and took a step. Immediately her injured leg gave way, and she collapsed in a heap on the floor. She howled with frustration and pounded the Old One's corpse with her fists.

"Hold these." I handed her the bottles of blood and then scooped her up in my arms like a child. I tucked Brown Robe's sword under my arm. As I carried Juliet out of the cell, she twisted around to stare at the headless, dried-out yellow corpse that lay on the floor. Then we were down the hall, up the stairs, and breathing the frosty air of a cold March night.

6

THE ALLEY BEHIND CREATURE COMFORTS, A MONSTER BAR in the New Combat Zone, is narrow and dark, piled high with trash and reeking with the scents of urine and vomit. Not the kind of place where you want to hang out at one o'clock in the morning.

Lucky for us. I was planning to hide Juliet here until I could talk to Axel, the bar's owner, about giving her refuge. The scarier and more deserted the alley, the better.

After we'd slipped out of the Goon Squad building, I headed straight for this alley, hugging the buildings and staying in the shadows. I was pretty sure no one had seen us. Now, I looked up and down the deserted alley. Certainly no one had followed us.

I set Juliet down gently, but her leg buckled and she collapsed on the sidewalk. She lay on her side, her face hidden by the robe's hood.

I checked her injured leg, unwinding the blood-and-pus-soaked bandage. The silver burn looked better—the blisters were gone, and taut, shiny skin covered the burned-raw places—but the gash looked worse than it had before. The stench of it made me gag, though I tried not to let Juliet see. The skin at the edges of the cut, a sickly shade of purplish-green, was ragged, like something had been eating at the wound. This wasn't right. Juliet should be healing. Had the Old One's blade been poisoned? What could poison a vampire?

Juliet struggled to sit up. I slid my hands beneath her arms and lifted her to a seated position. The hood fell back as she rested her head against the brick wall. Sweat plastered her tangled hair to her face. I wouldn't have guessed vampires could sweat—but when they did, it obviously wasn't good.

"Juliet, I'm going to go inside and ask Axel if he'll let you stay here." Creature Comforts was her best hope for a hiding place. The New Combat Zone was like Boston's version of the Wild West. Although the Goon Squad patrolled here, the Zone operated by its own rules. And nobody messed with Axel, the owner of Creature Comforts. Or if they tried to mess with him, they never tried a second time. Axel wasn't human—seven feet tall and solidly built, he looked more like a mountain than a man. Nobody knew what he was. There was a story that when government workers came to get a blood sample to analyze his DNA and determine his species—something everyone was subjected to in the months after the plague that had created Boston's zombies—one scowl from Axel's shaggy brow had sent the workers scurrying away, their vials empty.

Juliet needed protection, and I couldn't think of anyone better than Axel to give it.

Juliet was shaking her head. "Axel lets no one into his lair."

True. I'd seen him win a standoff with the Goon Squad when they'd threatened to break down his door. Yet that was precisely why Creature Comforts was the safest place in Boston for Juliet right now.

"Let me talk to him. He likes you." At the very least, he'd set up a cot for her in the storage room until I could come up with a plan B. I tried the back door, the one that led into Creature Comforts' storage room. Damn. It was locked. Well, I'd look at that as more evidence of Axel's first-rate security.

"I'm going to hide you behind some boxes here," I said. "Just for a few minutes, while I go talk to Axel." I couldn't risk carrying Juliet through the bar. Business throughout the Zone had been slow lately, with the code-red restrictions on zombies and fears of the Reaper keeping norms home at night, but once the story of her escape hit the news, even one witness could threaten Juliet's safety.

Juliet's face clenched with pain, and she didn't say anything else. I assumed she was okay with my plan.

But I wasn't—not quite. A pile of boxes wasn't exactly armor, and I couldn't leave her alone and vulnerable with the Old Ones after her. We hadn't been followed, but I couldn't be sure she was safe. For all I knew, her enemies could track her by smell.

I thought about leaving her Brown Robe's sword but decided against it. If the Old Ones arrived, it'd be too easy for one of them to use it against her.

I unwrapped the silver chain from my waist. The Old Ones wouldn't get within lashing distance of it. As long as it didn't come into direct contact with Juliet's skin, she could use it to fend off Brown Robe. Unless he arrived with an army.

The robe's sleeves were too long for Juliet's arms. I knotted the right sleeve at its opening so it couldn't slip up her arm and expose her skin. Then, feeling through the cloth, I closed her fingers around the chain's shackle end. "If that Old One comes, whip the chain at him. Show me you can do it."

"If an Old One comes, you'll never see me again." But she flailed the chain a few times. There was more strength and energy in her movements than I'd expected. Good. And I'd get her out of here in a couple of minutes.

Working quickly, I surrounded Juliet with a stack of empty boxes. I checked from several angles, rearranged some boxes, added a few more. Then I hurried to the end of the alley and down the street to Creature Comforts.

* * *

AS SOON AS I OPENED THE FRONT DOOR, ANY HOPE THAT Axel was having a slow night fled. Laughter and music blasted out. Creature Comforts was packed with women, dressed for a night of partying. They filled all the tables and spilled out of the booths. As I stepped inside, I was hit by the bar's characteristic perfume of beer, tobacco, and a slight whiff of human blood—shot through tonight with a strong scent of musk. On tables at the back, two half-naked, human male dancers performed an athletic bump-and-grind routine.

Oh, great. I'd walked into a werewolf bachelorette party.

Massachusetts was one of a handful of states that recognized marriages between paranormals. Other states had passed laws restricting marriage to humans only. Although some norms in "Monsterchusetts" objected to paranormal marriage, no one seemed to mind the money it brought the state. It had become fashionable among werewolves to have a norm-style wedding in addition to whatever ritual they performed at the full moon. In Boston, a whole industry had sprung up offering destination weddings to werewolves.

I scanned the crowd but didn't see a face I recognized. I knew most of Deadtown's werewolves through Kane. These were definitely tourists.

"Hey!" A woman pointed at me. She wore a tight, super-short, low-cut black dress and a crooked tiara sparkling with pink and white rhinestones. She flipped her glossy blond hair over her shoulder, managing to make the gesture an act of aggression. "This is a private party. The bar's closed."

Damn territorial werewolves. When they traveled in a pack, even out-of-towners acted like they owned the place.

I ignored her and walked toward the bar.

She was in front of me before I got halfway across the room. Her nostrils flared as she sized me up in a few sniffs. She bared her teeth—not a very impressive gesture in her human form—and growled. "I said it's a private party."

"Do I look like I'm here to crash your party?" I gestured at my ruined dress.

She didn't look at my outfit. She stared at the sword in my hand, the one I'd taken from the Old Ones.

Oh, that. Well, yeah, I could see how that might be interpreted as a threat.

I didn't have a sheath for it, so I stuck it under my arm, where I hoped it seemed less dangerous. I stepped to the left, intent on getting around her. "I need to talk to Axel."

She growled again and dropped into a fighting crouch. Jesus, the full moon was still three weeks away and she was going into feral overdrive.

"You want to challenge me? Fine." I dropped my purse on the floor and shifted the sword to my right hand, ready to use it. I wouldn't have minded two blades in a fight with a werewolf, but I wanted to teach her some manners, not kill her. Besides, it's bad form to rummage through your purse for a dagger at the start of a fight.

We circled each other. Someone cut the music. All I could hear was my heart thumping in my ears and the raspy breathing of my opponent—until Axel stomped over and got between us.

Axel isn't a guy you can easily ignore. Especially when he's wearing his pissed-off expression.

"No fighting." The werewolf tried to dodge around him, but his massive arm blocked her. "You fight, you're out. No refunds."

She pushed against his arm with both hands, snarling at me. Axel turned fully toward her, clamping his hands on her shoulders. A low, threatening sound issued from his throat. All at once, the werewolf relaxed. She dropped her arms, looked at the ground, and backed away.

Axel's not a werewolf, and he may not say much, but no one can beat him in a display of dominance.

The room remained silent for a few seconds. Then someone called out, "A toast to Kiana!" Other voices joined in: "To Kiana!" "To Kiana!" "To the bride!"

The werewolf who'd challenged me stood in the center of the room as everyone raised glasses to her. She lifted her gaze from the floor, broke into a wide grin, and grabbed a glass.

"Let's have some music!" she shouted, adjusting her tiara. Something started up, loud, with a heavy bass line I could feel through the floor. The male dancers gyrated, the female werewolves howled, and everyone went back to having a good time.

I'd almost gotten into a bar brawl with a werewolf bride on the eve of her wedding. Another day in the life.

Axel was back behind the bar, filling a row of plastic flutes with champagne.

"Axel, I need to talk to you. It's important." I had to shout to be heard over the music.

He kept pouring but nodded.

"Juliet—"

A redheaded werewolf in a green halter dress glared at me as she grabbed a glass of champagne from the bar. I didn't want to shout. Wolves have sharp hearing. Even with the music blasting, I'd be broadcasting a bulletin about Juliet's escape to everyone in the room. They might be out-of-towners, but they didn't need to know Juliet's business.

I climbed onto the bar and, kneeling there, cupped both hands around Axel's ear. He popped another champagne cork and poured as I spoke. I tried to sum up the situation as quickly and clearly as possible.

"Juliet's in trouble. The Goon Squad had her in custody in connection with that murder in D.C. A couple of powerful super-vampires killed some cops trying to kidnap her. She was chained to her cell with a silver shackle, and they almost cut off her leg trying to grab her. She's hurt, and she's not healing like she should. She needs a place to hide."

Axel stopped pouring. "Here?"

"I couldn't think of anywhere safer."

Axel pursed his lips behind his beard. He poured champagne into a flute, waited for the foam to die down, then topped it off. He filled three more flutes that way before he nodded.

"Okay."

Relief flooded me. "She's in the alley behind a pile of boxes, by your back door."

"Bartender! We need more champagne." The redheaded werewolf was back, waving two glasses and looking impatient.

He looked at the werewolf, then at me. At her, and then back at me.

"You want me to tend bar." A nod. "But Axel, I don't know anything about bartending." My taste ran to club soda and lite beer—the kind that comes in a bottle. They both taste about the same.

He opened a fridge stocked with green bottles topped with gold foil. "Champagne." He pointed at a cardboard box stashed under the bar. "Flutes." He grinned. Apparently he'd just taught me the secrets of his trade.

Axel patted me on the shoulder. He went to the back of the room and pushed a button on the portable stereo, cutting off the music. A few howls of protest went up but faded when they caught the look on Axel's face. Thirty female werewolves cringed under his gaze. "Going out. She's in charge," he said, gesturing toward me. "No fighting." He stalked down the back hallway, toward the storeroom.

Thirty glittering pairs of eyes turned toward me, and thirty werewolves straightened. You could almost hear the hackles rising.

The last thing you want to do when staring down a pack of werewolves is act intimidated. Even the norms know that. The best approach would be to emulate Axel's nonchalance. Just pour. It'd be nice if I could also emulate his height and muscle mass, but I'd work with what I had. Besides, I'd stashed the short sword within easy reach on a shelf below the counter.

Intimated? Not me.

I wished they'd turn the music back on, so they could ogle their beefcake dancers instead of stare at me.

I picked up a champagne bottle and peeled off the foil. The hairs on the backs of my arms stood up, making me all too conscious of my audience's intense gaze as I fumbled with the wire cage around the cork.

Why the hell didn't this stuff come with screw tops?

"I'm thirsty. Hurry up."

The bride-to-be stood at the bar, her tiara crooked again, her lips pulled back in an expression halfway between a sneer and a snarl. Oh, goody. More dominance games.

The wire came off. I grabbed the cork and yanked. It exploded from the bottle and flew from my fingers, missing the bride's head by a quarter-inch. Champagne sprayed out—and the champagne didn't miss. It hit the bride squarely in the face, soaking her hair, dripping from her nose and chin.

I righted the bottle and set it on the bar, foam flowing like lava over my fingers. In any other situation, I'd apologize. But you just don't say sorry to a soaking wet, angry werewolf. I gave her a hard stare and groped for my sword under the bar.

She grabbed the bottle, shook it hard, and blasted me with cold, wet spray. Sputtering, I snatched the bottle and emptied it over her head.

A roar went up. Werewolves rushed at me from all sides—running, vaulting over the bar. I went down. What a ridiculous way to die, I thought. Stomped to death by two dozen tipsy werewolves in stilettos.

A French-manicured hand reached toward me. I looked up. The bride, still dripping, smiled at me. What the hell? I grabbed her hand, and she pulled me to my feet. She offered me an open bottle of champagne.

The werewolves had raided the fridge behind the bar. Throughout the room, they sprayed each other with champagne. The poor dancers seemed to be getting more than their share. The wet look suited them, I had to say.

I shook the bottle and sprayed the bride, who laughed with delight.

Someone started the music, and the dancers resumed their gyrations. Drops of champagne flew from their bodies, catching the light. The werewolves started dancing, too, pushing aside tables to clear the floor.

The fridge stood open, empty. I shut the door. Then I found a recycling bin and started picking up the champagne bottles that littered the room.

"Don't do that." The bride put a hand on my arm, but her

touch was tentative, not aggressive. "Please. My girls will take care of it." She cupped her hands and shouted over the music. "Listen up, ladies! Everyone pick up two bottles and put them in the bin." She sat me down in her former seat, telling me to relax, and went behind the bar to find more recycling bins.

"Thanks." A werewolf with chin-length black hair sat down across from me. "You saved the party."

"You're welcome." I tried to look as though I knew exactly what I'd done, then gave up. "Um, how?"

"Ever since her engagement, Kiana has been a total bridezilla. Her mother stopped speaking to her weeks ago. She reduced her dressmaker to tears. She actually bit the caterer—the poor guy needed stitches." She shook her head. "The trouble is, she's not really all that dominant. Not by nature. It was stressing her out to be such a bitch."

Ah. The picture was becoming clearer.

"Somebody needed to challenge her. But you just don't *do* that to a mating female. She's like . . . like a temporary queen. Everyone defers to her. But everyone also saves up their grudges and takes them out on the bride's hide as soon as the honeymoon's over. Kiana knew how much trouble she was headed for, but she couldn't seem to stop herself."

"So a challenge from me released the tension."

"Exactly." She grinned, showing white, even teeth. "And you did it without spilling a drop of blood. Brilliant."

"Yeah, it always kinda sucks when a bachelorette party turns into a bloodbath."

The werewolf grinned again. "Now Kiana can relax and be herself. She'll still have some fights to face a couple of full moons down the road, but a lot of us will let our grudges slide. We've got our friend back." She got up and danced her way into the middle of the room.

TEN MINUTES LATER, AXEL RETURNED. HE STOPPED AND stared at me, sitting at the bride's table, wearing her tiara, and holding a bottle of my favorite lite beer, paid for by the bride. He turned to the bar, where Kiana was mixing a cocktail for one of her friends. "The champagne I paid for ran out, so it's a cash bar now," she called.

Axel turned back to me and raised a shaggy eyebrow.

"She said she was a bartender in college. I've been watching. She's charging for the drinks."

He sat down across from me. His eyebrow seemed to have found a permanent home halfway up his forehead.

"I, um, beat her in a challenge. Accidentally, kind of. There was no fighting involved," I added quickly. "Just champagne."

Axel surveyed the room. The place stank of spilled champagne, but there was no broken furniture or bleeding patrons. Better than a typical night.

"How's Juliet?" I asked.

"Safe." He placed the silver shackle and chain on the table. A nearby werewolf glanced at it, shuddered, and moved away. "She said you'd need this."

"Can I see her?"

He shook his head. "She's resting."

Shit. Axel wasn't going to let me into his apartment. As Juliet had said earlier, he never let anyone in. He was bending his usual rule to protect her, but his hospitality wouldn't extend to me. I'd just locked Juliet away even farther out of reach than she'd been with the Goon Squad.

And I still didn't have any answers.

"Axel—"

He shook his head, and I knew there was no use arguing.

"Okay, then tell her to call me as soon as she's feeling better, okay? Tomorrow, no later. I really need to talk to her. Can you do that?"

This time I got a nod.

I removed the bride's tiara and set it on the table, then stood. "Keep me posted about how she's doing, will you? I'm worried about her leg. And thanks. I know you . . . um, value your privacy. I'll try to move her to somewhere else that's safe as soon as I can."

I wrapped the chain around my waist, picked up my purse, and moved toward the door.

Axel's big paw shot out and grabbed my arm. "Come back after sunrise."

I nodded. I didn't know whether he'd let me see Juliet or whether he merely expected me to help clean up after these rowdy werewolves. Either way, I'd be here. Axel was good people—whatever species he was.

7

WHEN I OPENED THE DOOR TO HIS APARTMENT, KANE looked up from his laptop screen. He sat on the sofa, feet on the coffee table, papers spread all around him. He'd rolled up his sleeves, removed his tie, and even undone the top buttons of his shirt. *Mmm.* Sexy attorney at work.

But the alarm that leapt into his eyes reminded me I was the polar opposite of sexy right now.

"My God, Vicky. What happened?" He was up in a second, his strong arms around me, pulling me close.

"Careful. Silver," I said, stepping back and unwrapping the chain from my waist. I coiled it and added it to the arsenal in my purse. I leaned the Old One's short sword against the wall.

He sniffed. "Are you . . ." Another sniff, his nostrils flaring wide. "Are you *drunk*?"

"Of course not." He knew how little I drank. "I got caught in a little champagne fight at Creature Comforts."

"Creature Comforts? I thought you were going to see Juliet."

"I did."

Kane scowled, staring at my waist. "And that belt you were wearing looked an awful lot like a silver shackle. The kind they use to restrain vampires."

"Um. There's a reason for that."

Kane closed his eyes and shook his head as if clearing it. "Tell me what happened. Start from the beginning."

"Better sit down."

"How did I know you were going to say that?" He groped backward to find the sofa and sat on its arm. His eyes took inventory of my appearance. "You've got blood on your cheek."

Oh. That was from fighting the Old Ones. I suddenly realized how long it had been since I'd looked in a mirror—and wasn't sure I wanted to, ever again.

"All right." I took a deep breath. "From the beginning." I told him everything that had happened from the time he'd dropped me off until I walked through his front door. Well, I did gloss over the bachelorette party, saying only that some Creature Comforts customers, fooling around, had started spraying champagne at each other. The party, the bride-bitch, the idiotic dominance contests—somehow, discussing the commitment rituals of werewolves with my lone-wolf boyfriend would feel more than a little awkward. I didn't want him getting any ideas. Not now. I was comfortable with things as they were.

There are some areas where I'm perfectly happy being a craven coward.

"So Juliet's safe," I wrapped up. "I'm worried about her wound, but maybe with some rest she'll start to heal. I'll try to convince Axel to let me see her when I go back after sunrise."

Kane got up and paced in front of the sofa, rubbing his chin. He stopped abruptly and turned to me, his expression troubled. "She asked for me."

"What?"

"Juliet. She asked for me as her attorney."

"Yeah, so? You're a lawyer. You specialize in paranormal cases." Kane was the most famous paranormal-rights lawyer in the nation, possibly in the world. What vampire in trouble wouldn't want his counsel?

"Look at the timeline, Vicky. I get a call asking me to meet with her ASAP. Within two hours, these creatures—the same kind that attacked me in Washington the night Justice Frederickson was murdered—show up to bust Juliet out of jail."

It took me a second to process what he was saying. "You think she was setting you up?"

"Doesn't it look that way?"

"I can see why it does to you." *Even though you're wrong, wrong, wrong.* "You believe she was involved in Frederickson's murder, so of course you'd think she's out to get you. But we don't know what happened in Washington. What if she went down there to try to help you?"

"Did she tell you that?"

"No, she didn't get a chance to tell me anything. But she did try to tell me, several times over the past month, that she was working *against* the Old Ones, not with them." I described the postcards I'd received—the international postmarks, the hints that Juliet was trying to stave off some danger related to the Old Ones.

"You've gotten five of those? You never told me."

"If I had, what would you have done? You'd have wanted me to take them to the police. I wasn't going to do that." Juliet had already been running from the Old Ones. I wasn't going to put the cops on her trail, too.

I set my jaw, expecting to see anger in his face. Instead, what I read there was hurt.

"You didn't trust me," he said.

Shit. I'd rather have him fuming—anger I could deal with. This was harder, especially because he was right, about the postcards, anyway. I could have told him about them, but I didn't. I didn't tell anyone. I simply waited, hoping Juliet would find a way to let me know if she needed my help.

Now I didn't know what to say.

Kane stared at me for a moment. Then he sighed.

"All right. Talk to her. Find out her story." He covered my

hand with his, but I could see the doubt in his eyes. "I know she's your friend, Vicky. But I don't trust her."

In a way, I understood his distrust. Vampires are notoriously self-centered. Most vampires' personalities are an unholy blend of narcissism and deviousness that make Machiavelli look like Mister Rogers. Most of the time, I'd agree with Kane's caution. But this time, I thought he was mistaken. Juliet was no altruist, but she wouldn't betray a friend.

Kane raised his hand and touched my cheek, and I remembered my face was smeared with blood.

"I need a shower," I said, pulling away.

"I don't know," he said, tilting his head. "That whole blood-on-the-face look is kinda sexy to a werewolf."

"Good to know. But I'm still taking a shower."

I'd taken two steps toward the bathroom when he grabbed me from behind and pulled me close against him. "Need someone to wash your back?" His voice was soft in my ear; his warm breath against my neck sent little sparks through me.

I turned toward him and put my arms around his neck. "You know," I murmured, my lips brushing his, "that's the best offer I've had all day."

WHEN THE POUNDING ERUPTED ON THE FRONT DOOR, I was in the bathroom, wrapped in a towel, combing my hair. Kane had gone out to the living room to put away his work for the night.

He answered the door. Then it closed again, and I heard three voices: Kane's, a woman's, and another man's. The man's voice sounded familiar, but I couldn't place it.

I looked around the bathroom. I didn't have a bathrobe here (*note to self: buy second bathrobe for Kane's place*), and I wasn't going to put on the torn and stained dress that lay on the floor. Instead, I picked up Kane's discarded shirt and pulled it on. Under it, I rewrapped the towel around my waist, like a sarong, and strolled nonchalantly into the living room to see what was happening.

Kane sat on the sofa, wearing his bathrobe and looking

completely at ease. Across from him, in a leather chair, sat a female zombie dressed in a blue blazer, yellow sweater, and navy pants. Her straight, shoulder-length hair was blonde; she'd probably looked good once in that shade of blue. Slouching by the door stood a norm I recognized. One I wasn't exactly thrilled to see.

"Norden," I said, "I heard you were out of the hospital."

He snorted, not a pleasant sound. "Yeah, my insurance ran out so they booted me. Too bad. The food was lousy, but at least somebody else cooked it." Elmer Norden had been providing security for Deadtown's Paranormal Appreciation Day concert when Pryce loosed the Morfran to feed on the zombies. Norden tried to stop him, and my "cousin" had nearly killed the guy, slicing him up badly. Now, Norden seemed back to his usual caustic self: short and sneering, with a pitted complexion and piggy eyes. The scars on his face only made him look meaner.

I glanced at the zombie who'd arrived with him, then back to Norden. "You're back on the Goon Squad?"

"Yeah. They couldn't keep me off it, since the mayor gave me an award for my actions at that goddamn concert. I don't remember shit about that night."

"You were brave."

"Yeah? Well, I hope nobody expects me to act brave again. I've had enough of that shit. And now, my first night back on the squad, I manage to run into you. My luck stinks, you know that?"

"No worse than mine. So why are you bothering us, anyway?"

"We got some questions for your boyfriend here about a vampire who broke out of our holding facility. He looked at the notebook in his hand. "Juliet Capulet. Says here she's your roommate. So we got questions for you, too."

"Then I'm going to get dressed before you ask them. I'll be right back."

"Yeah, put some pants on, for God's sake. McFarren, go with her."

"What?" the female zombie and I asked at the same time.

"Go with her. This freak's into knives and shit like that. I don't want her charging out of the bedroom with a goddamn sword." He shooed at her with both hands. "Go on. Make yourself useful for once." He turned to Kane. "Can you believe it? Two chicks on the entire goddamn Goon Squad, and I draw one of 'em as my partner. See what I mean about my lousy goddamn luck?"

The zombie got up and followed me to the bedroom. We introduced ourselves on the way. Her name was Pamela McFarren—"But everyone calls me Pam"—and she'd been a corrections officer before the plague had turned her into a zombie. Like two thousand other Bostonians who'd woken up to find themselves zombified, she'd lost her job and her home when she was forced to relocate to Deadtown. "I didn't mind," she said, shrugging. "Moving out of the South Bay House of Correction and onto patrol was really a promotion."

"Even with Norden as a partner?"

She barked out a laugh. "Hey, I worked in corrections. He's a pussycat compared to some of the people I dealt with there."

"Norden" and "pussycat." Two words I never expected to hear in the same sentence, unless it was something like, "Norden ran over his neighbor's pussycat and laughed about it."

"Besides," McFarren continued, "his previous partner died. I can cut the guy a little slack while he deals with that."

"I knew his partner. Brian Sykes was a good man." And one of the zombies who'd been torn to shreds by the Morfran.

"Yes," McFarren agreed. "His death was a real loss to the force. I figure that's why Norden's kind of weird around zombies now. Twitchy, like. And mean."

"Pam, he's that way around everybody. Norden's one of those guys who comes across as a major-league asshole. He'll irritate the hell out of you and enjoy doing it. And then he says or does something that makes you think, 'Yup, it's true. He's a major-league asshole.'"

McFarren laughed. Then she did me the courtesy of turning around so I could get dressed.

I found a pair of my jeans in a drawer and pulled them on under the towel. I unwrapped the towel and hung it on the back of the door. I left Kane's shirt on. I liked the way it felt, big and slouchy and suffused with Kane's scent: hints of pine in a deep, moonlit forest.

When we walked back into the living room, Norden, notebook in hand, was questioning Kane. My stomach clenched at the thought that he might tell Norden where Juliet was. Surely he wouldn't betray her—not when I'd asked him to give her a chance. But he didn't trust her; maybe he'd rather see her in custody.

I swallowed the lump of worry in my throat and listened.

"At that time," Kane was saying, "I was in my office. I spoke with the security guard, when I signed in and again when I signed out. Several members of the night cleaning crew saw me, as well."

"Where's your office?"

"Near Government Center." He gave the address, and Norden scribbled it down.

"How come you were there at midnight?"

"I needed some papers I'd left on my desk. I went in to pick them up and then did some work while I was there." He looked up at the ceiling, as if calculating. "I passed through the checkpoints around . . . one thirty, I'd say, and then came straight home."

"We can verify all this, you know."

Kane looked Norden in the eye. "I'd think you were slacking if you didn't."

Norden turned to me, his trademark sneer in full force. "Oh, look. She found some pants. So where were you tonight, freak?"

"Me?" I kept my gaze on Norden's face to resist the temptation of glancing at Kane for a clue about what he'd already said. "When we got back to Boston after dinner with my sister, I asked him to drop me off at the checkpoint. I felt like a drink."

Norden's head snapped toward Kane. "You didn't say anything about being with the freak."

"You asked me where I was between midnight and one thirty. I told you." Kane's voice sounded calm, that of a law-abiding citizen being reasonable. But there was an undercurrent of threat that would make any werewolf's hackles rise. Not that Norden noticed. "And don't call Ms. Vaughn names." The threat deepened. "As an officer of the law, it's your duty to be respectful to the citizens you protect."

Norden's wheezy laugh showed what he thought of that idea.

"It's okay, Kane," I said. "Just part of Norden's unique charm." But now I knew that Kane hadn't mentioned me, or my visit to the holding facility, in his account of the evening.

They'd find out about the drive out to Needham anyway, when they checked for any permits we'd filed. But for now, Kane hadn't said a word more than he had to.

"Okay," Norden said to me, "so you went out in the Zone. Where?"

"A couple of places. The Wild Side. Conner's." Lying to Norden about visiting those places didn't worry me in the least. Every bartender in the Zone was an expert at fobbing off cops who came around asking questions. It was a matter of principle. "There was a party at Creature Comforts, and I stayed there for a while. Then I came here."

Norden's pencil flew across the page. "So you don't know where this Juliet Capulet is, either."

I shook my head. He issued a disbelieving snort in response.

"Okay, how about associates? Your roommate have any, um, unusual associates?"

That made me laugh. "She's an almost-seven-hundred-year-old vampire. I'd guess she's probably picked up a few unusual associates in her time."

"We're specifically interested in unregistered paranormals," McFarren said, in a tone that suggested she was trying to be helpful.

"I'm asking the questions," Norden snapped. "You're observing. Observing means you shut up and watch. Look it up in a dictionary."

I knew what they were fishing for, seeing as I'd left the headless corpse of an Old One on the floor of Juliet's cell. But I shrugged. I wanted to talk to Juliet and find out more about her association with the Old Ones before I gave any information to the police.

Norden didn't have any more questions. He grumbled about how much he hated his job again already, then barked at McFarren that they had other places to go.

McFarren offered me her hand. "Thanks for your cooperation," she said. We shook, even though she wouldn't be thanking me if she knew how much information I'd held back. But it was nice of her to make an effort—and unusual for a Goon.

Norden snorted derisively, so I grabbed his hand to shake, too. It was cold. Icy cold, like grabbing a metal railing on a subzero January day. The shock of it hurt my fingers.

Norden flung my hand away and pulled on a pair of gloves. "What?" he said. "I got circulation problems since I got cut up. That okay with you, freak?"

"Whatever." My fingers felt like they had frostbite. I clutched them with my other hand to warm them up.

"Come on, let's go." McFarren touched Norden's arm.

He yanked away, grimacing. "Don't touch me. Don't *ever* touch me. Not if you know what's good for you." He wrenched open the door. "Goddamn walking corpse," he muttered as he left.

McFarren was right. Norden *was* extra twitchy and mean around zombies, even by his own standards. We exchanged a look, then she followed Norden into the hall. When the door closed behind them, I turned to Kane. "Thanks for not giving Juliet away."

"I did that for you, not her." His face clouded. "Besides, I'm no friend of the Goon Squad."

I sat down next to him on the sofa. He put an arm around me, ran his fingers lightly along my collarbone, inside the shirt collar. "You know," I pointed out, "you say 'previously deceased human' instead of zombie. You say 'paranormal American' instead of monster. You even say 'human' instead of norm. But that's the second time tonight I've heard you call the JHP the Goon Squad."

"Well, they *are* goons. They patrol Deadtown to enforce laws that residents had no say in. Their purpose isn't to protect and serve; it's to intimidate and oppress."

"McFarren seems okay."

"Yeah. Maybe she'll do the world a favor and tear Norden's head off before the night is out." Kane sighed, and there was real weariness in the sound. "It's been one disaster after another tonight."

"I don't know." I snuggled in closer. "I kind of enjoyed our shower."

He leaned into me and inhaled deeply. "I like it when your hair smells like my shampoo." He inhaled again. "See, that's how we should've *started* the evening. We'd never have made it out of the apartment. No awkward dinner, no vampire jailbreak, no Goon Squad visit."

"I'm glad I got Juliet out of there. I'm glad she's safe." If I hadn't been there, the Old Ones would have grabbed her. I was certain of it.

"I'm glad she's safe, too. And I honestly hope you're right about her." He squeezed my shoulder. "Come on, let's get to bed. We've both got to be up early."

True. Dawn was a few short hours away. And as soon as the sun cleared the horizon, I'd be knocking on Axel's door.

8

A CLOSED SIGN HUNG CROOKEDLY IN CREATURE COMFORTS' window, but the door was unlocked. I pulled it open and stepped into the half-gloom of the unlit room. The bar had been cleaned up since the werewolves left. The tables were in their usual places; the smell of ammonia blotted out any lingering traces of champagne and werewolf musk. I wondered if Kiana had made her friends help Axel tidy up.

"Axel?"

He came forward from the storeroom, wiping his hands on a towel.

"How's Juliet?"

He flipped the towel onto his shoulder. "Stitched up her leg. Dunno if it helped."

That didn't sound good. Vampires shouldn't need stitches. When a vampire gets injured, the edges of the wound creep back together and knit up invisibly, not even leaving a scar. Of course, that *should* have happened before we left the holding facility.

Axel gestured for me to follow him. We went down the back hallway, past the ancient payphone, past the restrooms—Axel had labeled them BOOS and GHOULS to amuse tourists—and past the door to Axel's cellar apartment.

"Um, Axel?"

He stopped, turned around, and raised an eyebrow.

"Isn't Juliet in your apartment?"

I couldn't tell whether his grunt was negative or affirmative, but he kept walking toward the storeroom.

Had he actually set up a cot for her back there? It wasn't secure enough, not with the Goons and the Old Ones looking for her. After I saw Juliet, I'd try to convince Axel to let her into his lair.

But as we entered the storeroom, there was no sign of a cot. No sign of Juliet at all. Axel went over to some beer kegs near the back of the room. He twisted a cap on one of them, and a hidden door slid open. Beyond the door was a staircase descending into the cellar. Axel started down it.

"Wait, this is the door to your place? What about that triple-locked steel door with the oversized NO ENTRY sign?"

"Front door." He kept going. "This is the guest room."

"Guest room? You've got a guest room?"

At that he stopped and turned around. "For guests," he said, looking like he thought maybe he'd have to explain the concept to me.

Okay. So Axel was solitary, intimidating, and fierce about his privacy. That didn't mean he couldn't have company come to stay once in a while. I guessed.

As I descended the dark, narrow staircase, I couldn't see anything beyond Axel's broad back. So I was astonished to step into a room that looked like it belonged in an upscale hotel. A king-sized platform bed took up most of the far wall. To my left was a seating area, with a loveseat and two upholstered chairs. A desk, dresser, and bookcase filled out the furniture. To my right, a half-open door led into a marble-tiled bathroom. The windowless room should have felt like a cave, but the light woods and bright colors, along with well-placed lighting, made it feel cozy, even welcoming.

Axel's guest room. I shook my head. Yeah, it *was* a tough concept to grasp.

Juliet seemed tiny in the huge bed, propped up against a mountain range of pillows. She looked about the same as when I'd last seen her—pale and thin, with dark circles under her eyes. Again, not good. There should be more evidence she was getting better. But she was sitting up, and an empty bottle on the nightstand showed she'd eaten. That was something.

Axel muttered a few words about letting us talk. As he clomped up the stairs, I noticed those stairs were the only way in or out of the room. No connecting door to Axel's place. It was the only thing about Axel's guest room that didn't surprise me.

I sat on the edge of the bed. "How's your leg?"

Juliet winced. "Hurts like Hades."

"Do you feel up to talking? I've got a million questions for you." When Juliet closed her eyes, I added, "But I promise I won't ask them all at once."

A smile twitched her lips. " 'Ask me what question thou canst possible / And I will answer unpremeditated.' "

"Is that Shakespeare?" If it was, I'd take it as a sign that Juliet was feeling better. My roommate was the real Juliet Capulet, the one who'd actually lived in fourteenth-century Verona, and she had a serious Shakespeare obsession. She said she hated the guy because he'd twisted her story so much, but she'd gone on to memorize everything the Bard had ever written. She dropped Shakespeare quotes into conversations like other people add "um" and "you know."

She nodded, still smiling. "Of course. Nobody else talks like that. So there's one question answered." She opened her eyes again. "But I don't think that one was actually on your list. Let me guess. Question number one is: What are the Old Ones?"

"Sounds like a good place to start. My aunt told me a little about them." I'd asked Mab about them after they'd spirited away Pryce's comatose body. "She said they feed off you—off vampires, I mean—in the same way vampires feed from humans."

"Yes and no. The Old Ones slaughter humans for their physical needs—you saw what they did to those guards. They're so ancient and desiccated, though, they don't require much blood to live. What really sustains them is power. And power is what they drain from vampires."

"But why—?"

"Why do we let them? For the same reason. Power." I must have looked confused. Her voice took on a lecturing tone. "If you give them your power"—she held out her right hand, palm up, as if offering something—"they'll return it to you in a stronger form." She put her left hand on top of her right and clenched her fingers together. Then she broke her hands apart and let them drop back to the covers. "That's their promise, although I know now it's a lie. Just like their promise of eternal life."

I blinked, wondering if I'd heard her right. "Why do you need eternal life? You're undead."

"Undeath is not the same as life. The Old Ones claim they've discovered the secret of how to *restore* life—and make it last forever. They say they can create gods." Her eyes shone for a moment, then dimmed as she twisted the comforter in her fingers. "Do you know what the average life span of a vampire is?"

"I didn't know vampires have a life span. I thought you just keep on going forever."

"Seven hundred and fifty years." Her voice shook a little. "I'm approaching seven hundred."

"But . . . I thought vampires get stronger with age."

"We do—up to a point. And then we start to decline. It's not that different from living creatures. Humans gain strength as they grow into adulthood, but eventually they become weak and feeble. Let me ask you a question. Do you know any vampires older than I am?"

"Hadrian?" The vampire member of Deadtown's Council of Three was the most powerful vampire I could think of. Juliet shook her head, and I named a few others.

"Kids, all of them. Hadrian was turned in the eighteenth century—he's not yet three hundred." She twisted the comforter so hard it ripped. Bits of down floated around her. "I can feel it, Vicky. I've been at the height of my powers for centuries, and it was glorious. Now, those powers are starting to slip away. I don't want to die."

"You'd rather be like the Old Ones?" That hideous face—its yellow skin, its lidless eyes and oversized fangs—flashed through my mind. Juliet would never choose that.

"They're *twice* my age. Older, even. But you're right. I don't want to become like they are. They promised I'd stay as I am, but better. Alive again, and eternal. Like the gods." A piece of fluff landed in her dark hair. I plucked it out.

"I'll have to buy Axel a new comforter," she said, pulling another piece of down from the tear. "If I survive this." Her voice turned bitter. "I was a fool. They promised so much, but it was all lies. Instead of giving me power, they fed on mine. They . . . they had me in their thrall. They still do. It's why I couldn't react when they attacked me last night."

"That ritual in our living room—" Before Juliet had disappeared, I'd found her chanting with the Old Ones when she thought I was asleep. The next day she insisted I'd dreamed the whole thing. She'd nearly convinced me, too, even though I'm a lucid dreamer and can control my own dreamscape.

"I believed it would increase my power. Instead, it was intended to weaken me and make me their slave. If you hadn't interrupted, maybe they would have succeeded. Hades knows I came far too close to that state. But I managed to hold on to some tiny sliver of my own will. Eventually, when I realized what was going on, I called upon that sliver, focused on it, made it grow. It enabled me to escape. In all my centuries, that was the hardest thing I've ever done."

"So what *is* going on?" A few months ago, I'd never heard of the Old Ones. Most vampires would still insist they were a mere legend. They'd kept themselves hidden for centuries. I needed to understand why they were venturing forth now.

"The Old Ones have been recruiting the oldest vampires they can find. Others believed, as I did, that they wanted us to join them. But that wasn't it at all—they needed us to experiment on. To perfect some formula they're working on for eternal life. Four ancient vampires died before their time because the Old Ones tested the formula on them, and it failed. I would have been next."

"How did you learn this?" I couldn't imagine the Old Ones would say: *Oops, we killed four vampires so far testing our formula. You're up next, but don't worry—it* might *work this time.*

"The Old Ones communicate telepathically. Their fangs have grown so large it's hard for them to talk. When you interrupted that ritual, you surprised the Old Ones. In that moment, I felt . . . it was like an electric shock. Like it blasted away some barrier in my mind. I could hear their thoughts as they communicated with each other.

"At first, I was thrilled. I thought my new ability meant I'd become one of them, but on my own terms, without the ugliness." She touched her hair. It had been combed but still lacked its usual luster. "Believe me, I checked my appearance frequently.

"I tried communicating back, but they didn't pick up what I was saying. I assumed I just needed practice, but as I listened to them, I realized they'd never intended me to share their communication at all. They thought of me as . . ." She scowled, showing her fangs. "As some sort of lab rat."

"They didn't know you could hear them?"

"No. They communicated freely around me, and the more I learned, the more I realized how much they'd lied."

"You said they lied about strengthening your power. What else?"

"Eternal life, for starters. They claimed to be immortal. But you proved that was a lie when you killed that Old One. You *killed* him." Her eyes rounded and she shook her head, as though she still couldn't believe it, even though she'd kicked the thing's headless corpse. "Everything makes so much more sense, now that I know they can die."

"Did you overhear anything about someone named Pryce?"

She shook her head. "It didn't work like that. They didn't use names. I had to keep my own mind very, very still and listen for . . . it sounded like whispers in an adjacent room.

But they didn't communicate in words so much as in images, symbols, *understandings*."

"Not much room for Shakespeare in a language like that."

"You're right. The Old Ones would have no use for poetry. They have no use for anything besides their own power." Her eyes clouded for a moment, then refocused on me. "But tell me what this Pryce is like. Maybe I'll recognize something."

"He's a demi-demon, very old, from Wales." Juliet looked blank; no bells ringing so far. "I killed his demon half, and he went catatonic. After he fell, his human shell disappeared, and I'm pretty sure the Old Ones snatched it."

"Catatonic? There was someone they thought of as 'the sleeper.' They did take him. They wanted to use him as leverage against someone else, 'the wizard.' There was a lot of fear and hatred coloring their thoughts about this wizard, but they believed he'd help them because of the sleeper."

This wizard was news to me. "Who is he?"

"I don't know. By this time, you must understand, I'd run away. I was trying to stay a step ahead of them but also find out what they were planning. It was risky. As long as I only eavesdropped on their thoughts, I was fine. But if I saw one of them, even a glimpse, I'd be in their thrall again. Like I was last night." Juliet picked up a partially full bottle of blood from her nightstand, then put it down again. "I recall there was some reason that contacting the wizard would be immensely difficult, but I never found out why. That's all I know, I'm afraid."

"That's okay." The next time I spoke with my aunt Mab, I'd ask her if she knew of any wizard associated with Pryce. She knew more about Pryce's background than I did. I'd been too busy dodging his attempts to kill me to ask for his résumé.

Juliet yawned and stretched; the stretch ended in a wince.

"Are you okay?" I asked. "Do you need to rest?"

"Soon. But I know you're wondering what happened in Washington, so let me tell you that first."

Good. I really wanted to hear Juliet's side of that story—

and share it with Kane. But after last night's ordeal, I didn't want to tax her.

"I was still an enthusiastic new recruit when the Old Ones started murmuring about Kane and his paranormal rights case. They didn't like it."

"Yeah, we figured that out. But why?"

"I thought it was because the Old Ones wanted to keep the old ways, with vampires living in the shadows and treating humans as mere prey. I thought they were offended by the very idea that vampires and humans could be equal. And I'll admit those views appealed to me. Maybe it was because I was starting to feel my age, but I was nostalgic for the old days, before vampires came out into the open and found themselves subject to human-created laws."

"But Kane's trying to make that better, to give humans and paranormals equal standing under the law."

"Perhaps. I can see he believes that. But at the time, I was offended by the very idea of a panel of nine blood-bag judges deciding my fate."

My heart sank. "So you did try to help them frame Kane."

"I provided them with information about where he was staying, where he was working. They took me to Washington with them because they thought I'd be useful there. As we traveled, I listened to their conversation. The Old Ones don't want to keep the old ways—they're sick of the old ways. They want to come out into the open, but not like other paranormals. They want to be gods.

"Their plan was to murder a prominent norm and blame it on a prominent monster, with the aim of fomenting an all-out human-paranormal war. A war would weed out all the weaker vampires and norms. When it was over, the Old Ones would come forward and take control. They'd select the best vampires and humans to serve as their food supply—like farm animals, really—and annihilate everyone else.

"At the time, I still believed I was one of them. I wanted the power, yes, and the immortality. But not like that. What fun would it be reigning over a bunch of blank-faced vampires-in-thrall and cowering norms? And when they communicated about Kane, about the irony of using him to start a war and how much they'd enjoy humiliating him, something inside me altered."

"You wanted to protect Kane." The exact opposite of what he assumed.

She looked away, as though the very idea embarrassed her. "I told you I was getting weaker with age. For whatever reason, for the first time I began to doubt the Old Ones. I found that sliver of will within me. By the time we arrived in Washington, I knew I had to stop them. When the Old Ones left me alone—they had no reason to think I'd betray them—I tried to phone Kane. He never answered, and I couldn't exactly explain what was happening in a voice mail. I also tried to warn that woman they killed, Justice Frederickson. I stopped her on the street and told her she was a target. She laughed and said she'd add it to her collection of death threats." Juliet shook her head, and I wondered whether her amazement was because she'd bothered to warn a norm about a vampire attack or because Frederickson had laughed at that warning. "It took a few days before the Old Ones realized I'd defied them. It was incomprehensible to them that one of their vampire servants could think for herself. When they began to suspect me, I had to run."

"I know. I got your postcards."

"Oh, the postcards." She waved a hand dismissively. "Those were a ruse. I've been shadowing the Old Ones, first in Washington and then following them back to Boston. I've been here all along."

"Wait, a ruse?" Irritation surged through me. "You were lying to me about where you were?"

"I wouldn't lie to *you*. You're far too . . . goody-goody to betray someone's trust. Wait. That sounded like an insult, but I don't mean it that way." Her forehead puckered. "It's been so long since I thought in those terms. Moral—maybe that's what I mean. You're too moral."

"Thanks." I loaded up the word with sarcasm, but Juliet didn't seem to notice.

"I sent the postcards to let you know I was defying the

Old Ones. But the ruse wasn't to fool *you*. How many postcards did you receive?"

"Five."

"I sent twelve. So the Old Ones wasted their time running around the globe searching for me while I was right here. I could spy on them, and they never suspected. That's how I learned about the wizard and the sleeping one."

"If you didn't leave Boston, how did you manage to send cards from Brazil and Australia and all those other places?"

"Using a network of trusted vampires." The furrows in her forehead deepened. "Except one of them betrayed me. I don't know who, but when I find out, there's a stake with that vampire's name on it." The feral glow in her eyes showed she wasn't talking in metaphors. "It was nearly dawn. I'd been out to feed, and I was returning to my safe house. On the street outside, I stopped, getting out my key. As I did, I heard those soft, scratchy, psychic whispers. Two Old Ones were inside my no-longer-safe house, waiting for me. The sun was almost up, and I didn't have another place to stay. So I found a Goon Squad patrol and turned myself in. It was the only thing I could think of."

Juliet yawned again and sank lower on the pillows. "I'm tired. I think it's time for me to resume the shroud."

It was getting late for a vampire, and she did need to rest. "Can I take a look at your leg?" I asked.

She sighed and moved the covers aside as though she were doing me a great favor. Axel's stitches marched along the wound in a neat, even line. But the edges of the cut curled up slightly, away from each other, as though determined not to rejoin. Juliet's leg was hot and still smelled putrid.

I pulled the covers back over her leg. "When I was in Wales, my aunt gave me a salve that speeds healing. I brought some back with me. I don't know if it works on vampires, but it's worth a try. It's good stuff. I'll bring some next time."

"If you think it might help." Juliet lifted a hand, granting permission, then crossed her arms on her chest. "And now, 'to sleep, perchance to dream.' Although I'm no more eager for dreams than Hamlet was."

Before I could ask what she meant, her eyes closed. And that was it. She was dead to the world until sunset.

UPSTAIRS, AXEL SAT WAITING IN A BOOTH, RAPPING OUT A complicated rhythm on the tabletop. He stopped when he saw me.

"I don't know why she's not healing faster," I said. "I wonder if the blade of the sword that injured her was poisoned. I'm going to get it checked."

Axel nodded his approval.

"Can I use your phone?"

I don't carry a cell phone. When I change form, the energy blast of the shift is tough on electronic gadgets. After I obliterated three cell phones in a single month, I gave up. Axel nodded again and resumed tapping.

I went behind the bar and dialed the work number of Daniel Costello, a human detective who worked for Boston PD's homicide division. Daniel wasn't just a cop; he was a friend. Once I'd thought maybe we'd be more than friends. His curly blond hair and blue eyes, his easygoing manner and warm smile, had sent a flush of pleasure through me whenever we were together. But my world, filled with demons and monsters, had proved too weird for him—not to mention too threatening to his job under a paranormal-hating police commissioner. Now I was back with Kane, and Daniel was dating Lynne Hong, a television reporter. And this wasn't a social call. As I listened to the phone ring, I wondered why I still knew his number by heart.

Daniel wasn't in yet, but I left a message for him to call me, asking to set up a meeting for later this morning if possible. I was hoping he could have one of his forensics guys check the Old One's sword for poison. I couldn't get the antidote if I didn't know what the poison was. And I wanted to tell him my theory about the Morfran, how the South End Reaper could be possessed by that hunger-driven spirit. I wasn't sure what he could *do* with that information, but it seemed like something he should know.

After I hung up, I sat with Axel. "I know you must want to get to bed, but can you wait up a little longer? I want to go home and get a healing salve my aunt gave me, so I can use some on Juliet."

Axel quit tapping on the table and opened his hand. It held a key.

"That's to the front door?"

"Back." Even better. There'd be less of a chance someone might see me in the alley. Waltzing into Creature Comforts in the middle of the day would be sure to cause comment if anyone noticed.

Axel handed me the key, and I felt like I was getting the key to the city from the mayor himself. No, this was better. This key actually opened something important.

We went back into the storeroom, and Axel showed me how to open the secret guest room door. It was tricky; you had to twist the false keg's cap just the right distance and with just the right amount of pressure, or nothing happened. When I'd managed to open the door three times in a row, Axel grunted. I think it signaled approval. At any rate, he went down the hall and disappeared through the NO ENTRY door into his place.

I let myself out the back door. Juliet wasn't getting any better, but for the moment, she was safe.

9

SOMEONE HAD LEFT A PILE OF LAUNDRY ON THE SIDEWALK in front of my building. Or that's what it looked like until the pile stood up, put gloved hands on hips, and addressed me in an annoyed voice.

"Where have you been?"

"Oh, is that you, Tina?" Tina was the zombie who'd been my demon-fighting apprentice—until she ditched the whole idea for a chance at becoming a pop singer. "For a second I almost thought you were my mom."

"Ha. Ha." The laundry followed me inside. I nodded to Clyde, the zombie doorman, and headed for the elevators. Now that she was out of reach of the morning sunlight that could permanently damage a zombie's skin, Tina began discarding layers, dropping them on the floor as she went. She pulled off a wide-brimmed hat, taking a moment to fluff up her hair; unwound a long, multicolored scarf; and yanked off bright pink gloves. They formed a trail behind her like she was in a zombie version of *Hansel and Gretel*, making sure she could find her way home.

"Young lady!" called Clyde. "Pick up those clothes. The lobby is not a cloakroom!" Clyde's awfully prim and proper for a zombie.

"It's only for a minute. I have to get home—it's already past curfew there." Tina lived in a group home for underage zombies. She lowered her huge, round, pink-tinted sunglasses to make sure I could see her scowl. "I need to talk to Vicky for a minute."

When she didn't move to pick up her clothes, Clyde came out from behind his desk. He gathered the hat, the scarf, the gloves, and a jacket Tina had dropped in the meantime. He thrust the bundle into her arms, punctuating the action with a loud *hmmph!* Then he returned to his station.

Tina scurried toward me—although *scurry* probably isn't the right word to describe the stiff-legged way zombies walk—clutching her bundle of clothes. A glove dropped to the floor. She didn't notice. I retrieved it and put it on top of the pile.

"Okay, Tina, what do you want?" I might as well hear whatever she had to say here and now. If she followed me up to my apartment, I'd never get her to leave, curfew or no curfew. And I had things to do.

"You're *never* around anymore. How am I supposed to talk to you? You don't even have a cell phone."

"You know why I can't carry a cell phone."

"Well, then you should give me the phone number of what's-his-name, that werewolf dude. That's where you are all the time, with him. Right?"

"I see Kane sometimes, yes. And no, you can't have his phone number."

"So I'm supposed to sit around and wait until you decide to come home?"

I squinted at her. "Are you sure you're not my mother?"

"That's even less funny than it was the first time." She dropped her jacket and other gear at her feet and spun around to shout to Clyde, "Don't worry! I'll pick it up in a minute."

She turned back to me. "Okay, so here's the deal: I want to be your apprentice again."

Oh, no. Not that. Anything but that. "I thought you were writing your memoirs."

"I am. But I need, you know, more stuff to happen."

"So saving Boston from a Harpy attack and almost becoming a pop star aren't enough?" Tina's short-lived singing career had ended with her first concert, when attacking Morfran sent the crowd running through the streets in a screaming panic.

"Almost, almost, almost. See, that's the problem. I fought off some Harpies, yeah, but you defeated Hellion that commanded them. That's what really saved Boston. And there's as many 'almost' pop stars out there as there are MySpace pages. Who wants to read about somebody who *almost* did something big? You have to help me do something for real."

"Tina, fighting demons isn't something you can do halfway. It's not about gathering material for your memoirs. It takes hard work and serious commitment—"

"Yeah, yeah, I know. You said all that before. How it'll take a long time and how I have to be all single-minded and stuff. I get it." She bounced on the balls of her feet. "So when's our next job?"

"You really think I'm going to say yes, just like that? A month ago, you decided demon-fighting was your 'backup' career. What'll your new career be next month—fashion designer? Actress? Reality TV star? I can't pour my time and effort into your training if you're only going to give fifty percent."

Tina's expression grew thoughtful. "Reality TV," she breathed. "That would be awesome."

I pressed the button for the elevator. "Go home, Tina."

She stuck out her bottom lip. "Why are you so mean?"

"You think I'm mean? You should meet my aunt, the woman who trained me. Mab accepts no excuses, no weakness, no 'maybe, maybe not.' You wouldn't last ten minutes with her. That's the problem—I was way too soft on you." I'd taken on Tina as an apprentice because I felt sorry for the kid—zombified, abandoned by her parents, and most likely doomed to a life of manual labor. Zombies' strength was the only thing norms valued about them. But feeling sorry for someone didn't make her a good apprentice. Tina had stolen my most valuable weapon, tried to fight demons without proper training, and then quit with two seconds' notice. She just wasn't serious.

Her chin jutted out. "So get tough. I can take it."

"Why, so you can write about how 'mean' I am in your memoirs? No, Tina. You had a chance to be my apprentice, and you quit."

"But—"

"*No.* You made the decision, not me." The elevator door opened, and I got in. The doors closed on Tina's angry face. Well, that was her problem. I didn't have time to fool around with a half-assed apprentice. And more than once, she'd proved that was exactly what she was.

So why did I feel a sting at the disappointment in her eyes?

MY VOICE MAIL HAD THREE MESSAGES: ONE FROM A POTENTial client who needed some nightmare-causing Drudes chased out of her dreamscape; the second from Gwen, who wanted to meet for lunch. "Please call back as soon as you get this," she said. "There's something I need to discuss with you." I wondered if Maria had confided in Gwen about her dreams.

The third call was from Daniel. "I got your message," he said. "If you come by the precinct, I can meet you at ten. If you can make it then, call back to confirm."

I checked the kitchen clock. Ten would give me time to set up lunch with Gwen and return to Creature Comforts with some salve for Juliet. I called back to say I could meet him then, leaving yet another message.

I'd call the client later. The first phone contact with a new client often takes a while. It's not just a matter of listing symptoms and setting up an appointment; most clients need a lot of reassurance that their demons can be vanquished. That in itself is a sign of a demon infestation—it's in the demons' interest, after all, to make their victims believe no help is possible. From her message, this woman sounded like a talker. She could wait until after lunch.

Next I called Gwen. "You want to come into Boston for lunch on a Sunday?" I asked. That was usually a family day in the Santini household.

"Nick is taking Maria and Zack to a community basketball tournament," she said. "It'll last all day. That leaves me with the baby, and I'll call his sitter. You and I didn't have much of a chance to talk last night." I had a feeling Gwen wasn't in the mood for a sociable chat, but we agreed to meet at a diner near South Station at noon.

I got a cotton ball from the bathroom and swiped it along the blade of the Old One's sword. Brown Robe had sawed at Juliet's leg with one edge of the sword; I was careful to take the sample from the other edge. The cops had a sample of Juliet's DNA on file—as they did for every resident of Deadtown—and I didn't want to hand the Goon Squad any leads in their search for her. I dropped the cotton ball in a plastic bag, sealed it, and put it in my purse.

Next, I went back into the bathroom and rummaged through the medicine cabinet until I found the jar of salve Mab had given me. I removed the lid and sniffed the contents. It had a deep, earthy scent, overlaid with lighter notes of herbs and some kind of flower—lilac, maybe? It smelled like health, like spring. This salve had helped me recover from a Morfran attack without a scar. The attack had been bad: dozens of demonic crows swooping at me, tearing at my flesh with their beaks and talons. Yet the salve had made me whole again. My skin tingled with the memory of its healing coolness. I hoped it would do the same for Juliet.

BACK AT CREATURE COMFORTS, I STOOD OVER JULIET'S bed. She lay still, no rise and fall of the chest to suggest she'd ever open her eyes again. She looked so vulnerable. I thought of all the horror movies that showed a vampire looming over some sleeping innocent, eager to do harm. But Juliet was the defenseless one here. Anyone who managed to find her—Goon Squad cop, Old One, even a Humans First fanatic—could do her harm.

The thought made me feel creepy, since I was the one standing over Juliet's bed. But I was here to help her, and she'd given me permission to use the salve. Still, it felt wrong somehow to pull back the comforter and expose her leg as she slept, completely dead to the world. I did it, anyway.

I studied the wound, looking for any sign of healing, but I had to admit it looked worse. The leg was swollen and purple, still hot to the touch. If nothing else, the salve should cool it. I scooped some from the jar and spread it on the affected area as gently as I could.

Juliet didn't move, didn't even twitch.

I watched for a few minutes. The purple lightened a bit, grew a shade pinker. Or maybe I was imagining that in my hope of seeing some improvement. I spread on another layer of salve, then covered Juliet's leg with the comforter. I placed the jar of the salve on the nightstand where she could reach it.

"Sleep well," I said softly before I clicked off the light. "'Sleep dwell upon thine eyes, peace in thy breast!'"

Damn, listen to that. I'd come up with a good Shakespeare quote—from *Romeo and Juliet*, no less—and Juliet wasn't awake to hear it. Sometimes Juliet wanted to conduct whole conversations in Shakespearean. When she did, I could never cough up any apt lines. She wouldn't believe me when I told her. But that didn't matter. Shakespeare or not, the words expressed what I wanted to say.

WHEN I ARRIVED AT THE PRECINCT A FEW MINUTES BEFORE ten, Daniel was already waiting in the lobby. He looked restless, running his hands through his blond curls and checking his watch. Although we'd spoken on the phone a few times, I hadn't seen him since the Paranormal Appreciation Day concert a month ago. I was shocked to see how haggard he looked: his mouth grim, his bloodshot eyes smudged with dark circles.

The Reaper case must be running him ragged. Still, he smiled when he saw me. His expression brought back the old Daniel, the one whose smile always went straight to my core.

"Let's walk," he said, taking my elbow and ushering me toward the door. "It's a nice day, and I feel like getting outside."

"All right."

It was a nice day. I'd been so worried about Juliet that I'd barely noticed. Bright sunshine made the soft, early spring air feel almost warm on my face. Somewhere a robin was singing loudly enough to be heard over the passing cars. But even though he'd suggested the walk, Daniel didn't seem to enjoy it. His back was rigid, and a muscle twitched in his jaw.

After we'd gone half a block, he looked more relaxed. "I needed to get out of there. My new partner is driving me crazy. Foster. He watches me like a hawk. Anything out of the routine and he goes running to Hampson."

Fred Hampson, Boston's police commissioner, was a virulent hater of all things paranormal. He made no secret of the fact that he was a founding member of Humans First, and he'd publicly endorsed Seth Baldwin, the anti-paranormal candidate, for governor in the last election.

"Your partner knows I'm a shapeshifter." I was pretty sure he didn't like me, either. I'd been present when Foster had gotten into an ill-advised wrestling match with a zombie in Creature Comforts. I'd rooted for the zombie.

"And there's no reason Hampson needs to find out I'm talking to you. It's none of his damn business who my friends are." That twitch in his jaw started up again. "I can't stay out long. Everyone's working around the clock on these damn Reaper murders. There's a lot of pressure on the department to get results, and fast. Nobody's happy when there's a serial killer on the loose." His fingers combed his curls. "And I want to catch the bastard before there's another killing."

I was glad I had some information, that I wasn't just asking Daniel a favor. "That's one of the things I wanted to talk to you about. I don't know if this will be any help, but my aunt Mab told me that serial killers are usually possessed by the Morfran."

A crease appeared between his eyebrows. "You mean those giant crows that attacked the crowd at the Paranormal Appreciation Day concert?"

"They're not really crows. They're a spirit, a demonic spirit. But yes, that's what I mean."

Daniel stopped in his tracks. A woman behind us bumped into him and cursed. He didn't seem to notice. "But Vicky, that's great!" He grinned, and I wondered why he seemed so happy at the prospect of tangling with the Morfran again. "I saw what you did that night, how you used your black dagger to get rid of them. You can do that again, right? You can pull the urge to kill out of the Reaper."

"I wish." It was a good idea, but it wouldn't work. "The Morfran has to be loose—a free-floating spirit—for that ritual to imprison it. When the Morfran possesses someone, it becomes part of that person."

"Well, is there any way to . . . I don't know, call the Morfran? Flush the killer out of hiding?"

It might be worth trying, but I didn't know the answer. "I'll ask Mab. If it's possible, she'll know how to do it."

"Get back to me as soon as you can, okay? The Reaper's first two victims were forty-eight hours apart. We're worried he'll strike again tonight."

"He?"

"He, she, it. I wish we knew even that much. Your information might be our first break." He pulled back his sleeve to look at his watch, and we turned back toward the precinct. "So," Daniel said, "you mentioned a favor."

I crossed my fingers. If Daniel couldn't help me, I didn't know who to ask. "I was hoping you might be able to get one of your guys in forensics to analyze something for me. Check for poison—and whether there's an antidote."

"Possibly. But what—?"

"I can't tell you. Please don't ask."

"You're not . . ." The crease between his eyebrows was deeper this time. "You wouldn't use it against someone, right?"

"Of course not."

The crease disappeared, but no smile replaced it. "I didn't think you would."

"But you had to ask. I understand. And I don't mind addressing that. I'm looking to heal, not hurt." I pulled the plastic bag holding the cotton ball from my purse. Daniel took the bag and put it in his jacket pocket.

"I'll see what I can find out."

We were back at the precinct. We stopped in front of the glass doors, and I put a hand on his arm. "The sooner the better. All right? It's . . . it's important."

He started to say something, then cut himself off with a nod. He turned and went inside.

10

THE KNEELAND STREET DINER, WHERE I WAS MEETING GWEN, is a 1940s diner that's never aspired to join the twenty-first century. It's famous as a late-night hot spot, a place to go for munchies after the bars close.

If you stop by Kneeland Street at two a.m. on a weekend, you can expect to join a line stretching halfway down the block. Lunchtimes are a little less crowded, but not much, even on a Sunday. I was glad to arrive a little early and snag a place in line. You had to wait longer if you preferred one of the ten or so booths to a seat at the counter, and I suspected Gwen would want some privacy for our conversation.

I was second in line when I spotted Gwen coming from the direction of South Station, pushing a stroller. I waved, and she steered toward me. She must not have been able to get a sitter on short notice, but I was glad to see the baby. Actually, Justin wasn't much of a baby anymore, I thought, as Gwen came up. He was two already, a toddler with two settings: Go and Go Faster.

We snagged a booth right away. I held my nephew, who squirmed to escape my grasp, while Gwen folded the stroller. The waitress fussed over Justin, produced a high chair, and then fussed over him some more. She gave us menus and took our order for coffee, plus apple juice for the baby. "Big boy!" Justin shouted, pounding on his tray. I was hungry and in the mood for breakfast, which this diner serves round the clock, so I ordered the banana French toast. Gwen hesitated. She started to ask about the grilled chicken salad, then abruptly changed her mind. "I really shouldn't, but . . . Oh, what the hell—heck." She glanced at Justin, who was tearing up a napkin and dropping the pieces on the floor. "Bring me a cheeseburger with fries." She flipped a page on the menu. "And a strawberry frappe."

"Regular or extra-thick?"

"You know what? I'll go with extra-thick."

"Good choice." The waitress nodded, winked at Justin, and went to put in the order.

Gwen sat back and looked around, taking in the red-and-blue neon lights, the old black-and-white photos, the starburst aluminum panels behind the counter. She inhaled deeply. "I love that greasy-spoon smell, although I'll want to wash it out of my hair by the time we get home," she said. "I used to come here sometimes, back in my single days. My girlfriends and I would go out to the clubs, then stop here after they closed. It was fun."

"Fun!" Justin waved a scrap of napkin at her. Gwen took it away from him and replaced it with a coloring book. She shook some crayons out of a box. Justin picked up a blue crayon, examined it, then broke it in half and threw both pieces on the floor.

"No, honey, like this." Gwen opened the book to a picture of a teddy bear with an umbrella. She filled in part of the umbrella with red strokes. "See? You try it."

Justin snatched the red crayon and scribbled on the teddy

bear's face. Two seconds later, the crayon was on the floor. Gwen picked it up, along with the two halves of the blue crayon, and colored the umbrella as she talked. Justin watched her.

"I didn't expect to have him with me today. He's too young to go with Nick and the others, but his babysitter was sick. She said she has the flu." She stopped coloring and looked up. "Can you imagine not getting a flu shot? In this day and age?"

I knew what she meant. The fast-mutating virus that had caused the zombie plague three years ago was related to the flu. Since then, flu shots had become very popular. Norms tended to panic about *any* kind of virus.

"I feel like I should look for a new babysitter," Gwen finished.

"Well, if she hasn't dropped dead yet, it's not the plague. She'll recover."

"I know. But she was so careless, skipping her flu shot. I can't trust someone like that to take care of my kids."

She put down the crayon as the waitress brought our food. I drowned my French toast in maple syrup. Gwen took a bite out of her massive cheeseburger, closing her eyes as she chewed, perhaps remembering those single days. Justin whined. She put some French fries on a napkin in front of him and spooned a little of her frappe into his mouth. He smacked his lips and made happy *mmmmm* sounds.

"So what's up?" I asked, although I was pretty sure I already knew: Maria. "What did you want to talk about?"

"Can't I just have lunch with my sister? It's been so long since I've seen you, and we didn't get any girl time last night."

That wasn't why Gwen had asked me to lunch, and we both knew it. But I was happy to catch up with my sister until she was ready to talk about what was bothering her. I smiled to myself a little; Maria had acted the same way last night, letting me know she needed to talk and then having no clue how to get to the point. Like mother, like daughter. Justin waved his sippy cup and then bounced it off the floor. It landed near my foot. I scooped it up and handed it to Gwen. "Well," I said, "we've got plenty of girl time now."

For the next half hour, we swapped stories. I told some tales from work. Gwen laughed about the Drude victim who was terrified of cats, so his dream-demons took the form of cute, fluffy kittens. She talked about her boys—how Zack terrorized and charmed his kindergarten teachers by turns; how Justin had pointed at a cat and said, "Dog," making a neighbor laugh, and then Justin refused to speak for a week.

After a while, Justin got squirmy in his high chair. Gwen lifted him out, and he amused himself by sliding off Gwen's bench, crawling under the table, and climbing up onto mine. Then off my side, under the table, and back to Gwen. He repeated the expedition, over and over, with all the enthusiasm and determination of a mountain climber ascending Everest. I waved to Justin under the table, then looked up to see Gwen with tight lips and worried eyes. She was ready to get to the real subject.

"How's Maria?" I asked. "You haven't mentioned her yet."

The line of her mouth got tighter. "It took her a little while to recover from her . . . experience last October. But she's doing great now. Straight A's in school. She really loves dance class. She's got a recital coming up in a few weeks. I hope you can make it."

"Email me the date. I'll be there."

Gwen picked up her spoon and stirred the remains of her frappe, watching the spoon go round and round. Abruptly, she pushed the glass away. "I think Maria's becoming a shapeshifter."

Good. Now her fear was out in the open, where we could deal with it. "She's still so young, Gwen. It's too early to tell."

"She's eleven years old. Two of her friends have already started getting their periods—I overheard them talking about it. And Maria is . . . she's . . . starting to develop." Gwen blushed, like the whole subject of Maria growing up embarrassed her. "All the pre-shapeshifting symptoms are there. The mood changes. The secretiveness. And she's having shapeshifter dreams—she told me she spoke to you about those."

"That's just puberty. There's nothing specific to shapeshifting in what you call her 'symptoms.' Most eleven-year-old girls go through those things."

"Not the dreams."

"She's had a few flying dreams. Everyone gets those."

She sighed, exasperated. "I'm not a norm, Vicky. I went through the change myself. I know the signs."

"Okay, so let's say she is becoming a shapeshifter. Things are different now, not like when we were growing up. There's no shame in it, nothing to hide. Her friends will probably think it's cool."

"Yes. Things *are* different. And that's what scares me. Do you think the authorities have forgotten what happened in New Hampshire? They're watching us, watching Maria. If her abilities activate, there's *no way* they'll let her live a normal life. What if—" Gwen fumbled for a napkin from the holder and pressed it to her face. When she looked up, her eyes were wet. "What if they take my baby away from me?"

Finally I understood. I reached across the table and held Gwen's hand. "You think they'll force her to live in Deadtown."

Gwen nodded, sniffing. "We can't move there."

Yeah, I could see that. Nick was fully human. As an inactive demi-human, Gwen was legally the same as a norm. The boys, too—even if they carried the Cerddorion shapeshifter gene, they'd never develop the ability to shift; that was restricted to females in my race. Out of the whole family, Maria was the only one who might be "monstrous" enough to fit in.

"She could live with me."

Gwen quickly blinked the horror out of her eyes, but I'd seen it there. "Where would she go to school? Who'd be her friends? Zombies and werewolves?"

"They're people, Gwen. Just like you—and me." I knew what she meant, though. Gwen had always sheltered her kids, giving them the most comfortable suburban lifestyle possible. Maria wasn't ready for Deadtown.

"We'll have to leave the country. Emigrate to Canada, maybe. Or the UK." Those countries had more relaxed laws that allowed paranormals to mix with the human populace. "But I can't convince Nick. He doesn't want to move."

"I don't want you to move, either. Let me talk to Kane. Maybe you can apply for a waiver to allow her to stay in Needham." It didn't seem likely. When the monsters came out into the open, more than three years ago now, werewolf families in Massachusetts had been forced to move to Deadtown or one of the three secure "villages"—which were more like penitentiaries—adjacent to the state's werewolf retreats. The law had uprooted families who'd lived quietly among their neighbors for decades. It didn't seem like that law would make any exceptions for an eleven-year-old shapeshifter.

"Gwen . . ." I knew I'd regret what I was about to say. "You know that Mab would take her in." Gwen frowned. At the same moment, Justin bumped his head on the table and began to howl. She pulled him onto her lap and rocked him. I kept talking. I knew she was listening, even as she comforted the baby. Or was as close to listening as she'd ever get on this topic.

"I don't mean for training. Even if she's a shapeshifter, Maria's too young for that. And training would be Maria's choice, anyway. You know Mab would never force her." Gwen kissed the top of Justin's head and didn't look at me. "Mab has a beautiful home in a part of the world that accepts our kind. Jenkins and Rose still work for her—you remember what a softie Rose is, don't you? I don't know what went wrong between you and Mab, but—"

"I don't want to talk about that."

"Okay, okay. I wasn't prying. But Mab is a good person, loving in her own way. And she cares about family."

"I do not want my daughter anywhere near that woman. Do you understand?"

"But—"

"Off the table."

I heaved a frustrated sigh. Sending Maria to live with Mab was by far the best solution—if Maria did turn out to be a shapeshifter—and Gwen wouldn't even consider it.

Justin stared at me, his wide eyes still shiny with tears, as if he were trying to figure out why Mommy was mad at Aunt Vicky. I blew him a kiss. He smiled, then twisted and hid his face in his mother's shirt.

"I don't know what's going to happen with her, Vicky. But I might need your help. If Kane can do something on the legal side of things, that would be wonderful, and we'd all be very grateful. That's not what I'm talking about, though." Gwen stroked Justin's hair as he leaned against her chest, his eyes half-closed. "If Maria starts shifting, I . . . I don't think I can help her. It's been so long. When I made my choice to become a human"—her voice took on a bitter edge—"or as close to human as I can ever be, I was determined to fully live the life I'd chosen. I locked a lot away then. Maria will need someone who can show her how to deal with that side of herself." Her fingers stopped moving in Justin's hair. "I'm asking if you'll do that for her."

A warm feeling swelled in my chest. "Of course, Gwen. You don't even have to ask." But I was glad she had. For the first time in months, I felt like Gwen wanted me to be a part of her family, rather than shutting me out like I was some kind of threat.

"Promise me one thing, though," Gwen said.

"Sure."

"Promise me that you won't . . . you know, make it too much fun. You know how shapeshifting is at first. Like playing make-believe, only it's real. You have to promise that you'll explain the downsides to her, too."

"Wait." That warm feeling cooled off by several degrees. "You want me to discourage her?"

"Not that so much." But the way she toyed with her spoon, refusing to meet my eyes, showed it was exactly what she meant. "Just . . . well, you know what I mean."

"No, I don't. What downsides?" I took a sip of cold coffee

to keep my voice from getting shrill. "I'm a shapeshifter, Gwen—that's my choice. I'm not going to pretend I regret it because you chose differently. I won't try to influence her to embrace shapeshifting, but I won't push her to choose normhood, either. And neither should you. It's got to be Maria's own decision—and we don't even know for sure yet that she'll have any decision to make."

Gwen looked like she wanted to argue with me, but she remained silent.

"Besides, she'll have years of dealing with shapeshifting before she can make a choice." *Don't say it, Vicky. Don't.* "Unless you want her to get pregnant at twelve or thirteen." *Damn it all, you said it.*

"Of course I don't want that," Gwen snapped. "I just . . ." Her voice softened and tears reappeared. "I want to protect my little girl."

I took a deep, calming breath. I felt like a jerk. This wasn't about me or my sister's judgment of my choices. This was about a young girl who might be about to plunge into a very frightening and confusing time in her life.

"I'm sorry, Gwen. You can count on me. If Maria starts shifting, you know I'll do everything I can to help her."

"Thanks." Gwen smiled, but her eyes held even more doubt than tears.

11

THE DOUBT IN MY SISTER'S EYES HAUNTED ME AS I WALKED from South Station back to Deadtown. If Maria started going through the change, she'd need the unconditional support of her whole family, the kind of support that Mom had offered Gwen and me when we were that age. When I got home, I'd give Mom a call, ask her to talk to Gwen. My sister might appreciate the advice of someone who'd made the same choice she had. But Mom had also explored life as a shape-shifter, killing her share of demons before she met Dad and fell in love. If anyone could see both sides of the issue, it was Mom. And anyway, I'd been too haphazard about keeping in touch since she moved to Florida.

By the time I passed through the first checkpoint, I was feeling a little better. I'd take a minute to stop by Creature Comforts and check on Juliet, and then I'd go home and make that call.

During the day, the New Combat Zone is a ghost town. (Not literally. Although I'd had a run-in a few weeks back with a shade stuck in Limbo, there's no such thing as ghosts.) When the bars were closed, the only reason to be in the Zone was to pass between Deadtown and the rest of Boston. At this hour, most of the monsters were home, sleeping. Those who kept norm hours, like Kane, were at work. And most norms stayed as far away from Deadtown as they could get, even during the day.

Except for the vampire junkies. Those norms were a little too fond of the mild narcotic in vampire saliva that made donating blood feel so good. I passed one now, sprawled in the mouth of the alley, sleeping it off. His legs stuck out onto the pavement, and I had to choose between stepping over or walking around him. I walked around—and almost into another guy who materialized in front of me.

"Got a light?" he asked, feeling in his pocket for cigarettes. His greasy hair, parted on the side, was way past due for a trim. His eyes were dull, his neck ringed with vampire hickeys. Another vampire junkie, this one recently awakened from his beauty sleep.

"I don't smoke." I moved to step past him, but he blocked my way.

"How about change, then? Spare a few coins?"

"No." I shoved his shoulder, and he stepped back. As he did, his hand came out of his pocket, holding not cigarettes but a slim spray can. A cloud of choking mist hit my face. My eyes stung and streamed with blinding tears. I doubled over, trying to cough the junk out of my burning lungs. The ground tilted, and my knees gave way. The greasy-haired guy caught me before I hit the ground. The other junkie, on his feet now, grabbed my legs. They lifted me between them and moved into the alley. I struggled to get a breath but it was like my chest was squeezed by iron bands. Buildings bounced past. The light dimmed. I had a sense we'd entered a small, dark room or tunnel. Then I didn't know anything at all.

WHEN I CAME TO, MY FIRST FEELING WAS ASTONISHMENT and gratitude to be breathing. For several minutes I simply lay on my back, appreciating the rise and fall of my chest. A deep ache, like a fresh bruise, swelled with each motion, but I could do it. I could breathe.

But was I really awake? It was so dark. And silent. And warm. Just like the atmosphere I always chose for my dreams. I wrinkled my nose. There was something—an odor, a sharp chemical smell—that I'd never allow into my dreamscape.

I turned my head, looking for the familiar, comforting red numbers of my bedside clock. No, I didn't. I *tried* to turn my head. I couldn't. I tried to sit up, to turn on my side. I jerked my arms, my legs. I couldn't move at all.

Panic gripped me. I was strapped down, immobile, in a strange place with no idea of how I got here.

Wait. Those two vampire junkies I'd encountered in the Zone. I remembered the greasy hair, the spray can. They'd brought me here. But what the hell did they want from me? I'd never seen either one of them before.

Vampire junkies worked for vampires. Most of them would do anything to get their fix. And the only vampires I could think of who had a grudge against me were the Old Ones. I doubted they controlled the junkies directly. The Old Ones used humans solely for food. But the Old Ones kept vampires in thrall—Juliet had said how hard it was to break free of their influence—so they could make their vampire slaves command their human junkies.

The Old Ones might know how to control vampires, but clearly they didn't know squat about shapeshifters. Because you can't keep a shapeshifter captive by strapping her down to a table.

A shift would snap the bonds like thread. But I had to be smart about what I shifted to. I needed something dangerous—and fast. Something that wouldn't hesitate to attack whatever came through the door, and then could run like hell to get away. A cheetah—that might work. I'd have incisors to rival the Old Ones' fangs, and nothing can outrun a cheetah. Well, yeah, a vampire could. But I'd have the element of surprise going for me.

I drew my attention inward to begin the shift. I thought of

cheetah spots, of speed, of jungle foliage blurring at the edges of my vision as my paws beat the ground. I tensed, feeling for the change to begin, trying to make the images more vivid. Hunting. My teeth tearing into hot flesh. The smell of fresh blood . . . The images faded; I couldn't hold on to them. They fractured, swirling away like confetti. My mind went blank.

I tried again, but the same thing happened. I pulled up images, focused, tried to make them real. But before my imaginings had any effect on my reality, they dimmed, broke into pieces, and dropped from my mind.

I couldn't shift.

Now the panic really hit. I struggled and pulled against my bonds, bruising my own flesh but not feeling the slightest give. I bit my tongue to keep from screaming. My heart pounded like it would leap from my body and gallop across the room.

The door opened, and light flowed in. I stopped struggling and listened. Footsteps approached. Two sets, it sounded like, though I couldn't turn my head to see who they belonged to. All I could see was the stained ceiling panel directly above me. I shifted my eyes right, then left. On my left side, an IV bag hung from a metal frame. A dark head blocked my view of the bag for a moment, as a hand adjusted the drip. Then a face loomed over me. A man who looked to be in his early thirties, with black hair, pale skin, and eyes that seemed to suck in the light.

It couldn't be.

"Oh, good. You're awake," he said. The familiar voice had a strong Welsh accent.

I blinked, I squinted, but the face didn't change. The only thing different from the last time I'd seen him was that he now wore a beard.

"Pryce?"

He huffed, sending a blast of foul breath across my face. His teeth were rotted, and I realized the face didn't look like Pryce after all. Not really.

"Close," he said, "but no. I am not Pryce, though Pryce is of me. The poor lad remains an empty husk, a spiritless shell. Soon he'll return, but not to you. Of you, yes. To you, no." He laughed, a high-pitched giggle that made my skin crawl.

So there I was, strapped down in a windowless room, listening to a lunatic spew riddles. My day was definitely not looking up.

"I don't know what you're talking about." I tried to sound defiant, but my voice seemed far away. An echo, not the sound itself. "Who are you? And what the hell do you want from me?"

He seemed delighted with my questions. "My name is Myrddin Wyllt. I'd say, 'At your service,' except for the fact that it's so clearly untrue. If we're talking about service, you're indisputably at mine, wouldn't you say?" Another high-pitched giggle.

I barely listened to his gibberish. I was thinking about the name: Myrddin Wyllt. The name *Myrddin* is threaded throughout Welsh mythology; several different legendary characters with that name come together in a composite to create Merlin, wizard and adviser to King Arthur, in stories about the Knights of the Round Table. But Myrddin Wyllt was no kindly old man with a long white beard, a pointy hat, and a twinkle in his eye. Myrddin Wyllt was insane.

That Myrddin was a prophet and bard who'd gone mad with grief when a devastating battle slaughtered his lord, along with most of his army. After witnessing the carnage, Myrddin tore off his clothes and ran screaming into the woods, where he lived like a wild animal. Later, he foretold his own triple death: by falling, drowning, and impalement.

Myrddin Wyllt was crazy, wild, and as dangerous as a hungry predator. And my host had picked him as a role model.

"I'm not in any mood for riddles, 'Myrddin.' So why don't you just tell me what you want?"

Another face appeared over me and snarled, revealing vampire fangs. This one was gaunt, with bruise-dark circles under his eyes. "Where's Juliet?"

"If I knew, I wouldn't tell you."

He slapped me, hard. I couldn't turn my head to dissipate the force of the blow. My cheek burned and throbbed.

"Peace, Piotr, peace." Myrddin placed a calming hand on the vampire's shoulder. "We'll know soon enough. Pryce will give you whatever information you require from this one."

"Pryce is here?" Juliet had said the Old Ones called him "the sleeper." This "Myrddin" must be the wizard they'd allied themselves with.

"Here, here—is Pryce here? In a manner of speaking, yes. Although I'd hardly say that half-corpse of a man is 'here.' Poor lad can't even open his eyes and say, 'Welcome back, Papa.' "

Pryce's father. There was a family resemblance, as long as Myrddin kept his mouth shut to hide his bad teeth.

I searched my memory. Some stories claimed Merlin was the child of a demon father and a human mother. A demi-demon.

"Pryce doesn't like to admit it," Myrddin went on, "but there's a touch of the Cerddorion in him, as well. Of course, there'll be more soon. Much more." He rubbed his hands together and giggled again. The sound, plus the stench of his breath, washed over me in a nauseating wave. "You're going to help wake my sleeping son, you see. By donating your life force to him. I'm eager to see which parts of you will manifest in Pryce. He'll know the contents of your mind, of course." He tapped my forehead with a long, thick fingernail. "There may be a useful tidbit or two in there, although I'm not expecting much. He's already a better swordsman than you, so you've nothing to offer him there. But shapeshifting . . . Now, there's something that could be quite useful to a demi-demon. Our two forms, demon and human, are so limiting, you know."

He turned to the IV bag. "I need a little more time to prepare for the transfer. Hence this drug. It's a mild sedative to prevent you from concentrating enough to shapeshift. But doubtless you've already discovered that."

His words extinguished any last glimmer of hope I held. He must have seen the despair in my face, because he smiled.

"Victory. An odd name for one so completely defenseless, is it not? I've been watching you for years, you know, even though I couldn't come out to play. Pryce misread the prophecy, thought you were fated to bear his sons. No, no, no." He wagged a scolding finger. "You'll join with him in a different way. In just a few hours, I'll transfer your life force to my son. You'll be number three of the required five. Soon Pryce shall walk again, and Victory shall be no more." His insane giggle ricocheted around the room. "And there's nothing you can do about it."

12

I WASN'T USED TO FEELING AFRAID. UNCERTAINTY, WORRY, anxiety—those were emotions I knew well. But not fear. I didn't like fear. It tingled under my nails, convulsed my limbs, sent adrenaline charging through my veins. *Fight! Flee! Whatever you do, don't just lie there!*

I willed my heart to calm its wild beating. I would not lie in this room, stewing in fear. If Myrddin's sedative prevented me from shifting, I'd make it work for me instead. I'd rest. I'd sleep, even. And I'd use the dream phone to contact Aunt Mab.

The Cerddorion can communicate psychically through the mental pathways that open in sleep. A dream phone call would require some concentration, but not nearly as much as a shift.

I didn't know what time it was, but Mab was powerful enough to detect a dream-phone call even while awake. I needed to talk to her. I had no hope Mab could do anything to help me. I was beyond help—alone, immobilized, and without the vaguest clue about the location of this dark, locked room. Still, I wanted my aunt. I wanted to say good-bye.

The sedative stroked at the edges of my consciousness like a calm lake gently lapping the shore. I relaxed into the sensation, let myself sink into sleep. In my dream, I wasn't strapped down; I was free. I drew upon the image of the lake, picturing myself sitting beside still water. The day was sunny, the sand was warm. Thick woods grew around the lake, and the air was fragrant with scents of grass and pine. I leaned over and drew my hand through the water. It was warm, like bathwater, and I made patterns with the ripples. Tiny, rainbow-colored fish, attracted by the movement, followed my hand.

When my dreamscape felt real, I was ready to make the call. I pictured Mab in various contexts, as if I were paging through an old photograph album. Mab dressed in her fencing outfit, practicing swordplay on the back lawn at Maenllyd. Mab at the kitchen table, pouring a cup of tea. Mab reaching for a book from the top library shelf. And the image that always arose when I thought of my aunt: Mab sitting by the fireplace in her library, a book open on her lap. I recalled lightly—no anxiety, no straining—that Mab's personal colors were blue and silver. And I let those colors tinge my mental image of her. They formed a mist across her image, rising up in billows of blue and silver that swirled across my mind's eye, and then subsided. Mab sat in her wing chair, a fire crackling beside her, just as I'd imagined.

She put a finger in the book to hold her place as she closed it. Her gaze was alert as she waited for me to speak.

"Mab—" My voice cracked as the fear rushed back. I cleared my throat and tried again. "Mab, I'm in trouble."

Her expression didn't change, except for a sharpness in her eyes. "What is it, child? What's happening?"

"I'm being held captive—I don't know where. There's a man. He says he's Pryce's father."

The book slid from Mab's lap to the floor. "Myrddin."

"That's what he called himself. He . . ." I swallowed. I had to stay calm, keep fear from throwing me out of my dream. "He's going to transfer my life force to Pryce."

"Child, you must get out of there at once."

"I can't, Mab. I can't even move. I'm strapped down to some table, and Myrddin has given me a sedative so I can't concentrate enough to shift."

Mab jumped up from her chair and paced in front of the fireplace, both hands pressed against her face.

"It's okay, Mab. I'm not expecting you to solve this for me. It's hopeless. I called you because I wanted to thank you for everything you've done for me. To say good-bye." I paused. "To say I love you." Those were words I'd never said to my aunt. Love wasn't part of the vocabulary of our relationship, even though it was something I'd always felt for her. Not long ago I'd thought Mab had died, but even after I got her back I still hadn't managed to say the words. Saying them now gave me a measure of peace.

Mab didn't reply, but that didn't matter. I wasn't finished yet. "I want you to end your feud with Gwen. I don't care what caused it—you and she are family. It looks like Maria might become a shapeshifter. If she does, she'll need guidance. Promise me you'll give that to her."

Mab paced silently.

"Give Jenkins and Rose my love. And . . ." I took a deep breath, thinking about Kane. For a moment, he was next to me in the dream, his lips nuzzling my neck, his warm hand covering mine. His image faded. "Please contact Kane for me. Please tell him—"

"Stop it!" Mab's sharp voice cut me off. "Just stop. I don't want your farewell messages, because I am *not* going to let you die. Do you understand?"

"There's nothing you can do. So don't go blaming yourself."

"There *is* something I can do. However, it would be dangerous to you. And I'm not certain it will work."

Did she mean it? My aunt's expression was dead serious—and deeply worried. But a spark of hope flared inside me. "Whatever it is, let's do it. I've got nothing to lose."

She pressed a hand to her chest and spoke softly, as if to herself. "If you didn't survive . . . and I were responsible . . ."

"If we don't try it, I *won't* survive."

Mab gave me a long, searching look, like there were things she wanted to say to me and didn't know how. Then she nodded briskly. "All right," she said, sounding like herself again. "I'm going to get you out of there by pulling you through the dream."

"You can do that?"

"In theory. I've never attempted it in practice."

"Why not? You could've saved me a fortune on transatlantic plane fares."

"This is no joking matter, child." She put a hand inside the neck of her dress and pulled out a necklace. She reached back and unfastened the clasp, then let the pendant slide from the chain and drop into her palm. "Now, pay attention. I'm going to test the process by sending you this bloodstone." She held up the pendant. It was an oval stone, about two inches long, highly polished but irregularly shaped. The gray stone, mottled with spots of green and dark red, didn't look like jewelry—more like something a jeweler would toss onto the reject pile.

"Hold on to the bloodstone," Mab continued, "and whatever happens, don't let go. Do you understand? *Do not let go.* It will guide you safely through the dream regions."

I nodded. "What's so dangerous, Mab?" As a demon fighter, I was familiar with the dream world. I'd been in other people's dreamscapes hundreds of times.

"The danger is in traveling from your dreamscape to mine. You must pass through the collective unconscious."

Shit. Now we were talking dangerous with a capital *D*. An individual's dreamscape is generated from the dreamer's subconscious, the mind's basement that stores all the emotions, symbols, themes, and archetypes that emerge in dreams. That subconscious can be a terrifying place. I'd once fallen into a client's subconscious during a Drude extermination—and it was an experience I never wanted to repeat. But if the subconscious is bad, the collective unconscious is a hundred billion times worse. It's the storehouse for all the fears, nightmares, fantasies, and terrors of *everyone* who's ever lived. Worse, it's populated by forms. A form is an amalgam of essences—basically, it's a big blob that absorbs everything it touches, then burps out those essences in new configurations.

If I had to cross the collective unconscious, the forms would be the real danger.

Mab must have seen the change in my expression. "Listen to me, Victory. It's good that you understand the danger. But you must set aside fear. In the collective unconscious, fear will rip you apart." She gentled her voice. "Don't think about it now. You don't have to cross that territory yet. First, we must test whether I can pass the bloodstone to you. So take a moment to relax. Use the meditation technique I taught you."

Relaxation isn't easy when you're trying to decide which would be the worst fate: having your life force transferred to your enemy, being ripped to shreds by the worst nightmares humanity has ever imagined, or being sucked into a gross blob of nothingness. But even if the collective unconscious killed me, I'd die knowing Myrddin had failed. That alone was worth the risk.

I focused on the center of my being, going inward, counting my breaths. Slowly, my mind relaxed. My breaths became longer and deeper. When the last dollop of fear melted away, I nodded to Mab.

"Good," she said. "Now, look at the lake. Watch the water."

I did. All was still, except for the sparkles of sunlight playing across the surface. Then, several yards from the shore, ripples stirred the water. A hand emerged, curled into a fist. Its arm wore a tight-fitting sleeve of a white, silky material. I realized I no longer sat on the shore, but in a small boat. The arm glided toward me, and I marveled at its beauty and grace. The white fabric, shot through with gold and silver threads, caught the sunlight and made the arm glow.

The arm stopped beside my boat. I tried to peer into the water to see the rest of the person, but all I could make out was a hazy white shape. The fist shook itself—once, twice, three times—as though impatient. I held out my open palm.

A stone dropped into my hand. Immediately, the arm disappeared beneath the water.

The boat rocked gently under me as I examined the stone. It was gray with green and red spots, set in silver. Mab's pendant. I curled my fingers around it.

"Now, child, I need you to do something that's a bit difficult, so you must do it very carefully." Mab's voice blew across the lake like a summer breeze. I couldn't see her anymore, but I knew she was close by. "Stay in the boat—that will keep you in the dream. You must stay in the dream, but I need you to check your physical body. I'll hold you here, but take a moment to peek back into your waking world. See whether you have the stone there. Do it now." Her soft voice went on, murmuring a word-painting of my dreamscape, describing the lake, the sky, the woods on the shore.

Holding on to Mab's words like Ariadne's thread, I let a corner of my consciousness travel back to that dark, silent room. I still lay on my back on a hard table, unable to move. My right fingers were curled into a fist. I squeezed them gently. Yes. I could feel the pendant in my hand.

I shut my mind to grim reality and let Mab's voice reel me back into my dreamscape. I lay in the bottom of the boat, my heart hammering. My body felt rubbery, like I'd run hard for miles. But my journey hadn't begun yet.

"I've got it," I panted. "Out there, I mean. It's in my hand."

"Good." Mab's face hovered over me, huge, like a painting on the sky. Her lips curved as though she were trying to smile encouragement—an odd expression I'd never seen on my aunt's face—but worry lines creased her forehead and the corners of her eyes. "I'm going to steer this boat toward the far shore, out of your personal dreamscape. Relax as best you can."

Mab's face faded, and I felt the boat move. I lay back and watched the sky. It was blue and dotted with clouds—white, puffy, picturesque clouds, not the heavy kind that threaten rain or snow. The boat glided through the water with a gentle rocking motion. I smelled pine woods, and the scent reminded me of Kane.

A small bump, and the boat stopped. I sat up. Mab stood in water up to her ankles, holding a rope tied to the bow. The shore behind her looked nothing like the woods I'd conjured around my lake. Billows of dark smoke churned, lit by flashes of lightning. The smoke roiled, thick and opaque; my vision couldn't penetrate it at all.

I looked over my shoulder. Behind me, the placid lake reflected the blue sky. Tree branches swayed in the breeze. I wanted to stay there, but I couldn't. My dreamscape was an illusion, one from which I'd awaken into the reality of pain and death.

I had to go forward.

I stepped out of the boat into the water, warm around my calves. The boat disappeared. Right. No going back. I waded to the water's edge and stepped onto the shore. Mere yards away, the smoke obscured whatever was beyond.

"Okay, Mab, I'm ready. Lead the way."

Mab didn't budge. "I can't, child. You must go alone." Water rippled around her ankles. "This isn't me; it's a dream avatar."

A dream avatar is an image that can be projected into a person's dreamscape. But the avatar is part of the dream. And that meant Mab couldn't leave my dreamscape.

"Hold tight to the stone, child. It's our connection. It will lead you through the wilderness to my dreamscape. When you arrive there, you'll be safe." She reached for me, but her hand passed through mine like a ghost's.

Grasping the bloodstone, I plunged into the dense, swirling smoke.

BLIND AND COUGHING, I GROPED MY WAY FORWARD. SOMEthing brushed my right cheek. I jerked to the left. Footsteps pounded close by. Deep, evil-sounding laughter echoed. I spun around so much, trying to locate strange sounds, I had no clue which direction I was facing. Not that it mattered. Once I'd stepped outside my own dreamscape, I couldn't return. It was gone.

The bloodstone was my only chance for finding my way through this morass. I held it near my face and squinted at it through the dark, hoping it would glow to light my way to Mab. No such luck. The bloodstone, though polished, was dark, its colors dull. Mab had said it would guide me to her dreamscape, and I believed her. I just wished it had come with an instruction manual.

Out of the dark, something slimy wrapped around my ankle. I kicked it off and ran forward. Immediately, the stone began to vibrate. Galloping hooves pounded straight for me, and I swerved to the right. The stone's vibration ceased.

Something huge galloped past. Although the smoke didn't part, air rushed past my cheek. When the echo of hooves faded, I stepped forward. The stone vibrated. I turned ninety degrees to the left and took another step. The vibration stopped. When I turned back the way I'd been facing, the vibration began again.

I let the bloodstone lead me. At first, I proceeded with my left arm stretched out ahead, feeling for boulders or trees—or other, more sinister obstacles—that loomed suddenly from the darkness. But the stone guided me around those. I wished for a weapon, and a sword materialized in my left hand. It was a comfort to curl my fingers around its grip; the next time something tried to grab me, I'd slice the attacker in two.

There was no way to gauge my progress. I kept moving forward, following the vibrations of the bloodstone. The ground felt soft and springy under my feet, like a stretched-out trampoline. Each step sunk and rose, and I had to concentrate to keep my balance. Through the darkness came every sound and scent that feed people's imaginations: Howls of rage or pain. Deep-throated cacklings. A distant siren song. A baby wailing. A woman sobbing. One moment the smoke blowing across my face smelled of rotting flesh; the next it smelled of roses or camphor. I kept going.

I took a step, and the bloodstone's vibration changed to an electric pulse. The shock nearly made me drop the pendant, but I clenched it tighter. *Pulse, pulse, PULSE.* It felt like a warning. I turned my head wildly, my sword ready, but I couldn't see anything through the smoke.

Until what I did see made me wish the smoke would close back in.

A black blob emerged. A form, sucking up everything in its path, even the dense smoke. The form was right in front of me. I stabbed it with my sword, and the blade disintegrated. The form simply absorbed it and kept coming. I turned to run, but the form was there, too. And there. And there, wherever I turned. I felt like I was at the bottom of a deep well, and the walls were closing in on me. The bloodstone's frantic pulses cut through my hand.

The form touched my left arm. A sickening, liquid sensation shot through me, like I was melting, as my flesh began to merge with the form. The bloodstone flashed, delivering a teeth-clenching shock.

And I woke up.

13

USUALLY IT'S A RELIEF TO WAKE UP FROM A BAD DREAM. Your racing heartbeat gradually slows to normal as the familiar surroundings of your warm, safe bedroom come into focus. But for me, waking up meant returning to a reality worse than any nightmare.

I shivered; the room where I lay a prisoner had grown icy cold. My left arm felt bruised where the form had touched it. I wished I could move to rub some life back into the spot. I clenched my fingers and felt something. In my right hand, I still held Mab's bloodstone.

Maybe I could try again.

And I did try, but I couldn't settle back into sleep. As soon as my mind started to descend into my dreamscape, the form was back, surrounding me, cutting off air and light, pulling me in. Again and again, I jolted awake.

It was useless. I gave up and lay shivering in the darkness.

The door opened. Two Old Ones came in, their icy auras chilling the room even more. One of them bent over me, eyeballs rolling in the lidless sockets, fangs stopping just short of my face. His mouth stretched in a ghastly smile. Then they positioned themselves at the head and the foot of the table that held me and silently wheeled me out into a hallway. Harsh fluorescent lights blinded me; I closed my eyes against them, then blinked to get my vision back.

They steered me into a large room. As far as I could tell, there were no windows. What I could see of the walls were white-painted concrete blocks. Above me hung stained, cheap-looking ceiling panels. Then I could see myself, as the Old Ones wheeled me beneath a flat mirror that took up the space of two ceiling tiles.

I wore a hospital gown, its ties loosely closed in the front. Thick leather straps, fastened with buckles, held my ankles and legs, my wrists and arms, my waist and chest—even my forehead—tying me down more thoroughly than Gulliver among the Lilliputians. The table stopped. The mirror showed me another table right beside me. On that table, under a white sheet, lay Pryce.

This time, I had no doubt it was him. I recognized his pale skin and black hair, but in the month since we'd done battle, he'd gotten thin. His eyes were closed, the skin under them sunken. His tongue protruded slightly. Although the room was freezing and he was covered by a thin cotton sheet, he didn't shiver. His only movement was the slow, even rise and fall of his chest. If not for that, I would've thought I lay next to a corpse.

"Hello." Myrddin's voice was cheerful as his face appeared above me. His foul breath washed over me, and I could see the back of his head in the mirror. "And soon, good-bye. The sedative should be working its way out of your system now. Don't try shifting your shape; I can prevent it. Power over animals is one of my skills."

I double-checked in the mirror; the IV was gone. "Then why did you drug me?"

"Convenience. I had preparations to make. You don't think I'd trust these backstabbing Old Ones or their vampire puppets to make them for me."

He turned to Pryce, put a hand on his shoulder. "My only son. Do you know how difficult it is for my kind to reproduce? This boy is my most prized possession. I've followed him with interest over the years, of course, to the extent I could. But I was . . . away. And scrying is so passive. I couldn't help him, guide him, *mold* him as I wanted to."

Myrddin ran the back of his hand along Pryce's cheek. "Now that I'm back, we'll be gods together, my boy and I," he murmured. Then he raised his voice. "You hear that, Colwyn? Gods! True gods, not skulking shadow-dwellers like you desiccated fossils."

I guessed that Colwyn was one of the Old Ones who'd rolled me in here. He didn't reply to Myrddin's taunt.

Myrddin returned his attention to me. "And how is your . . . aunt, I believe she calls herself?"

His question took me by surprise. "Are you talking about Mab?"

"Mab. Yes, of course. So many names, one loses track over the years. At any rate, how is she?"

"None of your business."

"You think not? But your present predicament is my business, seeing as it's my doing, and Mab has everything to do with that. You see, I don't need *your* life force in particular to revive my son, although as I said, I'm interested to see whether the shapeshifting ability transfers. But a human would do just as well. Further, the process I'm going to subject you to is excruciatingly painful." He smiled, like this was good news. "It doesn't have to be. Your death could be quick and clean like the others'. Yet I'm putting in the effort to make it slow and agonizing because of your aunt."

He leaned over me, his stinking breath hot on my face. His eyes searched mine, looking for a reaction. I wouldn't give him one; I closed my eyes.

"Years ago, she did me an evil," he said, close to my ear. "And evil must be repaid with evil, don't you agree? Your 'Mab' deprived me of my family and made me suffer. So I must do the same to her. Nothing personal, my girl. Simply redressing the balance—or making a start, at least."

He must have straightened, because when he spoke again his voice was more distant. "It's a pity the Old Ones are so camera-shy. Won't allow them in the place." I opened my eyes to see what he was doing. He held a tangle of narrow plastic tubing. He pulled a tube from the mass and coiled it as he spoke. "Colwyn—he fancies himself chieftain of the Old Ones, you know—Colwyn is so unreasonable. I'd love to record this procedure. For science, of course, but also as a gift to your aunt. The Old Ones think they're eternal, but really they're quite backwards." He looked to his right. "Yes, you. I'm talking about you." He went back to coiling. "Colwyn and I have never trusted each other, so it's rather awkward to find ourselves in a position where each requires the other's assistance. I said I'd been away. Colwyn brought me back. He reunited me with my son and is providing support—locations, equipment, minions—so I can revive Pryce. In return, I'll give him what he wants."

"What's that?"

"What else? The secret to eternal life. I have it; he doesn't. Hah!" He spat that last word off to the side, toward Colwyn. "But the bastard has tried to tilt the scales in his own favor. You see, he released me from . . ." Myrddin's eye twitched. "From where I was. But only for a limited time. I have ten days of freedom before his spell wears off and I'm returned to that horrible place—unless I share my secret with him. But I won't share the secret until Pryce is restored, and Colwyn won't remove the time limit until I give him what he wants. And so we find ourselves at a stalemate." He giggled. "At least until one of us can figure out how to betray the other. Eh, Colwyn?"

Myrddin dropped the last coil on Pryce's table. He reached toward me and held open my right eyelid, shining a light into my eye. Then he repeated the process with my left eye. He leaned forward and whispered, "Colwyn thinks he's in charge, but he doesn't command me. There's recording equipment hidden in the mirror above you. You will scream nicely for it, won't you? Your aunt will want to know *exactly* what happened to her favorite niece, after all."

No screaming, I promised myself. No matter how bad things got. If Myrddin sent Mab a video of my last moments, she'd see that I died bravely.

He straightened and spoke in a slightly-too-loud voice. "I do believe you're ready. Well, *you* may not be, I'll grant you that, my girl." *Giggle, giggle.* "But the sedative has worn off enough to proceed."

I didn't believe Myrddin could stop me from shifting without the drug. If its effects had diminished, it was time to call the wizard's bluff and change into something powerful, angry, and deadly. I closed my eyes. The image of a grizzly formed in my mind—reared up, roaring, claws raised—and I poured all of myself into it. The image held. Energy buzzed through me. My limbs burned and twitched as the change began. I pushed more energy into it.

A hand settled on my forehead. It soaked up the energy like a sponge. I still held the grizzly's image in my mind, as vivid as if it stood before me, but my body remained unchanged.

"No," said Myrddin simply. He held his hand in place as the energy fizzled. I struggled, tugging on the energy, trying to pull it back from him, but I couldn't do it. He absorbed it all.

When there wasn't a spark left, the pressure of Myrddin's hand left my forehead. "It's time," he said. "Bring in the Reaper."

I DON'T KNOW WHETHER I BLACKED OUT OR GOT SWALlowed up by panic, but I don't remember the Reaper entering the room. The next thing I knew, a figure stood beside me, holding an evil-looking sickle. The figure was robed, like the Old Ones, but the hand that held the weapon was human. A man's hand.

I'll have to tell Daniel he was right, I thought, then laughed hysterically because I'd never get a chance to tell Daniel—or anyone—anything ever again.

Stay calm, Vicky. And don't scream.

The Reaper's face was too deep inside the robe's hood for me to make out his features. A distant cawing sounded. I opened my senses to the demon plane and was nearly deafened by the raucous sound of hundreds of crows. In the demon plane, a huge beak protruded from the Reaper's hood and ghostly black wings sprouted from his back. He was thoroughly possessed by the Morfran.

Sharp pain yanked me back into the human world. The Reaper had unfastened the ties at the front of my gown and was dragging the point of his sickle along my breastbone, tearing my flesh with the blade.

I gasped. But I clenched my teeth tightly before the pain tore a scream from my throat. I would not scream.

The Reaper cut further, carving symbols into my skin. In the mirror, all I could see was his robed back. I didn't know what the symbols were; all I knew was how much I hurt.

"Enough." Myrddin put a hand on the Reaper's arm. "That will do. This one is different."

A high-pitched whine issued from the Reaper's hood. The sickle sliced toward my throat.

Myrddin's hand stopped its descent. A few muttered words from the wizard, and the Reaper was lifted from his feet. Two seconds later, a grunt and cry sounded as he hit a wall.

"Keep him back," Myrddin said. "What? No, I don't need the jar. Didn't you hear me? This one is different." Working quickly and silently, he picked up a length of tubing and fitted it with a long, thin, wicked-looking needle. Then he moved between me and Pryce, and I couldn't see what he was doing. The mirror showed my chest as a mass of blood—so much blood I couldn't make out whatever patterns the Reaper had sliced into me. Myrddin turned back to me, needle in hand. The tubing trailed behind, somehow connected to Pryce. Myrddin used the needle to trace the symbols the Reaper had carved into my flesh. I felt every inch. He paused directly over my heart.

"The heart," Myrddin said, "is the center of a person's life force." He pushed. The pain sharpened. No, he couldn't be—but he was. He didn't stop. The needle slid into my heart and stayed there. My heartbeat went crazy, the muscle trying to push out the invader. "When the heart stops, so does life. Of course, I don't want you to die at once, so I've spelled the probe to minimize its physical damage. What we're going for here is the slow, painful draining of every last ounce of your life force."

It hurt. God, how it hurt. Like nothing I'd ever felt before. Sweat beaded on my forehead, and I gritted my teeth against my agony. I would not scream. I would not think about the needle thrust deep into my heart.

"Like the blood," Myrddin continued, "the life force circulates through the body. *Chi*, *prana*, *élan vital*—call it what you will. Every culture expresses the concept in some form. Now, these acupuncture needles"—he showed me a handful of fine needles with colored ends—"will be inserted at strategic points to slow down the flow of your life force. A sort of reverse acupuncture, if you will." He stuck a needle in my arm, another above my eyebrow. "The aim being, of course, to drag your life force from you. I want you to feel the wrench of that chi leaving every cell of your body."

He kept going, turning me into a pincushion. If I'd thought I hurt before, I didn't even know what pain was. Each needle magnified the agony, spread it throughout my body. It felt like my soul was being slowly pulled out by the roots.

"Now." Myrddin slapped my cheek to make me look at him. He showed me two thin tubes, each split into a Y shape with a needle at the branch of each Y. "They say, I believe, that the eyes are the windows to the soul. And since you're donating your soul to my son, that will be the final touch."

Oh, God. Not my eyes. My heart thumped wildly around the invading probe. I snapped my eyes shut, but his fingers forced the right lid open. I strained at the straps that held me immobile. I rolled my eyes in crazy, random directions.

And I screamed. I screamed and screamed because there was no other way to express the pain and horror.

"Hold still, damn it all!" Myrddin shouted. "I'd prefer not to blind you."

Maybe I shouldn't have cared. Maybe blindness would have been a mercy. But even now, some deep, primal part of me recoiled at the thought of losing my sight. I stopped screaming, stopped rolling my eyes. I lay still and watched the first needle descend.

Something clattered to the floor.

Myrddin froze. He took his hand from my eye, put down the needle, and bent toward the floor.

"Where did you get this?" he asked sharply. "You didn't have it when they brought you here."

I was shaking so badly that I couldn't focus on the object he held in front of my face.

"This bloodstone!" he shouted. "How did it come to be in your hand?"

If I could have had one wish right then, it would have been the freedom to turn my head away from him. I said nothing.

Pain coursed through me with each heartbeat.

Myrddin swore. His footsteps crossed the room. The door opened. "Battle positions!" he shouted.

Seconds later, he was back at my table. He yanked the probe from my heart. I groaned. It felt like he'd pulled the heart from my body with it. "We'll have to finish this later," he said, ripping needles from my flesh. Something cool passed over my chest, stinging my skin. Myrddin tossed a blood-soaked cloth aside, then refastened the front of my gown. "I must get you out of here before Mab arrives." He cackled, and an ugly light shone in his eyes. "Perhaps Mab herself will be number four—or five! Yes, five. What a pleasure that would be, for her to see my son open his eyes to the world just as hers close forever. A pleasure for me, that is, not for that bitch."

He turned toward Pryce and I couldn't see what he was doing, then he stood between us, coiling the tube whose needle had pierced my heart. The tube, spattered with blood, glowed with a silvery light.

The pain receded, leaving me weak and light-headed. My

ears buzzed. Myrddin's movements, as I watched him in the overhead mirror, were slow and fluid, like in an underwater ballet.

"I need attendants," Myrddin muttered. "Where the devil did Colwyn go?"

He stalked back toward the door. "Colwyn, whe—" The word ended in a grunt as the door banged open and Kane called my name.

Kane? Here? How had he found me? This had to be a hallucination, my dying mind conjuring up comforting images where everything could still be all right. Where escape and rescue were possible.

Kane's face hovered over mine. His gray eyes burned with fury and concern and something else.

"Are you real?" My voice came out in a croak.

The brush of his lips on mine felt real.

A commotion burst out near the door. Kane looked up, scowled, raised a pistol. He fired. Then something knocked him backward and I couldn't see him anymore.

A blast—gunshot? energy?—broke the mirror over my head. I closed my eyes as shards rained down, nicking and slicing my skin.

"Hello, Mab." Myrddin's voice sounded thick. Was he hurting? "Funny name you've chosen for yourself this time around."

"Myrddin Wyllt, you will not harm my niece." Mab sounded strong, certain. Now I knew I was hallucinating, because my aunt was two thousand miles away. Yet I felt a certain peace. I was glad my life was ending this way, in a fantasy of my aunt stepping in to protect me. And Kane. I always knew he'd come for me if he could. Still, I wished it had been real. His lips had felt so nice, so warm.

Where *was* Kane? If I was hallucinating, I wanted to imagine him beside me.

Fighting noises erupted from the other side of the room. It didn't sound like a sword fight. More like they were throwing bombs at each other. Energy blasted out again and again.

Then Myrddin's cackle rang out. "Colwyn, you lazy corpse. It's about time you—"

A furious snarl chilled me down to my fingertips. It was a primal, animal sound. Had Mab shifted to fight the Old Ones? Maybe I could help her. I concentrated, again summoning the grizzly bear image. But I couldn't gather the energy. I was too weak.

This was *my* hallucination, damn it. You'd think it would let me escape from the straps that held me down. Then I could at least imagine my death as an honorable one, fighting beside my aunt.

Shouts. Snarls. Running footsteps. Cursing. The thud and grunt of impact. More shouts—Mab's voice among them. "Get Pryce!" she shouted. "Kill him!" So she hadn't shifted. Yet the sounds of an attacking animal cut through the chaos. Something slammed into the table beside mine, shaking it. "No!" Myrddin shouted. A yelp of pain.

A slap stung my cheek and I opened my eyes. Myrddin stood over me. Blood smeared one side of his face and matted his hair. He was panting, slumped over. "Another time, my girl," he said to me, and winked. Then he disappeared.

"Victory, child, are you all right?" Mab's face appeared above me. Not huge and transparent, as she'd been in my dreamscape, but real flesh. Worry lines sharpened her gaze as her eyes roved over my face. She brushed glass off me. Her fingers loosened the strap across my forehead. She flung it aside and smoothed a warm hand over my icy skin.

I lifted my head, just because I could. The empty room looked like a battle zone. Scorch marks blackened the walls. Chairs and tables were scattered around like discarded toys. Something smoldered in a corner. I looked to my right. The table that had been next to me, the one that held Pryce, was gone.

Mab had unbuckled the strap across my chest and was working on the one that secured my right wrist. I was still shaking, and dizziness made the room spin. Weak, I let my head fall back.

"Myrddin has gone into the demon plane and taken Pryce with him," Mab said. "He knows I won't follow him there, not with you like this." She paused and laid her cheek against my forehead. I could feel her trembling. "Oh, Vicky, are you all right?"

"I . . . I can't stop shivering." I felt like I'd never be warm again. Mab put both her hands on my face, and I soaked in their warmth. "I thought I was hallucinating. Am I?"

She went back to work, unfastening the strap. She picked up my hand, bending the elbow and massaging my skin. "No, child. This is real. I'm really here. After you're safe and rested, I'll explain all."

"But I thought Kane was here, too."

"And so he was."

Was? I struggled to sit up through the nausea and dizziness. I snatched away my free hand and pulled at the strap across my waist. " 'Was,' Mab? Where is he?"

She smiled grimly as she unbuckled the waist strap. "The last I saw, he was in the hallway, making some Old Ones run in a most undignified manner." She tilted her head, listening. "I believe he's coming back. Here, child, you can sit up. I'll help you. Gently, now."

She got her arms around me and lifted. The room tilted, and I grabbed at her to keep from falling. I closed my eyes, waiting for the dizziness to pass.

Someone touched my leg, and I breathed in the scent of moonlit pine forest. Kane. His scent calmed me. I opened my eyes to see his gray ones.

In the face of a massive wolf.

Kane was in wolf form.

Mab gripped my shoulders. I looked at her, confused. The full moon was weeks away. "How long have I been here? Is the moon—?"

She shook her head. "Waning gibbous. Myrddin had you only for a few hours."

"So how . . . ?" Kane nuzzled my neck. I leaned into him and stroked his fur. It was thick and coarse, but soft. He didn't smell like a wolf. He smelled like Kane.

"Myrddin did it. He has some power over animals," Mab said, but didn't elaborate. "Most likely Mr. Kane's human form will return with the dawn."

Most likely. I didn't like the sound of that. But I put my arms around Kane's neck and buried my face in his warm ruff. He'd come for me. That was all that mattered. Whatever else we had to face, we'd face it together.

14

I SAT ON A DOUBLE BED, MY BACK PROPPED UP BY PILLOWS and my legs stretched out. The hard, lumpy mattress was uncomfortable, but it beat my previous resting place in Myrddin's guest room. I felt weak and tired, and every cell in my body ached. Mab sat in a chair beside the bed, holding my hand in both of hers. Kane lay on the bed beside me, his long wolf body pressed close against my leg. My hand rested on his shoulder, fingers burrowing into his warm fur. We were in a run-down motel somewhere north of the airport.

I was a little fuzzy on how we'd arrived here. I'd been too weak to walk—an attempt to stand up had made me faint. Flashes of scenes jumbled together in my mind. Being carried past white cinder-block walls and up a long staircase. Passing through a doorway into cool air that smelled of exhaust and wet cement. Darkness. Some kind of construction site. Mab buckling a seatbelt across me as she settled me into a car. Leather seats. I thought it was Kane's BMW, but I don't know who drove. Not Kane, who was lying across the backseat. I didn't think Mab knew how—Jenkins did duty as her chauffeur in Wales—but I sure as hell hadn't been in the driver's seat. As soon as the car door had closed, I'd slumped against it, dozing off and on as we moved through the streets of Boston.

Now, I smoothed the thin, stiff comforter over my legs. It was the cheapest kind, a hideous orange-and-brown floral print, pocked by cigarette burns.

"Are you still cold?" Mab asked, leaning forward.

"Not as much." I'd stopped shivering, at least. Mab pulled the comforter off the other bed and draped it around my shoulders. I probably looked like a pile of dead leaves.

"Warmth will return as your life force regenerates."

"That will happen?"

"It's happening already. I just thank all the heavens we reached you in time."

"How? How did you reach me at all? Where was I?"

"You were being held in an underground facility beneath a construction site. Stanhope was the name of the street, I believe."

I stared at her. It still seemed unreal that she was here. "But you were in Wales, right, when I called you on the dream phone?"

"Yes. I was trying to bring you there through your dream, remember? I thought the best strategy was to remove you physically from Myrddin's grasp."

"I didn't make it through the collective unconscious. A form almost absorbed me." I rubbed at my arm where the blob had touched me. "I woke up to get away from it."

"I was afraid something like that would happen. So I made a contingency plan. Always—"

"—have a contingency plan," I chimed in. She'd only told me that a million times over the years. We both smiled.

"As soon as you woke up," she said, "I could feel you'd left the dream realms. If you couldn't make your way to me, I'd come to you. That was the contingency plan."

"What did you do?" I asked.

"Jenkins called Mr. Kane—"

"Wait. You put in a phone at Maenllyd?" For my whole life, my aunt had refused to modernize her old stone manor house: no phone, no TV, no Internet. I always felt kind of lucky she'd allowed plumbing and central heating.

"At my house? No, of course not. Jenkins drove me to the pub. He went inside and called Mr. Kane, letting him know you were in danger and asking him to stand by. When he came back out to let me know he'd made the call, I attempted to contact your sister through her dreams."

Okay, if I hadn't been hallucinating before, I definitely was now. "*You* talked to *Gwen* on the dream phone?" That was even more remarkable than Mab's sudden appearance in Boston. Kind of on a par with an ice storm in hell or pigs taking to the skies.

"No, I did not. She wouldn't respond. I brought up her colors again and again. I tinged them with urgency. She ignored me."

"It's been years since Gwen used the dream phone. Maybe she's forgotten how."

Mab's brow creased in a frown. "There is no forgetting. Although she gave up her shapeshifting ability, she's still Cerddorion. She could have answered had she chosen to. So . . ." Mab paused, watching my face. "I contacted Maria."

"Wait, Maria? On the dream phone?" I didn't think my niece even knew what that was. The dream phone was part of the fun side of being Cerddorion—not the sort of information Gwen would volunteer.

"She's an impressive child. Brave and kind. She'll make a fine Cerddorion woman when she comes of age."

So Mab believed Maria was on her way to becoming a shapeshifter. Gwen would have a fit—right after she finished having a fit about the fact that Mab had contacted Maria behind her back.

"The child answered at once," Mab continued. "As I said, impressive. Apparently no one had ever explained our method of communication to her." She cocked an eyebrow at me.

I raised both hands. "Not my job, Mab. I can't interfere with how my sister raises her kids."

"Hm. We shall discuss that later. At any rate, Maria caught on quickly, and she allowed me to enter her dreamscape. I asked her to think of a place she knew in Boston, a place she could picture clearly. She chose the aquarium. While she imagined the spot, I roused myself enough to tell Jenkins the location. He communicated it to Mr. Kane. When I returned to Maria, she'd done a magnificent job of building a replica of the New England Aquarium in her dreamscape. I crossed through the collective unconscious and into Maria's dreamscape."

Crossed through. Somehow it didn't surprise me in the least that Mab had made it through that awful place as easily as strolling down a Welsh lane. "From there, I stepped into the aquarium's courtyard, but not before I took a moment to erase the dream-phone call from Maria's mind."

Good. Maria was having a hard enough time lately. I didn't want her to be traumatized by yet more dreams she couldn't understand.

"At the aquarium," Mab continued, "Mr. Kane was waiting for me."

Kane shifted position to put his head on my leg and stared at me. Even though I came from a long line of shapeshifters, it felt strange to see those familiar eyes peering from an animal face. I stroked his head.

"Okay, so you got to Boston the same way I tried to get to Wales. But how did you find me once you were here?"

"This." She pulled a pendant from inside her shirt, just as she had in our dream-phone call. It was the same one she'd worn then. "My bloodstone. I always know where it is. So you see, I couldn't simply call Mr. Kane and tell him where you were, but I could follow the pull of the bloodstone myself. It led us straight to you."

"You got it back." The last time I'd seen the bloodstone, it was in Myrddin's hand.

"Yes, Myrddin dropped it during the fight." She tucked the pendant away again. "But to tell the events as they happened: When we reached the construction site, we had little trouble getting inside. Mr. Kane had come prepared to fight the Old Ones. He brought a pistol loaded with silver bullets."

Kane? With a gun? I'd seen him with it, but somehow that still felt like a hallucination. I looked at the wolf who lay beside me. His intelligent eyes seemed to perceive my surprise. "I didn't know he could shoot. And how did he load it with silver bullets?"

Kane sat up and held out his right paw. The pads were blackened with silver burns.

I looked at him, surprised. "You can understand me?"

The wolf nodded.

That was odd. When I changed shape, the animal brain took over almost entirely. I could sometimes hold on to shreds of thought or glimmers of ideas, but I couldn't understand speech any better than whatever animal I'd become. I'd assumed werewolves worked the same way.

"Is that normal?"

The wolf shook his head.

"It's not a normal transformation," Mab said. "When Myrddin hit him with energy, the blast was intended to kill. Myrddin was more surprised than anyone, I think, when it forced a transformation instead. He obviously hadn't realized your young man was a werewolf."

I was glad Kane could understand what we were saying; it felt more like Kane—*my* Kane—was really present. But it must be killing him not to be able to talk. Kane without a voice was like . . . well, like nothing I'd ever experienced. Unthinkable. I stroked his head as he settled again beside me.

Mab explained what had happened when they stormed the Old Ones' hideout. They'd been attacked first by vampires and then by Old Ones. Kane's silver bullets had incapacitated the vampires, and a well-aimed heart shot had killed one of the Old Ones. After seeing one of their colleagues fall, the other Old Ones scattered.

"This vulnerability of the Old Ones to silver shows how weak they've grown," Mab said. "A century ago, silver would hardly have troubled them. Now, it burns and kills them. No wonder they've brought Myrddin back."

"Back from where?" I asked. "He said something about that. He also said his time was limited to ten days."

"Did he?" Mab looked thoughtful. But she didn't answer my question. She went back to describing the night's events.

Kane had found the room first. He shot Myrddin twice, hitting an arm and grazing the side of his head, but silver isn't lethal to demi-demons. Kane ran to me, but Myrddin blasted him with energy and he fell. By this time Mab had arrived. She and Myrddin fought, trading blasts of energy, the wizard slowed a bit by his bullet wounds. Even though the shots didn't kill him, they still would've hurt like hell. Then Colwyn, leader of the Old Ones, appeared in the doorway, with reinforcements behind him.

"I believe he thought Mr. Kane was dead and he was in no danger from the silver," Mab said. "Instead, a huge wolf leapt up and charged them." She gave a tiny smile. "The Old Ones are terrified of wolves—that's why there are no wolves in Britain to this day." A chuckle rolled past the smile. "I'd wager old Colwyn hasn't moved that fast since Stonehenge was new."

Beside me, Kane's ribs heaved in a silent, wolfish laugh.

"As we fought," Mab continued, "I held back a little energy each time I blasted Myrddin. It made him think, wrongly, that I was weak. But holding back also let me gather sufficient energy on the side for a double attack. I attacked Myrddin, and it staggered him. Immediately, I turned and blasted Pryce. But I tried too hard to be fast. It bungled my aim, and most of the energy missed Pryce and hit the table on which he lay. Pryce cried out, and Myrddin snatched him into the demon plane." She sat back, looking tired, as though she'd just fought the battle all over again. "And now you know what happened."

"What about the Reaper? What happened to him?"

Mab looked puzzled. "Who?"

I explained about the killings that had happened in the South End. "He was there tonight. Stanhope Street isn't in the South End, but I'm sure it was the Reaper. Myrddin called him that. He had a curved blade. And he carved these symbols into my chest." I opened the bloodstained hospital gown to show her.

Mab stared, and I wondered how bad it was. In all the rush

and confusion, I hadn't checked. "Victory," my aunt said. "There are no symbols there."

I looked down. The skin was unbroken. No scabs marked the lines the Reaper had cut into my flesh.

I stared at the smooth skin. "I don't understand."

Mab pulled the gown's front shut, tying the strings as though I were a toddler. "It could be that Myrddin used healing magic to erase any symbols when he figured out I was coming; he wouldn't want me to see them. And our kind heals so quickly. Or—and I'm afraid I must say this—it could be you imagined the whole thing. All that fear, all that pain . . . As you said, child, you were close to hallucinating. At any rate, you're tired. You need to rest to regenerate the life force Myrddin stole from you."

I did feel tired—and now confused. Even though I'd spent a good part of the past day drugged and dreaming, I felt like I could sleep for three or four days straight, even on a rock-hard mattress in a cheap motel.

Mab got into the other bed and lay on her back. Within minutes, gentle snoring filled the room. Kane gave me a quick, gentle lick on the cheek, then jumped off the bed and lay in front of the door, guarding it.

"I'll see you in the morning," I said to him as I turned out the light. And I hoped I would—the Kane I knew, not his human mind trapped in his wolf body.

Although I was tired, sleep didn't come. I lay in the dark, staring at the ceiling, my hand tracing a line along my breastbone. A vertical line, with a short branch at each end. Even if no marks appeared there now, I could feel the knife cut deep into my flesh. I could see the Reaper's hood falling forward as he bent over me, intent on his work, as the Morfran's frantic cawing urged him on. It was no hallucination. The Reaper had been there.

Pushing the image away, I turned onto my side. The freedom of movement felt like a miracle, and I shuddered at the memory of being held immobile as knives and needles violated my body. If Mab hadn't ventured across the collective unconscious and into Maria's dreamscape, I'd be dead now, my life force siphoned from me and poured into Pryce.

Myrddin hadn't managed to wrench away my life force tonight—but he did get some of it. My weakness, the bone-deep ache in every part of my body, confirmed that. What did it mean that some of my life force had gone to Pryce? For now, Pryce was still "the sleeper," but if Myrddin revived him, would Pryce have access to my thoughts? Would he always know my whereabouts, like Mab and her bloodstone?

No way was I going to let that happen. We'd just have to stop Myrddin before the Reaper struck again.

15

SUNLIGHT STREAMED AROUND THE EDGES OF THE DRAPES that blocked the room's picture window. I blinked against the light. Warm. The thought floated lazily through my mind. I felt warm, snuggled under blankets and two comforters. I felt alive again.

Kane. The thought hit me with urgent power. I sat up and looked toward the door.

Kane sat up at the same time. He was still a wolf.

I patted the bed, trying not to let dismay show on my face. He trotted over and jumped up beside me. He lay down, curling up, his head resting between his paws. His ears drooped. "We'll fix this," I said. I hoped my voice sounded surer than I felt.

"Indeed we will," said Mab. She sat at the table in the far corner of the room. "Assuming, of course, that it's possible."

I pressed a finger to my lips, looking down at Kane and back at Mab, to indicate she shouldn't say such a discouraging thing.

"Mr. Kane is well aware of his predicament." A bag sat on the table before Mab. She removed three paper cups and pulled the lid off one. The smell of coffee filled the room, and my stomach growled loudly. Mab smiled. "That's a good sign. Now, let's see how well you can get out of bed and walk over here."

I threw off the covers, but immediately felt like I'd stepped onto an arctic plain. I pulled one of the comforters from the nest I'd made on the bed and wrapped it around me like a cloak. Better. I was becoming almost fond of the orange-and-brown pattern.

Walking proved no problem. Aside from some lingering soreness, I felt steady on my feet and strong in my limbs. And the coffee tasted divine, its warmth spreading through me as I swallowed. Mab had a different appraisal of her tea. She sipped, then made a face. "I don't know where you Americans ever got the idea to call such swill 'tea.'"

Kane sat on the floor beside me. He looked back and forth between us and made an impatient noise that sounded almost like a whine, except not once in all the time I'd known him had Kane ever come close to whining.

"How does your young man take his coffee?" Mab asked.

"Black, no sugar. Like me."

Mab nodded as she picked up the third cup. She took off the lid and blew on the liquid. Then she held the cup out to Kane. He sniffed at the black liquid and then flicked out his tongue experimentally.

"It's all right," Mab said. "I had them put in a couple of ice cubes so it wouldn't burn." Kane stuck his muzzle in the cup and drank. I was glad to see it. Kane never did like to start the day without his coffee.

I took another sip of my own drink. "Mab, what can we do about . . ." I was going to say "the situation," but Mab was right. Kane knew there was a problem—hell, it was *his* problem. Trying to shield him with vague language was ridiculous. "What can we do about Kane?"

"As I see it, there are two possibilities," Mab said. Kane finished his coffee and licked his chops. Mab put the empty cup on the table. She dug around in the bag and pulled out three sugar packets. As she spoke, she dumped the sugar into her tea and stirred. "One: Wait until the full moon. At that time, the moon's power will most likely transform Mr. Kane into true wolf form, as usual. And when the full moon passes, he should return to his human form."

It was too long; the full moon was three weeks away. And I didn't like the sound of "most likely" and "should."

"What's possibility number two?"

"Myrddin's energy changed him to this form. Myrddin's energy can change him back."

Great. "So we just waltz up to Myrddin and say, 'Hey, old buddy, can you do us a favor?' "

"None of that cheek, young lady." She pulled some crullers from the bag and arranged them on a napkin. "Here, you must eat. The sugar will restore your strength."

She unwrapped an English muffin filled with egg, cheese, and ham and set it on the table in front of an empty chair. Kane jumped up onto the chair and, um, wolfed down the sandwich. Mab unwrapped another for him.

My stomach growled again. I picked up a cruller and bit into it. "Okay, sorry about the sarcasm. But what are we going to do? If I understand right, we can wait until the next full moon—" Kane let out a short bark to show how little he liked that idea. "And the full moon may or may not fix the problem. Or we can ask Myrddin to undo the damage he caused. That would be the same Myrddin who tried to kill me yesterday."

"I said nothing about asking him. We'll have to force him." Mab moved aside the food bag and opened a small laptop computer. "I've been reviewing the recording Myrddin made last night—"

I nearly choked on my cruller. "You know how to use a computer?" I'd always thought of my aunt as the original Luddite.

She didn't even bother to shrug. "One does what one must." Mab squinted at the small screen. "There was a camera behind the shattered mirror. It broadcast wirelessly to this . . ." She flicked a finger at the laptop. "To this contraption. I've been going through the files. Unfortunately, there seems to be nothing important there besides Myrddin's video." Her voice broke on the last word. She picked up her tea, but the cup shook and she put it down again. "Victory, child, I'm so sorry we couldn't get there sooner."

I closed my eyes against the image of a descending needle. "I'd say you arrived just in time." Then I thought of something. "The Reaper . . . ?"

Mab nodded. "Yes, child. You were correct. A hooded man attacked you with a curved blade. But whatever symbols he carved into your chest, I couldn't make them out. His back obscured what he was doing, and then there was so much blood." She grabbed a napkin and pressed it to her face, turning her head away.

I rubbed her shoulder, reminding her I was all right now. After a moment, she sniffed and balled up the napkin in her hand.

"The Reaper was possessed by the Morfran," I said. "In the demon plane, he looked kind of like a giant crow." That awful cawing, driving the Reaper to use his blade, echoed in my mind.

Mab nodded thoughtfully. She raised her cup with a steadier hand. "The Morfran is the essence of all demons. A Morfran-possessed hand drawing the symbols on the victims adds that demonic essence to the ritual. Without the Morfran, Pryce would be revived as a mere human. Myrddin wants his demi-demon son."

I remembered Daniel's question about calling to the Morfran to find the Reaper. "Is there some way we can make the Morfran come to us? Flush the Reaper out?"

Mab pursed her lips, considering. "Not that I'm aware of. Myrddin is using his demon side to control the Morfran—and with the Morfran, the Reaper. I can't break that connection unless the possessed human is in front of me. There's a ritual to exorcise the Morfran, but I can't do it at a distance."

Pity. We sat in silence for a minute. Then Kane jumped down from his chair and ran over next to Mab. He put his front paws on the table and nosed at the laptop.

I voiced his question. "You were talking about the video. Is there anything in it that could help Kane?"

"Perhaps." She sniffed again and cleared her throat. "As I watched the video, I paid careful attention to Pryce. He's not yet resuscitated. He cried out when my energy blast hit his table, yes, but it was merely a reflex, I believe. After that single cry, he sank back into his stupor."

"Myrddin said it would take the life forces of five people to bring Pryce back."

"Yes, I heard that on the video. And I was to be the fifth." She smiled grimly.

"I've been thinking about that. Myrddin and the Reaper appear to be working on a timetable—one victim every two days. Last night, I was supposed to be victim number three, but Myrddin failed to steal my life force. So maybe we screwed things up for him." I looked at her hopefully.

"We might have, child. Unfortunately, we did not."

She picked up a folded newspaper and showed me its screaming headline: *Reaper Strikes Again*. "It happened on Stanhope Street. The body was found three hours after we left. The police have discovered the underground facility where you were held captive. It was, of course, abandoned."

I grabbed the paper and scanned the article. The police weren't saying much, but the story claimed that the victim had suffered the same mutilations as the previous two. The reporter noted, somewhat hysterically, that the Reaper had moved beyond the South End. Now, no one in Boston was safe.

Mab took the paper and folded it again. "We know that two more victims are required before Pryce can be revived. That means Pryce is vulnerable. And the son's vulnerability makes the father vulnerable to us."

I saw where she was going. "If we can grab Pryce, we can force Myrddin to change Kane back." We could use Pryce as leverage, like the Old Ones were doing.

Mab nodded.

"And then what?"

Mab pursed her lips as though surprised I'd asked such a silly question. "Why, then we destroy them both."

* * *

AFTER BREAKFAST, WE CHECKED OUT OF THE MOTEL. MAB gave me some clothes—an oversized Red Sox sweatshirt and matching sweatpants—that she'd bought at a convenience store down the street. The best she could do for shoes was a pair of pink flip-flops. My toes would be chilly, but it didn't matter. I was happy to leave the bloodstained hospital gown in the trash.

We were barely out the door when Kane took my sleeve in his teeth and pulled me toward his car. He led me around to the driver's side, then sat and stared.

"You want me to drive?"

The wolf nodded. He looked back at Mab and shuddered. Mab handed me the keys. "As I said, one does what one must. I learned a great deal about driving last night, but I can't say I'm eager to repeat the experience, especially on your Boston streets."

If a wolf can heave a sigh of relief, that's what Kane did. I unlocked the doors and opened mine. Kane jumped into the back, and I slid into the driver's seat. The engine roared to life, then settled to a steady purr. Nice. I love my Jag, but she's an antique requiring frequent repairs. Kane's BMW was a dream machine.

I hit the gas. The car fishtailed a little as we sped out of the parking lot. Kane let out a short, sharp yip as Mab put a hand on her chest and exclaimed, "Oh, my." We headed back to town.

IF THE ANCIENT GREEK GODS HAD REALLY WANTED TO PUNish Sisyphus, they wouldn't have bothered with that rolling-a-stone-up-a-hill thing. They would have made him spend eternity trying to find a parking space on a downtown Boston street during business hours on a Monday.

I couldn't drive into Deadtown; we'd never get through the checkpoints. Myrddin and the Old Ones had taken my ID card, Mab had no identification at all, and Kane—well, Kane was a wolf. The Goon Squad would be all over us before I could back up and turn around. We'd have to sneak in. And that meant I had to find a place to park.

I was on Cambridge Street, circling City Hall Plaza, when Kane started yipping. I glanced at him in the rearview mirror. He stared down a side street. "You want me to take that right?"

His wolf's head nodded.

I turned right. A couple of blocks later, Kane yipped again, his eyes fixed on the entrance to a parking garage. I knew Kane had a parking space downtown somewhere. This must be the place.

Through barks and head gestures, Kane guided me to his parking space. I pulled in and turned off the car. I let my head fall back against the leather headrest.

"Good driving, child," Mab said. Kane howled his agreement.

"Driving was the easy part," I said, opening my door. "We've still got to sneak into Deadtown." And we had to do it in broad daylight with a wolf in tow.

There are several unofficial "back doors" that can get you into or out of Deadtown without having to pass through a checkpoint. Dead spots, for example, in the electrified fence that surrounds the area. I knew of one on Deadtown's north side, but it would be impossible to get there from here on a busy weekday without attracting attention.

Well, we'd have to try. Maybe passersby would think Kane was a very large dog. He jumped from the car and shook himself, then stood, head lifted, sniffing the air. The wolf was large, standing as high as my waist, his back broad, his muscles taut with strength. He exuded a barely restrained power, something primeval, that evoked deep forest and other wild landscapes. There was no way anyone would mistake this fierce, majestic creature for a domesticated puppy.

Yet what choice did we have? I made sure the car was locked up tight and started toward the garage exit.

Something tugged on the back of my shirt. I turned around to see Kane with his jaws clamped on the hem.

"You have a better idea?"

He let go of my sweatshirt and went deeper into the garage. Mab and I exchanged a look, then followed. We descended several levels. When a car drove by, Kane would duck between parked cars. Mab and I just stepped aside and waited for the car to pass.

At the bottom level, near the elevator, Kane stopped and sat beside a metal door, maintenance access for the elevator. He looked at me and yipped. I tried the door. Locked. He yipped again.

In the bottom of the door was a ventilation panel, with horizontal, louvered slats. Kane stood and pressed his nose against it. He looked at me, then touched the panel once more.

I hooked my fingers around some slats and shook. The panel gave a little. I pulled, and it came away in my hand. Kane licked my cheek and jumped through the hole. A moment later, he stuck his head out, staring at us like he wondered what was taking us so long.

I peered past him. I couldn't see much, just enough to know that Kane's route into Deadtown was dark and dusty and festooned with spiderwebs. Lovely. I nudged Kane aside and climbed in. The closet-sized room was deeper than I expected. Kane moved inside to make room for Mab, who crawled in a moment later. Together, she and I fitted the panel back into place.

"I hope you know what you're doing," I said to Kane.

He licked my cheek again and went farther back. In the stripes of light that came through the panel, I could see a low opening in the back wall, maybe a yard square. Kane disappeared into the tunnel.

A pitch-black, narrow, dirty tunnel. Several weeks ago I'd learned, in an abandoned Welsh slate mine, that I didn't do so great in dark underground spaces. And this tunnel looked too tight to even be called a "space." I calculated. On the surface, it took a brisk ten-minute walk to get from Government Center to Deadtown. Crawling the same distance through this tunnel would take approximately . . . forever.

An impatient bark echoed from the tunnel. I took a deep breath and crawled inside. Mab followed.

There was no light, but the tunnel felt cleaner than I expected. There was little grit under my palms, as if the floor had been swept. No cobwebs brushed my face. No horrible little creatures with too many legs dropped onto my neck. I let out a startled yelp when I bumped into something—it was Kane, who'd paused to wait for us. After that, I stayed close behind him. No more than a couple of minutes had passed before light flooded the tunnel as Kane nosed aside a curtain and leapt out.

I followed, trying to decide whether I felt more relieved to see or to stand up straight. We were in a cellar, with concrete floors and walls. It looked like some kind of storeroom, with cardboard boxes lined up on shelves and stacked on the floor.

"You must pay the toll to pass," croaked an ancient-sounding voice.

I turned around. Beside the tunnel we'd exited sat an old man in a folding metal chair. His leathery face was as lined as a road map, and he had a full head of white hair. A shock of that hair fell across his forehead as he sat hunched forward, holding a sharp-looking knife in one hand and a stick in the other. He smoothed the knife along the stick, whittling. A thin curl of wood joined others on the floor.

"We have no money," I began. "I was abducted and—"

"We'll pay," Mab interrupted. "What's the toll?"

The old man sized us up, his dark eyes glittering. "Ten dollars apiece. Double for the wolf."

"That's outrageous," I sputtered. I was ready to crawl back through the tunnel and take our chances going overland.

The man shrugged, then shaved off another curl of wood. "The authorities don't take kindly to wolves running around on city streets," he said in a bored voice. "Especially if a concerned citizen calls in a report." His eyes peered at me shrewdly from under his white hair.

"We can only go forward, child," Mab said. She produced a wad of bills and peeled off two twenties. "Here you are," she said, handing them to the man. "Now please allow us to proceed."

The old man took the bills, sniffed them, and stuck them

in his shirt pocket. Then he got up and shuffled across the room. His movements were slow, but something in them suggested he was faster and stronger than he appeared. I had a feeling that anyone who tried to cheat this toll collector would end up sorry.

He stopped in front of a metal storage cabinet. After fumbling in his pants pocket, he pulled out a key and opened the door.

"Have a pleasant journey," he said.

Kane led the way again, jumping into the cabinet and into the tunnel beyond. This tunnel was more passable, an underground corridor large enough that Mab and I could walk next to each other. There was even fluorescent lighting.

I'd heard about a network of secret tunnels in and out of Deadtown, but I'd always thought they were a rumor. It surprised me that Kane actually used them.

It also surprised me that Mab was carrying American money. She hadn't brought her passport with her through the collective unconscious—Jenkins was sending it by mail—so where had she gotten cash? I hadn't thought to wonder when she'd brought me breakfast and clothes, but the question hit home when I saw that stack of bills she was carrying.

"It's Mr. Kane's. He brought it when he picked me up," she said when I asked her. Kane, who was in front, turned his head back and nodded in agreement. "Of course, I shall pay him back when I'm able."

Kane snorted and shook his head.

It took us half an hour and two more toll payments to reach Deadtown. We must have zigzagged all over—or under—downtown Boston, but in the cellars and tunnels, it was hard to trace our exact route. Finally, we went up some stairs. I twisted a bulkhead handle and pushed open the steel door—and we were in Deadtown. I recognized the place right away, a small side street near the garage where I rented a space for my Jag. We were only a few minutes from my building.

It was daylight, so the streets were empty. Still, we took the back way, keeping Kane out of sight as much as possible. The citizens of Deadtown wouldn't panic at the sight of a wolf on the street, but they would notice. And the fewer people who saw Kane out and about in his wolf form, the better.

The tricky part, I thought as we approached my building, would be getting him past Clyde, who took his doorman responsibilities very seriously. Nobody snuck past Clyde's watchful eye. But then, he was watching for zombies, vampires, and other monsters, along with the occasional norm, not for animals. No one expects to see a four-legged werewolf in all his furry glory when the moon is waning. If I could distract Clyde, maybe Kane could slink past him.

We paused in a doorway half a block from our goal, and I told Mab and Kane my plan: "On the left side of the lobby there's a seating area. Clyde's desk is on the right. Mab and I will go in first. Kane, you come in right behind us and hide in the seating area. Keep low. I'll introduce Mab to Clyde. While we're talking, try to slip to the elevators." A partial wall blocked the lobby's view of the elevators, so he could stay out of sight while he waited for us there.

Nobody had any improvements to suggest, so we walked to my building. We were in luck; Clyde was on the phone. He glanced up as I opened the door, but when he saw it was me, he turned back to his phone call.

Kane brushed against the backs of my legs as he scooted toward the seating area. I didn't turn around to watch him, but I imagined him getting behind one of the potted palms that surrounded the leather chairs.

Mab and I proceeded across the lobby to Clyde's desk. By the time we got there he was hanging up. He straightened, brushing some potato chip crumbs from his uniform, and gave Mab a welcoming smile. That is, his greenish lips stretched back way too far in a skull-like grimace. Norms have fainted at the sight of a zombie's smile, but Mab is no norm. She offered her hand.

"Clyde, this is my aunt, Mab Vaughn."

He hesitated, staring at her hand as though he expected her to snatch it back, then shook.

"Delighted," he and Mab both said. This time, they shared a smile.

"Mab will be staying with me for a few days."

"Very good." He wrote her name down on a pad.

I heard the skitter of claws on the marble floor behind me, and I spoke up to cover the sound.

"Mab is from Wales," I said, a little too loudly. "I visited her every summer when I was a child."

He looked up. "South or north?"

"I live in north Wales," she replied.

"Beautiful country!" he exclaimed. "I climbed Snowdon as a young man."

"Did you? And what did you think of the experience?"

Clyde waxed damn near poetic on his experiences in the mountains of north Wales. Mab egged him on. After they'd talked for a few minutes, when I was sure Kane was in position, I said we'd better go up to my apartment.

"It's been a pleasure to meet you, ma'am," Clyde said to my aunt. He turned to me, still wearing the same smile. "I'm sorry, Miss Vaughn, but you cannot take an animal upstairs."

Busted. How the hell had he seen Kane? We'd timed it so well. But nothing gets past my doorman.

"Clyde—"

"I'm sure you're familiar with the terms of your lease. No pets. Tenants are not allowed so much as a goldfish, let alone a large dog."

He must have only glimpsed Kane to assume the animal running past was a dog.

Kane's head appeared around the partial wall that had shielded him from view. His ears went back and he bared his teeth. A growl rumbled from his throat.

"Come here," I said to him. "Please."

He slunk out from behind the wall. Lips pulled back to show his teeth, he moved across the lobby. The growl didn't falter.

"It's okay," I said. "Come on over. Let Clyde see you."

He did. As he approached, Clyde's red eyes widened. He opened his mouth, but nothing came out. Kane sat on the floor beside me. He stopped growling, but his hackles stayed up. I leaned across the doorman's desk. "Take a good look,

Clyde. That's not an animal. Or no more of one than I am."

His eyes stayed wide as they went back and forth between us. Tentative understanding dawned.

"That's . . . ?"

I nodded.

"But—" He picked up a calendar and squinted at it. "But it's not a full moon."

"Right. There's been a . . ."

"A magical mishap," Mab supplied. "We're working to set things right as soon as we possibly can."

"'Magical mishap'?" Clyde scratched his head as though the phrase made no sense. Or like it was a euphemism for something really nasty. "Oh, no," he said. "No, no, no. A transformed werewolf? That's even worse. I'm certain your lease—"

"Come on, Clyde," I said. "This isn't his fault. You know how it feels to be changed into something you don't want to be. You're not going to deny him shelter because of that, are you?"

Clyde exhaled noisily, puffing out his cheeks. He looked again at Kane.

Kane didn't whine or thump his tail. This was not an animal who'd beg. He merely watched Clyde, every muscle tense.

"All right," Clyde said at last. "But keep him in your apartment, and stay quiet. For heaven's sake, don't let any of the other tenants find out."

"Thanks, Clyde," I said. Mab nodded her agreement.

We hurried across the lobby, before he changed his mind. Clyde didn't have to worry we'd let the other tenants know. Whatever it took, I'd get Kane back to normal as soon as I could.

16

"WHAT ON EARTH IS THAT?" MAB POINTED AT THE SIXTY-three-inch screen that took up most of my living room.

"That's my roommate's TV."

"Surely not. I've seen television sets. Jenkins and Rose have one in their cottage. It's this size." Her hands shaped a box that estimated a little thirteen-inch screen. "Surely you're joking."

"No joke." I picked up the remote from the coffee table, and the picture snapped on. Mab winced. I turned the TV off again. "Good thing Juliet's not here right now. She leaves it on, with the volume way up, and wanders off."

"I wouldn't like that. Your roommate's away?"

"For the moment." I hadn't yet told Mab about Juliet's involvement with the Old Ones—there'd been so much to discuss—but I would. First, though, I'd show her my apartment and get her settled. I intended for her to stay in my bedroom, so she'd have some privacy.

Kane woofed at the blank screen. He went to the coffee table and, holding the remote with his paws, pressed the ON button with his nose. Then he carried the remote to me and dropped it at my feet.

"Let me guess," I said, "you want to watch the news."

He nodded.

"CNN or PNN?"

"I've heard of CNN," Mab said. "What's the other?"

"The Paranormal News Network. All monsters, all the time."

Kane growled when I said *monsters*, but I ignored him. I wasn't going to let a wolf take me to task for being politically incorrect. He wanted to watch CNN, anyway, as he let me know by jumping up and knocking the remote out of my hands when the TV showed that channel.

I picked up the remote and turned down the volume several clicks. "Okay?"

He nodded again and jumped onto the couch. He sat with his ears swiveled forward, already engrossed in a story about Congressional hearings on some banking scandal.

I took my aunt's arm. "Let me give you the grand tour," I said. "Not 'grand' in the same sense as Maenllyd, of course." My aunt's manor house would swallow up my apartment ten times over. But this place was home, and I was proud to show off the spacious, comfortable living room, with its separate dining area, and the eat-in kitchen with granite counters and cherry cabinets.

And then we came to my bedroom. I tried not to see the unmade bed and strewn-around clothing through my aunt's eyes—which was more or less impossible with her standing beside me.

"Um, this is my room."

"As I would have guessed by the unkempt bed. Honestly, child, personal habits are a reflection of character."

"I didn't know you were coming. If I had, the whole place would be pristine."

"That's no excuse. Character shines brightest when no one's watching."

You can't argue with that. I know, because I opened my mouth to do so and nothing occurred to me. Okay, time to move on. We went back out into the hallway.

"That door's the bathroom."

"And across from it, I presume, is your roommate's bedroom."

"Yes, that's Juliet's room, but—"

Mab reached for the doorknob. "Since she's away, she won't mind if I stay there." She opened the door before I had time to warn her that Juliet slept in a coffin. Halfway into the room, she froze.

"Your roommate is . . . a vampire?"

"Yes. Juliet Capulet." Surely I'd told Mab that at some point. I mean, sharing an apartment with Shakespeare's most famous heroine was too good a story to keep quiet. But Mab and I rarely engaged in personal chitchat; it just wasn't a part of our relationship. Maybe I *hadn't* told her.

Mab pulled the door shut, her face white. "I think I'd like a cup of tea, if you have any."

"Sure. Are you all right?"

She waved away my concern. "Yes, yes. Of course I'm all right. But I'm rather thirsty, if you don't mind."

We went back through the living room. CNN was doing an interview with Police Commissioner Hampson about the Reaper murders.

"Anything new?" I asked Kane.

He shook his head. Hampson was blustering about locking down Deadtown to protect Boston's human citizens. I tuned him out and continued into the kitchen.

Mab sat silently at the table as I put the kettle on, found the teapot, and spooned in some tea. As I worked, I snuck glances at her. My aunt's mouth was drawn into a thin, pale line, and the knuckles of her hands, folded before her on the table, showed white. What could have flustered her so much about Juliet's room?

I placed the teapot and a mug on the table. She pulled them toward her but didn't pour.

"Are you sure you're all right? What upset you in that room?"

"It wasn't the room, child. I . . . It was a bit of a shock to learn you live with a vampire. Some of the Cerddorion feel they're the enemy of our race every bit as much as demons. That they should be slaughtered without mercy."

I frowned. "Is that what you think?" I'd never heard Mab say a word against vampires before, but suddenly she was sounding way more like Commissioner Hampson than my aunt.

She poured some tea, and steam rose from her mug. She sighed. "No, that's not my personal view. But I can't say I trust them, either. You see, every vampire is a potential Old One."

That comment hit home. "Juliet came under their thrall," I admitted, feeling uncomfortable. "But she ran away from them. That's why she's not here now; she's in hiding."

"Are you certain she's broken with them?"

From the doorway, Kane barked, as if to say that's what he wanted to know, too. He came into the kitchen and sat beside me.

I related to both of them Juliet's account of her experiences with the Old Ones. And I told Mab what had happened when I'd visited Juliet in the Goon Squad cell, how the Old Ones had tried to saw off her leg to drag her out of there.

I wondered how Juliet was doing, if the salve had helped. I'd have to call Axel and check. Also Daniel, to see whether forensics had found anything on the swab of the Old One's blade.

"If her story is true," Mab said, "I'll be very interested to meet this roommate of yours. In all my lifetimes, I've never heard of a vampire who could resist the Old Ones."

"Why do the Old Ones have so much power over vampires?" It was easy to see why humans were attracted to the vampires who preyed on them—vampires were sexy, and their narcotic-laced saliva made feeding time an erotic pleasure. But the Old Ones . . . from their hideous faces to their icy auras, there was nothing attractive about those creatures.

"Vampires crave power and life. It's their nature. They cannot help that any more than you or I can help craving air, water, and food. But it's a craving that can get out of hand, and too many are prone to give in."

"The Old Ones offer them more of what they crave."

She nodded. "The Old Ones don't just prey upon vampires. Centuries ago, the Old Ones created them. In a sense, vampires belong to them."

"Explain, please."

Mab cleared her throat, going into storyteller mode. "In ancient times, shamans were the most powerful men in the world. They were prophets, priests, and rulers, or advisers to rulers. In Wales these shamans were the *derwyddon*, the druids." She poured herself another mug of tea, sipped. "Most druids were admirable men, loyal to a code of service and honor. But power corrupted then, as it always does. A druid named Colwyn became obsessed with the power of death. How could he have so much influence over men, and over the natural world through magic, and still be subject to death? The question possessed him, drove him mad."

"This is the same Colwyn who's working with Myrddin now?"

"Yes, but I can't imagine that either of those two is happy in their alliance. I'll explain why in a moment. When Colwyn was still human, still a druid, he began experimenting. He realized that power doesn't exist on its own; it's something you receive—or forcibly take—from others. And life, he reasoned, works the same way. Every sentient creature needs to consume life in order to sustain life. Predators eat other animals. Grazers absorb life from the living plants they eat. But that's consuming only a small amount of life, just enough to keep going for another day. Take more life, Colwyn reasoned, take it in massive quantities, and you could live forever."

"Sounds like a recipe for mass murder."

"Indeed. There have always been rumors of druids performing human sacrifice. Anthropologists still debate the question today. The druids did not sacrifice living humans." Her expression darkened. "Only Colwyn did. Hundreds of them. Eventually, he passed through death and turned himself into a vampire. The first one.

"Colwyn discovered how to create others like him. At first, Colwyn's little band of vampires were very much like the vampires you know today, possessing youth, beauty, and strength. There were arguments, of course, power struggles, splinter groups. Vampires spread across Europe, across the world. They went to war with each other. With the rise of the Roman Empire, they went underground. And then, about seven centuries after he'd corrupted himself, Colwyn began to weaken."

"Seven hundred years. That's about Juliet's age. She said the same thing, that she could feel herself growing weaker."

Mab nodded. "All living things have a life span. Vampires are a corruption of nature, but they haven't conquered death, merely traversed it once to postpone their ultimate end. Nature does win out eventually, as it must. But Colwyn couldn't accept that. So much power, so much life, and he was losing it. He pondered on his original transformation. If he'd cheated death once by preying on humans, perhaps he could cheat it permanently by preying on what he considered a greater life form."

"He started feeding on vampires."

"Yes. And you see what he became as a result." Colwyn traded beauty and youth for raw power. The Old Ones, with their skull-like faces and massive fangs, were vampires stripped to their essence: on the other side of death, craving power. "In a very short time, vampires became problematic as a food source. Although they'd spread, their population was relatively small, and Colwyn slaughtered most before he realized that he couldn't treat vampires the same way he'd treated humans. So he preyed upon humans to feed his physical body and vampires to feed his power. He selected his most loyal followers and converted them into the creatures we now call the Old Ones. And if they'd been hidden before, now they pulled back even further into the shadows."

"Let me guess. Fast forward to today, and their life span is once again coming to an end. That's why I could kill one."

Kane woofed.

"And Kane could, too," I added, stroking his fur.

"Yes," Mab said. "As vampires, they lasted seven hundred

and fifty years. As Old Ones, they doubled that life span. But again, they're weakening. I believe that's why they've become so vulnerable to silver. In their strength, they possessed all the powers of a vampire many, many times over. In their weakness, their vulnerabilities are similarly amplified."

I added up the numbers in my head. According to Mab's story, Colwyn was more than two thousand years old. "So two-plus millennia aren't enough for them." You'd think that even a vampire-god wannabe would get tired of the game after all that time.

"Obsessions do not fade with time, child. They intensify. Colwyn will never get enough power. And he'll never stop questing after eternal life."

Not until we stopped him. "So where does Myrddin fit in?" I asked. "You said he and Colwyn weren't exactly happy campers together."

Something flared in my aunt's eyes at the mention of Myrddin's name. But it was gone in a moment.

"He's the real Myrddin Wyllt, isn't he?" I said. "I thought he'd named himself after some crazy wizard he admired."

"Yes, he is. There can be no doubt about that." Again, a glimpse of something in her face I couldn't read. "You remember the story, correct?"

Uh-oh. Quiz time. "Myrddin was a prophet who worked for a chieftain named, um . . ."

"Gwenddoleu."

"I knew that. Give me a chance, Mab." I hated feeling like my knowledge was spotty in front of my aunt. But I did know this legend. "They lived in the sixth century." Nearly fifteen hundred years ago, around the time the Old Ones were weakening as vampires and trying to extend their life span. "Myrddin went insane after his chieftain's entire army was killed in battle. He ran off to the woods and lived as a wild man. Later, he prophesied his own triple death."

The triple death was how Myrddin Wyllt's story always ended. He predicted he'd die three times: by falling, by stabbing, and by drowning. And he did. A crowd of thugs, jeering at the madman, drove him off a cliff high above a river. He landed on a stake, which impaled him, and drowned with his head underwater. Three deaths for the price of one.

Mab nodded, and I felt a rush of relief at passing her pop quiz. "That's the gist of the recorded legends, yes. But the legends tell only part of the real story. Myrddin served as Gwenddoleu's bard, but he was actually working for Colwyn, who'd promised the wizard vast rewards if he could deliver the secret to eternal life. Myrddin believed he'd found it. He experimented on Gwenddoleu and his men and, thinking he'd made them invulnerable, summoned Colwyn to watch the battle. When Myrddin's magic failed and the army fell, Colwyn was livid. Myrddin fled for his own life.

"He went into hiding in the woods. There, he learned the languages of animals and gained power over them. He also began to give more and more control to his demon half. As you know, most demi-demons have a human form and a shadow demon that exists primarily in the demon plane. Myrddin merged his two sides into a single entity. That's where the name Myrddin Wyllt comes from. Wyllt is the name of his shadow demon; it means 'wild.' When he called Wyllt forth into himself, he added its name to his own."

"What does that mean, that he merged them?"

"Part of Wyllt is always present in Myrddin's human form, and part of Myrddin always dwells in the demon plane. As far as I know, no other demi-demon has achieved this feat, although Myrddin hasn't been around to teach anyone."

"The triple death." Myrddin Wyllt couldn't have died that way, not if he was running around Boston now. "So that part of the legend is untrue?"

"Myrddin Wyllt was indeed driven off a cliff, impaled, and drowned. But none of those things killed him. The so-called triple death was nothing more than a demi-demon's parlor trick."

"What for?" Killing yourself in three different ways didn't sound like a fun way to liven up a dull afternoon.

"He wanted to convince Colwyn he'd finally achieved immortality. For the reward. But Myrddin's means of surviving those injuries was nothing Colwyn could use. Merging with his demon half allowed Myrddin to enter and exit the demon plane almost simultaneously. For each injury Myrddin sustained, he blinked into the demon plane, healed there, and returned—too fast for the eye to perceive. Colwyn believed him."

"And Myrddin got rich by tricking him."

Mab shook her head. "He never had the chance. As you know, the character of Merlin is made up of many legends. What other ways did a wizard called Myrddin or Merlin come to his end?"

I searched my memory. "He was imprisoned in a tree or a cave by Nimuë." According to the legend, Nimuë was a beautiful young nymph who seduced Myrddin, stole his magic, and locked him up forever. According to my family history, she was Cerddorion. Not surprising that she'd tangle with a demidemon.

"It was a tree," Mab said. She wrapped her hands around her empty mug and stared past me, her eyes unfocused, her face sad. Then she shook it off. She stood up and carried the mug to the sink. "And there Myrddin stayed. Until Colwyn undid the spell and released him." Her voice took on a hard edge. "But I wish by all that's holy he'd stayed there forever."

17

I WANTED TO ASK MAB MORE QUESTIONS, BUT SHE SAID she wanted to rest. I couldn't blame her. Crossing the collective unconscious had to leave a worse hangover than transatlantic jet lag. So I changed the sheets on my bed and made it up neatly—gotta get that character nice and shiny for my aunt—and redistributed clothes into the hamper or the closet.

When Mab was settled, I went to make some phone calls. Kane was again absorbed in the news, so I went into the kitchen to use the phone. When I picked up the handset, a stutter tone indicated voice mail was waiting. I punched in the numbers to retrieve my messages. The first call had come in just after seven a.m.

"Hi, Vicky, it's Gwen. Maria's been having more dreams." My sister's voice sounded slightly embarrassed. "She woke up this morning absolutely convinced that you were in danger, and I promised I'd call and make sure you're okay. So that's what I'm doing. Give me a call when you get this, okay?"

A computerized voice announced that the next message was from the same number, recorded a few minutes later. This one was from Maria herself. "Um, hi, Aunt Vicky," she said, almost whispering. "It's Maria. Your niece. Sorry, that sounded dumb. I know you know who I am. You, um, said I could talk to you if I had any more weird dreams. And I did, but this one was *really* weird. There was this lady who said she was my aunt, and . . ." Maria paused, and her voice got so quiet and hurried I could barely hear her words. "I've gotta go. Don't call me back, okay? I'll call you later." The message ended, and there was no more voice mail.

Mab hadn't erased her presence from Maria's dreamscape as completely as she'd thought. I felt bad that Maria had worried about me all morning, but she'd be fine once she knew I was okay. The memory of the dream would fade—it probably had already.

I checked the clock. It was a little after one; Gwen would be at Justin's playgroup. I dialed her home number and left a chirpy message that I was just calling to say hi and would try again later. That should put Maria's mind at rest.

Next I called Creature Comforts, not expecting an answer since it was the middle of the norm workday—and that meant sleepy time for most paranormals. I figured I'd try, and then go over and let myself in to check on Juliet. Axel surprised me by picking up the phone.

"Yeah?"

"Axel, hi. I hope I didn't wake you."

"Nope. Deliveries." Talking with Axel was always an exercise in minimalism. Talking to him on the phone felt positively skeletal.

"Okay, well, I'll let you get back to work. I'm just calling to check on, um, your guest. How's she doing?"

"Holding steady."

"So the wound hasn't healed yet?" Damn. I was hoping to hear the salve had cured her.

"Hasn't gotten worse."

Huh. Somehow I'd never figured Axel for an optimist. Next he'd be telling me that Juliet's bottle of blood was half-full.

"So you've been using the salve?"

"Yep."

"Okay, good. I'll be in to see her tonight."

We hung up without any further chitchat.

I also needed to check in with Daniel, so I dialed his number at work. He answered right away.

"Any developments?" I asked.

"Not yet. The lab is swamped, as usual. No, worse than usual. But my friend there did say he'd look at it when he had a spare minute." Okay. I was a little less worried about poison now, since Juliet's wound had stabilized. "Did you get a chance to talk to your aunt?" he asked.

"She agrees that the Reaper is Morfran-possessed." I knew that from my own experience, but I didn't want to place myself at the most recent murder scene. Daniel would want me to come in to the precinct, and the questioning would last for hours. If the cops even believed me. I had no wounds to show for my run-in with the Reaper. "But she says the murderer has to be present for a Morfran exorcism to work."

"So there's no way to call it out, make the murderer come to us."

"I'm afraid not. But I think the Reaper is being controlled by someone else."

"You do? Who?"

A fifteen-hundred-year-old, half-demon wizard who'd spent most of his life sealed up in a tree. Maybe I wouldn't phrase it *quite* that way. I told Daniel about Myrddin, describing his appearance and explaining that Myrddin was using the Reaper in a ritual to harvest victims' life forces and resuscitate Pryce.

"How did you learn all this?"

Good question. For Daniel's sake, I wished I could answer it. "Can we make this an anonymous tip for now? Just follow up and see if there's anything to it. I promise there will be."

Daniel was silent for a minute. I could almost hear his reluctance over the phone; he didn't like going off the record. "Okay" he said finally. "Tell me where I can find this Myrddin Wyllt."

"I wish I knew, Daniel. I really wish I knew."

* * *

KANE WAS ASLEEP ON THE SOFA, THE NEWS CHANNEL STILL on. I muted the TV and watched him. His wolf form was beautiful, with a thick, silver coat, supple muscles, and intelligent features. As he lay on the sofa, his ribs gently expanding and contracting with each breath, the long, lean lines of his body defined animal grace.

But I missed talking with him. And I missed the feel of his arms around me, his hands on my skin. I wanted Kane, *my* Kane, back. And I didn't want to wait until the next full moon.

Maybe there was another option. I went back into the kitchen and picked up the phone.

Roxana Jade was one of Boston's leading witches. I'd met her last fall, when she helped me prevent a Hellion from destroying the city. She was beautiful—with long silky black hair and the kind of figure that makes men look not twice but five or six times—and also smart and accomplished. To tell the truth, I was a little envious of her. But she was an expert in magic, and she might have some ideas about getting a stuck werewolf unstuck.

I found her number, dialed, and we chatted for a few minutes. I wanted to work my question into the conversation casually if I could. But when you're talking about the spring weather and the movie you saw last weekend, it's hard to drop in a mention of werewolves. I blurted instead.

"Have you ever heard, hypothetically speaking, of a werewolf getting stuck in wolf form?" Not what you'd call smooth, but at least we were on track.

"Hypothetically? In folklore, there are stories like that. Usually the werewolf can't change back because someone hid his clothes." Kane had a couple of suits in my closet, so that wasn't the problem. Roxana continued: "It's funny how in those stories, the wolf is almost always a man—one with a cheating wife who finds it convenient to prevent her husband from returning." Nope, definitely not the case here.

"Anything else?"

"Well, there's wolfsbane. One of the reasons that plant got its name is that it's the bane of the wolf—in other words, it makes the wolf vanish and brings back the human form."

That sounded more promising. "How does it work?"

"From what I understand, it's compounded into an ointment and rubbed into the wolf's paws."

"So is this ointment for sale?"

"Oh, no, I don't think so. Wolfsbane is highly poisonous." She paused. "Why do I get the feeling we've moved beyond the hypothetical?"

I considered. I didn't know Roxana well, but she'd given me help and support when that Hellion threatened Boston. She'd had reason to doubt me then, but she'd decided to trust me. Okay. I'd make the same decision now.

"It's Kane. Last night he got hit with a blast of magical energy, and it knocked him into his wolf form."

"And he didn't change back with the dawn."

"Correct." I liked the way she got right to the heart of the problem. "I was hoping you might have an idea of how to help him."

"Well, the safest thing is to wait for the full moon. But I guess you called me because you don't want to wait. The wolfsbane could work. If I cast a strong protection spell before applying it—"

"I thought you said wolfsbane isn't available."

"It's a very pretty flower that grows in my garden. I have some preserved. Let me do some research. If I find a recipe for a wolfsbane ointment that I believe is safe, I'll call you back."

"Great. I'll talk to Kane about the risks and see if he's willing to try it."

The long pause made me think the call had been dropped. "Roxana?"

"Didn't you say he's in wolf form? How can you discuss anything with him?"

"He's still got his human consciousness. He can't talk, but he understands everything you say and responds as best he can."

"Interesting."

"How long will your research take?"

"It's hard to say. It could be an hour or two. It could be a day or two. It depends on how lucky I get."

I sighed. "I hope your luck is running better than mine."

I TOLD KANE ABOUT MY CONVERSATION WITH ROXANA, how she thought a wolfsbane ointment might reverse his transformation. He clearly liked the idea. He jumped down from the sofa, ran in circles, and then pointed his muzzle at the ceiling and howled. "Shh," I said. "We promised Clyde, remember?" He stopped howling and looked at me, eyes bright. I sat wearily on the sofa. "Wolfsbane is poison, Kane. Roxana said she'd only make up the ointment if she thought it was safe, but . . ."

He jumped up beside me and flicked his tongue against my cheek. I put an arm around him, pressing my face into his fur, breathing in the moonlight-and-pine scent, a link to the Kane I knew. It was his decision, but that didn't stop me from worrying.

Mab, awake after her nap, came into the living room. I asked her what she thought of Roxana's idea.

"Wolfsbane . . ." she said thoughtfully. "It could work. But it's dangerous. May I have her telephone number? I'd like to confer with her."

"I'll call her for you. But first, I need to take your picture."

Mab put a hand to her iron-gray hair. It was short, like mine, and mussed from sleeping. "Whatever for?"

"You need an ID," I said, "to get in and out of Deadtown. I know someone who makes fake IDs while you wait." Given the number of times my paranormal ID card had been shredded by the energy blast of a shift, I was one of his best customers. It had been years since I'd carried an honest-to-God official ID.

Mab went into the bathroom to brush her hair while I got out my camera. I positioned her against a blank stretch of wall and adjusted the lighting.

"Say cheese!" I said, centering her in the viewfinder.

"Whatever for?"

"All right, just smile." Mab's expression didn't change, and I knew that was as close to a smile as I was going to get. I took a picture, and then two more to make sure we'd have a usable one.

Mab stepped away from the wall and reached for my camera.

I smiled. "You want to choose your favorite?"

"Hardly. I presume you need a new identification card, as well. Myrddin and the Old Ones stole your belongings."

"You're right. But I don't need a photo. Mine's already on file."

Mab did smile at that.

I called Roxana again and gave Mab the phone. I put on my jacket, removed the storage card from my camera, and stuck it in my pocket. Kane sat up, ears swiveled forward, as I headed toward the front door.

"I'll be back in an hour," I said. "I'm going to 24-Hour Copy." I opened the door, then turned back to the room, my hand on the knob. "Kane, this wolfsbane thing. I want you back so much. But we're not going to try it unless it's one hundred percent safe. I'm not going to lose you."

The expression in his intelligent gray eyes stayed with me long after I'd closed the door.

A ROUND-THE-CLOCK COPY CENTER BEFORE THE PLAGUE, 24-Hour Copy hadn't changed much since. It was still always open, and it still had copy machines, high-quality printers, and rent-by-the-hour computers. But zombies and other Deadtown residents didn't need many photocopies. So the big change, the change that had allowed the business to thrive, was its trade in fake paperwork and IDs.

At the front counter, a bored-looking zombie attendant was reading a magazine and eating three chocolate bars at a time. She'd unwrap them, stack them, and they'd disappear into her mouth. She polished off six in the time it took me to walk from the door to the counter.

"Help you?" she asked around the chocolate that filled her mouth.

"Is Carlos here?"

She jerked her head to indicate he was in the back, where I'd expected him to be. As I thanked her and walked past the counter, she was already unwrapping more chocolate.

A locked door guarded the back room. I rapped three times, paused, rapped two more. The door swung open to reveal a zombie seated at a cluttered desk in the small room. Behind him, two large printers whirred. The desk held three wide-screen computer monitors, stacks of paper, crumpled lunch bags, and a coffee mug. The zombie who sat there turned toward the door, his hands still on the keyboard.

"Hi, Carlos."

Carlos had been a computer programmer before the plague. It was only after he'd been reanimated that he found his true calling. The man was an artist. Not only could he make perfect reproductions of ID cards and other documents, he had the skills to make sure that the city's database matched whatever his products said. He wasn't cheap, but he was the best.

Now, he smiled as I came in. Carlos was the only zombie I knew who had a genuinely pleasant smile—as opposed to one that made you want to run away screaming.

"Hey, Vicky. Don't tell me you've got more business for me already."

"I'm afraid so. I need two IDs."

"Two? You keep this up, and I'll be buying myself a yacht to cruise around Boston Harbor."

I laughed, but the joke wasn't all that funny. Zombies didn't get to cruise around the harbor, and I did hand over a good portion of my income to Carlos.

"So what do you need?" he asked.

"The usual for me. I also need an ID card for my aunt. She's a demi-human like me, but she's visiting from the UK and she doesn't have any papers." I handed him the memory card that held Mab's photos.

Carlos didn't ask how she'd arrived with no papers. Nosy wasn't his style. "You want her to be a visitor or a resident?"

"Which would be easier?"

"Depends on what you mean by 'easy.' Visitor's papers would be cheaper. But she'll run into fewer hassles going in and out of Deadtown if she's identified as a resident. Of course, that's where things get more complicated, getting her into the system. It'll take some hacking to establish her identity."

"She's only in town for a few days, but we can't afford getting tied up in red tape while she's here. I guess we'd better make her a resident."

Carlos grinned. "It's your money."

"Not for long." His grin broadened at my words. He really did have a nice smile—too bad it was at my expense.

"This will take longer than a while-you-wait job. The city's got their system locked down pretty tight now."

"Will that be a problem?"

"Not for me." Another grin. This was a zombie who loved his job. "How about you come back around ten tonight? I should have everything ready by then."

I paid half up front in cash, as usual. Maybe if I stopped by the bank I could get a loan for the rest before ten.

WHEN I GOT BACK TO THE APARTMENT, I WAS SURPRISED TO see Roxana there. She sat in a living-room chair, completely at ease, talking with Mab. Kane lay in what was becoming his customary place on the sofa, head on paws, ears pricked toward their conversation.

Roxana stood as I came into the room, smiling and offering her hand. She looked her usual gorgeous self: glossy dark hair, perfect makeup, a blue dress that showed off her curves. I felt like a scarecrow next to her.

I took her hand, and we gave each other a quick peck on the cheek. "I didn't expect to see you so soon," I said.

"Your aunt was a tremendous help. We agreed on the best recipe for the ointment, and I made it up and came right over. No point in wasting time."

"But . . ." Suddenly I didn't want to go through with the ritual. "Shouldn't you do more research? Don't we need to wait for a propitious time—the right moon phase or something?"

Mab came over and patted my shoulder with three quick pats: *onetwothree*. It was her way of reassuring me. "Child, I understand your reluctance. But the ointment is safe to use; I'll vouch for that. The only question is whether it's strong enough to counter Myrddin's magic."

"As for timing," Roxana added, "that doesn't matter. It's like taking a dose of medicine when you're sick—the sooner the better."

Kane sat up and barked his agreement.

I sat beside him and leaned my forehead against his. I put my arms around him, felt his warmth. "Are you sure you want to try this?"

He didn't even have to nod. His eyes showed how much he did.

We pushed back furniture to clear a space in the middle of the living room. Roxana summoned Kane to lie down in the middle of the open space. She gently pressed on his shoulder, so he lay on his side. When he was situated, she placed four small tea candles, each about a yard away from him, at the points of the compass: north, east, south, west. She stepped inside the circle they formed. Facing north, she bowed and closed her eyes in meditation. Her lips moved, but I couldn't make out what she was saying. She bent and lit the candle. After a moment she moved on to the east candle and repeated the process. Within a few minutes, she'd lit all four candles.

She stood beside Kane and pointed at the north candle. Going clockwise, three times she traced the perimeter of the circle with her pointing finger. When she'd finished, she closed her eyes and lifted her face skyward. Then she drew a jar from her pocket and held it upward, like an offering, to each of the four quarters, always turning clockwise. When she was finished, she knelt beside Kane.

Roxana removed a pair of gloves from her pocket and put them on. Gloves—to protect her own skin from the wolfsbane. I was half out of my chair, ready to stop the ritual, before I made myself sit back down. Kane wanted to do this, and Mab approved. Still, if Roxana needed gloves to apply the ointment, I wasn't so sure I wanted her putting that stuff on Kane's unprotected paws. But I bit my tongue. I didn't want to mess up the protection spell by breaking Roxana's concentration.

Please, please let this work.

Mab noticed my worry and nodded reassuringly.

Inside the circle, Roxana chanted as she rubbed the ointment into Kane's paws. Her voice sounded far away and muffled, like a mermaid singing beneath the waves. I watched Kane for any sign of pain or discomfort, but his eyelids drifted shut as she did her work. By the time she finished, he lay on his side, tongue lolling. I could see him breathing, and I kept my eyes glued to the up-and-down movement, as if watching alone could keep it going.

Roxana stood. She went to the east side of the circle and made cutting motions with her hand, first on her right side, and then on her left. She stepped outside of the circle. As soon as she'd crossed the barrier, she turned around and closed the door she'd made.

Roxana regarded Mab, then me. "Now we wait."

AND SO WE WAITED, WATCHING KANE, TALKING LITTLE, dozing in our chairs. Roxana had set up the circle to last as long as the tea lights burned—about two hours. While the candles burned, her circle formed a bubble of protection around Kane. When they went out, the circle would unmake itself.

I scrutinized Kane for any sign of change: a shortening of his fur, a change in the shape of his limbs or head. But no matter how much I hoped for change—any tiny alteration to show the ointment was working—I couldn't see it.

Eventually, the candles began to sputter. They extinguished

in the opposite order from Roxana's lighting of them: west, south, east, and finally north. When the final candle stopped burning, sending up a thin stream of smoke, a shudder ran through Kane. He twitched, and we all leaned forward. His eyes opened. He stood, stretched, and yawned. Then he stepped outside the circle—every bit as much a wolf as when Roxana had cast it around him.

18

"I'M SO SORRY," ROXANA SAID, PULLING ON HER COAT. "I really thought the ointment would work."

"You made it as strong as we dared," said Mab. "More wolfsbane would have been too risky."

Kane was fine, no worse for wear than if he'd taken a two-hour nap. I'd checked his paws: no burns or ulcerations. His heart beat normally, and he was alert, although he seemed despondent that Roxana's spell had failed. We all were. More than that, though, I was relieved he was okay—in any form.

"Well," Roxana said, "at least this might be helpful." From her coat pocket she pulled something that looked like a small crocheted snowflake. It dangled from the end of a string loop.

"What is it?" I asked, taking it. A buzz passed from the object into my hand.

"It's a diminution charm," Roxana said. "It makes something big and powerful look smaller, less threatening. I thought it might be helpful if Kane wants to go out." She looked around. "You have a great apartment, but who wants to spend three weeks cooped up in one place?"

"Thanks, Roxana. It's a great idea. I'm so glad you thought of it."

She glanced at Mab and smiled. "Your aunt suggested we have a contingency plan."

"Quite so," agreed Mab.

I slipped the loop over Kane's neck. The air around him shimmered. His appearance blurred and then altered. He looked like a German shepherd: still ferocious, but less so than a two-hundred-pound werewolf. A perfect disguise. I removed the charm and placed it on the coffee table. In a moment, Kane was back in all his wolfish glory. Roxana wouldn't take any payment for the charm. After she left, I went into my room, lay down on top of the comforter, and napped for a few hours. My sleep schedule is always erratic, living between the norm and paranormal worlds as I do, so I'm used to snatching a few z's when I have the chance.

When I woke up, it was dark out, and I was hungry. I ran my fingers through my hair, stuck my feet into slippers, and went into the living room. Mab sat in a chair, reading. Kane was stretched out on the sofa, watching PNN. The story told of a planned protest march through the streets of Deadtown, tonight. Zombies were gathering to protest the code-red restrictions. I felt for the zombies—they must be suffering cabin fever big-time by now—but nobody would give a damn about their march. Not if it was in Deadtown. In the eyes of Police Commissioner Hampson and other norms, they could do whatever the hell they wanted—as long as they stayed inside the boundaries of Designated Area 1.

"Who's hungry?" I asked.

Kane woofed, and Mab admitted she was feeling "a bit peckish," so we all trooped into the kitchen. I opened the freezer and peered inside. "Let's see. We've got lasagna, Salisbury steaks"—Kane howled at this point—"pizza, sesame chicken, fettuccine . . ."

"Heavens, child, is that how you get your food?" Mab

looked every bit as horrified as if my freezer shelves held human heads instead of frozen dinners.

"If I had Rose to do my cooking, I'd eat as well as you. But I don't cook." My kitchen skills were limited to knowing which buttons to press on the microwave.

Mab made a sour face, but she chose fettuccine Alfredo with chicken.

For the next fifteen minutes, I gave the microwave a good workout. Everyone ate their food as soon as it was ready. Mab even admitted that her meal tasted better than she'd expected. I noticed she scraped up all of her Alfredo sauce.

After dinner, it was time to pick up the IDs from Carlos. "I'll get those, then check on Juliet. I want to see how she's doing, but I also want to ask her some more questions about the Old Ones."

"I'll come with you," Mab said.

"You won't—" What would be the best way to phrase this? "It won't bother you that she's a vampire?"

"I solemnly swear I'll be on my best behavior," Mab said. "If your Juliet really managed to escape the Old Ones' thrall, she's someone I want to meet."

THE STREET WAS PACKED WITH ZOMBIES, ALL HEADED IN THE same direction we were. The protest march would start at the Old South Meeting House, proceed down Washington Street and along Winter Street, and finish at the Tremont Street checkpoints. Our goal, 24-Hour Copy, wasn't far from the meetinghouse. The march was due to start at eleven—still more than an hour from now—but the zombies were already on their way. Some carried signs with slogans like ZOMBIES AREN'T MONSTERS and PERMIT THIS, HAMPSON! Others walked along doing what zombies do best—stuffing their faces with junk food. Laughter rang through the night. The scene felt festive, like the march was a parade, not a protest.

One person bucked the crowd, plowing through with her head down, like a rowboat with an underpowered outboard putt-putting against a strong current. I recognized the blond hair first, pulled into a high ponytail that swung as she walked. She wore a curve-hugging white T-shirt with a green plaid miniskirt, torn fishnet stockings, and black combat boots. The gigantic tote bag she lugged—pink accented with zebra stripes—looked like it could hold half my worldly possessions, including my car. As she got closer, I read the bold pink letters on her T-shirt: LOVE IS THE ANSWER. She barreled right past us; on the back of her shirt, black letters asked, WHAT THE HELL WAS THE QUESTION?

"Tina!"

She stopped in her tracks and turned around, searching for the person who'd called her. When she saw me, she scowled in greeting.

"Aren't you joining the march?" I asked. It seemed like the kind of diversion that Tina would be first in line for. The closer to the front, the better the chances of getting on TV.

"Yeah, but I was going to your place first. Now at least I don't have to trek all the way over there." She knelt on the sidewalk and dug into her bag. She pulled out three celebrity gossip magazines, four tubes of lip gloss, a hairbrush, cell phone, assorted ponytail holders, and two pairs of sunglasses before she found what she was looking for: *Russom's Demoniacal Taxonomy*, the book I'd loaned her during the weeks she'd been my apprentice. "Here's your book," she said, thrusting it at me. "If you won't teach me about demons, I don't need it anymore."

I reached for the book, but Mab stepped between us. "Ah, so this must be the young lady you told me about a while back. The one who was your apprentice." Funny that I'd never mentioned Juliet to Mab, but I'd told her all about Tina on my last visit to Wales.

"Young lady?" Tina wrinkled her nose. "That's what my mom used to call me when she was mad." She shoveled items back into her bag. Then she stopped and squinted up at Mab. She looked at me, then at Mab again. "Wait. Are you Vicky's aunt? The one who taught her how to fight?"

"Yes," I said. "This is my aunt Mab."

"How do you do?" Mab said.

Tina stood, hauling the bag back onto her shoulder. She stared at Mab appraisingly. "So you must be, like, better than Vicky, right? At demon fighting? I mean, since you taught her and everything."

Mab didn't answer, but she favored Tina with her tiny, pursed-lip smile.

Clutching *Russom's*, Tina said to Mab, "Would you teach me? Vicky's all graduated and stuff, so you need a new apprentice, right? Plus my dad always said if you want something, you should go straight to the top."

"Mab's retired," I said. "Anyway, she's only in town for a few days before she goes back to Wales."

"Oh. That's another country, isn't it?" Even Tina knew it was virtually impossible for zombies to get visas to travel internationally. It was due to fear of the plague. Although the possibility of contagion was long past, there was still widespread terror of the virus that had killed and reanimated two thousand Bostonians. Boston had no choice about its zombies, but nobody else wanted them.

Tina looked down at the book in her hands, as if trying to memorize its cover. When she held it out to me, she didn't meet my eyes.

I reached out again to take *Russom's*, but Mab stopped me, putting her hand on my arm. "We're on an errand right now and can't be lugging books about," she said sharply. Tina stepped back as if slapped. "If you want to return my niece's book, bring it to her apartment after you've finished school for the night."

"But I don't go to school anymore."

"Did you earn your diploma?"

"No, but—"

"Then you have no business saying you're done with school. Go to class. Learn something. And then return *Russom's* in the morning on your way home."

Never before had I seen Tina at a loss for words. She gaped at Mab, red eyes wide, mouth hanging open, and stunned into silence. She held *Russom's* in front of her like a shield. Then she shut her mouth and gave a tiny nod.

"Tina," I said, "if it's easier, you can leave the book with Clyde. He'll make sure I get it."

"Not good enough." Mab waved away the very idea. "We'll expect to see you in the morning. Now, off you go to school."

Tina turned and fled. But not, I noticed, in the direction of her school. She joined the flow of zombies pouring toward the starting point of the protest march.

I watched her go. WHAT THE HELL WAS THE QUESTION? bobbed through the crowd until she was out of sight.

"Mab," I said, "I think you've just become the first mortal creature ever to terrify a zombie."

"Nonsense. I merely made some suggestions about manners and the importance of education. Things she'd do well to consider."

Tina, consider manners? That seemed about as likely as Commissioner Hampson stopping by Deadtown to link arms with protesters and lead the march. But I wasn't going to ponder that now. I wanted to complete our errand and see Juliet.

CARLOS WASN'T IN, BUT HE'D LEFT AN ENVELOPE WITH MY name and the amount I owed penciled on the front. Mab's eyes widened when she saw the figure, but I paid without telling her it was only half the total.

Outside, I gave Mab her card. She scrutinized it, and a most unladylike snort erupted from her. "Mabel!" she exclaimed, waving the card in my face. "He has me down as *Mabel* Vaughn."

"That's not such a bad thing, Mab. It puts a little bit of distance between you and your false identity."

"Hmph." Mab held the card as though it were a particularly slimy piece of garbage. "You won't have to call me that, will you?"

"No. You only need to show the card when you pass through a checkpoint. Or if a cop asks for it. Most people never see it."

"Good. Because I will not be referred to as 'Aunt Mabel.'"

She harrumphed again as she slid the card into her pocket. "Sounds like a Victorian charwoman."

I laughed and patted her shoulder. "Don't worry, Mab. Your secret is safe with me."

MAB PASSED THROUGH THE CHECKPOINT OUT OF DEAD-town like she'd lived in Designated Area 1 all her life. As we walked the half-block to Creature Comforts, I tried to prepare her for meeting Axel. "He's obviously not human, but nobody knows what he is. And nobody likes to ask, either. Axel doesn't say much, and his privacy is important to him. Like, *really* important." We stopped in front of the door. "So if he won't let you downstairs to see Juliet, please don't take offense."

I reached for the door handle, then paused. What would Mab see when I pulled it open and we went inside? A dingy dive bar with a surly bartender, most likely. That wasn't an inaccurate assessment. But Creature Comforts was more than its appearance—at least, it was to me. It was like a second home, and I didn't want Mab to judge it too harshly.

I opened the door and gestured Mab inside. I followed. The place was empty. No rowdy werewolves tonight; that was one good thing. Axel leaned on the bar and watched us approach. His small eyes glinted as he took in Mab.

"Axel, this is my aunt, Mab," I said. "She's come with me to see Juliet. I hope you won't mind if she visits your guest room with me."

Axel regarded Mab as if sizing her up—or thinking about having her as a snack. Mab appraised him just as coolly. For a minute, I thought we were headed for some kind of O.K. Corral showdown.

Then Mab stepped forward. She offered her hand and said something in a language I didn't understand. It sounded a bit like German, although it wasn't German.

A grin cracked Axel's face. He shook Mab's hand so vigorously it rattled my teeth where I stood beside them. He spoke in a rapid-fire barrage of words in the same language

Mab had used. In two minutes, he said more to her than I'd heard him say in three years.

Mab laughed, and Axel laughed with her. He came out from behind the bar, bowed, and offered Mab his arm. The two of them chatted away like old friends as they walked back to the storeroom together. I followed, feeling like a third wheel.

In the storeroom, Axel was showing Mab how to open the secret door. She clapped her hands together, impressed, then tried it herself.

Axel walked over to me, chuckling. "Lovely lady, your aunt," he said. He picked up a couple of cases of pretzels and, still laughing to himself, carried them into the bar.

Mab stood by the open door, smiling a private smile.

"What did you say to him?" I asked. "What language was that?"

"Trollspråk. It turns out Axel and I have some mutual acquaintances. I simply passed along news from the old country."

"Axel is a troll?" I'd wondered for years what species Axel was. And Mab had figured it out at a glance.

"Yes, of course, a *jötunn*, one of the Old Norse giants." She shook her head. "I must say I'm disappointed you never recognized him as such. But then, you were never a keen student of mythology. If it wasn't a demon, it didn't interest you."

"Hey, I was focused."

Her face softened. It may have looked about as soft as marble to anyone else, but I could tell the difference. "That you were, child."

Mab moved aside so I could go first, and then she followed me down the stairs. As we reached the bottom, I half-expected my aunt to start conversing fluently in whatever dialect they spoke in fourteenth-century Verona, but there wouldn't have been much point. Juliet was dead to the world, asleep.

A vampire's sleep resembles death so closely that it was always a little bit of a shock to see my roommate so absolutely still and silent. But vampires turn to dust when they die, so I knew death hadn't claimed her. Yet it wasn't good that she was fast asleep so many hours after dusk. She should be awake and active at this time of night.

I'd already described Juliet's wound to Mab; now I showed her. As gently as possible, so as not to disturb the sleeper, I pulled back the covers over her leg. The putrid stench still reeked, but it didn't faze Mab. She leaned forward to examine the injury more closely.

As Axel had said earlier, Juliet was holding steady. The wound hadn't really changed since the last time I'd seen it—swollen, purple, and hot. Axel's stitches held, but they were coated with seeping pus.

"How long since she was injured?" Mab asked.

"Two nights ago. It shouldn't take a vampire so long to heal."

"You're right, it shouldn't." Mab laid a hand on Juliet's calf. "And she's very hot." She nodded at the blue jar on the nightstand. "That's the salve I gave you?"

"Yes. I thought it might help."

"It was a good thought. It's not healing her, but it's prevented the injury from getting worse."

"Do you think the wound is poisoned?" I told her how I'd given Daniel a swab from the Old One's sword for analysis.

"Offhand, I can't think of any poison that would harm a vampire. Their system won't absorb most poisons. But I'm not an expert. I'll be interested to learn the results of the analysis."

So would I. Until then, I didn't know what to do—and neither did Mab. That was an odd feeling. I was used to relying on my aunt to have all the answers.

"Axel told me that the last four or five times he's checked on her, she's been asleep like this," Mab continued. "He couldn't rouse her."

"It's like she's in a coma."

Mab shook Juliet's shoulder, gently at first, then more vigorously. No response.

Resting her chin in her hand, Mab sighed. "I don't understand it. I suppose it *could* be a poison, something augmented by silver, perhaps. But at least she's stable for the moment."

Out of options, we let Juliet sleep. We went back upstairs and carefully closed the hidden door. In the main room, a customer had arrived. He sat alone at the bar, hunched over his drink. When he heard us come in, he looked up and sneered. I knew that sneer—it was Norden, the Goon Squad cop.

"Been to the 'Ghouls' room?" he said. "What the hell do you females do in there, anyway?"

"Powder our noses." I walked past him.

Mab sat on a stool and began talking to Axel in that troll language. He pulled out a bottle from under the bar—must be some kind of special reserve if he hid it there—and poured her a generous portion.

"Aquavit," Mab explained. "The Scandinavian 'water of life.' It's from Axel's private stock. Would you like some?"

She held out her glass to me, and I sniffed. The liquid smelled strongly of alcohol, but also of herbs. It had a licorice smell, and lemon, and something else—carraway, maybe?

I shook my head. "Too intense for me. Can I have my usual, Axel?"

He sighed and produced a bottle of lite beer. Mab made a face when she saw it, then sipped her aquavit. Axel watched her anxiously. She nodded, and they were off on another Trollspråk conversation. A troll. I couldn't get over it. Mab was likely bringing him up to date on the Billy Goats Gruff—they'd probably bought a condo together in Oslo or something.

Abandoned, I drifted down the bar and found myself talking to Norden. Or trying to.

"What brings you to Creature Comforts?" I asked. "I've never seen you here except when you're working." *Giving Axel and his customers a hard time* is what I meant by *working*.

"I'm on patrol later," he said. "Just killing time." He stared into his drink.

That seemed to exhaust our conversation. I sat there, peeling the label off my beer.

After a few minutes, Norden snorted. "If you're going to

sit there nursing a beer, at least get something that tastes like one."

"I don't like beer. This stuff is okay."

He replied with another snort. And we went back to having nothing to say to each other.

At the far end of the bar, Mab and Axel laughed uproariously. I wished they'd let me in on the joke. Axel poured more aquavit into Mab's glass. Great. If they kept it up, I was going to have to borrow a wheelbarrow to get "Aunt Mabel" home.

I turned back to Norden. "How come you're back on the Goon Squad? When I saw you last month, you'd quit to go solo."

"And you saw how well that worked out." He lifted one shoulder in a half-shrug. "It's a living."

"Yeah, but—sorry for being blunt—you hate paranormals. You call us freaks and monsters. Why do you even want a job where you spend all your time in and around Deadtown?"

Another half-shrug. "It was different when Sykes was alive. Or undead, or whatever the hell he was. When he was *here*. We'd been partners before the plague, back when he was human. Sykes was okay. But maybe I spent too much time with him, because after he died, I didn't know how to be with real people anymore." His eyebrows lowered, and he tossed back the contents of his glass. "Bartender! I'm dry here."

Axel sauntered to our end of the bar and poured a shot into Norden's glass.

"Make it a double," Norden said. "And gimme a beer chaser while you're at it." He glanced at my bottle and grimaced. "Make sure it's real beer."

"You sure you want to drink all that before a shift?" I asked after Axel had gone back to Mab. The two of them were singing now.

"What the hell is it to you?"

"Just saying."

Norden twisted away from me on his stool, grumbling something about nosy freaks who can't mind their own business. Then he twisted back. "You know why I'm back on the

Goon Squad? 'Cause I'm a freak, just like you. There's no place I fit in anymore. Ever since I got out of the hospital, nothing's been the same. I'm just a goddamn freak sitting in a goddamn freak bar."

Mab and Axel broke off their song and stared. Axel's eyes narrowed as he gauged whether it was time to throw Norden out.

Before he made his decision, the front door burst open. Throngs of zombies tumbled into the room, laughing and chanting, "Let us out! Let us out!" Norden tensed beside me, and I knew what he was thinking. Permits were rescinded. Zombies were restricted to Deadtown; they couldn't even go into the New Combat Zone. And he was the lone cop in a bar full of law-breaking zombies.

In the crowd, I saw a familiar face. I made my way over to him.

"Carlos, what's going on?" I said.

"We stormed the checkpoint! It was amazing. We marched to the border of Deadtown, and then people started chanting, 'Let us out!'" The chant still resounded through the bar. Carlos grinned and raised his fist in time to the chant. He turned back to me. "Why should we stay penned up in Deadtown? We're not criminals. We don't belong in jail. You should've seen it—the crowd surged right past the barriers. There wasn't a thing the border guards could do." He laughed at the memory.

The chant had changed. Now it was "Bring us beer!" Carlos called for beer, too, pounding on the table. Zombies don't get drunk, but for some reason they still like the taste of beer. Maybe reanimation damaged their taste buds.

Axel got busy filling pitchers. Mab went behind the bar to help, and I offered to carry pitchers to the tables of thirsty zombies. As I picked up a tray, I noticed Norden wasn't doing too hot. He was trembling, and sweat ran down his face.

"Are you okay?" I knew he should've slowed down on the drinking.

His lip curled, and he wiped a hand across his forehead. "Damn zombies. Too many of them. The smell. It makes me—" He covered his nose and mouth with both hands. "I can't stand it!" he screamed through his fingers. He jumped from his stool and ran out the front door.

Normally, you don't try to push your way through a crowd of zombies. But they moved aside to let Norden through. Everyone stared after him, silent. Then the chant of "Bring us beer!" started up again.

It was then I noticed that Norden's second drink was untouched. So was his bottle of beer. So what was the guy's problem? I knew he hated zombies—hell, he seemed to hate everyone—but I'd never seen him freak out like that before.

Axel cleared away Norden's drinks as a zombie took his spot at the bar. I carried pitcher after pitcher of beer to the euphoric protesters. Something told me their party wasn't going to last long. Sure enough, within an hour the Goons arrived to break it up and close down the bar. There was no trouble. The zombies went peacefully back to Deadtown—they'd made their point and downed a few beers besides. It was a good night for them.

We couldn't risk seeing Juliet again, not with Creature Comforts full of Goons. Axel promised he'd check on her before he went home for the night. Mab and I left with the protesters.

Outside, Goons lined the street, and the zombies walked between them as they filed back into Deadtown. I noticed Pam McFarren, Norden's zombie partner, among the Goons policing the crowd. But there was no sign of Norden.

Despite all the aquavit she'd consumed, my aunt was completely sober. Her walk was straight, her gaze steady, although I did catch occasional snatches of hummed Norwegian folk tunes as we made our way home.

19

WHEN MAB AND I GOT BACK TO MY APARTMENT, IT WAS two in the morning and Kane was watching live coverage of the zombie protest. There wasn't much left to cover, now that the march had ended and the zombies had all gone home. No violence, no arrests, no bloodshed. The media must have been disappointed. The last time hundreds of zombies had gathered—at the Paranormal Appreciation Day concert in February—a Morfran attack that was invisible to news cameras had caused mass panic, a stampede, and nearly a dozen deaths. The entire norm world thought the zombies had gone crazy. In comparison, tonight's event was a big snooze.

Still, after-the-fact commentators analyzed the march to death; talking heads who hadn't been there spouted off on the protest's significance, twisting events to fit their own political agendas. For some, the march ushered in a new era of freedom and autonomy for Deadtown's residents. For others, it was a clear signal that the government needed to crack down on the monsters. One crazy-eyed preacher from an obscure cult claimed it was the final sign that the world would end two weeks from tomorrow.

Sweet. Maybe I wouldn't have to pay my electric bill.

I picked up the remote. "Are you still watching this?"

Kane shook his head, and I clicked off the TV. He lay down with a sigh and put his head on his paws, staring at nothing.

It had to be hard for him, sitting on the sidelines. I'd called his office to let them know he'd be "away" for a few weeks, but I knew he hated missing out on this kind of action. Normally, he'd be in one of those television studios right now, setting the norms straight and advocating for PA rights. He'd point out that the march had been nonviolent, and that the zombies (he'd say previously deceased humans, or PDHs) weren't looking for trouble; they only wanted to stretch their boundaries a bit. And even though the zombies had pushed their way out of Deadtown, there'd been no Reaper murder tonight. Hampson's restrictions were meaningless.

But he couldn't say any of that. He could only sit in my living room and watch it on TV.

I sat on the sofa beside him and scratched behind his ears. It didn't solve anything, I knew, but I've always found that a well-placed scalp massage makes everything seem better.

Mab had gone to bed; I'd insisted she stay in my room. This should be snuggling time for Kane and me, but, well, things weren't the same right now. We sat on the sofa, his head pressed against my thigh, my fingers moving through his warm fur. A girl and her wolf. No, not the same at all.

Kane got up and stretched. He flicked his tongue against my cheek, then jumped down to the floor. He went to the front door and sniffed along its edge. Then he circled once and lay down. Protective, making sure the bad guys didn't cross the threshold. But I didn't want a guard dog, I thought as I turned out the light. I wanted Kane.

If Myrddin stayed true to his pattern, the Reaper would strike again tomorrow night. To prevent another murder—and to force Myrddin to change Kane back—we had to find

Pryce. If the Old Ones were hiding him, Juliet was our best chance for rooting him out. She'd been involved with the Old Ones for weeks; she must know where they were holed up. But Juliet was in some kind of vampire coma, and unless Daniel's lab guy came through with an antidote, I had no idea how to wake her up.

These thoughts circled my brain like sharks circling a shipwreck survivor in a rudderless boat. I would have sworn I didn't sleep at all, but when the phone rang, it jolted me awake. I blinked against the daylight streaming through the windows. I remembered I was on the sofa and fumbled around on the end table until I found the phone.

"Yeah?" I croaked.

"Vicky Vaughn, please," said an unfamiliar male voice.

"Speaking." I rubbed my eyes, wondering what time it was.

"Are you related to a child named Maria Santini?"

I sat straight up. My pulse surged as terrifying words like *accident* and *abduction* leapt into my mind. "She's my niece. Why, what—?"

"We've got her here at the Milk Street checkpoint, Boston side. She was trying to leave the city and enter Designated Area 1. To find you, she says."

"Don't let her through." The idea of Maria wandering around Deadtown by herself terrified me.

"No, ma'am. That's why I'm calling. She's an unaccompanied minor without the proper paperwork."

"What about her parents—shouldn't you call them, let them know where she is?"

"She won't give me her folks' number, and I don't have time to call all the Santinis in the phone book."

"My sister's number is unlisted, but I can—"

"Hang on." His voice grew distant and muffled as he spoke away from the phone. "Well, this is highly irregular," he said, coming back on the line, "but she wants to talk to you."

I waited a moment as he passed her the phone. "Maria?"

"Aunt Vicky, please don't call my mom. Please. I need to talk to you first." Desperation pushed her voice to the edge of tears.

"Okay, I won't. Not until we've talked. But you know she's worried about you."

Silence.

"Maria, stay right where you are until I get there. I'll be there in a few minutes, okay?"

"Okay." Her breath caught in a tiny sob. "Can you hurry?"

"I will, sweetie. I'll be there as fast as I can. Put the man back on the phone."

"Yes?" the guard said a moment later.

"I'm on my way. Please keep an eye on her until I get there."

"Of course. Make sure you bring proper ID. You must prove you're her aunt. I can't release a child to just anyone."

"You'd better not. I'll be there in ten minutes. What time is it now?"

"Almost ten thirty."

"Okay. Ten minutes."

Kane sat in front of me, watching, his ears pricked up. I told him where I was going and scrawled a note for Mab. I didn't want to disturb Mab in my bedroom, so I raided the bathroom hamper for clothes. I found a pair of jeans and a long-sleeved T-shirt that weren't too wrinkled and smelled okay—not that any of that mattered with Maria waiting, alone and frightened.

I grabbed my ID and my passport. In the living room, a bookshelf displayed a framed photograph of Maria and me from last summer. We'd spent the day at an amusement park near Springfield, and when we rode the roller coaster they snapped a photo at the steepest part. Maria and I sat together. She leaned forward, hair streaming back, her cheeks glowing pink, her eyes lit up with excitement. It was my favorite photo of her. I stuck it in my purse. It wouldn't mean a thing to the border guard, but to me it showed Maria and I were family.

MARIA SAT ON THE CURB BESIDE THE WALK-UP CHECKPOINT booth. She huddled there, her chin resting on a pink backpack propped in her lap. I called her name. Her head snapped in my direction, and she jumped up and ran to me. She hugged me like she hadn't seen me in years.

"Boston's big," she said, her face pressed into my shoulder. "It didn't look so big when my class took a field trip to the aquarium."

"No worries." I kept my voice light. "I know my way around."

As if suddenly remembering she was almost a teenager, not a scared little kid, she unwrapped her arms from my waist and stepped back. But she stayed close as I talked to the checkpoint guard.

"You live in DA-1?" the guard said, looking at my ID. "You can't take her in there, you know. She doesn't have the paperwork."

"Fine with me." I had no intention of escorting my niece through the zombie-filled streets, even though most of the zombies were home sleeping off the excitement of their protest. "We'll stay on the human side."

The guard swiped my card and squinted at his computer screen. He tapped some keys, then tapped a few more. I put my arm around Maria's shoulders and gave her a squeeze. She stood as stiff and rigid as a concrete pillar.

I thought the guard would insist on calling Maria's parents, but he didn't. He seemed more interested in getting the problem of an unaccompanied minor off his desk than in making sure she got home safely. When the database confirmed I was family, he printed out two papers and pushed them over for me to sign. One was an application for a permit to leave Deadtown under code-red restrictions. The other document stated that I was Maria's aunt and accepted responsibility for her.

The guard stamped the application and printed out a permit, which he instructed me to keep with me at all times. He nodded at me, indicating we were free to go. The problem was out of his hair.

I hoisted Maria's backpack over my left shoulder and hugged her close with my right arm. She was still stiff, but she relaxed a little against me.

"You must be hungry," I said. "How about some ice cream?"

It was one of those March days that made you think maybe winter would loosen its hold before too much longer. Not hot enough to be real ice-cream weather, but with enough promise of future warmth to make ice cream seem like a pretty good idea.

Maria started to shake her head, her eyes clouded with apprehension, but she changed her mind and nodded. Her lips curved a little, but the half-smile didn't push away the worry.

I kept my arm loosely around her shoulders as we walked the block or so to the ice-cream parlor. Neither of us said anything, but my mind roiled with questions. Foremost among them: Why on earth had Maria skipped school to try to visit me in Deadtown? And why didn't she want me to call Gwen?

Inside the shop, smells of coffee and vanilla greeted us. I moved toward the soda fountain–style counter. With its spinning stools, it was always the kids' favorite place to sit. But Maria stopped in the middle of the room. "Can we sit over there?" she asked, nodding toward a booth.

"Sure. Wherever you'd like."

When the waitress came over to take our order, Maria glanced at me, uncertain. So instead of getting a cup of coffee as I'd intended, I ordered a hot fudge sundae. Might as well pretend we were having fun until Maria was ready to open up. She ordered a sundae with chocolate ice cream and peanut butter sauce, yes to whipped cream, no to a cherry, her voice as serious as if she were giving a report at school.

"Hey," I said. "Remember this picture from last summer?" I pulled out the roller-coaster photo. "I brought it in case I needed to convince the guard I know you. That was a fun day, huh?"

She studied the photo. Something in her face suggested she barely recognized the people it depicted. She nodded politely and handed the picture back to me. Then she folded her hands on the table, examining them as though she'd never seen anything quite so fascinating. All at once she looked up.

"Promise you won't call Mom."

I made my voice gentle. "Honey, I can't promise that. If your mom doesn't know where you are, she'll worry." I didn't need to remind her of how frantic Gwen had been when Maria had been kidnapped and held in New Hampshire. I knew that was already on her mind. "But here's what I can promise: We'll talk first. You tell me what's going on, and then we'll figure out how to keep your mom from worrying, okay?"

She hooked a strand of pale blonde hair behind her ear. Her fingers trembled, but she nodded.

The waitress brought over our ice cream. Maria picked up her spoon and pushed it into her sundae, but she didn't eat.

I got started on my own sundae, scooping up a spoonful of whipped cream, hot fudge, and melting ice cream. After a second, Maria tasted hers, too.

Maybe this was about Mab's visit to her dream. "I was expecting you to call again," I said, trying to open up the topic without pushing. "And here you surprise me with a visit instead. It's not often I get to take an ice cream break so early in the day."

"What did he mean, paperwork?"

"Who? Oh, the guard at the checkpoint? Well, it can be a little complicated getting in and out of Dead— I mean, the part of town where I live. They don't let people in unless they have business there."

"Or live there."

"Right. Or live there."

She stirred her ice cream, making it soupy. "So the people who live there can't get out, either?"

"That depends. The zombies—" Fear flickered across her face at the word, so I backpedaled. "You know, the people they call the 'previously deceased.' They can't come and go whenever they feel like it. Someone has to sponsor them, get a permit, before they can leave."

"That's paperwork?"

"It's one kind of paperwork. If someone from outside wants to visit where I live, they need to get permission from the city, and that's the kind of paperwork he was talking about. It's sort of like getting a visa when you travel to another country."

"Do you have to do that?"

"Nope. I'm a different classification, a demi-human, so it's easier for me. I just have to show my ID card. They swipe it, and I'm through." I wouldn't go into the intricacies of traveling outside of Boston. "Piece of cake. You saw how easy it was."

"Mom thinks I'm one of those. What you just said you are."

"A demi-human."

"I heard her talking to Dad last night. She was crying. She said it would kill her to take me to Deadtown to live. So I . . ."

Ah. "So you thought you'd make it easier on her by coming to Deadtown yourself."

Brimming tears spilled from one eye, then the other, as she nodded.

I slid out of my seat and scooted in beside her, catching her in a hug. She pressed her face against me.

"You know how moms worry about everything, right?" I said, stroking her hair. "Your mom doesn't know what will happen yet. Nobody does. And nobody is going to make you live in Deadtown if you don't want to. Your mom and I won't let them."

"Are there kids there?"

"Some. Tell you what. One of these days, we'll do that paperwork and you can come for a visit. A sleepover, if you want—and if your parents will let you." I gave Maria a hug and then reached for my ice cream dish. "We've got even better ice cream over there."

"Really?"

"Uh-huh. Zombies are big eaters. It's junk food heaven."

Her smile was more genuine this time. "Maybe that's why Mom doesn't want me to live there. She'd freak if she knew I was having ice cream for lunch."

Oh, Maria. I could guarantee that Gwen would be freaking over far more than a late-morning sugar rush.

For several minutes, I watched my niece eat her sundae.

"You want to tell me about your dream? The one you called me about?"

She licked the last drops of peanut butter sauce from her spoon. "I don't remember it as much now. But it wasn't like those other dreams I told you about. I wasn't flying or running or swimming. It was . . . I remember there was this mist with different colors. It was so pretty. And a lady came through. She said you needed help. Everything else is kind of fuzzy. There was something about the aquarium, but I don't know how that fit in. Anyway, I woke up really worried about you."

"You had your mom call to make sure I was okay."

Maria nodded. "She said she left you a message, and when she went to yell at Zack to hurry up in the bathroom, I tried calling you, too. I wanted to tell you about the dream before I forgot it. But you weren't there. All day at school I felt kind of sick, but then after I got home Mom told me you'd called back. She acted like I was silly to worry about a dream, but she seemed kind of mad, too."

Maria had saved my life by answering Mab's dream-phone call—and she didn't even know what the dream phone was. Mab had called her an impressive child, and she was, but she was also a confused little girl. Gwen might not like it, but I owed Maria an explanation of what happened.

"So let me tell you about that dream. Your mom's part of the family—mine, too—is called the Cerddorion. We're part human, but we're also more than human. And that means we can do some cool things."

"Like shapeshift?"

"Yes, that's part of it. We can also communicate with each other while we're asleep. When we were your age, your mom and I called it the dream phone."

"Mom did?" Maria squinted at me skeptically.

"She did. Your mom loved the dream phone. We used it to keep talking about stuff—you know, school and music and boys—after your grandma told us to go to sleep."

"That's so cool."

"You know those pretty colors you saw? Everyone who's

Cerddorion has their own special colors. When you're asleep and you focus on somebody's colors, you can contact that person."

"But how can you do that if you're asleep?"

"It's not hard, but it takes some practice."

"So . . . the lady I dreamed about was real?" She frowned. "And you were really in trouble?"

I nodded. "Thanks to you, she was able to help me. And here we are having ice cream together. So, you see, everything worked out fine."

"Who is she?"

"Her name is Mab, and she's your great-aunt." Time to tread carefully. I didn't want Maria getting all curious about Mab if Gwen wasn't okay with it. "But Mab and your mom don't get along."

"That's why Mom got mad?"

"Probably. Did you tell her about the dream?"

"I just said I dreamed about an old lady who told me you were in danger."

"Well, you see. Your mom didn't like it that Mab contacted you without her permission." *Careful, careful.* "Mab is a good person. I don't know what happened between her and your mom, but you didn't do anything wrong by letting her into your dream, okay?"

"Because I helped you."

"Right. You helped me out a lot."

Maria smiled at that. "Can you show me how to do the dream phone?"

"If your mom says it's okay." At this point, there wasn't really anything Gwen could do to prevent Maria from experimenting with the dream phone, but I wasn't going to encourage it behind Gwen's back, either. "Speaking of your mom, I think we should call her now, don't you?"

Maria bit her lip, thinking, then nodded. "I guess so. She'll be worried when I don't get off the school bus."

Except try making a call when you don't have a mobile phone. Maria was supposed to carry one of those kids' cell phones for emergencies, but she'd left it home because she didn't want to turn it on and find it filled with frantic messages from Gwen.

I was the one who'd have the pleasure of talking with a frantic Gwen. But I could handle my sister.

I asked the waitress if there was a pay phone nearby. She scratched her head, as if trying to remember what a pay phone was, and then she said I could use the restaurant's phone if it was a local call and I was quick.

I was glad about the "quick" part when Gwen's voice exploded over the line. "Where are you? Where's Maria?"

"We're in an ice cream shop near Downtown Crossing. Everything's fine, Gwen."

"Put her on." Gwen's voice thrummed with anger. It seemed like a good idea to let her calm down before she spoke with Maria.

"She's on the other side of the room. It's okay, I can see her. But I'm using the restaurant's phone and I promised to keep this short."

"Her school called this morning to report that she was absent. I've been sick with worry ever since. Do you hear me? Sick!" Gwen voice kept creeping up the scale. It was a full octave higher than when she'd answered the phone. "When I called your apartment to see whether you'd heard from her, do you know who answered?"

"Gwen—"

"You tell that old bitch she is not to go anywhere near my daughter. Not in dreams, and not in the waking world. Got that?"

"We can talk about that later. Right now—"

"Do. You. Understand?"

"Yes. Yes, Gwen, I do. Now, let's figure out how to get Maria home."

"Wait for me at South Station. I'll be on the next train. No, damn it, I have to be here when Zack gets home from kindergarten. All right, I'll pick him up and then drive in—"

"Listen, there's no need to haul the boys into town. It might be easiest if I drop her off at Nick's office."

"He's not there. He's at a training seminar all afternoon."

"Okay, then how about I bring her out there? You and I need to talk, anyway. Let's do it at your house instead of in the middle of Boston." I didn't have the proper permit to go all the way to Needham, but I didn't care.

"You're right, we do need to talk. Again." Gwen's voice barely contained her anger. "All right, are you driving or taking the train?"

I hadn't picked up my Jag from the shop yet, so I told her we'd take the train.

Working out the details calmed Gwen down. Before we hung up, she said, "You should've called me earlier. But thanks for taking care of Maria. Tell her I love her."

"I will."

And I did. Maria rolled her eyes like she'd been practicing for just such an occasion, but she also looked pleased and a little relieved. And very, very ready to go home.

20

AS THE TRAIN PULLED INTO NEEDHAM HEIGHTS STATION, Gwen stood tiptoe on the platform, scanning the passing windows. Maria and I both waved, and as the train screeched to a stop, Gwen came over to our car.

Maria went down the steps a little hesitantly, but when Gwen opened her arms wide she flew to her mom. Gwen folded her into a hug as if she'd never, ever let go again. I waited, standing off to the side, giving them their moment.

Gwen stepped back, her hands on Maria's shoulders, and scrutinized her daughter's face as she held her at arm's length. "Don't ever, *ever* run away like that again. I don't care what the problem is, we can talk about it. Okay?"

"Okay, Mom." Maria looked at her tennis shoes but kept a hand on her mother's arm. "I'm sorry."

Gwen hugged her daughter again, pulling her close, both of them crying and laughing at the same time. Gwen buried her face in Maria's hair. They stood that way for several minutes. Then Gwen kissed the top of the girl's head and looked over at me. "Thanks for bringing her home."

I nodded, not trusting my voice to make it past the lump in my throat.

"Do you have time to come back to the house?" Gwen asked. "We really need to have that talk." There was no anger in her voice now. Just oceans of relief.

I nodded again. Before catching the train, I'd phoned Mab from South Station. She told me that Axel had called to say Juliet was still unconscious. No call from Daniel. I didn't have much time—and was fast running out of the little I did have—but with no way to find the Old Ones and no idea where to start looking, there wasn't much I could do about that.

Besides, this was family. I'd make time.

Maria threw her backpack into her mom's van and climbed into a middle seat. "Where are Zack and Justin?"

"Playing at the Henleys'." Gwen glanced at me as she buckled up and started the car. "They're our neighbors a couple of doors down. They have a boy Zack's age."

During the short drive from the train station to Gwen's house, the van was quiet. Maria stared out her window. Gwen turned on the radio, listened to two sentences of a news story about the zombie march, and turned it off again.

In the driveway, Maria jumped out with her backpack, slammed the door, and started toward the house.

"Maria," Gwen said, "go to the Henleys' and keep an eye on your brothers."

"But Mom . . ." Maria looked to me for backup. Her appeal wasn't lost on Gwen.

And there I was, stuck in a position I never wanted, wedged between my sister and her child. But I said what I thought was right. "I think she should stay, Gwen. This conversation concerns her."

Gwen gave each of us a long stare, as if trying to assess how much we were in league against her. *Not at all!* I wanted to shout. *You're her mom.* But until we played this out, my sister would see me as a rival.

"All right," she said, but in a voice that suggested we'd be sorry. "She may stay."

We went through the garage and took the side door into the kitchen. Gwen pointed at a chair, and Maria sat in it. My sister, ignoring her usual hostess instinct, didn't even offer a glass of water.

She sat at the head of the table and folded her hands, looking like a CEO ready to announce bad news at a shareholders' meeting. "So here's the situation as I see it. At this point, I think it's safe to say that Maria is developing Cerddorion tendencies. We have to plan for dealing with that." She turned to me. "You need to tell Kane to get started on the legal side of things. We have some time, but courts and government agencies move slowly, so we can't delay."

"He's, um, away right now, but I'll call his office and see what they can do. I'll fill Kane in as soon as he's back." If I ever got him back. The full moon still seemed a long way off, and after the failure of Roxana's ritual, I worried that even the moon wouldn't be enough.

"If Kane can help, fine. That would be our preference. But Nick and I agree we also need to have a plan B in place. If it looks like the courts may try to remove Maria from our home, we're moving to Canada. Nick says he can get a transfer to his firm's Toronto office."

Maria stood up. "But Mom—"

Gwen silenced Maria with a look, and the girl sat down again. She slumped in her chair and stared at the table.

I felt the same as Maria. Toronto was a long way from Boston. If they moved, I'd see Gwen and her family maybe once or twice a year. How was I supposed to help Maria get accustomed to shapeshifting if they moved so far away? Gwen's stony face brooked no arguments. All right, we'd figure it out. When Maria needed me, maybe I could take some time off and go up there to help her get through the first few months.

It felt like everything was moving way too fast.

"We do have time, Gwen, like you said. Maybe a year or longer."

"Yes. But I also said we need to have a plan in place. I'm

not going to wait until the authorities come knocking on my door."

Maria scrunched down farther in her chair. As the grown-ups talked, she'd made herself so small that she now appeared to be little more than a scared face hovering above the table.

"Okay, so we've covered plans and possible consequences," I said. "But we haven't discussed what's in store for Maria, what it's like to become a shapeshifter. Can I tell her what to expect?"

Gwen's eyes narrowed, but she nodded.

Maria sat up a little as I spoke. "Nothing is going to change right away. You'll keep having dreams like the ones you've been having, like the ones you told me about right here at this table."

"Will they get scary?" she asked in a tiny voice.

"No, because you're in charge. If a dream starts to feel scary or uncomfortable, just remind yourself, 'This is my dream; I'm in control.' When you do that, you can take the dream in whatever direction you want."

Maria looked dubious.

"Honest," I said. "These dreams are happening because your mind is starting to explore the idea of taking on other shapes. When you dream that you're flying or swimming underwater, what does it feel like?"

"Like it's me but not me."

"Exactly. When you get that 'me but not me' feeling, you know you're dreaming. So use that feeling to take control of your dream."

"It's called lucid dreaming," Gwen said. "I don't change shape like Vicky does, but I do control my dreams."

"*You* do it?"

Gwen smiled, a little ruefully, in my direction. "She used to think her mom could do anything." She cupped Maria's face in her hand. "If I didn't, worrying about you kids would give me nightmares, and I'd never get enough sleep to keep up with you all during the day."

Maria rolled her eyes, but she smiled.

"Try it the next time you have a flying dream," I said. "Pick a place to fly to, and see how easy it is to go there. Or switch: Go from flying to galloping or swimming. You don't have to wait for a dream to feel bad before you take control of it. You're always in control if you want to be."

"But if you do have a bad dream," Gwen added, "come and wake me up. I'll sit with you until you fall asleep again, like I did when you were little."

"Can I call you on that dream-phone thing?"

Something crossed Gwen's face, an expression like she'd caught an unpleasant smell. She scowled at me.

"She's already experienced the dream phone," I said. "She was curious about it, and I figured it was better not to keep her in the dark."

Gwen sighed. "I guess you're right." She turned to Maria. "Well, if you have a bad dream it'll probably wake you up, and you can't call on the dream phone when you're awake. But yes, you can talk to me that way. Vicky, too, if she's willing."

"Sure," I agreed, "we can chat about whatever you like. But I might be at work sometimes while you're asleep, so don't get frustrated or think you're doing it wrong if I don't answer."

"Start with me," Gwen said. "I'll teach you how. My colors are rose and gold. Vicky's are green and silver."

"What are mine?"

I let my eyes go out of focus and looked at the space just above Maria's head. Her aura shimmered into view. It spread around her, the size and balance of colors indicating she was healthy and generally happy, although some excess yellow showed she was prone to worry. Threaded through the aura, her Cerddorion colors were just beginning to show.

"A beautiful sky blue," I reported, "and . . . well, the other color is kind of pink now, but I think that'll deepen into a ruby red. Don't you, Gwen?"

Gwen, who'd also been reading Maria's aura, blinked. I couldn't imagine what she was feeling, getting her first glimpse of her daughter's Cerddorion colors. Her baby was growing up—and into something Gwen feared. She nodded, blinking some more. "Pink and blue. The colors we used for the nursery when you were born." She cleared her throat. "But Vicky's right. They're the base colors, and they'll take on your specific shades as you . . . as you grow."

"Are those good colors?"

"They're yours," I said. "Colors aren't good or bad, just like a fingerprint isn't good or bad. But they're part of what makes you, you." I touched the tip of her nose. "So, yeah, I'd say they're pretty terrific."

A bread knife lay on the table. Maria picked it up and peered into its shiny surface, tilting the blade this way and that, trying to glimpse her colors for herself.

Gwen closed her hand around Maria's and lowered it to the table. "Okay, we need to lay down some ground rules. First, you can use the dream phone only on the weekends. No calls on school nights. I remember how tired I used to get when Vicky and I stayed up talking for half the night."

"But you were asleep," Maria objected.

"It's a different kind of sleep. The kind you can wake up tired from."

"Oh." Maria seemed puzzled, but she shrugged. "Okay."

"Second—and this is important—you may answer a dream-phone call only if it's from Vicky or me. Green and silver or rose and gold. No other colors. Understand?"

"But what about the blue-and-silver lady? Vicky said she was my aunt."

Gwen looked so angry, for a moment I thought she would hit me. But she took a visibly deep breath, then another, and shook her head. "Just Vicky or me. If I find out you've been talking to anyone else, you'll be grounded."

"But *why* can't I talk to her?"

Gwen picked up the bread knife and toyed with it, her knuckles white. "Because many years ago, when I was a little older than you, I saw that woman do a terrible thing."

"What?"

"Gwen, it's been almost twenty years. Surely after all this time you can let go of whatever Mab did to upset you."

Gwen slapped the bread knife on the table, making Maria jump. "Let go of it? That woman should be in prison, not swanning around her fancy house in Wales. Not pushing her way into my little girl's dreams." Gwen shoved her chair back and went to the sink. She poured herself a glass of water and drank it in three gulps. She slammed the empty glass on the counter, fury seething in her eyes. "But I never could get anyone to believe what I saw. Not Dad, not the police—no one."

She pointed to the side door. "Maria, go outside. Go to the Henleys' house, ride your bike, do something. I need to talk to Vicky alone."

"But, Mom, you said I could stay. You said this conversation concerned me."

"You're right, it does. But you're still too young to hear what I have to say. Maybe later, when you're older, I'll explain."

"But—"

"No!"

Maria knew when she was beat. She slid from her chair and trudged across the kitchen. At the door, she turned around and said reproachfully, "I'm growing up, you know. You can't treat me like a little kid forever." She tossed her head and went out into the garage.

Gwen's laugh had an hysterical edge to it. "She sounds exactly like I did at that age—do you remember? If only I'd known then how good 'little kids' have it. I had to grow up way too fast, and I wasn't ready for it. Thanks to your precious aunt Mab."

"Gwen, what happened?"

"That's why I never told you, you know," she said, ignoring my question. "Christ, you were younger than Maria when it happened. I wanted to protect you, protect your innocence. And then later, you were so crazy about Mab and demon fighting and Wales that you wouldn't have believed me." She glared at me accusingly. "You won't believe me now, either."

"Try me. I promise I'll listen, at least."

Gwen didn't sit down. She didn't look at me as she spoke.

She stood by the kitchen sink, staring at a spot on the far wall, seeing into the distant past.

"Thirteen. I was only thirteen years old. A child. That summer in Wales, I was so terrified of Mab I felt more like her prisoner than her apprentice. I used to imagine that I was Gretel and she was the witch, getting ready to eat me alive. I was so unhappy. I'd take long walks whenever I could escape from the house, and on one of those walks I met a boy from the village. Eric." Her eyes softened. "I thought he was the handsomest boy I'd ever seen—black hair, dark eyes, and black eyelashes so long and thick I wished mine were like that.

"Eric was fifteen, and I knew Mab would never approve of him. So I'd sneak out at night and we'd meet. I thought I was being careful, but one night Mab must have followed me. I met Eric at our usual place, a stone wall where we'd sit and talk. It was all so harmless, so innocent. That night, he put his arm around me and said he wanted to kiss me.

"My heart was thumping like mad. I closed my eyes and waited for the feel of his lips against mine. Instead, something warm splashed onto my face. I opened my eyes. Eric clutched his neck, blood spurting from between his fingers. His throat had been slashed wide open. Mab stood behind him, holding a bloody dagger."

Here eyes locked onto mine like laser beams. "She killed him in cold blood, Vicky. A fifteen-year-old boy. And all because he tried to kiss me."

21

THERE HAD TO BE ANOTHER SIDE TO THE STORY. GWEN wasn't interested in speculating about what it might be. As far as she was concerned, our aunt was a brutal killer who'd murdered a young girl's first love. The set of Gwen's jaw, the absolute certainty in her voice—her mind held zero doubt about that night.

No, I thought, sitting on the train back to Boston, there must be more to it. I knew my aunt. Gwen's picture of her as a cruel butcher killing for spite simply wasn't *her*. Mab had once reminded me that I didn't know everything about her. But one thing I did know: She'd never do what Gwen accused her of. Mab was loved and respected by the villagers of Rhydgoch. She didn't go around slaughtering them.

She killed him in cold blood, Vicky. A fifteen-year-old boy. And all because he tried to kiss me.

Yet Gwen's words haunted me all the way home.

* * *

WHEN I WALKED IN MY FRONT DOOR, MAB LOOKED UP from the book she was reading. Kane came over and sniffed at my fingers, wagging his tail.

"You had a telephone message—" Mab began.

"I need to talk to you. Right now." My voice sounded harsh as I gestured toward the bedroom.

"The caller did say it was important."

"So is this."

Mab didn't argue. She stood slowly, her brow creased as she peered at me. She balanced her book on the arm of the chair and walked around the sofa to the bedroom.

Kane tilted his head, curious.

"I'm not trying to shut you out, but I need to talk to my aunt in private. It's a family matter."

He pressed against my leg, like he wanted to show his support, then went into the kitchen.

Mab sat straight-backed on the edge of my bed, hands folded in her lap. She kept her face blank, waiting.

I closed the door and leaned back against it. "Mab . . ." On the ride back from Needham, I'd imagined a dozen different scenarios of how I'd handle this conversation: a confrontation, a gentle question, a matter-of-fact request for her explanation. Now, it was hard just to get the words out. Gwen's story, so vivid when she told it, dimmed, and suddenly I wanted to say *never mind, it was a mistake, forget the whole thing*. The idea of Mab as a murderer was preposterous. But I needed to know the truth. I blurted, "Gwen told me you killed someone in front of her. A village boy named Eric."

Mab closed her eyes as if in pain. But then she nodded, once, and I had the feeling she'd expected my words. "Yes, I thought she might bring that up now. To enlist your help in keeping me away from Maria, I'd wager." She opened her eyes and regarded me calmly. No hint of guilt troubled her gaze. "Frankly, I'm surprised she's waited this long. She never told you before?"

"Don't you think I'd have asked you about it if she had? I'm asking now. I need to hear your side of the story."

"Well, your sister told you the truth. During the brief period of her apprenticeship, I became aware she was sneaking out of the house at night. I followed her, I saw her meet a boy. And I slashed his throat."

She looked at me fiercely, almost defiantly, challenging me to judge her acts. I put my hands behind me to hide their shaking, but I waited. There had to be more coming, and I was keeping my judgment—and my emotions—in check until I knew the whole story.

"There was no village boy, Victory. It was Pryce."

"Pryce?" The demi-demon who'd loosed the Morfran on Boston and tried to kill me had once upon a time courted my sister?

She nodded. "He somehow learned my niece had come to Wales to train with me, and his first thought was of the prophecy. He wanted to find out whether this young American niece was the Victory foretold in *The Book of Utter Darkness*."

The Book of Utter Darkness was an ancient text, written in the language of Hell, that outlined the origin of demons and was full of slippery prophecies about the struggle between the Cerddorion and demonkind. Pryce had attempted to use the book as his personal road map to power, believing that "Victory," mentioned in the book, was destined to be his mate and demon queen. In the end, though, his arrogance had caused him to misinterpret the prophecies and end up as he was now, "the sleeper."

Mab continued: "Pryce altered his human appearance to that of a teenage boy." Demi-demons can't shift into animals, but they can take on whatever human shape they choose. "In that guise, he courted Gwen. It didn't take him long to learn that she had a sister named Victory and to decide that you, not she, were the one foretold. Gwen was of no interest to him; he could have simply walked away. It would have broken the child's heart—she was a silly, romantic girl—but Pryce saw an opportunity to injure me through her. He intended to kill her."

I knew Pryce. I could believe it. But still I felt my jaw drop as I stared at my aunt.

"It's fortunate I chose that night to follow her. At first, he looked like a human boy to me, as well. I almost went home, thinking I'd simply keep the girl too busy to sneak out. But when Gwen closed her eyes and leaned forward for her first kiss, Pryce pulled a dagger. Moonlight glinted off the blade. His shadow demon loomed behind him, and I realized who he was. I drew my own dagger and ran over to them; I swear I never moved so fast in this lifetime. I grabbed Pryce's hair, yanked his head back, and slit his throat." Her face showed grim satisfaction. "My only regret is that the blade wasn't bronze. I could have destroyed that infernal demi-demon once and for all."

Her fists were clenched. She opened her fingers and smoothed out her skirt.

"Poor Gwen," she said. "All she saw was a mortally wounded boy. The look of utter horror in her eyes . . . I knew I'd lost her then. She ran back to Maenllyd and locked herself in her room. The moment she fled, Pryce disappeared into the demon plane to heal. Gwen didn't see that, of course. He returned moments later in his demon form—at a safe distance, I might add—and announced he'd be waiting for you."

No wonder Mab had kept such a tight leash on me for all those years of my apprenticeship. I never once went into the village alone, and my training left little time for walks through the woods and fields. Village boys? I never knew they existed.

Would I have been susceptible to Pryce's charms at that age? I was glad I'd never had the chance to find out.

"Gwen wouldn't open her door or listen to me. Over and over, she demanded to return home. That's all she would say. And so I sent her home."

Mab stood. "Your sister did see what she believes she saw: She saw the boy's slashed throat, felt his blood on her arms and face. Yet she'll never believe the rest. She wouldn't listen to me. She didn't believe the village constable, who said there was no such boy in Rhydgoch. She didn't believe your father, who tried to tell her about demi-demons." Mab sighed. "And should you try to explain, she won't believe you, either. I concluded twenty years ago that Gwen was lost to me. Her recent actions confirm that. I'm afraid there's nothing anyone can do about it."

And that was that. Mab moved toward me. I stepped aside to let her pass. She opened the door and went into the living room, saying over her shoulder, "You need to return that phone call. It was from a Detective Costello, and he said it was urgent." She picked up her book and resumed reading.

Kane's face appeared in the kitchen doorway. "We're good," I told him. "Everything's fine." But nothing felt fine. My heart ached for Gwen, who for twenty years had been forced to carry a ghastly secret because no one would believe her. And for Mab, branded a murderer by the niece whose life she'd saved, shut out of Gwen's life, her family. There ought to be something I could do to bridge the chasm between them. But they'd lived on their opposite sides of that chasm for twenty years. The tragedy of the situation was fresh to me; it had long ago been woven into the fabric of their lives.

I set the problem aside for now and went into the kitchen. I'd call Daniel and see if he'd learned anything that might help Juliet.

He picked up on the first ring. When he heard it was me, he dropped his voice.

"I can't talk now. I need to get to a secure location. You're at home?"

"Yes."

"Don't go anywhere. I'll call back within five minutes." He hung up abruptly.

Daniel's voice sounded strange, I reflected as I waited, phone in hand, for his call. Tense, but also with a coldness I'd never heard from him before. When the phone rang, I answered immediately.

"Where did you get that sample you gave me?" Daniel demanded.

"Why, what—"

"No, *I'm* asking the questions. Where did you get it?"

I considered how much I should tell him. Juliet was still

wanted by the police, and I wouldn't bring her into this unless I had to. "From a fight. The sample was from the blade of a sword I took from my opponent."

"Did it cut you?"

"No, but what—"

"Where, Vicky? Whose was it? Why did you swab the blade? That's a pretty unusual thing to do, wouldn't you say? I need details."

My head spun from his rapid-fire questions. I picked the one that seemed safest to answer. "The sword belonged to one of the Old Ones, those creatures who stole Pryce's body after the Paranormal Appreciation Day concert. Remember I told you about Myrddin? They're working with him."

"Who's working with the Reaper. Shit."

"Daniel, what's wrong?"

"When you brought me that cotton ball, did you have any idea what was on that blade?"

"Some kind of poison, I thought."

"It's worse than poison. It's a virus—a variant of the virus that caused the zombie plague."

The phone fell from my hand. It hit my boot and skated across the kitchen floor. I chased it and snatched it up.

"Daniel? Daniel? Are you there?"

"The whole lab is under quarantine. I'm lucky they didn't stick me in quarantine with them. I managed to convince them I didn't come into direct contact with the specimen. But you can bet I got a grilling about where it came from."

"What did you say?"

"I told them it was left anonymously in my mailbox, and I thought I'd better check it out." I let out my breath in a rush of relief. He hadn't linked the sample to me. I started to thank him, but he cut me off. "No more off-the-record stuff, Vicky. I can't do you any more favors. This is way too serious for amateur detectives."

I bristled a little at his suggestion that I was playing Miss Marple, but I let it go. He had a right to be angry. "Did anyone get sick?"

"Not yet." That was good news. The original plague had

killed its victims within minutes of exposure. "Don't tell anyone. We're trying to keep this out of the news to prevent widespread panic." I bet his girlfriend the TV reporter wasn't happy about that. "Each hour that goes by without symptoms is encouraging. This virus is a variant, so it may not be contagious to humans."

Just like the zombie plague hadn't been contagious to paranormals. My heart stopped. This virus hadn't infected any norms, but it sure as hell was affecting Juliet. "I've got to go, Daniel." I cut the connection.

The phone began ringing again almost immediately, but I ignored it. I skidded into the living room. Kane was at my heels, wondering what the hell was going on.

"Aren't you going to answer that?" Mab asked.

"No. Mab, do you know of any viruses that can infect paranormals?"

"What kind of paranormal? When you were a teenager, I recall you were ill for a week with chicken pox."

"Vampires. What about vampires?"

She considered, then shook her head. "I can't say I've ever heard of one."

The phone stopped ringing. Next the Goon Squad would be pounding on the door. We had to hurry. "You know that wound of Juliet's? The one that won't heal?"

She nodded and held up her book. "Yes, I've been reading about the toxicity of certain silver compounds, and—"

"Forget that. The blade that cut Juliet was coated with a variant of the zombie virus."

Mab's mouth dropped open. Kane sat on the floor. Both of them stared at me as though I'd just announced the beginning of the apocalypse. Maybe I had.

"The human victims of that plague were dead for three days before they rose again," I said. "Juliet was attacked three days ago."

Mab was already up and pulling on her coat. A minute later we were out the door.

* * *

IT WAS A LITTLE AFTER SEVEN IN THE EVENING, TOO EARLY for Creature Comforts to be open. I'd lost the key Axel had given me when those vampire junkies grabbed me, so I pounded on the back door, praying Axel would open it. He did. He didn't say a word when we rushed past him and opened the secret door. As I sprinted down the stairs, I wondered what we'd find: Juliet, awake and somehow changed? Or Juliet, reduced to a pile of grave dust?

Neither. She was still unconscious. There was no change at all.

I sank into a chair; Mab took another. I rubbed my temples. Ever since I'd hung up on Daniel, I'd been trying to figure out why the Old One who'd burst into Juliet's cell would carry a virus-coated sword. Was the blade tainted with the virus on purpose? If so, did that mean the Old Ones were behind the original plague? It made sense. Juliet had said they were experimenting with a formula for eternal life. What if that formula was a virus, one that killed its victims and then reanimated them? It would explain why there had been only a single outbreak of the virus, and in only one place—the Old Ones, damn them, had loosed it on downtown Boston and then sat back to see what happened. But that experiment failed. The virus infected only humans.

I voiced these thoughts to Mab. "I've been considering along the same lines," she said. "It seems they've been trying out different magical formulas and somehow binding them to a virus. The virus part would be important. It gets inside the body's cells and allows the formula to replicate there, spreading throughout the body. If the formula confers eternal life, every cell becomes eternal."

"But the Old Ones are basically vampires. Viruses don't affect them."

"And that's precisely what went wrong with the Old Ones' first attempt at an eternity virus—it didn't affect its true target. And it failed. The Old Ones don't want to become zombies. They want to become gods, with their former youth and beauty restored. In the years since that experiment, I'd wager they've been working to perfect the formula."

Two thousand people, along with their families and friends, had suffered—were still suffering—because the Old Ones had decided to use Bostonians as their guinea pigs. The callousness of it floored me.

And they weren't finished yet. "Juliet said they killed four vampires with their recent experiments." And that was just the number she knew of.

"I believe they've added silver to the mix somehow," Mab said. "Silver actually kills many viruses, but if they've found a way to make it work . . . The silver would weaken the vampire's immune system, making the vampire vulnerable to the virus and allowing infection to occur."

"That's why Juliet's wound isn't healing."

She nodded. "The Old Ones themselves are highly vulnerable to silver right now, but that's a good thing from their point of view: The silver will take them into death; the virus-based formula will bring them out of it. *If* they can get the balance right."

And they were trying out that balance on Juliet, no matter what it did to her. The whole point of breaking into the Goon Squad facility must have been to infect her, and then grab her and take her back to their lair—with one leg or two, it didn't matter to them—to observe what happened. Shit. Her odds didn't look good.

I walked over to the bed. Juliet was so still and pale: not alive, not dead, not undead. She was simply *there*, another object in the room, like the bed she lay in.

The jar of salve sat on her nightstand. I didn't know whether it was helping her, but Mab thought so. If she could just hang on a little longer, maybe we could find a cure, a way to force the silver out of her body so she could heal. I picked up the salve and pulled back the covers. Her leg was unchanged.

I scooped out some salve, cool and tingly on my fingers, and spread it on Juliet's calf. Her skin didn't absorb it. The salve smeared into a gray, greasy paste.

What the hell?

Wiping my hand on a tissue, I looked closely at Juliet's

skin. It was covered with an even layer of fine, grayish powder. I tried to wipe some off. The dust came off on my hand. More formed immediately beneath it. Brushing at it was like brushing Juliet away.

"Mab!" I shouted, holding out my dust-covered hands. "She's dying!"

Mab was at my side in a flash. She leaned over Juliet, and her breath puffed a powdery cloud into the air. The dust had spread. It covered Juliet's hands and face, clung to her eyelashes and hair. Grains flaked off and fell away, speckling the sheets, as Juliet slowly disintegrated.

My roommate was turning to dust before my eyes, and there was nothing I could do to stop it.

Mab shoved my arm. "Go upstairs, child. Quickly!" She tried to push me toward the staircase.

I planted my feet and stared at her. I wasn't going to leave Juliet here to die alone.

"Do as I say! There's a chance I can save her, but I must work alone." She reached inside her blouse, pulling out her pendant.

"The bloodstone? It can help her?"

"*Upstairs*, child! Before it's too late."

One foot on the stairs, I looked back. Mab dangled the bloodstone over Juliet's forehead. The room's light had softened to a silvery glow. It seemed to come from every direction, erasing all shadows. Motes of dust floated above Juliet's body, sparkling like stars. Mab murmured something in a low voice. I turned and hurried up the stairs.

22

I COULDN'T STAY STILL. I PACED THE LENGTH OF CREATURE Comforts: from the storeroom, along the hallway past BOOS and GHOULS, through the bar, to the front door. And then back the other way. Back and forth. Back and forth.

Axel wasn't in the bar. I didn't know where he'd disappeared to.

What was happening downstairs? I couldn't blot out the image of Juliet, lying so still, her body crumbling to dust.

Back and forth. Back and forth.

I was brewing coffee—for no reason other than it seemed like a semi-useful activity—when the bolts on Axel's private entrance slid back: one, two, three. A moment later, Axel stood in front of the bar. When he noticed me there, he did a double-take and scratched his head, eyebrows up.

"Want coffee?" I asked.

He nodded.

I poured him a cup and set it on the bar. "Okay, this is backwards," I said. "We're on the wrong sides of the bar."

He nodded again, and we switched positions. I sat on my usual barstool. He poured a second mug of coffee and slid it in front of me, where it sat untouched. I didn't want coffee. I wanted Juliet to be okay.

Axel sipped his coffee and waited.

"Juliet's bad," I said. "I think she's dying. Mab's trying to save her."

A large hand appeared on the bar, millimeters from my own. It was a strong hand, with square nails and long fingers. Axel wasn't the touchy-feely type, but I knew what he was trying to say.

He finished his coffee, and I helped get the bar ready to open, carrying in trays of washed glasses and setting them on shelves, scrubbing some of the customary stickiness from the tables. As we worked, I strained to listen for any sign of what Mab was doing, but the only sound was the clinking of barware. Axel didn't scrimp on soundproofing.

Time dragged its feet through half an hour. I could almost hear the minutes shuffling slowly along—until I looked up and saw Mab in the hallway, leaning against the wall. The shuffling footsteps were hers. She looked exhausted.

I ran to her side. Axel was right behind me. Together, we helped her into the main room and made our way to a table. Axel tested a chair to make sure it didn't wobble, and we got Mab settled in it. I pulled around another chair and sat next to her. She slumped, one hand over her heart as if checking to make sure it still beat. Her face drooped; her skin was ashen and papery. Whatever she'd done downstairs, it had taken a lot out of her.

I clasped her hand. "Are you all right? How's Juliet?"

"Juliet's alive. Or undead—whichever's appropriate to say about vampires. At any rate, she hasn't dissolved into a pile of dust." She took a long, shaky breath and attempted a small smile. "Although that's rather an apt description of how I feel at the moment."

Axel looked inquiringly toward the coffeemaker.

"Do you have tea?" I asked. "She doesn't drink coffee."

"Downstairs," Axel said. He went to get it.

Mab closed her eyes and inhaled a long, slow breath. She raised a hand to pat her hair into place. It scared me, seeing how badly her hand shook.

"How about some of that aquavit?" I tried to make my voice bright. "Water of life, right? Sounds like just what you need."

Mab shook her head. "A sip of tap water, perhaps." Her tongue darted across parched lips.

"Coming right up." I squeezed her hand and went behind the bar. As I took down a glass and filled it at the sink, I wondered what saving Juliet's life had cost Mab. Despite her age, my aunt was a strong, vital woman. I'd never seen her so weak.

Mab accepted the water glass in both hands. She gulped down a couple of swallows and set it on the table. She licked her lips again. "Better."

"Mab, what did you do down there? What's the bloodstone?"

She fingered the chain around her neck and pulled out the pendant. The bloodstone looked different, duller and shrunken in its setting. The green and red coloring had faded to a drab, flat gray.

"This stone," Mab said, "is my talisman. My object of power. It binds me to the land, and the land to me."

"I don't understand."

"The bloodstone possesses three qualities: it's sacred, it's powerful, and it's personal. Centuries ago, the stone was chiseled from an ancient altar—that's the sacred part. It was buried deep in the soil, where it absorbed power from the land. And it's personal to me, infused with my blood—the blood of numerous lifetimes."

Was she kidding? I knew the ancient druids believed in reincarnation, but I thought that particular belief had been put away in the filing cabinet of wacky ideas, somewhere between *Fairy, Tooth* and *Santa Claus*. Yet Mab's eyes were dull with exhaustion, not twinkling with a joke.

"The bloodstone is what gives me longevity," she said. "You might say it's the source of my power." The corners of her tired mouth twitched upward. "And I used that power to heal a vampire. You have some second cousins in Carmarthenshire who'd argue I should have staked her instead."

It was good to see Mab smile a little, because her appearance frightened me. Her skin was dull and sallow. Dark circles shadowed her eyes. The creases in her face had sharpened, and her jawline sagged almost into jowls. The past half hour had aged her twenty years.

"Can the bloodstone's power be renewed?" I asked.

"When I return to Wales, yes. I've drawn on it too much recently. First there was the injury to my heart"—Pryce had nearly killed her a month ago in a swordfight in a Welsh slate mine—"and then I used the stone to find you. And now this. I'm tired. The stone has dispensed much of its power without replenishment. When I get home, I'll bury it deep in good Welsh soil for a few weeks, give it time to regenerate. And we'll both be good as new."

"We could find a place to bury it here."

She shook her head. "I'm afraid that won't work, child. The bloodstone's power, and my own, is tied to the land of Wales."

"Then you've got to go back." Mab's passport had arrived in the mail. Carlos could forge an entry stamp, and everything would be in order for her to leave. If being away from Wales weakened Mab, she needed to go home, and as soon as possible.

"I have business to finish here. With Myrddin. The bad blood between us goes way back."

Way back. Myrddin was a fifteen-hundred-year-old demi-demon. "Have you really lived multiple—" I began, but Axel's heavy footsteps sounded on the stairs. Mab stuffed the bloodstone back inside her shirt and shot me a look that warned me not to talk about it now.

Axel reappeared, bearing a tray. He'd gone all out. Tea steeped in a delicate porcelain pot decorated with pink and white roses; a matching cup and saucer waited beside it. He'd put out cream, sugar, sliced lemon, and even honey in a plastic, bear-shaped squeeze bottle. I tried to picture Axel sitting downstairs in his lair, sipping tea from that cup. I failed.

As he set down the tray, Axel must have noticed me gaping at him. His face turned two shades redder and he disappeared behind the bar.

I poured a cup of tea, stirred in some honey, and handed it to Mab. She raised it, trembling, to her lips. She drained the cup and returned it to me for a refill. When she handed me the empty cup a second time, her hands were steadier.

"Ah, much better." She did look better. Some of the color had returned to her cheeks, and her eyes had reclaimed some of their sparkle. But she still looked much older and more frail than the woman who'd entered Creature Comforts with me an hour ago.

How much of Mab's vitality came from the bloodstone—and how much was left?

She stood, putting a hand on her back as though it pained her. "Now," she said, "there's no time to lose. We must speak with your roommate. Lives depend on it."

She set off toward the storeroom, moving with the awkward gait of someone trying to hide a limp. Axel came out from behind the bar, said something in his troll language, and offered his arm. Mab accepted it, and together they went down the hall.

JULIET HAD BEEN SO CLOSE TO DEATH THAT I EXPECTED TO find her limp in bed, awake but weak. So I wasn't prepared for the bundle of energy that paced the room like a tornado trapped in a box.

I was on the bottom step when Juliet ran over and threw her arms around me. She saw Mab behind me and cried, " 'O, then, I see Queen Mab hath been with you'!" And then she hugged Mab, too. My aunt stiffened, her face an almost comical picture of consternation. It was a pretty safe bet that Mab had never been hugged by a vampire before.

"That's Shakespeare," Juliet explained. Mab nodded and didn't reply, although she knew the Bard's plays as well as Juliet. "There's more to it, of course. The line is from my play, from a speech by Mercutio. I'm afraid he's not very complimentary of your namesake overall. But he calls you 'the fairies' midwife,' and I do feel like you've helped birth me."

Juliet kissed Mab on the cheek. Mab's eyes went wide, and I had to turn away to hide my smile.

"Glad to see you're feeling better," I said. I'd never seen Juliet such a bundle of energy. "How's your leg?"

"Oh, it's fine." She held it out, her arms positioned like a ballerina's. Her skin was smooth and pale, as normal. Not even a scar. She spun in a pirouette. "All better. Thanks to good Queen Mab. You don't mind if I call you that, do you?" She flashed a toothy grin at Mab, who was leaning heavily on the arms of a chair as she lowered herself into it. Axel went back upstairs to get her another cup of tea.

"So, when are we going to attack the Old Ones?" Juliet leapt around, shadowboxing. "Now that I know how vulnerable those bastards are to silver, I'll kill them all. I don't care if I burn myself to cinders doing it."

I stared at her. This wasn't just a surge of energy. This was like a whole new Juliet. And there was Mab, so drained. I hoped she hadn't given away too much. "Did Mab tell you what made you so sick?" I asked Juliet.

"Plague virus. But I feel fine now. And I didn't even turn into a zombie." She scrutinized herself in the mirror over the dresser, checking for gray-green skin or red eyes. But there wasn't a trace of zombie in her; she looked like Juliet. Pale skin, glossy hair. Even her curves had filled out again. "I feel better than I have in decades. Like I've started a whole new life." She laughed. "Does that make me *un*-undead?"

Axel returned, carefully balancing a teacup in its saucer, and sat next to Mab. She took tea and tried to sip it, but her hands were shaking again, almost as badly as before. She rested the cup and saucer in her lap. How much of Juliet's newfound vitality came from the bloodstone, I wondered, and how much from the Old Ones' eternity virus?

"Did you know the Old Ones caused the zombie plague?" I asked her.

"Not until Queen Mab told me I'd been infected with a similar virus. Then I realized the original plague must have been the 'failed experiment' the Old Ones were always going on about." She turned to Mab. "The Old Ones communicate psychically. I could hear their thoughts, but they didn't know I was eavesdropping. Anyway." She spun on her heel to address me again. "That was why they needed the wizard, because their experiment had failed and they were running out of time."

"We know now who the wizard is. Myrddin Wyllt. He's the father of Pryce, the one they call 'the sleeper.'"

Mab managed to lift the teacup to her lips. When she set it down, her eyes had brightened. "Colwyn believes that Myrddin possesses the secret to immortality," she said. "It took Colwyn centuries to find Myrddin and then centuries more to figure out how to undo the spell that held the wizard where he was. But the two of them are old enemies. I'm sure Colwyn would have greatly preferred to leave Myrddin there for all eternity."

"And where was that?" Juliet asked. She'd finally stopped pacing and spinning and dancing and perched on the edge of the bed.

"A hawthorn tree," I said. "He was imprisoned there by my ancestor Nimuë."

"Actually, it was a yew tree. And . . . well, the literature gets many of the details wrong. But that's not our concern now." She turned to Juliet. "Colwyn released Myrddin but put a time limit on his freedom: ten days. If Myrddin doesn't deliver the secret of immortality in that time, back he goes to the yew tree. In the meantime, they're assisting Myrddin in his attempts to revive Pryce. That's what's behind the Reaper murders." She gave a brief account of how Myrddin had attempted to transfer my life force to Pryce. "So, you see, we need to find where they're hiding 'the sleeper.'"

"I don't know." Juliet rubbed her chin. "The Old Ones have several bases in Boston. The one where I met with them is on Stanhope Street." She jumped up and began pacing again, gesturing as she spoke. "There's an empty lot there, across from that big parking garage, that's supposed to be a construction site. But the construction trailer is fake. The lair is under it, underground. It's set up like a big laboratory."

"We know that one," I said. "That's where they took me. It's abandoned now."

"Drat. That's the only one I visited. I know there are at least two more. They mentioned a safe house and also a headquarters, but not their locations." She stopped moving and closed her eyes. "They communicated in images. Let me see what I can recall. The safe house was in a brick town house, in the basement. But there's millions of town houses in Boston. The headquarters . . ." She scrunched her eyes more tightly. "Dark. Underground. Concrete walls." She shook her head. "Not helpful, I know, but it's all I can see."

"The murders follow a pattern," I said, thinking out loud. "They happen every forty-eight hours. The timing must have ritual significance for Myrddin. When he didn't manage to kill me, he sent the Reaper out to kill someone else that night, at that location. Could there be a pattern to the murder sites, too?" Since one murder site had also been the site of a known base of the Old Ones, if we could identify the pattern, maybe we'd flush them out of hiding.

"A pattern . . ." Juliet closed her eyes again. "There was a symbol that dominated their conversations. I don't know what it means, but it always came with the number five."

Mab and I exchanged glances. "Myrddin said there had to be five victims," I said, "that Pryce would open his eyes when he received the life force of the fifth. Maybe the symbol is related. What did it look like?"

Juliet's eyes popped open. "Give me something to write with and I'll draw it for you."

Axel fished a pencil from his shirt pocket, and Mab handed Juliet the napkin from her saucer. A few splashes of tea had sloshed onto it, but most of it was dry.

Juliet sat on the bed and smoothed the napkin flat on the nightstand. Her tongue poked out from one side of her mouth as she concentrated on her drawing. She held it out so we could see. It was a simple figure, a vertical line with diagonal branches forming a point at each end:

ᛇ

"Eihwaz," said Axel.

"Yes." Mab nodded. "I believe you're correct."

I stared at the symbol. I didn't care what it was called. I felt it burning in my chest: a long, vertical line along my breastbone, with a diagonal cut at each end. The Reaper had carved that symbol into me as I'd lain strapped to the table.

"Child, are you all right? You've gone deathly pale."

I put a hand to my chest. "That symbol—the Reaper carved it into my chest."

Mab peered at me, her eyes dark with concern. In a moment, the burning sensation faded. I reminded myself that the symbol wasn't there now, not even as a scar. "Tell me about the symbol," I said.

Mab watched me for several seconds before she answered. "It's a rune. It represents the yew tree, symbol of triumph over death." She took the napkin and smoothed it on her lap. I wondered if it was a coincidence that Myrddin had been imprisoned in a yew tree. "The Old Ones' focus on this rune may simply show their preoccupation with defeating death."

"But the number five. Five victims, five points on the rune." I glanced around the room. There was no computer. "Is there any way I can get online right now?" I asked Axel. "I need to see a map of Boston."

Axel scratched his chin through his shaggy beard. Then he trundled over to the bed's nightstand and opened a drawer. He pulled out a neatly folded paper map. "This okay? I keep it for guests."

"Perfect." I unfolded the map and spread it open on the bed. "Juliet, give me that pencil. Now, the body of the first Reaper victim was discovered here, in the South End near Rutland Square." I drew a circle on the site and filled it in.

"The second body was also in the South End, at the intersection of Harrison and East Newton." I squinted at the map until I found the place, and drew another dot. "If a third murder happened at the site of the Stanhope Street base, that would be just about here, more toward the Back Bay." Dot number three appeared on the map.

"Now, if we connect the dots . . ." I drew a line from the first murder site to the second, and then from the second to the third, the place that could have been the site of my own death. A chill hit me. I was still worried what it meant that Pryce had absorbed some of my life force. But I couldn't afford to dwell on that now.

A lopsided V appeared on the map, with one branch longer than the other. It looked like the bottom half of the eihwaz rune.

"Extend the vertical line northward," Mab said. "Make it the same length as from the Harrison Avenue site to Stanhope Street."

I sketched the line upward, then folded the map at Stanhope Street to make sure I located the end point correctly. From there, I drew a diagonal line, branching off to the southeast, and folded the map at an angle to verify that it mirrored the bottom branch. A corner of Boston Common at Boylston Street. The eihwaz rune stood out on the map, connecting five separate sites.

"If they're using this rune as a pattern, the next murder will happen here," I said, pointing to the dot at the top of the map. It was on Back Street, a sort of alleyway between Beacon Street and Storrow Drive, near where the Back Bay becomes Beacon Hill.

Mab stood. Axel jumped up to assist her, but she was much steadier on her feet. "We must go there at once. It's our best chance to ambush Myrddin."

"And stop the Reaper," I added.

Juliet grinned. "And kick the Old Ones' bony asses straight to hell."

23

JULIET SAID SHE NEEDED TO HUNT AND WOULD MEET US AT Back Street. I wasn't sure joining us was such a great idea. Right now, she was the Amazing Perpetual Motion Vampire, but two hours ago, she'd been dying. The surge of vitality she'd gotten from the bloodstone wouldn't last forever—Mab warned it would wear off. And who knew what the longer-term effects of the virus might be? Besides, Juliet was unarmed and I couldn't spare any weapons.

Axel thunked two silver stakes with polished ebony handles onto the bar. "Crowd control," he said. Juliet picked one up, hefted it, and made a lightning-fast downward strike, stopping just above the bar's surface. She almost looked like she knew what she was doing. "Now I'm armed," she said, "with silver. See you there." She was gone before I could argue with her.

I didn't even attempt to convince Mab to go home and rest. She seemed to be gradually recovering, and I knew she wouldn't let me face Myrddin alone. Whatever was between my aunt and the demi-demon wizard, it was personal. She wanted her shot at him.

We checked our weapons. Ever since Myrddin's little helpers had snatched me off the street, I'd carried a small arsenal for defending myself against demons, Old Ones, vampires, and whatever other nasties might come at me. I carried two guns: one loaded with bronze bullets, the other with silver. In addition, I had a bronze dagger and a second dagger with a silver-plated blade. Mab didn't like pistols; she preferred old-fashioned weapons. She also carried two daggers: one for demons, one for vampires. We were as ready as we were going to be.

WE FILLED OUT A SMALL MOUNTAIN OF PAPERWORK AT THE checkpoint into Boston, but we made it through. Beyond the checkpoint, several taxis waited. I snagged the first one. Mab got in and sat with her head against the seat, eyes closed, while I gave the driver an address on Beacon Street, about half a block past the intersection with Berkeley. He nodded, pulled away from the curb, and turned up the radio.

Some talk-radio host was ranting about the Reaper. "Three murders in five days. Only a creature with no respect for life—for *human* life—could commit these horrible, disgusting, inhuman crimes." His voice rose with outrage. "Only a monster could commit these murders. And every Bostonian knows where the monsters are: Deadtown. I say call in the military. We've got precision bombers. Burn the whole place down to the ground. Purge Boston through cleansing fire, and then start over. Let the filth of Deadtown perish, and let Boston, like a phoenix, rise from the ashes."

I leaned forward. "Can you turn that down?"

The driver scowled into the rearview mirror, his eyes narrowing under bushy salt-and-pepper eyebrows. He reached forward and reduced the volume by maybe half a decibel. The talk-radio ranter speculated on how many megatons of explosives it would take to wipe out Boston's zombie population.

"No, I meant *turn it down*. I really don't want to listen to that nutjob right now."

"Nutjob? What nutjob? The man has a point." The volume stayed where it was.

I glanced at the cabbie's license for the driver's name: Ferris Mackey. "Listen, Ferris—"

"Mack. Everybody calls me Mack."

Okay, fine. "Listen, Mack, I live in Deadtown. So I'm not all that thrilled to listen to some lunatic who wants to blow up my home and my friends, all right?"

Mack shrugged, but he switched off the radio. A couple of seconds later, his eyes returned to the rearview mirror. He studied me so intently he almost ran a red light.

"Watch the light!"

He slammed on the brakes, throwing Mab and me forward, the taxi's nose a third of the way into the intersection. He turned around in his seat to gawk at us. This time, his scowl seemed puzzled.

"So what are you, a werewolf?"

"No."

"You're not vampires."

"No, we're not."

The light changed, and the car lurched forward. "Vampires and werewolves, them I don't mind. Good tippers, usually. So are the people who've been out to the bars—real people, I mean, you know, humans. Usually the humans are so relieved to get the hell out of there, they show their appreciation with cash, know what I mean? That's why I wait for fares outside the checkpoint. But I won't let a zombie in my cab. Those things . . . they're unnatural."

I didn't want to listen to this crap for the couple of blocks we still had to go. "How about you turn your own volume down? You're as bad as the nutjob."

The salt-and-pepper eyebrows climbed his forehead. "There's a serial killer running around Boston, and she calls *me* a nutjob. Nice. Hey, I'm just telling it like it is. This city has got its problems. Political corruption. Muggings. Gangs out in Roxbury and Dorchester. But we ain't had a serial killer since, what, the sixties? Seventies?"

"The Boston Strangler was a human."

"Yeah, and he was a good, old-fashioned crazy-type killer. Him I can understand. But now all these zombies appear, and next thing you know there's this weird, ritualistic, carve-'em-up killer on the loose. Everybody knows the zombies got bloodlust. That's what happened. The bloodlust, it got to one of 'em. For humans to be safe, we gotta get rid of the zombies. Us or them." He took another look at me in the rearview mirror. "I don't believe you live in Deadtown. I saw you come out of that bar. You ladies are human, ain't you? Out looking for a little paranormal excitement. Well, take my advice—stay out of the Zone. Unless you want to end up as monster chow."

He pulled over to the curb and threw the cab into park, as if to underline his point. He stopped the meter and told me the fare. I got out and handed him exact change, down to the last quarter. He scowled as he counted the money, and I smiled sweetly. "Add shapeshifters to your list of lousy tippers." I shoved the door shut.

He shouted something, but I didn't hear him through the closed cab window. His gesture was clear enough, though. The cab peeled away from the curb, but slammed to a stop at the red light at Clarendon.

A nutjob *and* a lousy driver. I was glad to be out of his cab.

When I turned around, I didn't see Mab. She wasn't standing on the sidewalk where I expected her to be. My heart lurched. We were a block away from where the Reaper would strike, and I'd turned my back on my aunt.

"Here, child."

I tracked the sound of her voice. There she was, sitting on the steps of an elegant, four-story brick town house. I went over and sat beside her. "I liked the way you handled that bigot," she said. "Some people aren't worth arguing with."

There were a lot of those in Boston. Like Police Commissioner Hampson. You'd never convince a guy like Mack the taxi driver, because he was so totally in love with the sound of his own voice spouting off his opinions. Anything you tried to say presented a chance to spout off some more.

But I didn't really care about norms and their opinions right now. I was worried about Mab. We hadn't even made it to Back Street, and she was already sitting down to rest.

"Are you okay to go on? Be honest," I added before she could reply. "I know using the bloodstone took a lot out of you. If you're too drained, I can run and get that taxi before the light changes. He'll take you back to Deadtown."

Mab's expression showed she had no intention of listening to any more of Mack's monologue. Too late, anyway. Down the block, someone ran over from Clarendon Street, hailing the cab.

"I'm fine," Mab insisted. "And I'm not letting you proceed without backup. Your roommate seems to have forgotten us."

It was true. I looked up and down the street, but there was no sign of Juliet. I hoped she was okay. Most likely she was fine. She hadn't fed properly in days, and I could see how hunting would distract her. Vampires weren't what you'd call team players; they were survivors who put their own interests first. Juliet could easily get sidetracked and assume I'd handle my own problems. Like stopping the Reaper.

I stood, and so did Mab. She moved easily, but something haunted her eyes. How much pain was she hiding? If I asked her, she'd deny she hurt at all.

Side by side, we walked down Beacon Street to Clarendon, where we turned right, toward Storrow Drive and the river. The spot I'd marked on the map, the top point of the eihwaz rune, was a block east, just past Berkeley Street. We'd approach the site slowly, looking for places where Myrddin could be hiding, alert for any sign of the Reaper.

Back Street was deserted. To our left, past a narrow strip of grass and trees, cars zipped by on Storrow Drive, but traffic was light. To our right, Beacon Street town houses and apartment buildings showed us their backs. Grand and elegant in front, they were much plainer from this vantage point, crisscrossed with metal fire escapes. Parked cars lined the street and crowded into tight lots. We kept to the shadows, peering into the windows of garages and basements, looking for any sign that the Old Ones might be in residence. Slowly, we made our way east.

We were about to cross Berkeley Street when headlights shone down that road. Probably a car headed to the Storrow Drive on-ramps. I grabbed Mab's arm, and we ducked into a small parking lot, getting between an SUV and a car. We crouched there, peering through the SUV's windows, as the beams grew brighter. The car, a taxi, rolled slowly into view. It didn't accelerate like it was going to get on Storrow Drive. As it crossed Back Street, it drifted to the right—past the on-ramps—and hit a signpost. The overhead STORROW DRIVE EAST sign shuddered. The car halted, kissing the post, its front bumper crumpled.

A drunk taxi driver? Just what we needed stumbling onto the scene when we were trying to stop a serial killer.

I hesitated. Should we go over and make sure the occupants were okay? Find a phone and call 911?

Before I could decide, the taxi's front passenger door flew open, and a man—at least the silhouette looked like a man from where I crouched—jumped out and ran east on Back Street, away from us. Guess he wasn't going to pay a drunk driver who crashed the cab.

I started to move from our hiding place, but Mab grabbed my arm and pulled me back. "Wait," she breathed in my ear.

Across from the taxi, a garage door opened. Four figures streamed out and silently surrounded the car. One pulled open the driver's door, and then gestured in the direction of the garage. A fifth figure emerged.

Myrddin.

I pulled out my pistol, the one loaded with bronze bullets. Mab's restraining hand weighed on my arm.

The demi-demon carried a lidded jar. He held it close to his chest, one hand beneath and one on top, keeping the lid in place. He moved swiftly but carefully, gliding across the street like he didn't want to shake the jar's contents.

He'd said something about a jar—told someone he didn't need it—when he'd tried to kill me.

My God. We were witnessing another Reaper murder.

Beside me, Mab moved to stand up. About halfway to her feet, she gasped and pressed a hand to her back. She cursed softly in Welsh. She yanked out her pendant and grasped the bloodstone with her left hand, murmured some words I didn't catch, and sprang to her feet. When she hurled a blast of energy at Myrddin, it was like Zeus throwing a thunderbolt.

Myrddin didn't even turn. He clutched the jar to his chest with one hand and flung out the other toward us, palm out like a traffic cop. A pulsing rectangle of energy met the blast and held it back. Sparks skittered against it. The energy streaming from Mab's hand sputtered, then failed. Her knees buckled, and she collapsed against the car behind us.

Myrddin made a pushing motion in our direction. The shield sped toward us, accelerating as it came. "Get down!" I yelled. I ducked and curled into a ball on the ground, covering my head with my arms and trying to shelter under the SUV. The energy shield blasted into that vehicle and tossed it into the air. The SUV somersaulted over half a dozen other cars and landed on its roof.

I looked behind me, checking for Mab. She motioned that she was all right. She clasped the bloodstone, preparing for another blast.

I leapt to my feet. The hell with tossing energy around. I had a gun.

Shielding myself behind a van, I popped off three bronze bullets in fast succession. All three struck the target, hitting Myrddin once in the shoulder and twice in the back. The jar dropped from his hands, but he swooped and caught it before it hit the ground. As he moved, he changed. His human flesh split open to reveal ash-gray scales. His features twisted into glowing yellow eyes above a tusked snout. Horns shot forth from his head, leathery wings from his back. And he grew in height—ten, fourteen, eighteen feet.

On Storrow Drive, brakes screeched and metal slammed metal.

Myrddin's demon form still clutched the jar. It looked like a dollhouse toy in the thing's monstrous hands. The lid had gone askew, and taloned fingers fumbled to straighten it. I fired again, aiming for the jar, but the demon twisted and the bullet gouged its arm instead. Melting demon flesh dripped from the wound.

Protecting the jar with one hand, the Myrddin-demon pointed toward us with the other and roared. The four figures that surrounded the car simultaneously turned our way. I tried to duck out of their sight, but I wasn't quick enough. They knew where we were. A creature thumped onto the roof of the van directly in front of us. It crouched there, eyes glowing orange, drool hanging in strings from its fangs. Vampire.

One shot knocked him off the car roof. The bullet was bronze, so it wouldn't slow him down for more than a minute, but it gave me time to draw my dagger and silver-loaded gun. Another vampire landed on the roof of the car behind us, and two more figures stood between us and Back Street. With a brick wall behind us, we were surrounded.

But I still had a gun.

The second vampire sprang at us. I shot him with silver in midair. His arms and legs pinwheeled, and he hit Mab square in the chest, knocking her onto her back. The vampire, squirming with pain, crumpled in a heap on top of her. Mab stabbed him with her silver dagger and strained to push him off her, but he didn't budge. She was too weak. He reared back his head and sunk his fangs into Mab's side. I buried my dagger in his neck, half-turning as I did to face the two who rushed us from the street. I nailed the first with a dead-on head shot. He fell, and his buddy tripped over him. I tracked the fall, aiming at his head. He looked up, terror in his eyes. "Please," he said, "I'm human."

I recognized this guy—he was one of the vampire junkies who'd grabbed me in the Zone. He'd shown no mercy then, handing me over to Myrddin and the Old Ones for torture and death. Why should I show any now? My gun didn't waver.

A tremor shook the human and he vomited in the street.

Something hit me from the side, slamming me against a car

so hard my head shattered the driver's side window. Blood streamed into my eyes, blinding me. A hand grabbed my wrist and banged it, over and over, against the side of the car. Bones cracked. I dropped the gun.

A body leaned into me, pinning me against the car. Fingers tangled themselves in my hair and yanked my head forward. I blinked frantically, trying to clear the blood from my eyes. Fetid breath, rank with grave rot, washed over my face. A hand wiped my eyes, and the vampire I'd shot with bronze came into focus. He sniffed at my cheek. Fast as a snake's, his tongue flicked out to taste my blood. He pulled back, nose wrinkling. "Shapeshifter," he said with disgust. Vampires won't drink the blood of weres or shapeshifters. It makes them lose control of their physical forms, turning them into hybrids of other creatures.

The orange eyes narrowed. "I can still rip out your throat."

"Do not!" thundered a voice. The vampire's head snapped to the right. Myrddin, again in his human form, stood over the two humans sprawled on the pavement, holding his jar and looking smug. Blood stained his clothes around several bullet holes, but he held himself as though uninjured. He glanced down at the human who'd pleaded for his life, then gave the prostrate form a vicious kick. "Get up," he said. The human scrambled to his feet and scuttled behind Myrddin.

Myrddin turned back to the vampire who held me. "No throat-ripping. Not here. I want both of them in the safe house. We'll use that one to complete the reawakening spell. For this one"—he jerked his chin toward Mab—"I have other plans." The vampire snarled, but he pulled back.

I looked at Mab. The wounded vampire still pinned her down. She should have been able to lift him off and throw him across Storrow Drive into the Charles, but she struggled under him. She was so weak. I should have made her go home.

"Get me the pendant the old woman is wearing," Myrddin said. Mab's bloodstone lay on the ground by her shoulder.

The vampire holding me threw me onto the ground and pressed his foot on my neck to keep me there. I landed on something that dug painfully into my shoulder blade. Gravel pressed into my cheek. My broken wrist throbbed. The vampire bent over Mab.

My right hand was useless, and though I tried I couldn't lever his boot off me one-handed. The lump under my shoulder blade, I thought, was my gun. I groped around on the asphalt for my dagger, but I couldn't locate it.

The vampire straightened, Mab's pendant dangling from his hand. He tossed the bloodstone to Myrddin; it sailed over me, chain trailing behind it like a comet.

Mab quit struggling and lay limp on the ground.

"Excellent." Myrddin giggled behind me, where I couldn't see him. "Now I wear the bloodstone. How does it look—does it suit me?" His lips made smacking noises. "It's been a long time since I had a taste of that power. Very nice, old thing. I can even taste the old days." More smacking. "But dilute. Funny, I thought your power would be richer. I expected vintage wine, but it's more like small beer. I guess you had me fooled, old girl. Now . . ." His voice darkened. "Speaking of weakness."

The whimpered response could only be from the terrified human who cringed behind him.

"You groveled before an enemy. You begged for mercy. You are not worthy to serve your masters."

"No, I'm sorry. I'll do better. Please—" The man's words were cut off by an agonized scream. A second later the scream, too, was cut off.

"I cannot abide weaklings," Myrddin said, as casually as if he were expressing a distaste for broccoli. "Now, you, vampire. I can never remember all these ridiculous vampire names. Pull that silver out of your friend and have him help you remove the two shapeshifters." A siren sounded in the distance. "Do it quickly."

The crushing pressure on my windpipe shifted as the vampire stretched to reach the silver knives that impaled his companion. I arched my back a little, just enough to allow some space where my pistol dug in. With my left hand, I reached behind me, feeling for the gun. I touched its grip. If I could move my shoulder a little more . . .

Pain sharpened as the vampire stepped harder on my neck. "Stay still," he growled, "or I'll—"

There was a grunt. The pressure on my neck let up as the vampire toppled over. I grabbed the gun and sat up, my finger on the trigger, praying I could aim left-handed.

"Don't shoot!"

Juliet raised her hands, still holding a silver stake. On the ground beside her lay the vampire, writhing, the other stake protruding from his chest. Juliet pouted. "You started without me."

I exhaled. Then I turned the gun on the fallen vampire and shot him four times. At such close range, left-handed didn't matter. The vampire jumped and jerked and then lay still. Four silver bullets through his heart would make sure he never got up again. Already, he was disintegrating into dust.

The siren was on top of us. Flashing lights splashed the landscape as a police car pulled onto the shoulder of Storrow Drive. Cops had arrived to assist the crashed cars on Storrow Drive, but it wouldn't be long before they came over to check out Back Street.

"Where's Myrddin?" I asked Juliet. "Is he still here?"

"That fellow with the jar? Is he the wizard? He's gone. Disappeared. He moves fast for someone who's not a vampire."

"He went into the demon plane." Mab's voice issued from beneath the vampire who pinned her. I couldn't shoot this vampire with the cops right on Storrow Drive, but I yanked him off her and tossed him over a couple of cars. Mab sat up, rubbing her forehead.

She looked terrible. Worse than before, like someone had stolen my aunt and replaced her with an ailing centenarian. Drooping eyelids and puffy bags turned her eyes into slits. Age spots mottled her skin, and wrinkles creased every inch of her face. Her head shook with palsied trembling.

She touched her chest where her pendant had hung. "Myrddin took the bloodstone with him. We must get it back."

"We will. We know where to find him." At the fifth and final point to complete the rune.

"There's little time." Mab's voice was a mere croak.

More sirens were headed our way. Not a good idea to be found at a murder scene. I kicked the decomposing vampire at my feet. Let his friend take the blame. It would send human-paranormal relations back to the Dark Ages—and wouldn't the Old Ones love that? But there was nothing I could do about that now. I needed to get Mab home.

I got Mab's arm around my shoulders and helped her to her feet. She seemed a couple of inches shorter, as though she'd shrunken. She leaned heavily on my arm as we made our way out of the parking lot to Back Street. I lifted her over the body of the human who lay at the entrance. "I thought he was a vampire," I said. If I'd realized he was human, I wouldn't have shot him in the head.

The other human servant—what was left of him—lay on the pavement. Myrddin's magical attack had blasted his head from his body. Fragments of skull, teeth, and brains littered the ground and stuck to cars and trees.

The sirens were getting closer.

"Juliet," I said. "Take Mab's other arm."

"Ah, Queen Mab," Juliet said. "'Reach me thy hand, that I may help thee out.'"

"'No strength to climb without thy help,'" Mab wheezed, taking her arm.

"Now's not the time for your Shakespeare game," I snapped at Juliet. "We have to go."

"Take me to the taxi," Mab said. "I need to look inside."

The sirens sounded like they were a block away.

"Mab, there's no time."

"Don't argue with me, child. Do as I say."

Juliet and I carried her to the taxi between us.

Mab pulled open the driver's side door. A body spilled out sideways and lay half in the cab and half on the ground. I stared into the blank eyes of Mack, the taxi driver who'd wanted to bomb Deadtown out of existence. His favorite talk-show ranter shouted from the radio.

I recalled a man hailing the cab down the block from us, when I'd tried to send Mab home. Had that passenger been the

Reaper? When the taxi crashed, I'd assumed the driver was drunk. I was wrong. He wasn't drunk—he was under attack. The Reaper had done his work and run off, allowing Myrddin to trap the dead man's departing life force.

I shivered, feeling like a cold gust had blown in from the river. Juliet gasped and stepped back. The sight of human death didn't usually bother vampires, but I could see why this one might.

A crescent-shaped slash grinned across Mack's throat. Symbols had been carved into his face and hands. Blood soaked the front of his sweatshirt. Mab lifted his shirt to reveal another symbol scored deep in his chest, over his heart: the eihwaz rune.

My own chest burned.

She nodded, as though she'd seen what she'd expected, and pulled Mack's shirt back down. She straightened—as much as she could in her aged state.

I took her arm and turned to ask Juliet to take the other. She wasn't there.

She wasn't anywhere on Back Street.

Juliet's gasp. That sudden cold. A chill lingered in the air, along with the stale smell of ancient grave dust. The Old Ones had snatched Juliet away, and I hadn't even noticed.

The sirens were almost on top of us, and flashing lights splashed across the Berkeley Street intersection. I lifted Mab into my arms, ignoring the pain that gripped my wrist, and ran.

24

AT THE CHECKPOINT BACK INTO DEADTOWN, THE ZOMBIE guard eyed Mab's ID. He flicked a glance toward her face, then blinked and stared hard. He looked at the ID then back to Mab. ID, Mab. ID, Mab. He typed into his computer and squinted at the screen. He waited, tapping his fingers on his desk, until the computer beeped. He squinted at the screen again. Once more, he compared Mab's picture with her actual face. Finally, he shrugged. "You should update your photo, ma'am." His polite voice held a warning. "It will prevent future delays at the checkpoint." He handed both IDs back to me.

The photo on the card in my hand, taken yesterday, showed someone who could be the daughter of the woman at my side. With each minute that passed, Mab was aging almost visibly. A dowager's hump had sprouted between her shoulders, and her spine curved like a shepherd's crook. She clutched my arm with ropy, liver-spotted hands. She could barely walk; I picked her up again so I could carry her through the streets of Deadtown. She turned her face to my shoulder and let me.

At the door to my building, though, she insisted I put her down. "I'll walk across the lobby myself," she insisted. Even her voice had aged, to a thin, tremulous, almost-whine.

Clyde came over to assist us. "Another relative, Ms. Vaughn?" he asked, offering Mab his arm.

"No," said Mab, all dignity. "We met yesterday. I'm Vicky's aunt, Mab."

Poor Clyde nearly choked on his mortification. "I . . ." He coughed, swallowed, opened his mouth, closed it, then coughed again. "I do apologize."

Mab harrumphed and accepted his proffered arm.

"She's had a rough night," I said. "She'll be better tomorrow." I sent up a silent prayer to whatever gods might be listening that it would be so.

Mab harrumphed again. She shuffled across the lobby, leaning her whole weight on Clyde and me.

"Would you like me to accompany you upstairs?" he asked, pressing the elevator button.

"No, thank you, Clyde. We'll be fine," I said.

"Very good." When the elevator door opened, he helped Mab inside, then stepped back out into the lobby. The doors closed on his puzzled face.

"Almost home." I patted Mab's arm, hoping the gesture gave more assurance than I felt.

Mab sighed. The sound seemed to hold all the weariness of the ages. "This place, child, is very, very far from home."

IN MY APARTMENT, KANE CIRCLED MAB, SNIFFING, GIVING me inquiring looks. I told him I had to get Mab to bed, and he backed off as I helped her into my bedroom. Once she was settled under the covers, Kane came in and sat on his haunches, staring at my aunt. She lay back with her eyes closed. *There's little time,* she'd said. Right now, she looked like someone with no more than a few grains of sand left in her hourglass. Kane lifted his muzzle. His nostrils flared, as though he were trying to catch the scent of what had happened.

Two people I cared about, both so drastically altered. Tears pressed at my eyes, and I pinched myself to make them stop. I couldn't afford to cry. I had to figure out what to do.

"Myrddin stole Mab's bloodstone," I told Kane. He cocked his head, asking what exactly that meant. I wanted to know more, myself, but now wasn't the time to exhaust Mab further.

I laid a gentle hand on my aunt's arm. "Mab?" Her eyes fluttered open. They were cloudy with cataracts. "What can I do to help you? Are there herbs I can get? Roxana—the witch—should I bring her back?"

"No, child. None of that would help."

"Can you shift? Would that bring back your strength?" But even as I asked, I knew that the feeble old woman lying in my bed could never summon the energy for a shift. Mab merely shook her head.

"Well, maybe you'll feel better after you get some rest." It was the lamest thing I'd ever said in my entire life, but I couldn't admit there was nothing we could do.

"I taught you better than that, child," Mab's thin voice admonished. "Wishful thinking means nothing. Unless you can retrieve the bloodstone, I'm finished. I will continue to age until my body gives out."

"I'll get it back." But how? I didn't know where Myrddin's safe house was, and I didn't know if I could face Myrddin—and his army of Old Ones, vampires, and human servants—alone. Saying I'd get the bloodstone back felt like more wishful thinking. But I needed to try to comfort Mab. "I won't let Myrddin . . ." I couldn't finish the sentence.

"Won't let him what, child? Kill me? If only that were all he had in mind." Her rheumy eyes closed, and her voice, barely audible, trembled with weariness. "Myrddin won't kill me. He'll bring me to the very end of life, to the point where death is the only thing still desired. And then he'll use the bloodstone to imprison me, as I did to him fifteen hundred years ago."

MY HEAD SPUN WITH QUESTIONS, BUT I COULDN'T TROUBLE Mab with them now. She was sleeping; a quiet snoring buzzed from my bedroom. Sitting on the living-room sofa, I listened, cherishing those snores. Each one meant another breath.

I checked the splint I'd put on my wrist. My kind heals quickly—the pain had already diminished—but it takes time for bones to knit back together. Keeping the wrist immobile would make sure they healed properly. Right now, though, I had more to worry about than a broken wrist.

Mab said she'd imprisoned Myrddin fifteen centuries ago. Was she telling me she was—or had been—Nimuë? According to legend, Nimuë had seduced Merlin and imprisoned him in a hawthorn tree. No, a yew tree, Mab had corrected. I guess she'd know. She also said she'd had many lifetimes. That was how she knew so much about Myrddin—she'd battled him before and won. No wonder Myrddin was obsessed with revenge.

He wouldn't succeed. I'd promised my aunt I'd get the bloodstone back. And I would, somehow.

In forty-eight hours, the Reaper would claim another victim. The final point of the eihwaz rune was on the edge of Boston Common, near the Boylston Street T station. Myrddin would be there with his lidded jar. I couldn't be sure he'd have the bloodstone with him—but I could be damn sure he'd expect me. He wanted my life force for Pryce.

It would be better if I could ambush him where he *wasn't* expecting me: at the safe house. Myrddin must be there now, waiting until he could complete his ritual. It was probably where the Old Ones had taken Juliet, as well. But I didn't have the slightest idea where the safe house might be. All Juliet could tell us was that it was in the basement of a brick town house—and Boston was full of those.

Kane settled on the cushion beside me, resting his head on my thigh. Gray eyes, a man's eyes, regarded me from his wolf's face. "How can we find the safe house, Kane?"

His head lifted, ears alert, and he jumped from the sofa and ran to the front door. He turned and looked back at me expectantly. When I didn't move, he let out a frustrated yip.

"I can't take you with me." Even with Roxana's charm to

disguise him, it felt too risky to have Kane running around Boston in his wolf form. "I need you to stay with Mab."

Kane barked again, more aggressively this time.

"Stop it. We promised Clyde that no one would know you're here." Besides, I wasn't going to argue with a wolf.

Kane came back over, caught my sleeve in his teeth, and pulled. When I shook him off, he nipped my skin.

"Ow!" I rubbed the spot. No broken skin, but it stung. I glared at him.

Seeing he had my attention, he put his nose to the floor and ran around in circles, sniffing exaggeratedly. Okay, so in wolf form he was an expert tracker. But Myrddin had left the scene through the demon plane, and Kane couldn't track his scent there. I told him so, and he yipped again.

He had a point. The Old Ones who'd grabbed Juliet were vampires, not demons. They couldn't travel through the demon plane. And they had a very distinctive scent. Kane could track them, find out where they went. Even better, I could let him get Juliet's scent from an item of her clothing and he could track her specifically.

"But what about Mab?" I didn't think Myrddin would try to attack her here. He didn't need to when he had the bloodstone. But I couldn't leave her on her own, weak and ill as she was.

The phone rang, interrupting my thoughts. I snatched it up before the noise could wake Mab.

"Hello?"

It was Clyde. "Tina would like to pay you a visit?" There was a reason he phrased the statement as a question. Tina never, ever paused to let Clyde call upstairs. She always breezed past his desk, assuming (a) he'd know where she was going and (b) I'd be delighted to see her. Clyde must be questioning why she'd stopped to let him call up.

Tina's voice sounded in the background. "That's *not* how I said to say it. Give me that."

There was a squeak—from Clyde, I assumed—and then Tina came on the line. "What he was *supposed* to say was 'Tina requests your royal permission to come upstairs and return your stupid book.' I wrote it down and everything. Since, you know, you made it clear that you don't want to see me and all. I'm only doing it because I told your aunt I would."

I closed my eyes. I had an idea, one I was sure I'd regret, but I was short on both time and options. "Yes, fine, Tina. Please come up. Tell Clyde I said it's okay."

She hung up without another word.

"What do you think?" I asked Kane, who sat by the door. "Am I crazy?"

He thumped his tail on the floor and nodded. Then he nuzzled my hand.

I put Roxana's charm around Kane's neck and watched as he took on the appearance of a German shepherd. Then I opened the door to watch for Tina. The elevator dinged, and she stepped out, holding *Russom's* in both hands.

"Here," she said, thrusting it toward me. "Here's your book. I've gotta go."

I opened the door wider. "Come in, Tina. I need to ask you a favor."

Tina rolled her eyes, but she huffed past me into the living room. She dropped *Russom's* on the coffee table with a bang.

"Shh!" I said. "My aunt's asleep."

"Oh! Sorry." Tina spoke in a whisper. "But I don't see why I should do you any favors, not after you dropped me—" Her eyes widened when she saw Kane, and she forgot about whispering. "You got a dog?"

Kane growled, and I patted his head to make him stop. It was better that Tina didn't know his real identity. She wouldn't exactly be my first choice if I were looking for someone to keep a secret.

"I'm watching him for someone. Just for a few days." Or until the next full moon, I hoped.

"He's cute. What's his name?" Tina got down on her knees and scratched behind Kane's ears, burying her face in his ruff. "Are you a good doggie?" she asked in a baby-talk voice. "Are you a good boy?"

Kane growled and pulled out of her embrace. He backed away a few steps and crouched, ears back, teeth bared, looking ready to spring. I stepped between them.

"His name? Um, Killer. He's not a pet."

"A working dog, huh?" Tina sat back on her heels and leaned to see around me, looking wistfully at Kane. "I used to have a dog, when I lived with my family. Buddy. He was a crazy hound dog, but a lot of fun to play with." She climbed stiffly to her feet. "One time, Buddy got hold of my little sister's favorite teddy bear, and—" She frowned, remembering she was mad at me. "I've gotta go. Sorry, but I don't have time to do you any favors right now." She headed toward the door.

"The favor isn't for me, Tina. It's for Mab." As soon as I said it, I bit my tongue. Mab's brusqueness had intimidated Tina when they'd met. Being alone with Mab was probably the last thing Tina wanted.

She paused, one hand on the doorknob, and turned around. "Your aunt?"

"Yes. She's not well. I need someone to stay with her while I . . . uh . . . while I take Killer for a walk."

"Oh. Okay, I guess I can do that. I don't really have to go anywhere." She headed toward the kitchen. "You got anything to eat?"

"Whatever's in there, it's yours. I might be gone a couple of hours, but Mab will probably sleep until I get back."

"A couple of hours? That's a long walk. But I guess a big dog like Killer needs lots of exercise." She pulled open the freezer. "Ooh, ice cream! Chocolate—is that all you've got? No mint chocolate chip or butter pecan or anything?"

"Tina. Listen to me." I took the ice cream carton from her hands and set it on the counter, then closed the freezer door. "This is important. Until I get back, don't let anyone in the apartment. I'll tell Clyde, too."

"Sure, okay. Nobody gets in." She opened drawers until she found a spoon. "Is your aunt, like, in danger or something?" Her eyes widened. "Are there demons after her?"

If only you knew. "Not immediate danger. And no, you

won't have to fight off any demons, so stay out of my weapons cupboard." I hoped the lock was strong enough to keep Tina out if she got curious. "Like I said, my aunt isn't feeling well. I want to make sure she gets her rest."

Tina nodded. I picked up the ice cream and handed it to her.

"What did you do to your wrist?" she asked, looking at the splint.

"I broke it in a fight with a vampire."

She rolled her eyes. "Yeah, right. You probably slipped in the shower or something. You know," she said over her shoulder as she carried the ice cream into the living room, "you don't have to make up stuff to make your life seem more interesting than it really is."

"I'll keep that in mind."

Kane, waiting by the front door, bared his teeth when he saw her.

Tina sat on the sofa and grabbed the remote. She flipped to a talk show. Then she put her feet up on the coffee table and pulled off the ice cream carton's lid. "Killer wants ice cream. I'd give him some—you know, to make friends—but chocolate is bad for dogs."

Kane growled deep in his throat. I had a feeling it would be bad for Tina if I didn't get him away from her.

"Thanks, Tina. I'll be back as soon as I can." I ran into Juliet's room, grabbed one of her sweaters, and stuck it in a plastic bag. Back in the living room, I pulled on my jacket. "Come on, Killer."

When I opened the door, Kane ran out into the hallway and jumped up to press the elevator button. I hoped we'd get him through the lobby without Clyde noticing. The thought made me turn around.

"Tina, one more thing. Don't tell anyone that Killer's staying with me, okay? We're not supposed to have pets in this building."

She answered through a mouthful of chocolate. "That's two favors you owe me now. Don't think I'm not counting."

25

WE DIDN'T EVEN TRY TO HIDE KANE AS WE CROSSED THE lobby. Clyde's eyes bugged out and he turned a new shade of zombie green, but he must have seen something in my face, because he didn't say a word. He went back behind his desk and shuffled papers, pretending we weren't there.

The checkpoint presented no problems. Kane stayed low, and the guard didn't notice him. Besides, German shepherds didn't need permits. At Back Street, police had cordoned off the murder site. Portable floodlights illuminated the scene. Police cars flashed their lights, contributing an almost carnival-esque atmosphere. Uniformed cops stood at the perimeter, keeping reporters and curious citizens back. The crowd spilled into Berkeley Street. Kane and I threaded our way through the onlookers until we got to the front.

Roxana's charm held. No one shouted "Werewolf!" and ran away screaming.

I bent down and spoke quietly in Kane's ear. It twitched as he listened. "The last time I saw Juliet, we were standing by that crashed taxi. Mab was inspecting the driver's injuries, I stood beside her, and Juliet was behind us. We stood there for a minute, tops. But when I turned around to leave, Juliet was gone."

Kane nudged at the plastic bag I held. I removed Juliet's sweater and held it out to him. He sniffed at the fabric, taking his time. Then he put his nose to the ground. He moved back and forth along Berkeley Street, nudging people out of the way or scooting between their legs, trying to find the scent. It must have been hard trying to sniff out one vampire in that jumble of confusing odors.

Before long, though, Kane froze. He raised his head and yipped quietly, looking back at me.

"You got it?" I mouthed.

He nodded and lowered his head to the ground again. He broke out of the crowd and moved toward Beacon Street at a swift trot.

At the intersection, Kane turned right on Beacon. He went maybe a dozen yards and then veered toward the curb. Beside a parked car, he stopped and raised his head. He looked up and down the street, nostrils flaring, trying to catch a scent on the wind. Then he squeezed between two parked cars, stepping into the street. He walked slowly along the street side of the cars, sniffing the ground. There wasn't much traffic on the one-way street at this time of night, but I watched for cars coming from Beacon Hill.

Kane bounded across the street and paced up and down the sidewalk there. After a few minutes, he returned to where I stood. He sat and shook his head.

"So the trail disappears right here?"

He nodded. He got up on his hind legs, leaning his front paws against a car, and then looked down the street.

"Yeah, that must be what happened. They put her in some vehicle and drove off." I slumped against the parked car. Damned dead end. Now what? The Old Ones had Juliet. Myrddin had the bloodstone, and Mab was aging by the minute. Kane was stuck in wolf form, thanks to Myrddin's magic. And in forty-eight hours, someone else would die.

It was more than I could handle. Maybe I could do something to stop the Reaper—and frustrate Myrddin's plans. But I couldn't do it alone.

"I'm going to look for Daniel," I told Kane. I couldn't imagine Detective Costello would be happy to see me, the "amateur detective" who wasn't good at much besides handing over mysterious virus samples and getting in the way. But if I told him where the Reaper would strike next, he could flood the place with cops and, with luck, prevent the final murder.

And I'd be there, too, to settle things with Myrddin.

We made our way back to the crime scene. The crowd had thinned. There wasn't much to see: crime scene technicians crawling over the place, a photographer taking photos, cops standing around talking.

Standing beside the Channel 10 On-the-Scene News van was Lynne Hong, investigative reporter. Lynne had been dating Daniel since the Paranormal Appreciation Day concert. She was pretty and petite and, right now, mad as hell. I went over to talk to her.

She nodded in greeting when she saw me, then turned her annoyed gaze back to the crime scene.

"Is Daniel here?" I asked.

"Yes. Not that it's doing me any good. There's been no official statement yet, and he won't talk to me unofficially. What good is dating a cop if you can't get inside information?"

I'd gone out with Daniel a few times, and I could think of lots of good reasons to date him. "He's under a lot of stress right now—" I began.

"They're keeping all the reporters way back," she said, as if I hadn't spoken. "We couldn't even get a decent shot of the ambulance crew removing the body."

"I need to talk to Daniel. Can you point out where he is?"

"Why?" Her head whipped around, and she looked at me as though she'd only just realized I stood beside her. "Do you have information? Can give me something to follow up on?"

Her eyes shone with eagerness. A month ago, when a mysterious force was killing Deadtown's zombies, "eager" had nothing to do with Lynne Hong, who'd been slow to cover the story. Now that humans were the victims, she was all over it. I wasn't going to give her any scoops. I shook my head and walked away.

"He's over there," she called. I turned around to see where she was pointing, then waved my thanks.

As I walked in the direction Lynne had indicated, I noticed that all the police activity was on the strip of grass between Back Street and Storrow Drive. There were no cops in the place where Mab and I had been cornered by Myrddin's vampire allies. That area wasn't marked off as part of the crime scene. The vampires were gone. No bodies lay in the street. Not even the SUV Myrddin had blasted remained.

The Old Ones had done one hell of a clean-up job. And fast. But why bother?

I could think of only one reason. They must have feared the vampire, the one I didn't kill, would betray them. They'd lost their grip on Juliet, who'd run away. Maybe they worried their power was slipping.

At the crime scene's perimeter, a uniformed cop stood with his arms folded across his chest. He was young and trying to look tough. Probably not the best cop to approach, but he was closest to Daniel. I stopped in front of him, and he gave me a distinctly unfriendly look.

"I need to talk to Detective Costello."

"Who are you?" His sneer looked like he'd been taking lessons from Norden.

"My name's Vicky Vaughn. He knows me. I have some information for him."

He didn't turn around, didn't even blink. "I'm sorry, ma'am, but Detective Costello is busy right now. This is a crime scene."

"Oh, really? I thought you'd strung up all that black-and-yellow tape for a birthday party."

He still didn't blink. "If you call the department, you can make an appointment to see him tomorrow."

I could see Daniel right now, standing near the taxi, his partner beside him. They were talking to a woman who stood with her back to me. Long black hair cascaded down her back. For a second, I thought it was Juliet, but then I realized this woman was taller. It was Roxana Jade. I wondered what a witch was doing at the crime scene.

"Daniel!" I shouted, my hands cupped around my mouth. He turned, and I waved my arm over my head.

The cop standing guard pivoted to see Daniel's reaction. When he did, Kane bolted from the shadows and into the crime scene.

Daniel held up a finger, telling me to wait. He touched Roxana's arm. She turned, her eyes scanning the crowd until she saw me, and nodded. The two of them came over. Daniel's partner moved off to talk to the photographer.

"Vicky." Daniel's voice was wary. "What are you doing here?"

I decided to play the concerned citizen, not the amateur detective: Give my information to the professionals and let them handle it. I certainly wasn't going to tell him it was my second visit here tonight.

"My aunt and I plotted the murder sites on a map. We thought we recognized a pattern, and then we heard that there'd been another murder, right where the pattern indicated. I figured you'd be here, so I came to tell you."

"What pattern?" Roxana asked.

"It's a rune."

"Eihwaz." Roxana nodded. "That rune was carved—"

"Roxana." Daniel's sharp voice cut her off. He wouldn't be giving me any free information, that was clear. Suddenly, I understood Lynne's frustration. Daniel turned to me. "What do you know about this rune?"

"It represents the yew tree."

"It's a complex symbol," Roxana said. "It symbolizes both death and transcendence over death. Yew trees are planted in cemeteries throughout the British Isles. They belong to the dead, yet the trees themselves are some of the oldest living things on the planet." She traced the symbol in the air with her finger. "Death not as an ending, but as a beginning. That's how I've always thought of eihwaz."

That made a whole lot of sense. It meshed with what the

Old Ones wanted, passing through undeath into eternal life. It also expressed what Myrddin was trying to do—use the deaths of others to create a new life for Pryce.

I asked Roxana what she was doing here. Daniel gave her a sharp glance and answered for her.

"Roxana's an expert in magical symbols. She's working for us as a consultant." His tone said that she had a reason to be here—and I didn't. The implication stung. Well, I wasn't here to win Daniel's approval. I just needed to make sure he knew where the next murder would take place. "I came to tell you about the rune. But since you already know about it, you can see why the pattern is important: It predicts the next murder site. The Reaper will kill again near the Boylston Street T station, the night after tomorrow."

Daniel nodded, and I drew in a deep breath of relief.

I decided to push my luck. "I told you that I think that a wizard named Myrddin is using the Reaper to try to resuscitate Pryce Maddox."

Wary, yet interested, Daniel nodded. Since the Paranormal Appreciation Day concert, there had been an arrest warrant out for Pryce, who was wanted for using sorcery to incite terror. I knew that Daniel would love to be the one who arrested him.

"There will be some sort of facility near the murder site set up to do the ritual transfer," I continued. "It will be dark"—the Old Ones didn't like sunlight any more than vampires—"probably underground. In fact, I bet if you check the basements of these buildings, you'll find something like that here."

Daniel's expression made me suspect they were already doing just that. It made sense. They'd found an underground facility at the previous murder site. Roxana caught her breath. "There's an abandoned subway tunnel right near that T station," she exclaimed. "It runs south from Boylston under Tremont Street. An ex-boyfriend of mine—he belongs to an urban explorers' club, and they check out abandoned buildings and tunnels and such—anyway, he told me about it. You get into the old tunnel through the emergency exit at the Boylston Street station, inbound side."

Bingo. That had to be the Old Ones' headquarters. I could

have hugged Roxana. Now I'd find Kane and we'd check it out together. I started to move away.

"Vicky." Daniel's voice held a warning. "Stay away from there. I mean it."

Before I could reply, a voice shouted from the crime scene. "Get that damn dog out of here!"

I looked in the direction of the yelling. Daniel's partner flapped his arms, making shooing motions. Kane ran out from behind the taxi and into Back Street.

"Here," I shouted. "Over here!"

Kane swiveled in midstride and trotted over to where we stood. He sat down and looked at me. His tail thumped on the pavement. Roxana's charm dangled from his neck, resting against his chest.

Roxana didn't say anything. Her almost imperceptible nod told me she wouldn't give us away.

"That's your dog?" Daniel asked, surprised.

"I'm just watching him. Temporarily."

Daniel's partner came puffing over, looking furious. "You're responsible for that animal? What the hell do you think you're doing, letting it run all over a crime scene?"

"Sorry. I thought he was waiting for me over there." I gestured vaguely toward Berkeley Street. "With a serial killer in Boston, I figure I'm safer with him along."

"Give her a break, Foster," Daniel said.

Detective Foster narrowed his eyes at Kane. "What the hell kind of dog is that, anyway?"

The air around Kane shimmered. He still looked like a German shepherd to me, but someone with clairvoyant abilities might be able to see through Roxana's charm. If Foster had clairvoyance . . .

"He's a German shepherd," I said.

"Looks like a goddamn werewolf to me."

"That's ridiculous," I scoffed. "We're weeks away from the full moon."

Hand at her side, Roxana made surreptitious gestures with her fingers, strengthening the charm. "My grandparents used to breed German shepherds," she said. "This animal is a beautiful example."

Foster stared at Kane. Roxana's fingers moved faster. *Don't growl at him, Kane. Whatever you do, don't growl.* Kane's hackles rose, but he managed to swallow any growl before it escaped. He turned away from Foster, flicking out his tongue and licking my hand.

The detective grunted and looked away.

"I'll take him home."

"What the hell are you doing here, anyway?" Foster directed his glare my way. His neck veins looked ready to pop as he swiveled his head to Daniel. "And why are you consorting with a known paranormal?" He made *paranormal* sound like the equivalent of *criminal*. Talking to me could get Daniel in big trouble with Hampson.

"I was taking my dog for a walk," I said, regarding Foster levelly. "I saw the commotion here and came over to see what was happening. Then I noticed Roxana and called her over. We're, um, going shopping together next weekend and I wanted to confirm our plans."

Foster dialed back his expression from furious to annoyed. He believed me. "We've got more important things happening here than a goddamn shopping trip."

"I know. I'm going." I slapped my thigh. "Come on, Killer." We turned toward Berkeley Street.

"And that dog shouldn't be running around like that!" Foster yelled behind us. "Boston has leash laws, you know."

At that, Kane did growl, but we were already leaving. If Foster heard, he didn't give any indication.

Even under the cloak of Roxana's diminution charm, Kane looked sleek and powerful. He moved with graceful strides, muscles rippling, each step strong and sure. Just try putting a leash on that.

26

KANE AND I HURRIED THROUGH THE STREETS OF BOSTON, trying to get to the Boylston Street T station before it closed for the night. As soon as we were out of sight of the crime scene, we broke into a jog, staying on Berkeley until we turned left on Boylston. We made one stop, at an all-night convenience store where I paid an exorbitant price for a portable flashlight. It was a rip-off, but I figured a flashlight was the must-have accessory for exploring abandoned subway tunnels. Well, that and a fistful of weapons, but I was already armed. A couple more blocks and we were there.

The entrances to the Boylston Street T station are housed in two small, narrow concrete buildings—one for the inbound track and one for the outbound—on the edge of Boston Common. Roxana said her ex had explored the old tunnel from the inbound station, so that's where I headed. I pulled open the glass door and trotted down the stairs. The warm scent of the subway, exhaust and oil and urine, puffed up to meet me. Kane glided down the staircase beside me, silent as a shadow, keeping close to the wall. Near the bottom, he waited, crouching. I went over to talk to the attendant, who sat by the entry gates in a folding chair. He wore a tweed cap with his MBTA uniform and looked to be in his sixties.

"What time is the last train?" I asked, positioning myself between him and the stairs.

He checked his watch. I didn't turn around, but I could feel Kane dash from the staircase.

"Should be through in about five, six minutes," said the attendant. I thanked him and bought a ticket from the machine. I fed the ticket into the fare gate and passed through to the platform.

"Have a nice night," the attendant said.

"You, too."

"I will soon as I get home." He grinned, displaying a gold tooth.

The narrow platform faced the tracks, where the train would arrive. At the back of the platform was a display of some old trolley cars, from when the T was called the Boston Light Railway. I pretended to be interested in them. The trolley in front of me was orange and cream, a bit dented and old-fashioned but not all that different from a modern subway car. The old trolleys sat on tracks that disappeared into a tunnel that ran behind the wall, curving out of sight. Was that the abandoned tunnel? I didn't see any other candidates.

A fence separated the platform from the trolley display. It would be easy enough to climb except for one thing: The station attendant was watching me.

I turned my back on the old trolleys, strolled to the edge of the platform, and peered down the tunnel, like I was impatient for the train to arrive. I glanced at the attendant. He still watched me—there wasn't much else to look at this time of night. I smiled. He smiled back, his gold tooth catching the light. I put my hands behind my back and rocked impatiently on the balls of my feet.

A rush of warm air ruffled my hair, and I heard a distant rumble. The breeze got stronger as the train approached. A few seconds later, I could see its headlight. I walked down the platform, away from the entry, like I wanted to get on the train near the driver.

The attendant stood and folded his chair. As soon as his back was to me, I vaulted the fence and scrambled behind one of the old trolley cars. The last train rolled into the station, brakes screaming, and slowed to a halt. I heard the doors slide open and footsteps cross the platform. Warning bells bonged, and the doors slid closed. The train revved, then pulled away from the station. I waited, rubbing my right wrist. Even with the splint, I'd hurt it again climbing over the fence. A shapeshifter can heal a broken bone within a day or two, but not if I kept reinjuring it. I needed to be more careful.

Within two minutes the station was silent. I crept along between the antique trolley cars and the wall, until I stepped into the tunnel beyond the display. The tunnel curved to the left; a triangular head poked around a corner on the right. Kane was waiting for me. He stood in a narrow corridor that led back into the station, coming out behind the stairs. Roxana had said part of the tunnel served as an emergency exit; Kane had discovered the easy way in.

As we moved farther into the tunnel, I pulled out a silver knife and held it ready in my left hand, my fingers tight on the grip.

The tunnel was a narrow, arched passageway, just big enough for a trolley to clear the walls. Lights, spaced every twenty feet or so, cast a yellow glow over the concrete. The old track was still embedded in the floor, but the place was swept clean. Nothing about the tunnel suggested a hidden lair for the ancient undead. It looked like what it was: a clean, well-maintained emergency exit.

Even so, I got that squeezed-in feeling, the weight of the walls and ceiling pressing on me. It wasn't as bad as crawling into Deadtown the back way or being stuck deep in a pitch-black slate mine, but the constant pressure made me crave air and space.

Focus, Vicky. Watch for the bad guys. I shook off the claustrophobia as best I could, took a deep breath that wasn't deep enough, and moved forward.

Kane went first, and I was happy to let him lead, with his sensitive nose and keen hearing. He'd be able to smell trouble before it leapt out snarling at us.

Regularly spaced, arched indentations appeared along the walls. The indentations were both narrow and shallow, no more than a foot deep. Perfect for a worker to squeeze into when a trolley passed, but lousy for hiding. Good. The fewer hiding places here, the better.

When the curve straightened out, I could see a long way down the lighted tunnel. There was nothing that looked like a hiding place for the Old Ones.

We went swiftly but cautiously through the tunnel. After a few minutes, we came to some stairs leading upward. It was the emergency exit, heading toward street level and safety. Beyond it, the tunnel stretched into darkness.

The walls crowded in a thousand times more closely.

I glanced up the brightly lit staircase, then squinted into the dark tunnel. Kane was already so deep into the shadows that I couldn't see him. I took the flashlight from my pocket and flipped it on. I pointed the beam straight down at the floor, trying to keep the light as unobtrusive as possible.

A paw appeared in the circle of light at my feet, and then Kane ducked his head into the beam and gazed up at me. I'd never thought of wolves raising their eyebrows, but that was his expression. And I knew what he was thinking: that I could wait here, in the light, as he checked out the tunnel and reported back.

"No," I whispered, "we stay together. I'm fine." Kane could probably hear my heartbeat from where he stood, a riotous thumping that sounded anything but fine. "Give me a second." Okay, so the lights stopped at the emergency exit. I had a working flashlight. And even if it failed, I wasn't alone. Kane was here. His eyes shone with intelligence and loyalty, telling me I could rely on him.

I willed my heart to calm down. When it slowed to something like its normal rhythm, we stepped past the emergency exit staircase, beyond the light. Kane continued in the lead, and I stayed close behind him. The narrow tunnel's walls and low, curved ceiling pressed more heavily with the weight of the darkness, and each breath required conscious effort. *In, out. In, out. Don't forget to breathe.*

It was slow going. Like the lights, the tidily swept floor ended at the exit, and I had to watch carefully so I didn't trip on the tracks or the debris that covered them in this part of the tunnel. Every few feet, Kane would pause and look up, his ears straining forward, his nostrils working to sift through the scents ahead. Then he'd put his nose back to the ground and keep going.

I couldn't smell anything besides mold and the old dust that covered every surface. But that was the scent of the Old Ones, that deep, underground scent of ancient decay. I stayed on edge, unable to tell whether I was smelling an old, empty tunnel or a black-robed, fanged monstrosity about to attack.

Yet nothing did attack. We reached the end of the tunnel without finding any sign of the Old Ones. At the far end, a huge pile of cans, ranging in size from soup cans to ten-gallon barrels, was heaped up against the wall almost to the ceiling. It looked like debris from a landslide. I shone my flashlight on a label. Pear halves. Judging from the dusty, peeling condition of the label and the rust that marked the seams of the can, it was decades old. There were cans of other fruits and vegetables, crackers and biscuits, and drums marked POTABLE WATER. I didn't think it would be all that potable now.

Homeless settlement? Fallout shelter? Whatever this tunnel had become after it was closed, these supplies had long outlasted whoever had carried them in. I sheathed my knife. The Old Ones weren't here.

As we backtracked to the emergency exit, the pressure lessened. We were on our way out.

By the exit, I turned off the flashlight, happy to stand again in the lights of the emergency exit. I set my foot on the first step, but Kane leapt up in front of me and blocked my way.

"What?" Fresh air and open sky were calling me, and I was eager to say hello.

He jumped down the stairs in a bound and pulled at the back of my sweater.

Reluctantly, I stepped back into the tunnel and turned around. "Why can't we go? Did you spot something?"

He stared at the tracks. I did, too, looking for a secret switch or something that might open a hidden door, like the door to Axel's guest room. I didn't see anything like that, but after a minute I realized what Kane was trying to tell me. There was only one set of tracks.

"This tunnel has room for just one train. There must be an old track on the outbound side, too." Kane yipped and ran along the lighted tunnel. After a longing glance up the stairs, I followed him.

Since Boylston Street Station was closed, we could hunt for the other tunnel without anyone bothering us. I was glad the station attendant hadn't turned out the lights when he went home. The platform was deserted. We walked along the tracks a little way, then crossed to the outbound side. At the end of the platform, we squeezed around a gate and into another disused tunnel. No lights here. I pulled my knife again, shone my flashlight straight down to the floor at my feet. A little ways into the tunnel was a door marked PUMP ROOM. Cautiously, I tried the handle. It was locked. Kane spent a long time sniffing around the edges of the door, but eventually he continued down the tunnel. Although we followed the tracks to the end, we found nothing else besides dust and scattered debris.

No Old Ones here, either.

We crossed back to the inbound platform and followed the route to the emergency exit. This time, we took the stairs to the street-level door. When I pushed it open, an alarm sounded at the same moment the cool night air hit my face. It took only a second to get my bearings—we were on Tremont Street near the Wang Theatre—and move quickly away from the clanging exit toward Deadtown.

"Just to make sure," I said to Kane as we walked. "You didn't scent Juliet in there, did you?"

He shook his head.

"Myrddin?"

Another shake.

"What about the Old Ones?"

He stopped and sat on the pavement. He reared up and lifted his shoulders in a canine approximation of a shrug.

"Not sure, huh?" I could understand that. The entire subway system smelled like an age-old tomb.

Kane nodded, and we continued our progress toward Deadtown.

Although the night was chilly, the breeze blowing from the Common felt warm, carrying smells of spring, of damp earth and life stirring. I inhaled deeply, savoring the sweetness that cut through the usual city smells. It was a good antidote for the dust that clogged my lungs.

The tunnel had been the perfect location for the Old Ones' base—near the final point on the rune, deep underground, old and dusty enough to feel like home to a bunch of creatures that should've been corpses centuries ago. But there'd been nothing. It was hard not to feel discouraged. Juliet was still missing, Pryce was one victim away from coming back to life, and Mab's life-giving bloodstone was still in Myrddin's clutches.

We did have one advantage, though. Myrddin wanted my life force to revive Pryce. If I showed up at Boylston Street at the appointed time, Myrddin would be waiting for me.

A guaranteed date with a crazy wizard who wanted me dead—some advantage. But it was my best chance to defeat Myrddin and save my aunt.

27

BACK AT MY APARTMENT, TINA WASN'T IN THE LIVING ROOM. The TV was off, and the empty ice cream container sat on the coffee table. A trail of candy wrappers led down the hallway toward my bedroom. Tina's laugh, never what you'd call subtle, boomed from that direction.

I threw my jacket on the sofa. What the hell was Tina thinking? One thing I had asked of her. One. Let Mab rest. And there she was, in the bedroom, bothering my aunt. As I stormed down the hallway, Kane slunk off in the other direction, into the kitchen. I couldn't say whether he was avoiding my scowl or Tina's "nice doggie" routine. Either way, I couldn't blame him.

Outside my bedroom, I paused to take three deep breaths. Calm. I had to stay calm and reasonable for my aunt's sake. No point in upsetting Mab because I was annoyed with Tina. One more deep breath and I stepped through the doorway.

Tina sat on the edge of my bed, one leg tucked under her, facing Mab, who sat propped up against the pillows. I flung a peeved glance at Tina. "How about you let me talk to my aunt?"

Tina stood up slowly and stretched like a cat. Well, stiffer than that—a zombie cat. I had to squeeze past her to get near Mab.

My aunt didn't look any better. A little more rested, maybe, but so old and ill. Her hands, folded on top of the sheet, were rough and crisscrossed with veins. Those hands had always been so strong, able to deal any problem, from treating scrapes and bruises to fighting off Hellions. Now they were frail and trembling. It was hard to imagine them lifting a cup of tea.

I sat where Tina had been and patted Mab's hands. They were cold. "How are you feeling? Are you warm enough?"

"Don't talk to me as though I'm an invalid, child." Coming from Mab, the quavering voice still managed to sound sharp.

Behind me, Tina brayed a laugh. I turned around to tell her off at the same time Mab said, "Be respectful, young lady."

"Sorry," Tina mumbled at the floor.

"Wait for me in the living room," I said, pointing. "I'll be there in a minute. I want to speak to you before you go."

Tina gave a sulky nod and stepped into the hall. But she turned around immediately. "It was nice talking with you," she said to Mab.

Mab nodded regally.

"And . . . you won't forget?"

"I'll not forget. But you have some things to remember as well, do you not?"

Tina's eyes flicked to me, then away. She bit her lip and nodded. Then she turned and fled down the hall.

"That young lady—" Mab began.

"I'm sorry she was in here bothering you. But I don't want to talk about Tina right now. I want to talk about you." I caught her hands and held them between mine, warming them.

"I'm as well as can be expected under the circumstances. Rest did help. But unless the bloodstone is returned to me, I shall continue to age at an accelerated rate." She spoke matter-of-factly, as if commenting on the weather. But that was Mab.

No matter how bad the situation, she always cut through emotional distractions to focus on the practical. "So tell me, child, what have you learned?"

"We didn't find the bloodstone."

"I assumed as much. If you had, I'd have felt it."

I briefed her on what Kane and I had learned. Since that was virtually nothing, it didn't take long. But as I spoke, I had an idea. "Can you use your connection with the bloodstone to locate the safe house?"

Mab shook her head. "Myrddin has cloaked it. Its whereabouts are as much a mystery to me as they are to you."

"How can we get it back?"

"I'm not happy with your plan to put yourself at risk to draw Myrddin out. Let's be up front about that. But I can't see any alternative. Myrddin intends, I believe, to pour your life force into Pryce and then shut me away forever, suffering from the knowledge of your fate." Her cloudy eyes looked down at our joined hands. "So there's one piece of good news, at least."

I attempted a smile. "I think your definition of 'good news' must be different from mine."

"We've time to plan, child. My body is giving out, but my mind is keen. Now, let me think, and then we'll discuss strategy." She drew her hands away. Three quick pats on my arm let me know I was dismissed.

The bed shifted as I stood. When I was at the doorway Mab said, eyes still closed, "By the way, I told Tina you'd most likely let her keep *Russom's* a bit longer."

"You did? Why?"

"She's adequate on her overview of the *Inimicus* genus but needs to spend more time on the characteristics of individual species. If the child wishes to study demonology on her own time, surely you can allow her to borrow a text that would otherwise only gather dust on your bookshelf."

I opened my mouth to respond, then decided not to bother. I wasn't going to argue with Mab about anything right now, least of all Tina. And really, I thought as I pulled the door shut, Mab was right. What harm could it do to let Tina keep *Russom's*? As long as she understood that borrowing the book didn't mean she was still my apprentice, I had no problem with it.

Something looked different as I walked down the hallway back to the living room. As soon as I saw Tina holding a trash bag, I realized what it was.

"You're cleaning up." The words sounded strange, directed as they were at Tina.

"Yeah. Your aunt said I should. She was all about how an orderly environment is important."

That did sound like Mab. If she could get Tina to pick up after herself, she was stronger than I was, even in her weakened state.

I put out my hand for the bag. "Here, give me that. I'll take care of it."

Tina handed it over, her eyes thoughtful. "What's wrong with your aunt? The last time I saw her, she didn't look so . . . I mean, I knew she was old and all. That's how she got all that awesome demon-fighting experience. But she didn't look *old* old. How sick is she?"

"She'll be better in a couple of days." I'd make sure of that.

"Whew, that's good. 'Cause I thought she looked like . . . I don't know, like she was about to die any minute or something. She didn't sound that way, though. Um . . ." Tina ground the toe of her boot into the carpet. "Did she say anything about me?"

"Right now, Mab and I have other things to talk about."

"Oh. Sure. I guess you do. I mean, she's visiting from another country and all." Tina picked up a discarded pizza box. I held open the trash bag, and she dropped it in. "Well, I guess I'd better get home. I have to clean my room—that whole orderly environment thing."

Making Tina's home environment orderly would probably require a bulldozer and a hazmat team, but if the kid wanted to clean her room, good. It would keep her out of trouble for a month or two.

"Where's Killer?" she asked, looking around. "I want to say good-bye to him."

I made a point of not looking toward the kitchen. "Probably sleeping. We took a long walk."

"Oh. Well, rub his tummy for me, okay?"

Heat rose in my face as my color turned beet-red. Any tummy-rubbing I gave Kane would have to wait until things were back to normal. And it would not be on Tina's behalf.

Tina headed for the front door. I picked up *Russom's* from where it lay on the coffee table. "Wait a second," I said. "Mab did mention you. She said you needed to work harder on the individual species of the *Inimicus* genus."

"That's what she told me, too."

"So I guess you can hang on to my copy of *Russom's* a little longer. I'm not using it right now."

She grinned and reached for the book.

"But," I added, pulling back slightly, "we need to be clear on one thing. I'm still not taking you back as an apprentice. You do understand that, right?"

Tina nodded, her eyes on *Russom's* like it was a container of butter-pecan ice cream and not some dry old textbook about demons. "Yeah, sure. I understand. I just want to, you know, brush up." I let her take the book, and she hugged it to her chest. "If you need somebody to stay with your aunt again, give me a call, okay?" She let herself out.

Wow. Tina offering to do somebody a favor. I stood and stared at the closed door like maybe another miracle would happen. I could use one right about now.

I WENT TO BED BEFORE DAWN, BUT FOR A LONG TIME I LAY on my back on the sofa, unable to sleep. When I did drift off, I found myself in my usual dreamscape, an endless space of soft twilight. Sort of how I imagined it would feel to float in a warm ocean at midnight. Empty and restful.

Something stirred in the darkness, a small pulse in the air like a soft sigh. It pulsed again. As I watched, it took on form and color, becoming a small pink cloud. The cloud hiccupped and grew a little larger. Sky blue streaks swirled up among the pink.

I peered through the colors to see a young face peering back at me.

"Hi, Maria."

"Yes! I did it!" She pumped her fist. "I called you." My niece stood in the middle of a vast, colorless dreamscape, like an actor on an empty stage.

"You certainly did. But isn't it a school night?"

"Nope. Tomorrow's an in-service day. That means the teachers have to go to school, but the kids stay home." She did a little happy dance. "I really called you! It wasn't too hard, either."

"It gets even easier with practice. For example, you can fill in your dreamscape with whatever scenery you want. You can make it look like you're in your bedroom at home, or you can make it look like you're a princess sitting on a throne in a big castle."

"Princess stuff is for little kids."

"Well, whatever you want."

"Can you show me how?"

"Sure. Start by closing your eyes."

"My eyes are already closed. I'm sleeping."

"Inside your dream. When you're getting started, imagining is easier with your eyes closed."

She screwed her eyes tightly shut.

"Relax a little. Believe it or not, the harder you try, the more difficult it gets."

Her face smoothed out as she let some of the tension go.

"Good. Now, think of somewhere you'd like to be. Somewhere fun."

"The beach." Each summer, the Santinis spent a week's vacation on Cape Cod.

"Good choice. Now, imagine you're there. Feel the sand under your toes, the warm sun on your back. What do you hear?"

"Seagulls. And the waves coming into the shore." She turned her head a little and sniffed. "Vicky! I can smell the salt water!"

"Perfect. Hold all that in your mind." As she did, a seascape sketched itself around her. Colors and shapes filled in—a beach umbrella, a plastic bucket, a sandcastle decorated with shells. "Ready? Open your eyes."

She did, and her eyes went wide with amazement. Her pajamas had changed to a bright pink bathing suit, and pink-framed sunglasses perched on top of her head. She spun around, laughing, and ran to splash in the water. "It's cold!" she shouted. "Just like at the Cape!"

"You can warm it up if you want. It's your dream."

"Really?" She closed her eyes again. Then she opened them and threw herself into the water. She dived into the waves, arcing through them like a porpoise. Briefly, a gleaming porpoise superimposed itself on her as she swam. I saw both Maria and the animal she'd be if she shifted right now.

Interesting. Maria's shapeshifting abilities might be developing faster than we'd realized.

But when she ran back up the beach, water streaming from her hair, she was all Maria, an eleven-year-old girl having fun. She looked around for a towel, but there wasn't one. She closed her eyes, and a towel patterned with seahorses draped itself around her shoulders.

"That's what your mom and I were talking about when we said you're in charge of your dreams. Eventually, you won't even have to close your eyes to make things happen."

"Cool!" She sat down on the sand and tipped her head back to look at the clear blue sky. "Thanks for teaching me, Aunt Vicky."

"I think that was a pretty good first lesson. Now we should both get some real sleep."

Maria drew lines in the sand with her finger. Studying them, she asked, "What did Mom tell you about my great-aunt? When she made me go outside."

One thing Gwen was right about—Maria shouldn't hear that story. I did my best to answer without answering. "Your mom is a good person. Aunt Mab is a good person. But there's a misunderstanding between them that probably can't be fixed. It's sad, but sometimes things happen that way."

"If it's a misunderstanding, can't you talk to Mom?"

"I don't think it would help. Not after all this time."

"Aunt Mab's colors were so pretty. And she wanted to help you. I don't believe she'd do anything bad."

"She didn't. But you still have to obey your mom. When she says that she and I are the only people you can talk to on the dream phone, you listen." In her current condition, I didn't think Mab had the strength to use the dream phone, and I didn't want Maria trying to call her.

"Okay. But maybe Mom will change her mind."

Not on this issue. Not unless she could travel back in time and turn around at the right moment, to see what Mab had saved her from.

"Now I'm going to show you how to hang up the dream phone. You know what you did to call me?"

"I thought about your colors."

"Do that again." She immediately closed her eyes. "In your mind, make them rise up so it looks like I'm standing in the fog." As she concentrated, her own colors rose up around her where she sat in the sand. They swirled around her waist, then her shoulders. When the pink and blue tendrils of mist touched her face, I said softly, "Good night, Maria."

My dreamscape returned to its empty, dim twilight. I heard the faint cry of a seagull, and then Maria's voice, like an echo from far away, bidding me good night.

28

WHEN I WOKE, IT WAS LATE AFTERNOON. I REMOVED THE splint from my wrist and moved my hand. It was a little weak, but it felt fine. I crept down the hall to check on Mab, who slept. I couldn't see her in the darkened room, and I didn't want to wake her by turning on the light, but I listened to her breathing for a while. Slow and even, punctuated from time to time by a tiny snore. No wheezing or struggling for air. Mab was hanging on. It was the best I could hope for right now.

I pulled the bedroom door shut and went back down the hall. I brewed a pot of coffee and turned on the TV to see what the press was saying about the Reaper murders. Mostly, it was what you'd expect: shots of the latest murder site, a profile of the victim (Mack had been in his fifties, unmarried, and a member of Humans First), and a summary of the other murders. CNN aired an interview with a motorist who'd been traveling on Storrow Drive and claimed to see a "monster" through the trees at the time of the murder.

"The thing was about fifty feet tall," he said, stretching a hand way above his head. "It looked like the devil, with horns and everything. Like a monster out of a nightmare."

Kane jumped up on the sofa beside me and growled at the screen.

"It was Myrddin," I said. "I shot him, and his injuries made him change into his demon form." The demon had been closer to twenty feet tall than fifty, but otherwise the witness gave a pretty good description.

But the problem was his use of the word "monster," and not just because Kane found it politically incorrect. A press conference held by Police Commissioner Hampson came on.

Hampson stood at a podium, tugging at his necktie and reading from a prepared statement. "For the next forty-eight hours, an emergency containment order will be in effect on all paranormals throughout Massachusetts."

Kane and I gaped at each other. A containment order meant that all residents of Deadtown had to be present and accounted for within its borders by sundown on the day of issue. And they had to stay in Deadtown until the order expired.

"In addition," Hampson went on, "a curfew will be enforced on Designated Area 1 during that time. All residents of that designated area must be off the streets between ten p.m. and four a.m. during the period of the containment order. The Joint Human-Paranormal Task Force will conduct random compliance checks."

Hampson's curfew covered the times the murders had been committed, but slapping a curfew on Deadtown in the middle of the night was like shutting down the norms' business district between eight and five on a weekday. Hampson had put all of Deadtown under house arrest, sending out the Goon Squad to knock on people's doors and make sure they stayed home.

The containment order would make it harder, but not impossible, to get myself into position at Boylston Street tomorrow night. It would mean sneaking out again. Myrddin wanted my life force to complete his ritual, but he'd make do with that of some random victim if I wasn't around. And I wouldn't let that happen.

Kane paced the length of the living room, growling, and I realized that Hampson's containment order was a bigger problem for him. He couldn't be accounted for, not without revealing that he was stuck in wolf form. The very idea that a werewolf could change when the moon wasn't full would send the norms into a panic. I could already hear the speeches calling for a mass werewolf internment, permanently restricting the entire species to the secure retreats.

"Kane," I said. He paused in his pacing and looked at me. "The night you and Mab rescued me—did you go through the checkpoints when you left Deadtown?"

He nodded.

"And then we sneaked back in. That means there's no record of your reentry. So as far as the authorities know, you're still outside Deadtown." That didn't matter for the containment order—not if he was thought to be in Massachusetts. All paranormals would have to report to one of the state's designated areas: Deadtown, a werewolf retreat, or one of the smaller paranormal-only sections in cities like Worcester and Springfield. If another murder happened, any "monster" who wasn't accounted for would be a suspect.

But maybe we could convince them he was out of state.

I dialed the number for 24-Hour Copy.

"Vicky," Carlos said, when he came on the line, "don't tell me you need another ID already. I'm going to have to start offering you a volume discount."

"Nope, I've still got the last card you made for me. But I thought maybe you could help me with another little problem."

He chuckled. "Your 'little problems' are usually big news for my bank account. What's up?"

"You've heard about the containment order?" He had. "I need to come up with evidence that someone left the state a couple of days ago."

"And stays out of state for at least the next forty-eight hours. Gotcha. Where?"

"D.C." Kane had rented an apartment there when he'd been working full-time on his Supreme Court case. The lease hadn't yet expired. I explained as much as I could without telling Carlos that Kane was currently a wolf.

But Carlos was never one to ask for inconvenient details. "Here's what I can do," he said. "I'll call a norm I know who might be willing to take a quick trip to D.C. on Kane's ID. All expenses paid, of course." Of course. "Guy I have in mind has the right height and build. Just needs to dye his hair. I can . . . Let me see, what time is it? Less than two hours to sunset. Damn, girl, you're not giving me much time. Okay, if my guy can make the trip, he'll drive down as himself—you know, as a human—some time tonight." The states didn't keep records of the humans who crossed their borders, only paranormals. "I'll get busy with the state databases to add a few records showing that Kane drove down . . . you said a couple of days ago. When, exactly?"

"Make it Monday morning."

"Monday morning. Let me write that down." He paused, and I pictured him searching for a pencil and paper on his cluttered desk. "Okay. Get me the key to Kane's apartment so I can pass it on. I won't get the fake ID done in time, but I'll email the file to an associate of mine in Washington, along with the number of a credit card in Kane's name. The credit card will already have some charges on it—groceries, meals, that sort of thing. When the new 'Mr. Kane' gets into town, he can pick up the cards at my associate's establishment. He buys some more dinners on the credit card, flashes his ID a few places, and—ta da!—plenty of evidence he was outside of Massachusetts during the containment order."

The whole scheme hinged on the availability of Carlos's norm friend, so he said he'd call back to confirm. I explained the plan to Kane, and by the time I finished, Carlos had called back to say everything was a go. I managed not to faint when he told me how much it would cost, not including expenses.

Kane would be accounted for, that was the important thing. Besides, he was paying.

Next I called Daniel. "What's Hampson thinking with this containment order?"

"What do you expect, Vicky?" He sounded both exhausted

and exasperated. "There's no secret lair in the abandoned subway tunnel—we checked." No surprise that Daniel hadn't found anything, either. "Hampson was furious about time we wasted on that dead end. I told him about Morfran possession and how it pointed to a human killer. Roxana showed him the rune and how it fit the pattern of murder sites. He blew it all off. Called it 'mumbo jumbo' and fired Roxana as a consultant."

"So he locks down Deadtown?" It was the stupidest response possible.

"What else would he do? He won't listen to me. He's convinced the murderer is from there. The motorist who said he saw a 'monster,' the mutilation of the bodies, even the fact that a variant of the damn plague virus has appeared in the wild—in his mind, it all adds up to a paranormal killer."

"Is the lab still under quarantine?"

"Yes, until the end of the week. But no symptoms yet. Feels like the only piece of good news I've had all year."

What a mess I'd made for Daniel—the virus sample, a German shepherd in his crime site, information that did nothing but infuriate his boss. But the information was important, and I needed Daniel to act on it. Lives depended on it.

"Daniel, you know that rune pattern is valid. Tomorrow night, the Reaper will be looking for a victim somewhere near the Boylston Street T station. No matter what Hampson thinks."

"I know. I'll do what I can, but Hampson has directed nearly all our resources to patrolling the perimeter of Deadtown. He's even convinced Governor Sugden to call in the National Guard."

"Are you serious?"

"Dead serious. Hampson argued that the zombies are likely to riot. Apparently, after that protest march got out of hand, the governor agreed with him."

Wow. Sugden, whose own daughter was a zombie, was usually a friend to the paranormals. Now he'd ordered the tightest lockdown since the plague. And all because some zombies pushed past the first checkpoint to have a beer in the Zone?

Nothing had gotten out of hand; they hadn't even tried to march into the human part of Boston.

Hampson had to be feeling a lot of pressure from his Humans First buddies to use these murders to advance the cause. But his focus on Deadtown was ridiculously shortsighted. "So while the cops and the National Guard tighten the noose around Deadtown," I said, "the Reaper will get on with his work behind their backs."

"Like I said, I'll do what I can." Tension strained his voice. "And Vicky, I'm not kidding. I know what you're like—stay away from this. Don't try to sneak out of Deadtown. Don't try to catch this guy yourself. Let the police handle it." He hung up, making sure he got the final word.

Let the police handle it. Those same police who'd be playing ring-around-the-rosie around Deadtown? Somehow, I didn't think so.

I WAS OUT FOR HALF AN HOUR GETTING THE KEYS FOR Kane's D.C. place and delivering them to Carlos. When I got home, I heard Mab moving around in the bedroom and went to see how she was doing. I knocked on the door and pushed it open. The creature who sat on the edge of the bed barely resembled my aunt. She looked like a wizened gnome, or one of those preserved bodies that archeologists dug up from peat bogs. Her gray hair had thinned; I could see her scalp through it. Her feet dangled over the side of my bed, not touching the floor.

"I'm afraid I need some help getting to the lavatory."

I lifted her to her feet. Mab was normally a couple of inches taller than my five foot six, but she'd shrunken so much she barely came up to my shoulder. Although she leaned heavily against me as we crossed the hall to the bathroom, I barely felt her weight.

When I returned her to bed, she patted the mattress. "Sit, child."

"Can I get you anything first? A cup of tea?"

"I'm past any need or desire for nourishment." She patted

the bed again. "Come, sit close. I can barely see you. Give me your hand, child."

I sat and took her hand. Mab had said that, without the bloodstone, her body would rapidly catch up with her true age. But she looked older than any living person I'd ever seen. "Mab, how old are you?"

"In this lifetime? A shade over three hundred years." Most of the Cerddorion lived human-length lifespans, but Mab had told me once that some of our kind live much longer. And with the bloodstone, perhaps she'd pushed the limit even further. "You probably think I'm no different from the Old Ones, trying to live forever. It's not that, child. I've had to hold on; I've waited so long for my successor." She gave my hand a squeeze. "There have been many apprentices over the years, many fine demon fighters. But always I waited for Victory."

This speech sounded way too much like she was getting ready to say good-bye, to pass her demon-fighting mantle to me. Gently, I released her hand. "I'm not ready to be your successor."

"Not yet, it's true. There is much you need to learn, and I still hope to be the one to teach you. I haven't given up, child. Not when there's a chance we can retrieve the bloodstone." That was good to hear. It sounded more like the Mab I knew. "Still, when one looks back over the past, there are things one feels the need to explain."

I thought about the twenty-year-old misunderstanding between her and Gwen, who'd never accept any explanation other than what she'd seen with her own horrified eyes. But nothing like that stood between Mab and me.

"You don't have to explain anything to me."

"Yes, I do. I want you to understand what's behind my feud with Myrddin."

I hadn't wanted to tire Mab out with my questions about that. But now she wanted to talk. "Were you Nimuë?"

She shook her head. "Nimuë was my sister." Her face looked sadder than I'd ever seen it. "Myrddin killed her."

For a long moment, neither of us said anything. Mab's

murky eyes went distant, and she held out a hand, as though reaching across time. I folded my hand around hers, and she turned to me.

"What happened, Mab?"

"In that lifetime, I was Viviane."

"The Lady of the Lake." I recalled the white-sleeved arm that rose from my dream-lake to hand me the bloodstone. Mab had taken that form in my dreamscape.

She nodded. "It was all so long ago. Several lifetimes, and my lives are long. I was a demon fighter and priestess of Ceridwen. Not much different from how you know me, although I was much, much younger." Her voice softened. "So very young. I was eighteen, Nimuë was all of sixteen. We'd heard rumors of a handsome, mysterious man who lived in the woods. Being silly girls, we went to find him. We wanted an adventure, but there was no challenge to it. Myrddin meant for us to find him." She glanced at me sidelong. "And handsome he was indeed. His teeth were better then."

I could believe that. A millennium or two without dental care would take its toll.

"Myrddin charmed us. He flattered and entertained us. And he tried to seduce me. You see, what he really wanted was a son." Demi-demons have a very low rate of reproduction—most of their females are barren, and when they do manage to conceive and carry to term, the death rate for infants is high. Myrddin must have felt he'd have a better chance of success with a Cerddorion female.

"I resisted. I was a shapeshifter and a demonslayer; I didn't want to risk having a child. He tried to ensnare me with magic, but I could feel the tendrils of his spell. I refused to see him anymore. I forbade Nimuë from going anywhere near him." She sighed deeply. "But my sister was sixteen and thought she was in love."

"He got Nimuë pregnant."

"She trusted him, and he used her, not caring how it might hurt her." She scowled. "The pregnancy tore her apart from the inside. How she cried from the sheer pain of it. The baby clawed at her, she said; it burned her. I tried to give her herbs that would end the pregnancy, but she wouldn't take them. She ran away to be with Myrddin, to give him his son. She said she wanted them to be a family." Her voice caught in a tearless sob. "For weeks, I searched for her."

"Did you find her?" I was afraid I already knew the answer.

"I found her corpse. Myrddin had ripped the child from her womb and left her to bleed to death on the ground." Mab rocked back and forth, moaning softly, as if she'd just this minute discovered her sister's mutilated body. But then she straightened. "I vowed to make him pay for what he'd done."

Mab lifted her chin, and a defiant pride showed in her face. "I shifted my shape to become the exact image of Nimuë. Not as she died, but as she looked when Myrddin first saw her. In that shape, I entered Myrddin's dreams. Do you know what happens when a beautiful young girl enters a man's dreams?" She smiled. "She gets whatever she wants."

"So that's why the legends say Nimuë stole Myrddin's magic."

"Yes, but it was I, in Nimuë's image. Myrddin gave Nimuë his secrets—and gladly—but it was Viviane who took them. Only one thing did he withhold: the location of his son. Whenever I mentioned the child, Myrddin would remember that Nimuë was dead and banish her image from his dreamscape. I tried entering his dreams in other guises, but it didn't work. He refused to divulge that secret."

"But he taught you the spell you needed?"

"He did, and I used it." Again, her eyes looked into the past. "One night, Myrddin slept in his forest under a yew tree. I sent an avatar of Nimuë into his dreams to distract him. As Viviane, I stood beside his sleeping body and wove the binding spell. When the spell was too far advanced to resist, I woke him. I didn't want that bastard spending eternity in happy dreams of Nimuë; I wanted him to suffer. He saw me, felt the binding spell, knew I'd trapped him—and why. I made certain he knew why. The tree began to absorb him. He struggled, but I told him it was no use. I told him I'd find his demon spawn and kill it. He laughed at me then, said

I'd never find the boy. Just before the tree took him, his arm shot out from the trunk. He pointed at me, his face straining forward so he could speak. And Myrddin cursed me."

I shuddered. "What was the curse?"

"That I'd remember. No matter how many lives I lived, I'd remember that one, as vividly as when each moment was new. When he returned to take his revenge, he wanted to be sure I knew why."

It was a terrible curse. To experience that trauma, lifetime after lifetime, the pain never dimming. Even if he never returned, Myrddin had taken his revenge.

"I never did find Pryce," Mab said. "Not in that lifetime, though I searched far and wide. Myrddin had fostered the boy with a human family. After several years and many rumors, I discovered the family's name. But when I traveled to them, I learned that Pryce had murdered them all and run away. The boy wasn't yet ten years old. And so it went for many years. Pryce left a long trail of death and destruction, but I was always a step or two behind him."

"So how did we get so lucky to have him in our lives?"

"Eventually, he found me. He came to Maenllyd, called me 'auntie,' and told me he wouldn't rest until he'd destroyed everything I love—and finally me."

I WANTED TO LET MAB REST, BUT SHE INSISTED SHE HAD more to say. "Let me speak now, child, while my memories give me strength. I know how you can kill Myrddin."

I sat up and paid attention at that. After what he'd done to Mab, I wanted to kill him three times over—a triple death for real this time.

"Myrddin is not immortal. We know that."

"But he might as well be, the way he can zip in and out of the demon plane."

"There is no 'might as well be' when it comes to immortality." She rubbed the withered flesh of her arm. "Think back to last night, child. How did Myrddin react when you shot him?"

"He shifted to his demon form."

"Yes. Why did he not simply exit to the demon plane and return, as he did when he fooled Colwyn with the triple death?"

I pictured last night's scene. I remembered firing, the black blood flowing from the wounds, the demon growing. "Because the bullets were bronze?"

"Precisely. The bronze prevented Myrddin from entering the demon plane in his human form to heal. Before he could slip away into that plane, he had to take on his demon form. Only in that state could he exit to the demon plane and heal his wounds there."

"Why?"

"I believe it's because of the way he merged those two forms: demon within the human and human within the demon. It's made his human form vulnerable to bronze in a way other demi-demons are not."

I thought about the legend of the triple death. None of those fake deaths—falling, impalement, and drowning—had involved any bronze implements. "So I can use bronze to force Myrddin to change to his demon form . . ."

"And then you can kill the demon, just as you did with Pryce. With his demon half dead, Myrddin will be as mortal as any human."

I stood up. "I'll need the Sword of Saint Michael." Saint Michael was the enemy of all demons, and the bronze-bladed sword bearing his name, a weapon my family had owned for centuries, would shimmer with celestial flame in battle. It was the surest way to kill a powerful demon. And I couldn't wait to for Myrddin Wyllt to feel its bite.

29

I WANTED TO DO A TRIAL RUN, SLIPPING OUT OF DEADTOWN and getting into position at Boylston Street, before we had to do it for real. The sun had set on Deadtown an hour ago, so the containment order was now in force. We still had several hours left before curfew. Now was the time to give our plan a try.

I called Tina and asked her to come over and stay with Mab. She let out a whoop of excitement before she cleared her throat and tallied up another favor I owed her, so I didn't think I was inconveniencing her too much. Then I called Clyde and told him I was expecting her, so he wouldn't get too apoplectic when she breezed past his desk.

Next, weapons. To make the trial run as close to the real thing as possible, I needed to arm myself the way I planned to be armed tomorrow night. I unlocked my weapons cabinet and made my selections. I strapped on a double shoulder holster and filled it with pistols: bronze bullets on the right, silver on the left. Two thigh sheaths held daggers: I stuck with the pattern of bronze on the right and silver on the left. I slid a silver throwing knife into each boot. Last, I strapped on a vertical back sheath designed for the Sword of Saint Michael. It held the sword straight up-and-down, the hilt behind my neck. To draw it, I just had to reach back, grab the hilt, and pull the sword up and out in an arc. I practiced a couple of times.

A knock sounded on the door. "Just a minute!" I called. I took a coat from my closet—the coat was leather and mid-calf length, with a hood—and pulled it on. I flipped up the hood to hide the hilt of my sword. Then I answered the door.

Tina came in, carrying a thermos. "Chicken soup," she said. "For your aunt. My mom used to make it for me when I got sick."

I took the thermos. "Feels kind of light."

"I only had a little, to make sure it tasted okay." I set the thermos on the coffee table as she made a beeline for the kitchen. "Did you get a chance to buy more ice cream? Because—" She stopped and spun on her heel, gawking at me. "*What* are you wearing?"

"My coat. I'm taking Killer out again."

"No, no, no. You can't wear that. You look like Little Goth Riding Hood." She came over, examining me.

"The coat is fine. I'm going—"

"Well, at least don't pull the hood up like that. Here . . ." She yanked on the hood, pulling it down and exposing the hilt of my sword. Her eyes grew wider. "You're carrying a sword to walk your dog?" Her hand flashed out, and she pulled my coat half off my shoulder. "Oh my God, you are *totally* armed. Where are you really going? To fight some demons?"

No need to tell Tina I was sneaking out of Deadtown in violation of the containment order. "Yeah, that's right. I've got a quick demon extermination to take care of. I'll be back before curfew."

I headed for the door. Tina stepped in front of me.

"What kind? I've been studying. Go ahead—quiz me."

"Um, Harpies. I don't have time to quiz you now." I pulled my hood back up.

"Harpies, really?" She wrinkled her nose. "Those weapons are, like, total overkill for fighting revenge demons. What are you going to do with that big sword, shish-kebab them?" She lifted the side of my coat. I slapped it back down. And you're carrying silver, too—what's that supposed to do against Harpies?"

What a time for Tina to get all smart about demon fighting.

"Gotta go," I said. "Come on, Killer." I opened the door. Kane, wearing Roxana's charm, shot out from wherever he'd been hiding and ran to the hall. I was right behind him.

"You're taking your *dog* on a demon extermination? What—?"

I shut the door on her incredulous face.

There's a saying that a little learning is a dangerous thing. But who'd have thought that Tina's little bit of learning about demons would be so dangerous to my sanity?

DEADTOWN'S STREETS WERE CROWDED. NOT ONLY HAD every single resident returned to Designated Area 1, they all seemed to be rushing to get groceries and light bulbs and beer and whatever other emergency supplies they thought they'd need before curfew confined them to their homes.

We pushed through the crowds and made our way to the side street where Kane's network of secret tunnels began. There were so many people around, I thought I'd never get a chance to pull open the bulkhead door and slip inside. Kane sat on the ground, and I lounged against the wall, trying to look nonchalant. Of course, since everyone else was out running errands, standing still made me stick out as much as a huge boulder in the middle of a rushing stream. Zombies shot curious glances my way as they passed.

One man stopped in his tracks as he came even with us. He turned his head sharply, nostrils flaring. *Uh-oh.* Werewolf. And he smelled Kane. A charm wouldn't disguise his scent to one of his own kind.

Kane stood, hackles rising with him. He barked sharply. Then he lowered his head and growled.

The werewolf stepped back. He glanced at me. "Sorry," he muttered, and hurried away.

"Nice dominance display," I told Kane. He sat and thumped his tail. I wished it had been that easy with the werewolf bachelorettes.

After several more minutes of waiting, the crowd thinned and I saw our chance. I grabbed the handle to the bulkhead door and pulled. And nearly wrenched my back. I pulled again. The door was locked.

"Is there another way in?"

Kane shook his head.

"Okay, let's try plan B." Always have a contingency plan.

I led the way to Deadtown's northern boundary, where there was a dead spot in the electric fence. What I found was a big, new sign that read: DANGER. HIGH VOLTAGE. DO NOT TOUCH. I didn't stand around long wondering if the sign was for real. A moth flitted past, attracted by portable floodlights trained on Deadtown from the other side. It bumped the wire, and got zapped into oblivion.

So much for our contingency plan.

"THERE *MUST* BE SOME WAY OUT," I SAID. WE WERE IN THE bedroom, having a strategy meeting with Mab. Tina was in the kitchen, cleaning up. Again. I could hardly believe it.

"You could shift," Mab said. "Become a bird, for example, and fly over the fence. Although there would be several drawbacks."

"I've thought about those. I couldn't carry out any weapons, and there's no telling how long the shift would last." Not to mention I'd wake up naked in some strange place, perhaps miles away from my goal. My human mind and personality didn't have much control over whatever animal I shifted to, so if the bird decided it was time to fly up north to its nesting grounds in Nova Scotia, that's what it would do.

"What about the man who made my ID? Can he help?"

"I already called him. He can smuggle documents, but not people. He didn't have a clue."

My shoulders sagged. Kane, lying on the floor, put his head on his paws.

"Think, child. We must get you past the boundary."

The door opened, and Tina stuck her head in. "Is that all you want to do? Get out of Deadtown?"

"Tina, this is a private conversation," I said.

"Sorry, I couldn't help overhearing."

"Through a closed door?"

Mab held up a hand. "Let her speak, Victory. We need all the ideas we can get."

Tina came in and sat at the foot of the bed. "I sneak out of Deadtown all the time. It's easiest in the winter, because then everyone's all bundled up with hats and scarves and stuff and nobody can even tell you're a zombie."

"Are you thinking of that dead spot in the north fence?" I asked. "Because it's got lots of juice now."

"I've used that spot, but there are lots of other ways." She bit her lip and looked at each of us, considering. "Okay, I'm not supposed to tell anybody this, but there's this club. We sneak out of Deadtown and visit different places in Boston. It's fun." Sort of like a zombie version of the urban exploration club Roxana mentioned.

"Tina, do you know how much trouble you'd be in if you got caught outside of Deadtown without a permit? They'd call in the Removal Squad." Zombies who got removed were never heard from again. And that was true even when there wasn't a containment order in place.

She shrugged. "So we don't get caught."

"And right now it's too dangerous. They've fixed the electric fence. They've added police patrols. They've even called in the National Guard." I turned to Mab. "I'll have to shift. It's not ideal, but it's the only way."

"It's *not* the only way. Some of us are sneaking out tomorrow night." Tina flipped her hair behind her shoulder. "What? If it's too easy, it's no fun."

Mab laughed. "That young lady," she said, shaking a finger at Tina, "reminds me of myself at that age."

Tina puffed up like a preening cockatoo.

"Okay," I said. "Where are you planning to sneak out? I'll go take a look now."

"I don't know yet. I haven't heard from Brendan. He's the one with all the maps and police information and stuff. He'll text us tomorrow and tell us when and where to meet."

"I don't like it," I said to Mab. I didn't want to be caught with a bunch of teenage zombies trying to sneak out of Deadtown on a lark. And if I had to wait until tomorrow, there would be no chance for a trial run.

"Let's reserve judgment until we learn of this Brendan's plan," Mab said. "If it doesn't seem feasible, you can still get out by shifting."

"Awesome!" Tina said, bouncing on the bed with excitement. "This will be *so* fun. It'll almost be like we're out fighting demons again." She got up. "I know, I know. You don't have to say it. I'm not your apprentice anymore." She grinned. "But it'll still be fun."

TINA LEFT TO MAKE IT BACK TO HER GROUP HOME BEFORE the curfew took effect. About two minutes past ten, there was a knock on my door. I went to answer it, wondering why Clyde hadn't called to announce the visitor. Then I realized he was under curfew, too. He'd be home, like everyone else.

Everyone but the Goon Squad. Because that's who was at my door.

Pam McFarren, the female zombie Goon, stood outside, a clipboard in hand. "Curfew compliance check," she said.

Lucky me. Right at the top of the list.

"Mind if I come in?" she asked.

"Do you have to? You can see that I'm home."

She held her clipboard at arm's length and squinted at it like she needed reading glasses. "Says here this apartment has three residents. I don't need to go inside if they all come to the door."

Three. Carlos had done a good job of putting Mab in the

database. But I wasn't going to drag her out of bed just to parade her in front of the Goon Squad. They'd insist on checking the apartment, anyway, since Juliet wasn't here.

I opened the door wider. McFarren walked past me. Behind her came a human cop I'd never seen before. He was tall and thin, with a shaved head and an oversized Adam's apple. He nodded as he passed.

"Where's Norden?"

"Elmer quit the task force," McFarren said, shrugging. "He said he wanted to go back to working in the human parts of town."

Yeah, right. What he'd actually said was probably more along the lines of "just get me away from those goddamn freaks."

"I felt kind of bad for him," McFarren said. "I really think his old partner's death got to him. It was like he couldn't stand being around PDHs anymore. Last time we patrolled together, he wouldn't even walk on the same side of the street as me." She shook her head sadly. "The department's got good psychological resources. I hope he'll make use of them." She tapped her clipboard with her pencil. "Now, I'm looking for three residents. You're Vaughn, Victory." She made a checkmark on the page. "Where's Vaughn, Mabel?"

"That's my aunt. She's in the bedroom. Do you have to disturb her? She's sick."

"Just a peek." McFarren cracked open the bedroom door and looked inside. "Sorry to bother you, Mabel, dear," she said, pulling the door shut. I hoped Mab was asleep. It wouldn't be good for her condition to have steam shooting out of her ears at being called Mabel.

"And what about Capulet, Juliet?" McFarren asked.

"Is that supposed to be a trick question? You know as well as I do that she's missing."

"So that's an X then." She marked the clipboard. "Where's her room?"

I showed her. She and her partner took a quick look inside. They also checked the bathroom and the kitchen. I didn't know where Kane was, but I was glad he was keeping out of sight.

At the front door, McFarren tucked her clipboard under her arm. "You still don't know Ms. Capulet's whereabouts?"

"I wish I did." I'd give a lot to know where Juliet was right now.

"All right. Let me leave you with a reminder that all residents of Designated Area 1 are to remain in their residences between now and four a.m. Failure to do so could result in a fine, a lengthy prison term, or both."

"Have a nice night," her partner said as they left. Watching them move down the hall to the next apartment, I almost missed Norden. At least he didn't pretend to be polite while stomping all over your nonexistent rights.

30

THE NEXT DAY, LYNNE HONG WAS ON CHANNEL 10 ON-THE-Scene News, reporting rumors that the Reaper was expected to strike on Boston Common. "If you must be out after ten," she said, "use extreme caution, and avoid Boston Common and the surrounding area."

Go, Daniel, I thought. He may not be able to assign extra patrols to the Boylston Street side of the Common, but he was doing his best to keep potential victims out of the area. Giving Lynne the rumor to report probably kept the peace in their relationship, too.

Around five in the evening, Tina called. "Brendan says to meet at Munchies at nine. Can you be there?"

Munchies, a popular zombie snack shop with a seemingly endless supply of junk food, was on the north side of Deadtown.

"He does know they fixed that dead spot, right?"

"Yeah, yeah. He's got a different plan."

"What is it?"

"He'll tell us at Munchies."

An hour before curfew, Kane and I stood in the doorway of Munchies, watching a roomful of zombies chow down before they had to go home for the night. Waitresses carried trays overflowing with nachos, cheese fries, sliders, onion rings, popcorn—anything that fits into the category of "munchies." You'd think the zombies believed they'd never have a chance to eat again. But it was probably a pretty typical night.

Tina waved to me from a table of teenage zombies. The plague had happened on a school day, so not many kids had been zombified. But there were a few. Some, like Tina and her friend Jenna, had cut school to go shopping or hang out in Boston. Others had been in town for college or job interviews. Now, they all lived in a group home in Deadtown.

Tina wore a tight, strapless pink dress with rhinestone accents. She looked like she was going clubbing. Maybe that was the plan after they slipped outside. Maybe college kids were dressing up like zombies these days when they went out to dance, and this group would fit right in.

More likely, I'd be flying out of Deadtown tonight.

Kane sat on the sidewalk outside while Tina introduced me to her friends. I knew a couple of them already, but Brendan, the group's leader, was new to me. He was about five ten, with curly red hair and a complexion that had probably been freckled before he got the plague. "Sit down," he invited.

"Thanks, but I'll stand." Sitting down was a little iffy with the Sword of Saint Michael strapped to my back.

"Don't ask her to take off her hood," Tina said. Everyone stared at her for a moment, then went back to eating. Tina says Tina-type things. Sometimes it wasn't worth the effort to try to understand.

"Okay," said Brendan to the group. "Name something Boston's famous for."

"Baked beans."

"The Red Sox."

"Clam chowder."

"Lobsters."

"Boston cream pie."

I noticed a disproportionate number of the answers were food-related. But then, we were in a place called Munchies at a table full of zombies.

"Try this," Brendan said. "Potholes."

Everyone nodded, including me. Neither I nor the Jag would argue with that one.

"So I was thinking about our little problem with the fences," Brendan went on. "Can't go over it, can't go around it . . ."

"Gotta go *under* it," someone finished.

"Exactly. And the best way to get under the fence is with the help of our friend the pothole." He surveyed the group, making sure everyone was with him. "I went online and checked the street-repair schedule for the Department of Public Works, with a special focus on their pothole remediation crew. And I found the mother of all potholes, right here in Deadtown. It's low on the priority list, because it isn't on an active roadway." He leaned forward. "It's under the fence."

"So we're going to crawl under the fence through a pothole," I said. My voice sounded skeptical; I'd seen some big potholes in Boston, but this sounded a little nuts.

He nodded. "After we help the pothole along a little bit. I checked out the site. We need to make the pothole deeper and longer. After we do, it'll be a snap to get through."

"What about the cops?" asked my skeptical voice. A couple of the kids glanced at me like I was a spoilsport. So be it.

"I timed the patrols. They go by every eight minutes. That gives us six good minutes of digging time between passes. With zombie super-strength and two people digging, it'll take two, maybe three patrols to make the hole big enough."

"You don't think they'll notice the pothole getting bigger?"

"No, I don't, actually. They'll be looking at eye level, not checking the ground."

"What makes you think that?"

"That's my job," Tina said. "Distract the cops."

Ah. So that explained the tight dress. Tina had a sexy figure. If she were still human, she'd have legions of boys eating out of her hand. But did she really think human cops would ogle a zombie?

I'd promised Mab I'd give the kids' plan a chance. But now that I'd heard it, I wanted to tell them to give it up and go home. The norms weren't fooling around. There were cops with guns, soldiers with guns. They carried the exploding ammunition that could kill a zombie. There'd be serious consequences for any paranormal caught outside of Deadtown tonight. Consequences, hell. Some of these kids could die.

I'd check out the site, and then I'd try to talk the zombies out of it. Whether or not I managed to dissuade them, I'd go home and lock up my weapons. I'd go up to my building's roof, shift into a bird, and fly out of Deadtown.

But when I arrived at the site and saw Brendan's pothole, damned if I didn't think it might work. It really *was* the mother of all potholes. And the site itself was isolated, without a lot of activity on either side of the fence. We moved a little way down the block and waited for the patrol to pass. After it did, Brendan checked his watch. Two zombies grabbed shovels and started digging, being careful to stay clear of the fence itself.

After six minutes, Brendan signaled, and they faded back into the shadows. The patrol went by. The changes to the pothole were on the Deadtown side, and neither cop noticed. They didn't care what was on our side of the fence.

A minute after the patrol passed, Brendan gave the signal. Two other zombies rushed forward and started digging. They made good progress. I saw gravel fly up on the other side of the fence.

This time, when the patrol was due, Tina sidled up to the fence. She struck a sexy pose, jutting out her hip and showing a lot of leg, and asked if either cop had a light for her cigarette.

Cigarette? I was planning a future lecture against smoking when I remembered zombies couldn't get lung cancer. Okay, whatever.

One of the cops said, in kind of a nasty voice, that she should try touching her cigarette to the electric fence. She laughed like she actually thought it was funny, flinging back her hair, and then walked with them as they moved on. She asked if they liked monster rock and talked about how she used to sing with Monster Paul and the Zombie Freak Show. Down the block, one of the officers laughed, and Tina joined him.

The girl had a talent for flirting.

The zombies finished digging the hole, and the first ones slipped through. "You next," Brendan said, touching my elbow. It was a little difficult with all the weapons, but I wriggled through. Kane was out a minute later. We ran toward the Common, staying close to the dark buildings.

Somewhere down the block, Tina's laugh rang out.

THE BOYLSTON STREET T STATION WAS CLOSED, BOTH INbound and outbound. I didn't know how Daniel had managed that, but it was a good idea. Anyone waiting on the platform would be a sitting duck for the Reaper.

Printed signs taped to the locked glass doors directed would-be passengers to Arlington or Park Street T stations or the Silver line bus stop. Not that anyone was around. The Common was completely deserted. Lynne Hong had gotten the message out, and Bostonians weren't taking any chances tonight.

For an hour, Kane and I wandered the park's paths and ventured down Boylston or Tremont a little way, never straying far from ground zero between the two subway entrances. Just a woman out walking her dog. I'd brought along Juliet's silver chain because it looked a little like a leash—but more important, it had been a good weapon against the Old Ones. It hung from my coat pocket.

Two patrol cars passed. One slowed when it saw us; the other cruised right on by. There were no taxis—not surprising after what happened to Mack—and very few cars. The occasional bus that went by was empty except for a single uniformed cop in one of the front seats. Getting cops on the buses that traveled through this part of town must have been Daniel's doing, too, like the shuttered T station. Shops and restaurants were closed. I'd never seen the streets so quiet and empty.

The *slap-slap* of footsteps heading toward us from the heart of the Common echoed like gunshots in the silence. With a glance at each other, Kane and I took our positions. He crouched in the shadow of the low brick wall that marks the edge of the Common. I drew my gun—bronze bullets, no vampire made that much noise—and slipped behind the outbound T entrance, where I could peer around the corner without being seen.

The footsteps were hurried but irregular: *step step pause, step, pause, stepstepstep*. Within moments, a man's figure staggered from the shadows into the light. He appeared to be about forty, balding, with glasses and a scruffy beard. He wore a light khaki jacket over a sweatshirt and jeans, and he carried a bottle in a brown paper bag. About three steps into the light, he tripped on the pavement and sprawled facedown. There was the crash and tinkle of breaking glass.

Not the Reaper. A drunk.

I holstered my gun and stepped into the light. The man had pushed himself into a sitting position and was holding up his dripping bag, staring at it sorrowfully. The smell of whiskey washed over me from ten feet away.

Down the street, headlights approached. I glanced at my watch. One o'clock. It was the last Silver line bus of the night. And I'd make sure this drunk was on it.

"Come on," I said. "You've got a bus to catch."

He squinted at me through crooked glasses. "Are you the Reaper?"

"No, I'm your ticket home."

"I'm here to fight the Reaper." He dropped the sopping bag and gave a couple of exaggerated punches. I grabbed his outstretched arm and hauled him to his feet.

"Wow," he said. "You're strong. Wanna fight?"

I didn't answer, just dragged him toward the bus stop.

"Noooo!" he howled. "Where's the Reaper? Lemme at him! I'm gonna kill the bastard!" He swung at me with his free arm, dug in his heels, let his knees collapse. Nothing slowed our progress. And nothing short of a knock-out blow would shut him up, either. I was tempted, but I just kept dragging.

"What the hell is all that noise?"

I knew that voice. Beyond the struggling drunk, Norden glared at me. It was kind of good to see his scowling face. The bus was almost at the stop.

"He wants to be a hero," I said. "Help me get him out of here."

Norden waved the bus to a stop, then grabbed the drunk's legs and helped me carry him on board. While I gave the bus driver two bucks for the fare, Norden and the uniformed cop wrestled the guy into a seat and handcuffed him to it. He yanked at the cuffs and yelled for the Reaper to come out and fight.

"Don't let him out until the end of the line," Norden said. "If you can stand his racket that long."

"If he doesn't settle down, he can spend the night in the drunk tank," the cop replied. "You hear that?" he shouted over the yelling. "No Reaper for you tonight. I'll have a patrol car waiting at the end of this bus ride unless you shut it right now."

They were still arguing as the bus closed its door and pulled away.

Norden wiped sweat from his scarred face with the back of his arm. "Damn crazy drunk." His voice sounded breathy, like dealing with the guy had winded him.

"McFarren told me you quit the Goon Squad. You're the first cop I've seen all night. Other than the ones on the buses, I mean. Where's your partner?" No cop would be patrolling this area tonight without backup.

"You're here alone." Norden couldn't seem to get a breath. "What the hell are you doing out here, huh? You should have stayed in Deadtown. With all the other freaks."

I felt, more than saw, Kane's ears prick up. A growl rumbled from his throat.

Something felt wrong. What *was* Norden doing here by

himself? He mopped his face, his handkerchief wiping the scars. Scars he'd gotten at the Paranormal Appreciation Day Concert, in the middle of a Morfran attack.

I heard a distant cawing, like a flock of crows perched somewhere in the Common.

Oh, no.

I reached for my gun.

Kane growled again, and sprang. So fast his movement was a blur, Norden pulled out his gun and shot him. Kane backflipped and, with a piercing yelp of pain, landed on the far side of the wall.

Norden knocked my gun from my hand and jammed his own under my chin. "Hands up, where I can see them both."

I raised my hands, straining to hear anything from Kane.

"Let's go see the werewolf," Norden said. He dragged me over to the wall. Behind it, Kane lay on his side, bleeding from his shoulder. His ribs moved rapidly as he panted. Norden let go of me, but the barrel of his gun still pressed into the flesh under my jaw. He pulled a second gun, aiming it directly at Kane's head.

"Don't move," he said. "You so much as twitch, and I blast a silver bullet through this werewolf's skull. Understand?"

"Yes," I whispered.

"You tried to make it look like a dog," he muttered. "But I know it's a wolf. They said there'd be a werewolf."

"Who did?"

"They. Them. The voices, the birds. *You* know." He voice rose in pitch, and he pressed the gun into me so hard I had to rise up on my toes. "Or they know you. They told me you'd be the fifth."

"What birds, Norden?"

"Black birds. Big ones. They live in my head and caw at me. They scratch the inside of my skull. They . . . they tear at my nerves with their beaks." He shuddered. "When I'm around zombies, the birds scream with hunger. They make me . . . they make me want to eat dead flesh." I could smell the fear and desperation in his sweat. "And kill. I never killed before, not even on the job. But the birds . . ."

He shook himself, and I squeezed my eyes shut, expecting a bullet. But he stepped back. He removed the gun from my jaw but kept it pointed at me. He kept the other gun pointed directly at Kane. His voice lowered to its normal range. "You've got one gun left, four knives, and that big-ass sword. Put your right hand on top of your head, and use two fingers, left hand, to pull out the other gun. Then throw it behind me."

I complied, moving very slowly. I opened to the demon plane. Norden was all beak and wings. Crows dove at his head; others perched on his shoulders, his arms. Beneath it all, Norden's spirit struggled—shaking, flinching, trying to pull free. His aura radiated pure agony. "Norden," I said gently. "This isn't you. You're a cop, one of the good guys, remember?" Blue—hope—flared in Norden's aura. It was pale, but there. I kept talking. "Those birds. They're not part of you. They're the Morfran. Remember the night of the concert? Remember the crows that attacked Tina?"

The crows plaguing Norden stepped up their attack. Their shrieking tore at my ears. The thin plume of blue faded from Norden's aura. I pulled back to the human plane. Norden was bathed with sweat, his eye twitching, but he held both guns steady. "Now the knife strapped to your right leg," he said.

"You tried to help Tina. You held the kid when she was hurt. Remember? I made the crows go away then."

"I . . . I don't remember none of that. Other knife."

I had to make him remember, give him hope that the Morfran could be defeated. "That night, at the concert, the Morfran got inside you somehow. You were cut up pretty badly. Okay, maybe you don't remember that, but you've got the scars to prove it. Some of the Morfran entered your wounds, got inside you."

"Right boot, then the left." In the demon plane, crows pecked at Norden's aura, gouging out big chunks. Other crows opened their beaks and poured blackness into the spaces.

"It's not you, Norden. We can get the birds out. My aunt—"

"Shut up! Now the sword. Don't touch the weapon. Just unbuckle the sheath and let it fall."

I fumbled with the buckles one-handed.

"Faster!" His voice was frantic, high-pitched. "The damn birds are pecking inside my head!"

"Fight them! You can do it. I can help—"

"No, you can't!" he screamed. His aura was completely black. "Nothing makes it stop. Nothing but killing. And I'll kill this goddamn werewolf *right now* if you don't shut up and do what I say!"

The last buckle let go. The Sword of Saint Michael clattered to the ground.

The Morfran shrieked in triumph. In the demon plane, I could see nothing at all of Norden—just a flock of crows swarming the place where he stood. I closed to that plane. Norden was right. I couldn't help him.

"Both hands on your head now. Kick the sword away." I did, not as far as I might have. But the distance was too great to dive for the sword and charge Norden. Kane would be dead before I was halfway there.

"Face that way." He gestured with his chin, indicating he wanted me to turn my back to him. "And drop to your knees." The gun he pointed at Kane didn't waver as he holstered the other gun and pulled out a knife with a long, curved blade.

I didn't move. I stood and stared Norden in the eye. I would not die on my knees.

"Look, Vaughn, it's nothing personal, okay? I *have* to."

"You don't."

"Yes, I do!" he screamed. His breathing was labored again. "It's . . . nothing . . . personal. Yeah, I've called you a freak . . . but I always thought you'd make . . . an okay partner, ever since . . ."

"Ever since what, Norden? Ever since the concert? You *do* remember. Those crows. I got them away from Tina. Remember?"

"They tore up that kid." He cocked his head. "That's what's inside me?"

"Let me help—"

"No, they're tearing *me* up. I have to. I *have* to!"

The curved blade flashed as it fell from his hand. Norden brought up the gun, jammed it under his own chin, and pulled the trigger.

31

BEFORE NORDEN'S BODY HIT THE GROUND, THE GLASS doors of the T station shattered. Myrddin came out, carrying the jar he'd had at the last murder site. Two vampires stood behind him.

"Kill her," Myrddin said.

I lunged for my sword, but I'm no match for a vampire in overdrive. One of the vampires slammed into me, knocking me off my feet. I twisted out of his grasp, rolled, and came up with the silver chain in my hand.

It was the only weapon Norden had left me.

I lashed out with the chain like a whip, striking the vampire's face before he knew what hit him. A ghastly scream rang out as he staggered back, clawing at his cheek. The other vampire stopped and stared. I lashed out again. The chain nicked a chunk of flesh from his neck, and he knew what his friend was screaming about.

I stood with my back against the subway building, whipping the chain to hold the vampires back. They dodged it, and fear of the silver prevented them from trying to snatch it away from me. But I couldn't rest for a second, or else one of them would dash in and snap my neck. And I couldn't get any closer to Myrddin.

In my peripheral vision, I could see the wizard pick up the curved blade and bend over Norden's corpse. He slashed at Norden's chest and then opened the jar. Loud cawing erupted as the Morfran left Norden's body. Immediately the sound grew muffled; Myrddin was capturing the Morfran, along with whatever remained of Norden's life force.

A vampire grabbed for my arm, clawing me. I knocked him back.

"I can't wait for you buffoons," Myrddin called. He stood, holding the jar in both hands. "I must complete the transfer before the life force loses potency. After you've killed her, meet me below. I require your assistance."

"We could use a little assistance here, wizard. Hit her with a magic bolt; we'll take care of the rest."

"It's taking all the magic I can summon to keep these spirits contained. The ritual won't wait. Do as I told you, then come." He stepped through the shattered door and disappeared down the stairs, into the subway.

The vampires spread out. The distance between them made it harder for me to use the chain. I had to turn between them, and as I lashed at one there was an extra fraction of a second for the other to move in. A fraction of a second is plenty of time to a fast vampire. One of them got his claws into my throat.

I grabbed at his hands and struggled for air as he lifted me from the ground. The silver burned him, but he laughed and squeezed tighter.

There was a pop, like a car backfiring. The vampire's fingers spasmed, then let go. We both fell to the ground.

His friend stared, eyes bugged. But only for a moment. A second pop dropped him, too.

I looked toward the Common. Leaning on the wall he'd fallen behind, holding one of my pistols, was Kane.

Except it wasn't Kane, not fully. He was half-changed. Pointed wolf ears sat above a face that looked like Kane's except for the silver fur that covered it. Coarser fur, matted with dark blood on the left side, covered his human chest and shoulders. He slumped, the gun dangling from his clawed hand.

I ran over. "The wound," he said. His voice sounded rough and gravelly. "Where Norden shot me. It's forcing a change. But the silver—" He winced in pain.

The silver bullet lodged in his shoulder was interfering with the shift. If the silver didn't come out, Kane would die, stuck between his two forms.

I ran past Norden's body, looking for the weapons I'd thrown. A bronze blade gleamed in the streetlight. I snatched it up and went back to Kane.

"Let me dig it out." I touched his shoulder. Beneath the fur, his skin was burning up.

He closed the fingers of his right hand around mine. "I'll do it. You stop Myrddin." Gray eyes gazed steadily at me. They were clouded with pain, but they were Kane's eyes. I'd always seen him there.

I nodded, not trusting my voice. I kissed his lips—human lips, despite his half-changed form—and gathered up the rest of my weapons.

I strode back to the fallen vampires. The first was dead, the body already crumbling. Kane had sent a silver bullet straight through his heart. Better make sure he stayed dead—you never knew with vampires. I unsheathed the Sword of Saint Michael and struck off his head with a blow.

The other vampire moaned. His prone body cringed away by an inch or two. Kane's bullet hadn't hit this one as squarely.

I wrapped the silver chain around the vampire's neck, pulling it tight, and hauled the creature to his feet. "Let's go," I said. "You're taking me to Myrddin."

The vampire let out a strangled cry. He nodded, then cried out again as the silver abraded his undead skin. Keeping one fist wrapped in the chain, I shoved him toward the subway entrance. In my other hand, I brandished the Sword of Saint

Michael. I whispered the invocation, and the blade burst into flame. It lit our way as we descended into whatever hell waited below.

THE VAMPIRE STAGGERED TOWARD THE TUNNEL KANE AND I had explored the other night, the one with the emergency exit.

I yanked on the chain and shook him. "Stop wasting my time. I know this tunnel is empty. Where did they go?"

"Hidden," he croaked. "The entrance is hidden."

I didn't trust this vampire, but I didn't have a lot of options. Myrddin had fled into this station. He and Pryce were down here somewhere.

I pushed the vampire, and he stumbled forward.

We moved swiftly. The tunnel was bright and clean and empty, as it had been the other night. Until we reached the emergency exit. Two vampires emerged from the staircase. Two others came forward from the darkness beyond.

I jerked my captive vampire to a halt. "You led me into an ambush!" I ripped the chain from his neck and pushed him away. At the same time, I touched him with the flame from my sword. Fire flared and took his body. He lit up like a torch, dancing and jerking in the flames. He staggered toward his friends, who drew back. His screams echoed through the tunnel.

Vampires burn fast. He collapsed in a pile of charred bones and ashes.

I swung the sword in front of me. The flames brightened and whooshed with the motion. "Who's next?"

The vampires backed away.

Except for the one who got behind me. I never saw him move. Hands clutched my throat, the grip so tight I couldn't tell whether he was trying to strangle me or squeeze my head off. I whipped the silver chain behind me and simultaneously kicked back, connecting with his shin.

His grip loosened, and I followed through with an elbow

strike, turning as much as I could to throw my weight behind it. The vampire let go and staggered back, and I stabbed him with the flaming sword. He burned as brightly as the first.

Two vampires, both females, split and came at me from both sides. I spun to the right, sweeping my sword with the motion. At the same time, I lashed out with the chain to the left. The sword caught one vampire in the side; she howled as she went up in flames. The chain wrapped itself around the other vampire's calf as she came at me in a roundhouse kick. The kick missed my head but connected with my shoulder, knocking me sideways. As I fell, I tightened my grip on the chain, pulling her off balance. I thrust out my sword to avoid landing on it, and got a lucky hit on the fifth vampire, just as he moved in to attack. He burst into flame but kept coming, impaling himself deeper on my sword, reaching for me.

I grabbed the hilt in both hands and arced the sword sideways to the ground, forcing him to fall with it. His burning fingers stretched toward me, blackening.

A metallic clatter sounded to my left. The female vampire had unwrapped the chain from her leg and was hobbling away, into the dark tunnel.

Pain seared my arm as the burning vampire grabbed it. I hit at his fingers and shook him off. My sleeve smoldered, and I batted out the flames. The vampire's hand curled into a tight, skeletal fist and dropped away.

I yanked my sword from the charred body and ran into the tunnel after the escaping female. The silver burn on her leg kept her from going into hyperspeed, but she still moved fast enough that I was afraid I'd lose her. I ran harder, my breath rasping through my bruised throat. I could just see her ahead, in the light cast by my sword.

She ran-limped to the pile of rusty cans of old provisions piled up against the wall. And then she disappeared.

Was it a trick? Had she led me to this dead-end, pretending to be injured, and then run off at vampire speed? The Sword of Saint Michael lit up the tunnel. No vampires lurked anywhere that I could see.

The vampire I'd forced down the stairs said the entrance to the Old Ones' lair was hidden. This mountain of cans must hide it somehow. Some kind of magical illusion, maybe? I looked closer. I poked at a rusty can with my toe, then kicked it. The can rolled across the tunnel. It was real enough. I kicked at another, and another. Cans went flying. And then I kicked one, and my foot went right through it.

I tried again. The same thing happened. I stepped forward—just half a careful step—and met no resistance. Shifting the sword to my left hand, I took a deep breath and drew a silver-bladed throwing knife. Demon or vampire, I was ready. I walked forward through the illusion, into the Old Ones' lair.

THE FIRST THING I SAW WAS A BLACK-ROBED OLD ONE, ARMS wide, coming straight at me. My silver knife sailed through the air and hit him in the throat. The Old One sank to the ground.

Now I could see the room. It was large, although its low ceiling made it feel cramped, and divided into two sections. To my right, a cluster of Old Ones huddled together. To my left, Myrddin stood in the middle of a setup I recognized from when he'd tried to steal my life force. Pryce lay on a table, tubes entering his body. Before, I'd been on the other end of those tubes. This time, it was the jar in which Myrddin had captured Norden's life force.

Myrddin seemed annoyed to see me. "Aren't you dead yet?" he asked irritably.

"Not yet." I pulled my pistol and shot a bronze bullet. Myrddin ducked. But I wasn't aiming at him. The jar containing Norden's life force shattered.

A blue-tinted vapor spiraled upward from the fragments.

"No!" Myrddin batted the vapor toward Pryce with his hands. But the spiraling stream didn't waver. It rose up and out of sight.

Rest in peace, Norden.

"Bring her here!" Myrddin shouted. "The ritual must be completed tonight. I'll use her life force to finish it."

The knot of Old Ones to my right stirred. Keeping an eye

on them, I stuck my gun in my belt and reached down to retrieve the silver throwing knife from the one I'd killed. I touched the ice-cold body; my fingers groped for the knife.

Pain slashed through my palm.

The Old One wasn't dead. He'd pulled the knife from his throat and used it to slice a deep cut into my hand. Now he grasped my wrist and pulled me to my knees.

I wrenched my arm away. Ignoring the pain, I got my gun in my right hand. It was slippery from the blood. I pressed the gun against his forehead and put a bullet between his eyes. Bronze, but at this range it should do some damage.

It didn't. The Old One's skull spit the bullet back out at me. The hole closed at once. The Old One sneered and knocked the gun from my hand.

All right. Silver didn't work, a close-range pistol shot didn't work. Let's see how he liked fire.

I swiped the flaming sword at his neck. Blade cut into flesh, but then it stopped. The Old One's flesh pushed out the blade. The wound filled itself in.

The creature felt the sting of fire, though. It screamed and scooted backward, away from the touch of the flames. Its flesh sizzled and blackened. Unlike the cuts, the burn didn't heal. It sizzled and bubbled and blistered. The smell of burned, rotten flesh filled the room.

I waved my sword at the other Old Ones. They cringed and stayed where they were. Then, as if one of their psychic signals had passed among them, they parted like a curtain, taking a few steps to the left or right.

Behind them, Juliet was pinned to the wall. A dozen silver spikes held her in place: through her neck, her arms, her hands, her torso, her legs. A silver plate covered her mouth, rendering her silent. Her eyes were wide with terror and pain.

What the hell were they doing to her?

I roared and charged the Old Ones, slashing my sword. Maybe I couldn't kill them, but I could make them hurt. *You want to be gods? Eat fire, assholes.*

They scattered, and I went to Juliet. Keeping them at bay with my sword, I pulled the spike from her throat.

An Old One flew at me, and I set its robe on fire. It screamed and dropped to the floor, rolling to put out the flames. I hoped the fire barbecued its yellow hide.

I removed the spike from Juliet's left hand. The Old Ones gnashed their fangs at me but stayed back.

"Victory"—Myrddin's voice cut across the room—"cannot win." He giggled at his little pun.

I looked across the room at him. Mab's bloodstone dangled from his hand.

He laid it on the table where the jar had stood. And then he lifted a hammer above it.

"Do you know what will happen if I smash this bloodstone?"

"Don't—"

"Your aunt's life force shatters into little pieces, as well. She dies. Instantly." He tapped the stone lightly with the hammer. Each tap was a blow to my heart. "I think I can gather enough life force from the shards to finish the job with Pryce. Would you like that, to have part of Mab's soul trapped within my son?"

"Don't do it, Myrddin."

"All right. Then I'll need your life force instead. You or Mab. It's one or the other." He stopped tapping and raised the hammer again. "Hurry up. I don't have much time. If you won't decide, I'll decide for you."

"Let Juliet go. If you promise not to hurt her or Mab, I'll cooperate."

"What Colwyn and his corpses do with that vampire is none of my concern. My offer extends only to your aunt."

I hesitated.

The hammer descended.

"No! Stop!" I screamed. "Don't kill her."

An inch above the stone, he stopped. He glared at me from under his brows. "Extinguish your sword."

I let the flames die. One of the Old Ones—Colwyn, I think—snatched the sword and tossed it aside. Cold hands wrapped around my limbs like shackles of ice. The Old Ones hoisted me and carried me toward Myrddin.

A howl sounded. It started low and rose in pitch, full of anger and desperation. The Old Ones carrying me halted as it reverberated, filling the room.

"Kane!" I screamed, twisting toward the entrance. "In here! Go through the—"

An Old One stuck his hand in my mouth. I choked on long-dead flesh. Pushing aside revulsion, I bit down hard, but it didn't faze the Old One. I couldn't hurt it.

"Get her over here, now!" Myrddin said, his voice low but brimming with menace. The Old Ones carried me, bucking and struggling, to the table.

"Hold her down," Myrddin said. "So I can finish this."

Four Old Ones restrained me, pressing my arms and legs hard against the table. At my head, Colwyn covered my mouth, holding my upper arm with his other hand. I fought to breathe. Each hard-won inhalation reeked with the smell of the grave.

Myrddin bent over me. He'd hung the bloodstone around his own neck again. The pendant dangled from its chain, the bloodstone still small and dull. "No time for fun and games tonight, my girl," he said. "No slowing down the chi and maximizing the pain. A pity, but it's time to bring my son back." He carved the eihwaz rune into my chest. Then he plunged the metal probe into my heart.

The pain convulsed me. My head strained against the Old One's hand as I tried to scream. My right arm broke free; my grasping hand fastened on the bloodstone.

It pulsed.

The stone grew warm as blood from my slashed palm seeped into it.

I yanked, snapping the chain that held the stone around Myrddin's neck.

The bloodstone vibrated in my hand, drinking in my blood. A silvery light glowed from between my fingers. The light spread, running up my arm, lighting up the rune cut into my skin. It seeped into my heart, spreading warmth through my chest.

With a mighty heave, my heart rejected the probe, expelling it from my body.

From the entrance, a roar pierced the room. The heads of all four Old Ones whipped toward it. I looked, too.

Kane towered there, still a hybrid of man and wolf. He stood at his full height, powerful, his shoulders broad. But his head had wolfish features and his fingers sprouted wicked-looking claws. He wore clothes he'd taken from one of the dead vampires, but somehow that made him even more terrifying.

He roared again, and the Old Ones scattered like cockroaches. They scuttled deeper into the room. Kane howled and ran after them.

Myrddin drew back his arm to hurl energy at Kane. I kicked him, knocking off his aim. His fireball missed, exploding against the wall. I rolled off the table, away from Myrddin, and crouched, ready to dodge his next fireball, gauging the distance to my sword.

But Myrddin didn't throw another fireball. His mouth dropped open as he stared at the light emanating from the bloodstone.

I opened my fingers a little to let the light stream out. A beam shot upward and spread into a nimbus. Its center glowed with an intensity that almost hurt to look at. The light pulsed. It fractured, spun, and came back together in an image. In the center of the nimbus stood a young woman, clothed in a white gown, a silver circlet crowning her flowing hair.

"Viviane," whispered Myrddin.

"Betrayer," she spat. She lifted an elegant hand. Her finger pointed at him, and a torrent of energy shot out. It picked Myrddin up and hurled him against the wall. When he hit, his skin split open and his demon form emerged. It twisted out of his body, like some scaly reptile emerging from an egg, growing by feet each second. Myrddin's human form disappeared.

Now. I had to act now, while Wyllt, Myrddin's demon form, was forced to materialize in the human plane. I ran for my sword, shouting the invocation. Flames licked the blade. Holding the bloodstone high with my right hand, I snatched up the sword with my left. I charged the demon.

Viviane directed the stream of energy with laserlike precision. Wyllt glowed, held here somehow by the beam. The demon crouched, too big for this low room. I drove the Sword of Saint Michael through its hide and into its stomach. Flames burned demon flesh; sulfurous smoke billowed. I withdrew the sword and thrust it in again, moving it around to slice up as much of the demon's innards as I could.

Wyllt doubled over, clutching its abdomen. Black, stinking bile gushed from the wound. Demon flesh melted. Smoke surged. I kept striking and slashing. The demon's body wavered. It softened and grew spongy, then melted into a waterfall of black blood and liquefied flesh. The remains of the demon puddled on the concrete floor.

From the puddle, a form took shape. Myrddin, his demon half gone, reemerged. He lay slumped against the wall, his body broken, his eyes closed. I checked for a pulse and found none.

In the glowing light from the bloodstone, Viviane nodded, grim satisfaction on her face. Her image faded, along with the silvery light.

Screams echoed from somewhere deep in the underground network of rooms.

I ran over to Juliet and pulled out the spikes that impaled her. I worked as quickly as I could, but carefully. Too much of her weight on the wrong spike would cause more damage.

She was too weak to stand. I lowered her to the ground and removed the silver gag. She licked her lips. "I was the first one to survive the virus," she said. "So they were trying to see if they could kill me." Her eyes fluttered. "I think maybe they succeeded."

The bloodstone pulsed. I opened my hand. Red with my blood, glowing, it was larger than before. The setting had cracked and fallen away in places, but the broken chain was still attached. I tied its ends in a clumsy knot, then lifted the chain over her head and positioned the pendant so the bloodstone hung over her heart. Then, without knowing why, I traced the eihwaz rune on her forehead like a blessing.

Juliet gasped. Her body went rigid, then shuddered. Her

wounds shrank and closed. Her eyes flew open and she looked around the room.

"What's that wizard doing?" she cried.

Myrddin wasn't dead. He still slumped on the ground, but he held the metal probe with both hands. The probe protruded from his chest, where he'd stuck it deep into his own heart.

I raced over and tried to tug it out. He fought me with surprising strength, struggling to keep the probe in his own heart. I kicked him and tugged harder. Inch by inch, the probe gave.

Kane appeared at the back of the room, bruised and bloody, his clothes torn.

I looked at him. "Are you—?"

Myrddin wrenched the probe from my hands and drove it deeper into his heart.

Kane fell to his knees. On the table, Pryce convulsed.

Myrddin giggled. "I win, my girl. Tell Viviane I'll see her in hell." The giggle cut off abruptly as the triumphant light faded from his eyes.

32

"FATHER!" PRYCE GASPED AND SAT UP ON THE TABLE, LOOKing around, pulling needles from his body. His face twisted with hatred when he saw me.

"You," he sneered. With amazing agility for someone who'd been comatose for a month, he jumped from the table. To his left, he saw Myrddin's corpse. "What did you do to my father?"

I grasped the Sword of Saint Michael; its flames blazed to life as I raised it. "The same thing I'm about to do to you." I raised my sword and charged, aiming to plunge the point into Pryce's heart.

He dodged to the far side of the table. As he did he raised his hand, palm out, and pushed toward me. A rectangle of energy pulsed out. The Sword of Saint Michael passed through, but when the energy hit me it knocked me backward. My ass landed hard on the concrete floor.

I'd never seen Pryce do that before. But Myrddin had used the same gesture when Mab attacked him at Back Street.

Pryce looked as surprised as I was. He looked at the ceiling, then at the floor where Myrddin lay, then back at the ceiling again. "Father?"

I got to my feet.

Pryce laughed. The sound emerged as a giggle.

I charged again. And again, Pryce used magic to knock me back.

He hurled a fireball at me. I sliced it in two with my sword.

Throwing fireballs, Pryce edged toward the entryway. His aim was bad, but the strength and sheer number of his missiles kept me back.

Near the door, the fireball he tried to throw fizzled and extinguished in his hands. He turned and ran.

I ran after him.

"Vicky!" Juliet yelled behind me. "Kane needs your help!"

I stopped in my tracks and turned around. "There's silver in him," she said. "I can't get it out. It's killing him."

Outside, cans bounced and rolled as Pryce found his way out the hidden door.

Behind me, Kane groaned, the sound weak and shot through with pain.

I let Pryce go and ran back to Kane.

KANE LAY UNMOVING ON THE FLOOR, HIS EYES SHUT, HIS skin ashen. His breath tore from his throat in ragged gasps. The flesh around the bullet wound had blackened and blistered, classic signs of silver burn. He felt hot all over, and his heart beat erratically, like it had lost its normal rhythm and couldn't find it again.

Around his neck, he wore the bloodstone.

"He was having seizures," Juliet said. "The pendant helped me; I thought it would help him, too. But he's not getting better."

At least the seizures had stopped. But we had to get the silver out. There must be a fragment of Norden's bullet still inside him. I needed something to dig it out with.

I rushed back to the table where the Old Ones had held

me down. Myrddin had cut me with something. I found it on the table where he'd dropped it—a scalpel.

In the few moments I was gone, Kane had gotten worse. The silver burn had spread across his chest and down his arm to the elbow. It would be spreading inside, too.

Mab's bloodstone wasn't healing Kane. I took it off and put it around my own neck. First, remove the silver. After it was out, maybe the bloodstone would help Kane, as it had Juliet. If it wasn't too late.

Sweat beaded on Kane's forehead as I searched the wound. His unconscious body spasmed as I hunted for the fragment. I was hurting him, and I hated that, but the silver was hurting him more. I had to get it out.

I saw blood and flesh and bone. But no scrap of silver. I cut a little more. Kane groaned, and I felt sick inside.

The scalpel revealed a tarnished point. I dug a little deeper, trying to get the scalpel under it, and I could see more of the fragment. I attempted to lift the fragment with the blade, but it wouldn't come. Some jagged part was caught in the flesh. As gently as I could, I cut a little more. It still wouldn't come; I'd have to grip it somehow. Holding back the flesh with the scalpel, I reached in with my thumb and finger. Unsanitary, but werewolves aren't vulnerable to many infections. Right now, a few bacteria were the least of Kane's worries.

Blood smeared my fingers, making them slippery, but I got the edge of the fragment between my fingernails. When I had a good grip on it, I pulled gently. Kane shuddered as I drew the silver through his flesh. Slowly, carefully. And then it was out: an inch-long, twisted piece of blackened, bloody silver.

As soon as the silver left his body, Kane gasped. His back arched. His eyes opened, and then immediately squinched in pain. The half-man, half-wolf writhed on the floor, his limbs twisting. An energy field built around him.

I scrambled backward, out of reach of the blast of energy that would come at the moment of change.

Which way would he shift? I couldn't tell. Fur grew, then receded. His arms shrank to forelegs, while his legs stayed human. His skull shifted so fast, to so many different forms, I couldn't tell what shape it was taking.

The energy blasted out. I closed my eyes and shielded my face with my arms. Energy flared and pulsed for a long time—so long I was afraid it would burn him up, consume him entirely so that there'd be nothing left, man or wolf.

Finally it subsided. A naked man lay on the floor, bloody and silver-burned and absolutely beautiful. Kane was back.

He sat up, and I tackled him in a hug. His strong arms encircled me, and I covered his face with kisses. His human face. Everything about him—his skin, his features, his limbs—was a miracle. I looked into his gray eyes. They were the same eyes I'd searched for some sign that Kane would come back to me. Man or wolf, Kane had always been in those eyes.

He pulled me to him. His lips found mine. His tongue was in my mouth, hungry, frantic, hot. He pulled back and held my face in both his hands.

"Do you know how long I've been wanting to do that?" His voice, rough and husky with disuse, sent a thrill through me.

Somewhere behind us, Juliet cleared her throat. "Um, pardon me for interrupting," she said, "but do either of you hear anything?"

Kane turned toward the hidden entrance and listened. "There are people out in the tunnel," he said. "Probably cops, but I don't think we should wait around to find out." He pulled the sheet from the table where Pryce had lain and wrapped it around himself. "Come on, there's a back way out. I chased some Old Ones through it." He took my hand and we ran toward the back of the room.

I carried the Sword of Saint Michael before me like a torch, partly for light and partly to keep back any Old Ones or vampires who might be hanging around. Kane walked beside me, holding my hand. Juliet followed, and I kept turning around to make sure nothing had snatched her away. Shouts of "Police!" erupted behind us as we quietly moved deeper through tunnels and turnings. No one leapt out at us; no one came after us.

Kane's hand was warm in mine. As we walked side by

side, my flame held aloft, his broad chest gleaming in its light, I felt like we were the first explorers of some ancient world.

After a while, the three of us emerged onto a deserted platform at South Station. The station clock read 4:47 in the morning. It felt like I'd left Deadtown a century ago.

"Juliet," I said, removing the bloodstone from my neck. "Take this to Mab. She needs it as soon as you can get it there." I hoped we weren't too late. I didn't know how Viviane had appeared in the bloodstone's glow, but I was worried about what her appearance had cost Mab.

Juliet took the pendant. I also gave her the Sword of Saint Michael to take home for me. "'Your bidding shall I do effectually.'" It was good to hear her spout Shakespeare. She made an elaborate stage bow, and then she was gone. Damn, I wished I could move that fast. I'd be at Mab's side now.

Kane caught me in his arms. His skin was warm despite the early-morning chill. I ran my hands over his back, feeling its muscles, amazed at the smoothness of it. Amazed to have him with me again.

But time was short. We couldn't be here embracing on the platform when the first train pulled in. Hard as it was, I stepped away.

"I have to get back to Mab," I said. "I need to know she's all right."

Kane traced one finger along my cheek. Desire lit his eyes and reached out to me, but he nodded. "How are you going to get there?"

"The only way I can think of. I'm going to shift into a bird."

"Are you sure you'll know to fly to Deadtown?"

"I think so. The moon isn't strong right now. I'll hold the idea of going home in my mind and hope it leads me there." I touched his arm. "Will you be all right?"

He nodded. "I'll hide out in my office for a few days. I practically live there, anyway. I've got a change of clothes, food, coffee." Kane's staff was all paranormal, so no one would be coming in to work for another day. "Once the containment order is lifted, I'll call Carlos and have him bring my impersonator back from D.C."

We walked outside, our arms around each other. On the sidewalk, we kissed. Then Kane turned toward Government Center. He kept close to the buildings, out of sight of any passing cars, but the streets were quiet. Soon, he melted into the shadows, and I couldn't see him anymore.

I walked out Summer Street, toward the water. The sky was beginning to brighten in the east, and somewhere birds were singing. I stood and listened. I pulled their song into me, letting the notes fill me with lightness. I imagined stretching out my wings, letting the air hold me up, the currents carry me over the city, toward home. It was time to go home. Then energy blasted out, and all I knew was that I was flying, soaring over the water, happy it was spring.

33

I CAME BACK TO MYSELF ON THE ROOF OF A BUILDING. The sun warmed my back and my first thought was, "Maria was right. Flying dreams are the best."

My next thought was of Mab. Had Juliet returned the bloodstone to her? Was she all right? Could I get to her?

I got up and went to the edge of the roof to see where I was. Deadtown lay below me. It was daytime, so the streets weren't as crowded as at night, but the curfew seemed to make people want to get out while they could. Bundled-up zombies trundled along in twos and threes, an occasional werewolf or other paranormal threading their way through them. I recognized the street below—mine. In fact, I was on the roof of my own building. I'd made it home. I stepped back from the edge before someone looked up and pointed out the naked woman on the roof.

Naked. That presented a problem. I wasn't used to streaking through the halls of my building, and I'd prefer not to bump into any neighbors au naturel. I glanced around the roof. I'd never been up here before. If I was lucky, maybe somebody had set up a clothesline to give their laundry that fresh-air smell. I didn't see anything like that, but I did see a red, blue, and yellow beach umbrella. Odd. I went over to investigate.

Under the colorful umbrella sat a beach chair, a cooler, and a half-full wading pool. On top of the chair was a neatly folded pile of clothes: knee socks, long pants, a long-sleeved turtleneck, gloves, scarf, ski mask, and wide-brimmed hat. Zombies are oblivious to temperature, but the spring sunshine had obviously made someone yearn for the beach. Sunbathing, zombie-style. Only in Deadtown.

I pulled on the pants and shirt. I'd return them later, but now I needed to get to Mab.

I hurried down the stairs to my floor, worried about my aunt. Had the bloodstone reached her in time? I had to believe it did. But what condition would she be in? Would she still be the Mab I knew? Or had the last several days wrought some permanent change even the bloodstone couldn't undo?

My heart pounded as I knocked on the door to my apartment. Juliet answered. She hugged me and then threw the door wide open. Inside, two figures sat on the couch, their heads—one gray-haired, one blond—bent over a book.

"There," Mab was saying, "there's the answer you want. Reread this section, and pay attention this time. I'll quiz you again in ten minutes."

"Mab?"

"Victory? You're home?"

Mab stood, and she wasn't the Mab I knew. She looked younger.

I'd always thought of my aunt as a very youthful sixty, but the bloodstone's restoration had taken ten or fifteen years off that. Her hair was still gray, but her face was unlined, her complexion glowing, her eyes sparkling clear. She stood straight and tall and rushed over to me with a vigor I almost envied.

We met in a hug. My aunt isn't the hugging type, but she clasped me to her like she'd never let go. She even lifted me off my feet. I felt the bloodstone's warmth between us. Finally, with her customary *onetwothree* pat, she put me down and stepped back.

"And once again I have to ask," Tina said from the sofa, "*what* are you wearing?"

I looked down. Gauzy purple harem pants an inch too short and a fuzzy orange turtleneck. Focused on Mab, I'd barely noticed the clothes as I put them on.

"You know," Tina continued, "you should be *my* apprentice. Like, in fashion school."

Tina stood. Her oversized T-shirt showed a skull and crossbones sporting a glittery pink bow. Um, yeah. If that had been my only option on the roof, I'd have come downstairs naked.

"Tina, Juliet," Mab said. "I must have some time alone with my niece."

"I was about to resume the shroud, anyway," Juliet said. She went into her bedroom and closed the door. Tina, pulling on gloves, said, "Just wait 'til you hear how good I've gotten with *Inimicus*. You'll tell her, won't you, Mab?"

"I'll give her a full report," Mab replied, and Tina left beaming.

I couldn't stop staring at my aunt. "You look amazing," I said.

She smoothed her hair, seeming pleased and a bit flustered. "That's thanks partly to you," she said. "Sit, child, and we'll talk."

We sat together on the sofa, where Mab had been sitting with Tina. I put an arm around my aunt's shoulders and squeezed.

"What happened last night?" I asked. "I realize my blood helped to renew the stone, but how did Viviane appear like that?"

"Yes, your blood did renew the stone. When that happened, I felt its power surge, demolishing Myrddin's cloaking spell. Once I felt the stone again, I was able to reconnect with it." She looked at me sideways. "Thanks to some help from your sister."

"From Gwen?" Maybe I'd heard wrong. I only had one sister. "What do you mean?"

Mab examined her hand, as she had the other day, turning it back and forth, looking at skin that was now firm and smooth. "Do you recall how, when my body was failing, I said there were things I needed to explain?"

"Yes, but I thought Gwen would never listen." Twenty years is a long time to hate someone.

"You're right, she wouldn't have. For all those years she clung to her belief in what she saw—or what she thought she saw." Sadness crossed Mab's face, hinting at how much the rift with Gwen had pained her. "A traumatic event like that leaves a deep scar, the kind that marks our dreams. So I monitored Gwen's dreams. I guessed that, especially with my arrival stirring up the past, she'd dream about that night. When she did, I extended the dream."

"You showed her the part she didn't see." If seeing is believing, show her the whole thing.

Mab nodded. "In her dream, Gwen ran for the house, as she'd done that night. She never looked back—then or now. When I sensed she was about to wake up, I called to her, in Eric's voice. She stopped. I held my breath, hoping she'd stay in the dream. And then she turned around. For the first time, Gwen saw Pryce in his demon form. She stared and stared at him until the dream faded."

"So now she understands what really happened?"

"I don't know, child. It will take some time and reflection, I think, for her to truly understand. But she has been thinking about it. Last night, she contacted me via dream phone."

I wouldn't have been more astonished if Gwen had suddenly appeared in the middle of my fight with Myrddin, offering tea and cookies. Gwen, using the dream phone to call Mab? Impossible.

"She was angry," Mab said. "She accused me of poisoning her dreams with lies. She warned me to stay away from Maria. She upbraided me on every topic she could think of. I was so depleted, so exhausted and weak even in my own dreams, that I had no defense against her. I let her rant." Mab chuckled. "That confused her. She wanted to know what was wrong with me, why I wouldn't argue back. I told her I was dying. She said, 'Good.' " Again, a shade of sadness. "I wanted to end the call at that point, but I had no strength even to call up the mist. I lay in my dreamscape, Gwen staring at me. That's when I felt the bloodstone surge. I was too weak to respond to its call. I knew you needed help to defeat Myrddin, but there was simply nothing I could do.

"Gwen felt the change, as well. She accused me of playing some trick on her. I told her it was no trick, that you were under attack by a demon, like the one in her dream. I told her you needed help, but I was too weak to give it to you. And I asked her to lend me some of her strength. All she had to do was stay in my dreamscape and give me her hand."

"What did she say?"

"She told me to go to hell and started to end the call. Her colors rose up, and I reached out to her, pleading." Mab held out a hand now, as though Gwen were in the room. "Her colors rose some more. I could barely see her. I thought I was losing you both. And then she walked straight through the mist. She came back."

Mab dropped her hand to her lap and shook her head in wonder. "I don't know why she did. Maybe the demon from her dream remained vivid in her mind. She stepped out of the mist and took my hand. She let me draw upon her strength so I could project myself as Viviane before Myrddin. The effort drained her, I think, but she held on. She didn't let go until you'd killed the demon."

Mab paused. She watched my face, making sure I understood. "Your sister didn't do it for my sake, child. She did it for you."

ONCE AGAIN, THE REAPER WAS ALL OVER THE NEWS. NORden was listed as the fifth victim, and the containment order was extended for another forty-eight hours. But when the clock ticked down and no murder occurred, the police changed their tune. They identified Elmer Norden as the Reaper.

According to the news, his fingerprints were on the curved blade found at the site and matching the other victims' wounds.

They theorized that Norden, driven to despair by his psychotic urge to kill, had taken his own life. Reporters interviewed endless people who'd known Norden. Neighbors, coworkers, his barber, even past teachers. Everyone described him as mean, rude, bullying, and bad-mannered—all pretty accurate descriptions. The only one who had anything halfway nice to say about him was Pam McFarren.

But nobody said the one thing about Norden that I knew to be true. In the grip of a murderous spirit that tormented him unbearably, he tried to hold on to some little piece of what made him human. However much a jerk he'd been in life, in death he'd sacrificed himself for that bit of humanity.

Juliet went back into hiding. With the Reaper case closed, the police were putting more resources into other cases, including tracking down vampire fugitives from justice. The Washington police still wanted to question her about Justice Frederickson's murder, and the Goons still wanted to find her for breaking out of their facility. Juliet stayed at our apartment for a couple of days—the cops had already checked for her there so many times it was becoming the last place they'd look—then left. She wouldn't tell me where she was staying, but she'd pop up from time to time when she thought it was safe.

The Old Ones had scattered, she said. Many of them were dead, killed by the virus they'd used to infect Juliet. When they'd seen her that night on Back Street, apparently unharmed by the virus, several Old Ones had immediately infected themselves with it, expecting the same results. All were dead now. Others, including Colwyn, had been more cautious, torturing Juliet with more silver than any vampire could survive to test her immortality. Those Old Ones were still out there somewhere.

"I thought they'd really done it," I said. "Really achieved immortality. When I hit that Old One with silver and he didn't die . . . why didn't it affect him?"

"I'm not sure," Juliet said. "That was one of the Old Ones who infected himself. I think it had something to do with the bloodstone. The stone has so much power, and the Old Ones were in its presence for more than a day. My guess is that they absorbed some of that power. But obviously the effects were temporary."

I wondered if they'd be temporary for Juliet and asked Mab about it later. She didn't know. "You must understand, child, that the bloodstone has never been used in such a way before. The stone is life-giving, and I employed it in an emergency to counteract an artificially engineered, death-dealing virus. There's no telling what the long-term effects could be."

For now, Juliet said she felt like a kid of three hundred again. I don't think she noticed Mab's smile.

WITH THE CONTAINMENT ORDER LIFTED, KANE RETURNED to Deadtown. I left Mab grilling Tina on *Inimicus* demons and went to his place to wait for him. I opened all the windows to let in the fresh spring air. I hung a brand-new bathrobe on my side of the closet—and then I stepped back to marvel that I had a side of the closet here. It felt good.

I was sitting on the sofa, leafing through the latest copy of *Paranormal Rights Law Journal*, when the key turned in the lock, and Kane opened the door. I looked up—and then just looked. He was the same Kane I'd known for years, and yet I felt like I was seeing him for the first time. I let my eyes linger on every part of him. His silver hair. The broad shoulders that made him look so damn good in a suit. His strong hands, their square-nailed fingers. Everything. But especially the eyes that had helped me hold on to Kane when I was so afraid I'd lost him.

"Hi, Killer," I said. "Wanna see my new bathrobe?"

He grinned and closed the door. "Maybe afterward," he said.

He scooped me up and carried me to the bedroom. And then there was no need to say anything at all.

THE NIGHT BEFORE MAB FLEW BACK TO WALES, AXEL THREW her a farewell party in Creature Comforts. The aquavit flowed freely. Mab and Axel sang songs in Trollspråk and even demonstrated a traditional folk dance. Tina jumped up to try it, too. As the three of them thumped around the room, customers clapped their hands to keep time. After tonight, it would take years for Axel to recover his scary reputation.

Kane sat beside me, his arm around my shoulders, tapping his foot as he watched. I reached up and laced my fingers through his. Since he'd been back, I couldn't touch him enough.

Axel went back behind the bar to pour some drinks. He put on some quieter music.

Juliet popped in and out—in that sudden, "now you see me, now you don't" vampire way—to offer a toast to Queen Mab. "'Fair thoughts and happy hours attend you,'" she said. "'Heaven give you many, many merry days!'" Mab nodded, accepting the good wishes, and replied with something equally Shakespearean.

For the few minutes she stayed, Juliet sat at our table. "I'm going to Washington," she told us. "I think Colwyn may be hiding out there. I want to expose them. If I can find Colwyn's lair, I'm certain I'll find evidence linking the Old Ones to Justice Frederickson's murder. It's time to put that matter to rest." She looked around and slowly licked her lips. "I want to get back to trawling the bars for hot blood."

Kane cleared his throat. "Juliet," he said. "I'm sorry I mistrusted you. I owe you an apology."

She waved her hand dismissively. "'Sorry,' 'apology'—please. Vampires don't know the meanings of such words." But she looked pleased he'd said it.

I asked Juliet if she'd come across any news of Pryce while she was tracking the Old Ones.

"Nothing," she said. "Nothing at all." Then the door opened. Juliet disappeared in a blink, before the new customers came inside.

Pryce was out there somewhere, plotting. If he hated Mab for imprisoning his father, he now hated me exponentially more for killing him. I didn't know how the life force he stole from me would affect him. When I reached out with my mind, searching, I got a big blank. No connection to him at all. But could he sense me? Did he know where I was right now? The questions creeped me out, but I couldn't dismiss them.

A waltz came on. Kane stood and asked Mab to dance. As he whirled her around the room, I felt a twinge of sadness that Gwen wasn't here. I'd invited her, even though I knew she wouldn't come. Gwen would never set foot in Creature Comforts, let alone for a bon voyage party for Mab.

Tina sat down in Kane's seat and bugged me to quiz her. "Go on," she said, nudging me with her arm, "ask me anything about *Inimicus*. Anything at all."

"Not now, Tina."

She pouted. "Then give me a sip of your beer."

"You're not twenty-one yet."

"So? I just want a sip. Zombies can't even get drunk."

I picked up the bottle and looked at the pale yellow contents. Nobody—zombie, human, or otherwise—would ever get drunk off this stuff. "No, Tina. If Axel won't serve you, I'm not sneaking you beer."

She threw herself back in her chair. Then she leaned forward again. "Come on." Another nudge. "Just one question." Her red eyes gleamed with eagerness.

I put my bottle on the table. "Mab says you're going to school again. Is that true?"

Tina nodded, looking almost embarrassed to admit it.

"Tell you what. Next Monday, come over after school. We can go over *Inimicus* then."

"Really? Does that mean—?"

"Don't push it, Tina."

And for once, she didn't.

MAB RETURNED TO WALES. I WAS SAD TO SEE HER GO, BUT it was where she belonged. Her strength came from the land there, she'd said, and I wanted my aunt to stay strong for a good, long time.

It didn't really feel like she was gone. I was conscious of her in a way that was new. It wasn't like I could hear her thoughts or see through her eyes, but an awareness of my aunt was a constant presence in some corner of my mind. Adding my blood to the bloodstone had helped to renew the stone; it had also brought us closer. I cherished the connection.

That night as I slept, a rose and gold mist filled my dreamscape.

"Gwen?"

The mist cleared. My sister sat in a rocking chair, wearing her nightgown. The chair glided rhythmically back and forth. "I used to rock Maria to sleep in this chair when she was a baby."

"How are you doing?" I asked. "How's Maria?"

"She told me she called you, and that you showed her how to control her dreamscape." Her laugh sounded sad. "Want to show me, too?"

I waited.

"I can't stop dreaming about that night. It's like a looped tape that plays endlessly, over and over and over and over . . ." She pounded her fists on the arms of her chair. Then she closed her eyes and rocked for a few minutes. She stopped and looked at me.

"I talked to Mom," she said.

"What did she say?"

"That you should pick up a phone once in a while."

"She's right." I'd intended to call Mom and ask her to talk with Gwen about Maria, but events had gotten in the way. But events always do that, even when you're not stopping a murderer. They were no excuse. "I'll call her tomorrow."

"She also said that Maria's not my baby anymore. That I should give her time, let her explore and make her own decisions. Like she did for us."

"She did pretty well with her kids. Both of us."

Gwen lay her head back, as if she were looking at the sky. "Mab's gone?"

"I took her to the airport last night."

She nodded and rocked a few minutes more. "Too many things are changing—Maria, my feelings, even the past." She shook her head in bemusement. "You'd think the past, at least, would stay put. How on earth did that woman manage to change it?"

"She didn't. She just showed you something you missed at the time."

"I know. And I even know it's the truth. Gut-level." She smiled distantly. "I may have lost shapeshifting when I became a mother, but I gained intuition."

Silence settled again.

"I can't let go of the past all at once, Vicky."

I thought about Myrddin's curse on Mab, how she carried the pain of her sister's death with her through time. "But you can let it go eventually. Just do it a little at a time."

"Should I have said good-bye to her? I thought about it. I had the keys in my hand to drive to that farewell party before I chickened out."

In that corner of my mind, my sense of Mab stirred, like she could feel Gwen's regret. "I don't think she's bothered you didn't say good-bye. I think she'd rather you start with hello."

Later, after Gwen had gone, a dream unfolded in my dreamscape. I didn't try to shape or control it. I just let it happen. It was a simple dream. Mab stood beside me. Then Gwen appeared on my other side, holding Maria's hand. Four Cerddorion women, each one different, but standing together and looking forward, not back.

ABOUT THE AUTHOR

Nancy Holzner grew up in western Massachusetts with her nose stuck in a book. This meant that she tended to walk into things, wore glasses before she was out of elementary school, and forced her parents to institute a "no reading at the dinner table" rule. It was probably inevitable that she majored in English in college and then, because there were still a lot of books she wanted to read, continued her studies long enough to earn a master's degree and a PhD.

She began her career as a medievalist, then jumped off the tenure track to try some other things. Besides teaching English and philosophy, she's worked as a technical writer, freelance editor, instructional designer, college admissions counselor, and corporate trainer.

Nancy lives in upstate New York with her husband, Steve, where they both work from home without getting on each other's nerves. She enjoys visiting local wineries and listening obsessively to opera. There are still a lot of books she wants to read.

Visit Nancy's Web site at www.nancyholzner.com.

Explore the outer reaches of imagination—don't miss these authors of dark fantasy and urban noir who take you to the edge and beyond . . .